The reason these stories are being published only now, rather than 40 or more years ago when they were first written, is that Gil Brewer's markets have come back to him. Brewer published his first great noir story in 1955, and he kept writing great noir stories for more than 20 years, long after there were magazines eager to buy them. . . . Now, in 2019, with Brewer's reputation as an important figure in 20th-century American crime writing continuing to grow, the time has come for his later short stories finally to find their audience.

—from the Introduction by David Rachels

"Simultaneously unique and iconic, [Brewer] managed to invest in the best of his stories a genuine sorrow, anguish and fear. His protagonist is often a luckless, working class, Average Joe. And Joe's downfall has less to do with the femme fatale or the duffle full of money than it does with his inability to transcend the ignorance, weakness, greed or lust that resides in his own heart."

—Jack O'Connell, author of *Word Made Flesh*

DEATH IS A PRIVATE EYE

Unpublished Stories of Gil Brewer

Edited by
David Rachels

Stark House Press • Eureka California
www.starkhousepress.com

DEATH IS A PRIVATE EYE

Published by Stark House Press
1315 H Street
Eureka, CA 95501
griffinskye3@sbcglobal.net
www.starkhousepress.com

DEATH IS A PRIVATE EYE
Copyright ©2019 by Marvin N. Lee and Mary V. Rhodes.
Printed by permission of the Estate of Gil Brewer.

Original introduction and notes copyright ©2019 by David Rachels.

ISBN: 978-1-944520-77-9

Book design by Jeff Vorzimmer ¡caliente!design, Austin, Texas
Cover Illustration by John H. Fay, 1955

First Stark House Press Edition: August 2019

Table of Contents

Introduction

On the morning of December 23, 1960, Gil Brewer awoke to find a "tall, cold glass of vodka" waiting for him on his bedside table. He drank the vodka on an empty stomach and sneaked out of the house without waking his wife. He was going to have breakfast at a friend's. An hour later, five miles from home, Brewer crashed his silver 1957 Porsche 356A Coupe. Later that day, the *St. Petersburg Evening Independent* reported that Brewer had been admitted to the hospital "in fair condition with several broken ribs, bumps and bruises" and that "[charges] were withheld pending further investigation." The next day, the *St. Petersburg Times* reported that Brewer had been charged only with failure to yield the right of way. So much for the investigation.

This was the end of Gil Brewer's first decade as a professional writer. Ten years earlier, he had signed with literary agent Joseph T. Shaw, the legendary former editor of pulp magazine *Black Mask*, who had big plans for his new client's career. For much of 1950, Shaw critiqued Brewer's fledgling attempts at writing crime fiction, and by the end of the year, Shaw had sold Brewer's first two stories, which would appear in *Detective Fiction* and *Detective Tales* in March and April of 1951. Brewer would publish a third story in October 1951, and by the end of the year, he had also published three novels, including *13 French Street*, which would sell more than a million copies. After one year as a professional writer, Brewer had reached the peak of his commercial success.

Sadly, Brewer's alcoholism was already taking its toll. When the publisher's contract was issued for *13 French Street*, Brewer was in a sanitarium drying out. By the time of his drunken crash in 1960, Joseph T. Shaw was long dead, and Brewer was the client of Scott Meredith, to whom he was nothing special. While Shaw wanted to help Brewer "chart [his] course" as a writer, Meredith did not care what Brewer wrote as long as it sold, and in 1960, sales were increasingly difficult to come by.

The 1960s and '70s brought mostly frustration and more booze. By the time Brewer died in January 1983, he no longer had an agent—Meredith had dropped him in May 1982—and he was publishing almost nothing. Thus, the wrecked Porsche becomes an easy metaphor for the coming wreckage of Brewer's career. But this metaphor is far too romantic, especially as far as Brewer's drinking is concerned. Some commentators have portrayed Brewer as a tortured artist, a writer of great talent who aspired to great things but who managed to achieve only brief success as a genre writer before his genius, never fully tapped, sank under the weight of the bottle. The problem here lies with cause and effect. To be sure, Brewer *was* a talented writer whose career was wrecked in part by alcoholism, but he was an alcoholic for *all* of his adult life. He was *not* driven to drink because of his frustrations as a writer. He was an alcoholic before he was a published writer, and he was an alcoholic at the peak of his success, and he was an alcoholic when his career shriveled up to nothing. The drunken car crash could have happened at any point along the way. The date of 1960 is poetic happenstance.

As well, in 1960 Brewer had a major problem beyond his drinking: His markets were disappearing. During the 1950s, his primary market for short stories had been noir digest magazines, of which *Manhunt* was the most popular. By 1960, most of these publications had folded. In 1956, Brewer's most successful year as a story writer, he had published a total of 15 stories in *Accused, Hunted, Justice,* and *Pursuit*; all four digests ceased publication that year. *Guilty* and *Trapped,* where Brewer published a total of five stories, would last until 1963, but they both published Brewer for the final time in 1958. Alone in the field, *Manhunt* would hang on until 1967. Brewer published 11 stories in *Manhunt,* but none after 1958.

At the peak of his story-writing career, from September 1954 to October 1956, Brewer kept a log of the stories that he completed. This log appears to have been kept in real time with Brewer noting when he finished each story, sent it to his agent, and then waited for news. Usually, the news was good, and Brewer would record who had paid how much for his work. Sometimes, however, the news was bad, and Brewer would note that a particular manuscript had been returned to him.

In the 26 months covered by Brewer's log, he sold 39 of the 55 stories that he wrote. These are the 16 stories that his agent *failed* to sell: "Pawnee" (written in September 1954, eventually published by *Zane Grey Western Magazine* in 1969); "I Tried to Tell You" (October 1954); "The Hunter" (completed 23 January 1955); "The Heat" (13 April 1955); "Too Tight" (17 April 1955); "It's the Kid!" (20 April 1955, eventually published as "The Mountain Kid" by *Zane Grey* in 1969); "Recall—U.S.A." (27 May 1955); "Green Promise" (4 June 1955); "The Green Umbrella" (6 June 1955); "Somebody Goofed" (12 June 1955); "Tea for Two" (16 July 1955); "Winner" (20 July 1955); "Twilight in Brass" (4 October 1955); "Tired of It All" (12 October 1955); "A Present for Cleo" (February 1956); and "The Pitch" (19 June 1956). Unfortunately, beyond the two stories that eventually appeared in *Zane Grey,* only one of these stories survives. Brewer kept the manuscript for "A Present for Cleo" because, at over 18,000 words, it was the longest of the bunch and might have served as the basis for a novel.

In sum, Brewer's writing log reveals that, even when things were going well, he was still striking out with nearly 30% of his stories. He left behind no records from the 1960s, but it seems safe to assume that his rate of sales must have been much worse. While he published 57 stories in the 1950s, he published only 13 in the 1960s (excluding condensed novels and the *Zane*

Grey westerns written in 1954 and 1955). In an author's questionnaire that Brewer completed for Monarch Books on April 5, 1963, he reported that his hobbies were "Painting, collecting jazz records, writing, thinking about writing, writing, writing, all not necessarily in that order. Also—writing." Unfortunately, few (if any) of Brewer's unpublished stories from the 1960s survive. Given that, in 1969, Brewer published the two westerns written in 1954 and 1955, he must have kept his unpublished story manuscripts at least until the end of the 1960s. But at some point after then, it seems that he could no longer see any reason to keep the manuscripts of unpublished stories unless they were long enough to be launching pads into novels.

Therefore, the overwhelming percentage of Brewer's unpublished manuscripts come from the 1970s, including dozens of unsold stories that Scott Meredith returned to Brewer upon dropping him in 1982. Reams of manuscripts show that Brewer had periods of prolific production, though he managed to publish only 27 stories between 1970 and 1979. While these 27 stories represent a small fraction of Brewer's 1970s output, he nevertheless seems to have done better than he had done in the decade before. The 1970s, however, were essentially the end. The only story that Brewer managed to publish in the 1980s did not appear until after his death in 1983.

II.

This collection gathers Gil Brewer's two unpublished novellas from the 1950s along with 20 of his unpublished later stories. As we have seen, of the 14 unpublished stories listed in his writing log of September 1954-October 1956, Brewer kept only one manuscript until his death: "A Present for Cleo" from February 1956. He hung on to this story because of its length, which was 91 pages in manuscript. When his agent failed to sell the story, Brewer noted in his log, *"REUSE."* (As well, Brewer kept one other story from late 1956, "The Golden Scheme," a 35-page western, which was also longer than the unpublished manuscripts he chose not to keep.)

In addition to "A Present for Cleo," Brewer kept an earlier unpublished novella, "Death Is a Private Eye," a 98-page manuscript that was written no later than 1950. This is the earliest surviving crime manuscript in Brewer's papers. (The only older manuscript of any kind is *House of the Potato*, a literary novel from 1946 or early 1947.) "Death Is a Private Eye" will seem familiar to Brewer fans who have read his novel *Gun the Dame Down*, which was first published by Stark House Press in 2015. While Brewer only considered expanding "A Present for Cleo" into a novel, he actually did so with "Death Is a Private Eye." The result, which was originally titled *Gun the Man Down*, was rejected by Gold Medal Books in late January 1951. The rejection said that the novel had "too much sex, and most of it is of a pretty filthy kind. But the pace is fast, there is plenty of action, and when the language isn't dirty, the dialogue is good." The surviving manuscript of *Gun the Man Down* contains sloppy penciled edits on its opening pages, which include replacing *Man* with *Dame*.

Gun the Dame Down and its source material "Death Is a Private Eye" see Brewer attempting the mode of Raymond Chandler. Narrator William Death is a wise-cracking private eye from the school of Philip Marlowe, and elements of the story's plot and cast of characters recall *The Big Sleep*. For example, the well-to-do Carters stand in for the Sternwoods with Nora Carter in particular indebted to Carmen Sternwood; *Sexual Customs of Savages the World Over* might have come from Arthur Gwynn Geiger's bookshop; and Cadillac Smith seems to be Death's version of Mona Mars. A different sort of parallel connects Death with Brewer himself. In 1950, Brewer was a novice crime writer trying to find his way, much as Death is a novice private investigator. Death does have a gun, but he runs into trouble for not having a holster. One of the bad guys tells him, "You act like a kid." In fact, Death has been hired as a dupe, a hapless *soft*-boiled detective, chosen for his lack of experience. As a result, it somehow seems fitting that Brewer was unable to sell either manuscript.

William Death may have been Brewer's first attempt to launch a series. The detective's memorable if silly name, along with the identity-announcing title "Death Is a Private Eye," suggest that Brewer had high hopes for this character, but Gold Medal's rejection of *Gun the Man Down* was an early hint that private investigators would be an artistic dead-end for him. As a novelist, Brewer's breakthrough would come with *Satan's Rib*, which he sold to Gold Medal in March 1951, only two months after they had rejected *Gun the Man Down*. Gold Medal would change the novel's title to *Satan Is a Woman*, a fair advertisement of its contents.

Brewer's agent at the time, Joseph T. Shaw, knew that novels were the surest path not only to a sustainable career but also to literary glory, so once Brewer was established with Gold Medal, Shaw saw short fiction as a distraction from his goals. This is why Brewer published no short stories in 1952, 1953, or 1954. His mode would change, however, when he signed with Scott Meredith. With Meredith wanting him to produce anything he could sell, Brewer began keeping his writing log. Brewer's first story sold by Meredith, "Moonshine," appeared in *Manhunt* in March 1955. With "Moonshine," Brewer found his voice as a writer of noir short stories. (A pitch-black tale of a cuckolded family man, "Moonshine" appears with the rest of Brewer's best 1950s stories in *Redheads Die Quickly and Other Stories: Expanded Edition*, also from Stark House Press.)

Brewer's talents as a writer of short stories paralleled his talents as a novelist. He was noir, not hard-boiled; he was James M. Cain, not Raymond Chandler. Cain once observed that, in the short story, sympathetic protagonists are not required. Neither Philip Marlowe nor William Death is necessary. Cain wrote that "in one respect, not usually noted, [the short story] is greatly superior to the novel, or at any rate the American novel. It is the one kind of fiction that need not, to please the American taste, deal with heroes. Our national curse, if such a perfect land can have such a thing, is the 'sympathetic' character. . . . The world's greatest literature is peopled by thorough-going heels."

So it is with the short stories of Gil Brewer, though this is not to say that his stories are devoid of sympathetic characters. Rather, the sympathetic characters are usually not the memorable characters. "A Present for Cleo," for example, is memorable neither for Cleo, a generic damsel in distress, nor for her boyfriend Tom, who tries to save her. Paul Stapleton, the story's spurned lover turned murderous stalker, is the real attraction. As well, Brewer's most memorable characters, while they may sometimes be sympathetic, are often not heroic, and sometimes when they attempt heroism, their attempts lead only to disaster and misery. Furthermore, sometimes Brewer's most sympathetic characters, as in his breakthrough story "Moonlight," can test the limits of reader sympathy in shocking ways.

This is the vein of classic noir found in the 20 stories that comprise the bulk of this collection. The reason these stories are being published only now, rather than 40 or more years ago when they were first written, is that Gil Brewer's markets have come back to him. Brewer published his first great noir story in 1955, and he kept writing great noir stories for more than 20 years, long after there were magazines eager to buy them. When he died in 1983, his unpublished stories were worthless, but his family could not bring themselves to throw them away. Instead, they found someone willing to take them (*not* buy them), and they heaped Brewer's unpublished stories and other papers into boxes and shipped them from Florida to the University of Wyoming. Now, in 2019, with Brewer's reputation as an important figure in 20th-century American crime writing continuing to grow, the time has come for his later short stories finally to find their audience.

Sources

"tall, cold glass of vodka": Gil Brewer to Russell Galen, 17 October 1977, Box 3, Collection 8187, Gil Brewer Collection, American Heritage Center, University of Wyoming.

"in fair condition": "Two Men Hurt in 2-Car Crash," *St. Petersburg Evening Independent*, 23 December 1960, page B1.

"failure to yield": "2-Car Crash Injures Two," *St. Petersburg Times*, 24 December 1960, page 11-B.

"chart [his] course": Joseph T. Shaw to Gil and Verlaine Brewer, 11 June 1952, Box 4, Collection 8187, Gil Brewer Collection.

"Some commentators": See, for example, Bill Pronzini's essay "Forgotten Writers: Gil Brewer" in *The Big Book of Noir*, ed. Ed Gorman, Lee Server, and Martin H. Greenberg (New York: Carol & Graf, 1998), 191-200.

"a log of the stories that he completed": in Box 9, Collection 8187, Gil Brewer Collection.

"Painting, collecting jazz records, writing": Monarch Books author questionnaire, 5 April 1963, Box 3, Collection 8187, Gil Brewer Collection.

"too much sex": Quoted in Joseph T. Shaw to Gil Brewer, 31 January 1951, Box 4, Collection 8187, Gil Brewer Collection.

"in one respect": James M. Cain, introduction, *For Men Only* (Cleveland: World Publishing Company, 1944), 8.

A Note on the Editing and Dating of Stories

The stories in this collection are reprinted as they appear in Gil Brewer's original typewritten manuscripts, which are held at the American Heritage Center at the University of Wyoming. Typographical errors have been silently corrected. Idiosyncrasies of punctuation have been altered when necessary to clarify confusing sentences.

A few of the stories in this collection can be dated with precision based on evidence in Brewer's letters and other papers. Most of the stories, however, can be dated only generally to the early 1970s based on the addresses of his literary agent during that decade and the fact that, at some point after 1969, Brewer appears to have purged his files of all unpublished story manuscripts other than the novellas "Death Is a Private Eye" and "A Present for Cleo" and the long story "The Golden Scheme." This evidence, however, is not sufficient to rule out the possibility that some of the stories dated here to the early 1970s might, in fact, be earlier.

A Present for Cleo

February 1956

Paul Stapleton parked his three-year-old black-topped convertible in the sparse shade of a slash pine, on the shoulder of the seldom-traveled dirt road, got out and stood looking at the palmetto field. The air was heavy with the odor of dry grass and hot sand under the dazzling sun-white Florida sky. A boggy area with a stand of moss-draped cypress showed about a half mile beyond the road across the field. Stapleton smiled sadly, but his blue eyes mirrored a deep satisfaction.

He held the car door open, reached behind the seat and brought out a four-foot length of Burma pole. Brass eyelets gleamed along the pole to the tip, threaded with woven white cord. One end of the cord was fastened to the tip, forming a loop that could be drawn tight. He leaned the pole against the car, picked up a shiny red box about the size and shape of a cigar box, patted it with his fingers, then laid it gently on the seat. He closed the car door, grasped the pole, and walked down into the field.

He wore Army combat boots, his tan gabardine trousers neatly tucked into the tops of the boots, and a lightweight yellow sport shirt. Once in the field he experienced the hard hot pressure of the sun and opened his shirt. He was of average build and height, with tanned, regular features that were neither strong nor weak. His blond hair was trimmed in a neat flattop crew cut. He looked patient, dependable. Everything about Stapleton seemed personable except for the eyes.

He smiled again. It was odd how her name was Cleo. Like Cleopatra. Cleopatra was supposed to have died of snakebite—the pretty worm of Nilus. That's what had given him the idea; that and the fact that he worked at Ford Lyons' Animal Ranch. Ford had taught him a lot about snakes. It had taken some consideration as to exactly how he would do this thing, but now any other way seemed somehow unfitting. Wouldn't his sister, Esther, throw a fit if she knew he planned to bring Cleo to their home? to his blue bed, even? The last field trip with Ford, when they were out for a fresh supply of rattlers in this very area, had tipped him to the answer. It was so right. He had seen the very one he wanted in here.

Only not a rattler. Rattlers were for babies to play with. They weren't beautiful, either—not truly. Everything about this must be beautiful and tragic.

Stapleton slowed his pace, stepping almost silently. The heat was baking. His clothes stuck to his skin; sweat trickled down his ankles into the boots. He looked sharply, watching for a blend of color, carrying the rigged pole in both hands, tip slanted out and down.

His expression became sad and he paused, rested the pole on the ground, took out a handkerchief and mopped his face, neck and arms. He stared across at the moss-choked, sun-burnished cypress trees.

Finally he rammed the handkerchief into his pocket and moved toward a thick clump of sunny palmetto. There was nothing by the palmetto clump. He ran a brown-fingered hand across his chin, then moved off toward more swampy ground.

He was nearing the cypress trees when something flashed at the corner of his eye, a sunny wink. He stopped still, slowly moved his head. It was a young rattler. Discouraged, he moved on.

You had to know how to look, Ford always said. They could be all around and you couldn't see them. Someone had to show you first; you had to hold them in your hands, study them. After a while you could spot them easily.

He came along a stretch of white sand, then stopped rigid, pole poised, holding his breath. He did not move at all—did not even blink.

The brilliantly colored coral snake paused, head up, tail half hidden in a knee high bush of green grass. The red-, yellow- and black-striped body was over a foot long, the black bullet head absolute and deadly.

Stapleton did not move. The pole would not reach. He had fashioned this rig himself, unlike the ones they used at the ranch that you jammed down over the snake, holding it to the ground, because he'd thought it safer. He waited, breathing soundlessly through his mouth, his lower lip trembling. Sweat formed on his forehead, upper lip and chin, like fine young pearls, and his eyes were dry, pale blue agates.

The coral snake inched briefly, hesitated, then slithered in a swift rush of silence across the sand. The pole shot out and Stapleton keened high in his throat as the noose snapped taut. The snake twisted, writhed, then hung deliberately alive at the end of the pole in the white glare of sunlight.

Cleo Monohan turned toward her bedroom door and frowned when her mother called from downstairs. Then she moved slowly toward her bedroom window, brushing rich auburn hair that swept her shoulders, a tall girl even in her bare feet, eighteen years old, vital. She wore soft blue denim shorts above slimly curved legs, an unbuttoned, sleeveless white blouse that clung to the youthful symmetry of her body as her arms lifted with the brush. Her expression was faintly troubled, the face oval, the lips full and just this side of pouting, the dark blue eyes extremely gentle, yet very alert. Her skin did not tan and was of that fine ivory-white texture, absolutely pure, so seldom found, and then only in the true auburn-haired girl. Everything about her was lovely, but she moved with hesitance.

"Honey? Lunch is ready."

"Please, Mom—I'll be right down."

She stepped over to her dresser and looked at herself in the mirror, forced a smile, then let it go. She laid the brush down too carefully, gripped the hair at the back of her head, then quickly fastened it with a gold clip into a pony tail. She secured the open blouse by one button over the full white brassiere, left the room and moved swiftly along the upstairs hall.

Mrs. Monohan spoke reprovingly from the foot of the stairs as Cleo came down. "You've been in your room for hours."

"Sorry."

"Is anything wrong?"

"No."

Mrs. Monohan moved aside, then stood there looking at Cleo. She resembled her daughter in many ways, but the flesh had become heavier with time, though the years had been gentle. The auburn hair was darker now, more brown, without the fire—just hair. She wore a thin gray cotton dress with white trim, and her face was kind, the eyes touched with resignation. Cleo knew her as a thoughtful, knowledgeable person who could, with the aid of Mr. Monohan who was an investment broker with Littletons, answer just about any question under the sun. The trouble was, Cleo had long since vacated the questioning period of her life. She and her mother had never really been close.

"Hungry?"

Cleo smiled, padded rapidly into the bright yellow kitchen where they usually ate lunch. The table was set by a window; sandwiches, salad, and a pot of tea.

Cleo plumped into her chair, bit into a sandwich and began to chew slowly as her mother sat down across from her.

"Honey—what's the matter?"

"Nothing. Why?"

"Well, Tom's coming for the weekend again. I'd think you'd be doing things—getting ready."

"He won't be here before seven. He doesn't leave Gainesville till after his last class, and it's a three-hour drive."

"Well," Mrs. Monohan said, smiling as she poured two cups of tea. "I suppose love's like that."

Cleo did not speak.

"Of course, I didn't meet your father until after he'd long finished college. Things weren't so hasty then, I guess." She shrugged, still smiling, and wiped her hands on a pink paper napkin. "You kids get married so early these days."

"Now—for gosh sakes—who said anything about that?"

"You really love Tom, don't you?"

Cleo swallowed, reddened slightly, then looked at Mrs. Monohan and nodded. "Yes," she said. "Yes, I love the guy."

Mrs. Monohan sighed, picked up her cup and sipped. It was quiet for a time. The china clock in the living room on the mantel slowly chimed twelve. Outside, a jay screamed in the azalea bushes.

"Tom's a fine boy," Mrs. Monohan said.

Cleo was silent.

"Honey? Whatever happened to that other one—that nice-looking boy who was always phoning you? Did he stop bothering you? What's-his-name? Stapleton? Remember, he came into church that time, shoved right by me and sat whispering to you all during service? Your father didn't like that at all. Did you tell him to leave you alone?"

Cleo moved uneasily on her chair. "No, mother."

"Well, you should. Emphatically. I remember he called up all your friends—asking those silly questions. Whether you loved him. My goodness!"

"Mom, please."

"He's not bothering you again, is he?"

Cleo said nothing.

"If that's what's got you down, honey—you just tell him. Tell him to leave you alone."

"I couldn't do that."

Mrs. Monohan sighed heavily. "Cleo, you make too much of a little thing. Just tell him and be done with it."

"Will you please stop? I told you, there's nothing the matter."

"Oh, all right. Well," Mrs. Monohan said, "I'll sure be glad when Tom gets here. Maybe he can wake you up. What do you two have planned for the weekend?"

"Nothing special. Listen—Mom?"

Cleo gripped the edge of her chair with both hands, her face slightly flushed. Mrs. Monohan looked at her and began to smile, then did not.

"Mom, if anybody—if anybody phones this afternoon—anything like that, tell them I'm not home, will you?"

"But, why?"

"Just—do it for me, will you?"

"Well, for goodness' sakes," Mrs. Monohan said.

Cleo rose from the table, jarring it roughly with her knee. Tea splashed from her untouched cup. She moved swiftly from the kitchen. Mrs. Monohan watched her with faint concern, said something under her breath, frowned, then shook her head with a smile of dismissal and took a big bite of lettuce sandwich.

Esther Stapleton was hurriedly clearing up her luncheon dishes in the kitchen, when her brother Paul came in the driveway and parked at the rear of the small cottage in the suburbs. Esther glanced toward the kitchen door, then began running water in the sink, a very thin woman of twenty-seven, who looked shopworn. Her face was long, angular, the once-smooth blonde hair darkened to a splotchy brown. Her red knitted dress hung a bit awry, belted with a flat silver chain, a silver broach at the throat. The large, fawn eyes were touched with hurt, and there was deep tiredness about the too heavily rouged orange-colored mouth.

It would never do to tell Paul that she wasn't returning to work on the switchboard at the telephone company this afternoon, was, in fact, going to try one more afternoon with Gregg Tillotson. Paul did not like Gregg. Paul didn't much like anybody, except the way he sometimes went on about that pretty Monohan girl—and lately all this talk about Cleopatra. For Lord's sake.

Esther glanced at the clock on the stove. She had to meet Gregg outside of town at the Big Niter Café, and she was already late. Gregg would be furious.

The kitchen door rattled and Paul came quickly inside. He saw Esther, moved something behind his back, and started for his room down the hall.

"Can't you even say hello?" Esther said, running water in the dishpan. She turned the water off and looked at him as he paused.

"Hi," Paul said.

"What're you hiding there?"

"What?" Paul said, vanishing into the hall. His bedroom door closed.

Esther snatched a hand towel, walked rapidly down the hall wiping her hands, then opened his bedroom door and said, "When are you going to start being civil?"

Paul was sliding a shiny red box under the edge of his bed on the floor. Esther watched him. Paul stood up and looked at her, unsmiling, breathing heavily.

"Oh, knock it off," he said. He moved to his bureau and regarded himself in the small, brown wooden-framed mirror on the wall above. He glanced at his watch, his back still turned to her. "Better snap it up, Essy. You'll be late."

"What's that red box, there?"

"Nothing."

"It must be *something*."

"It's nothing. For God's sake, leave me alone, will you?"

Esther moved across the room and sat down on the edge of the double bed. The room was very neat, with yellow hardwood floors, two colorful throw-rugs. The walls were bright blue, the spread on the bed the same color as the walls. The one window at the head of the bed, hung with blue curtains, revealed a blossoming azalea bush, a small withered sago palm, some of the rear yard, the garage, and the front of Paul's blue convertible.

Esther looked outside, then up at Paul again, stretching the towel across her knees.

"Paul?"

"Yeah. What now?" He had taken a flat brown notebook from the top drawer of the bureau, opened it and was pouring over a page with his back still turned. He closed the notebook, laid it on top of the bureau where it lay precariously near falling. He turned and leaned against the open drawer, closing it, his gaze moving from Esther's eyes to her feet, and around under the edge of the bed.

"Oh, never mind," Esther said.

"*Now*, what's the matter?"

"Paul, why can't we be nice to each other? I mean, we live together like this—we fight all the time. What sense is there to it?"

She looked up at him. He ran his hand over his chin, watching her wryly now. Then he came across the room, slumped into a chair opposite the bed, on the other side of the window, and began unbuckling the combat boots.

"All right. We'll be nice. Consider it done, Essy."

Esther brightened somewhat, with effort. "Where've you been today?"

"Oh, no place. Just around."

He kicked one boot off, began on the other.

"Aren't you working?" she asked.

"Took the rest of the day off. I'm beat, Essy, beat."

"I see. Well—" She started to move from the bed, but did not. She kept watching him, the eyes very large, brown and hurt.

"You'll be late," Paul said.

"Yes. I'm going."

Paul looked at her. "I know about you and that Tillotson fellow, from Willowville," he said. "You're not fooling me, Essy. I know what you two been doing."

Esther stood up, started for the door. Paul lay back in the straight chair, regarding her with casually bitter eyes. "You know I don't like that, Essy. Mother and Dad wouldn't like it if they were alive. You'd better quit seeing him, you hear?"

"I'll do what I like." She paused by the door, turned and looked at him. Her face began to color and the flesh around her lips paled slightly. "If it's necessary, I'll find a place of my own, Paul."

"No, you won't, Essy. We'll live together till we find the right guy for you. Just remember that. O. K.?"

"Paul, I'm older than you—you've got no right—"

"Haven't I, Essy?" Paul said, standing up. He did not look toward her now, picked up his boots, set them under the bed in front of the small red box, then flopped down on the bed and closed his eyes. "Haven't I?"

Esther Stapleton watched him for a time, regarding the steady breathing, the absolute unconcern. For a moment the artery in her throat pulsed noticeably, then she turned and walked loudly down the hall into the kitchen. She stood by the sink, staring at her hands clenched in the damp towel. With a gasp, she threw the towel into the sink, picked up her black purse from the table and moved through the house. She hesitated by the telephone stand in the front room, then hurried on outside to her car at the curb, a maroon bantam coupé, five years old, with a slightly dented right front fender. Driving off, she pressed hard on the gas pedal and was overly reckless.

"Hello?"

"Is Cleo there? May I speak with her, Mrs. Monohan?"

"Oh? Who is this?"

"Just wanted to speak with her a moment."

"Oh, all right—*Cleo*—*telephone . . . Cleo . . . What? . . . I know, but you'd better speak with him, anyway. Now, honey—you do as I say . . .*"

"*. . . Mother, I told you not to tell*—Hello?"

"Cleo?"

"Who is this?"

"Guess."

"*. . . Mom, don't stand there!* Is this Paul?"

"Uh-huh."

"What do you want?"

"I know how you feel about me, Cleo."

"What do you mean?"

"It's all right. Is your mother still there?"

"No. What do you want, Paul?"

"I'd like to talk with you. Not over the phone—I mean, I'd like to see you this afternoon. Just for a little while."

"I'm sorry, Paul. That's impossible."

"Cleo, look. I said I understand how you feel about me. Isn't that right?"

"I can't see you."

"It's not asking much. There's just some things I want to talk over with you—tell you. I thought you could spare me a few minutes, anyway. I'm not asking for a date. What's the matter, somebody there you can't break away from him?"

"No. It's not that. Paul, you've got to stop phoning me—and everything. It's not very nice, all the things you've done. I've tried to tell you."

"You wouldn't have said that last summer."

"Please, Paul!"

"I'm sorry. I really am. I mean, that's what I wanted to talk to you about. Some of it. Listen, Cleo—do this one favor for me—huh? Meet me this afternoon. I'll pick you up by the mailbox on Tangerine, where we always used to . . ."

"I told you, Paul—I can't."

"It's the last time. I won't ever bother you again—if you'll just meet me this afternoon. Just so I can tell you something. Just for a talk."

"What's so important about this afternoon?"

"Nothing. Nothing at all. It's just I've got something important to tell you. I promise, I won't phone you again. Ever."

"Important about what?"

"Something. Something you should know."

"Paul?"

"I can't talk over the phone. I've got to talk to you. Look, you met my sister, Esther. Remember? Well, Esther and I live together now. I told her I was bringing you around to the house, and she'll be there, and we can talk. I'll pick you up by the mailbox. We'll run over to the house and then I'll bring you right back. That's all—just for a few minutes. You can spare me that, can't you?"

"You'll want to go out you know where—out to the mill."

"No. Nothing like it. Straight to the house, then straight back. Pick you up in fifteen minutes—"

"It's pretty late, Paul."

"For gosh sakes, am I poison? Please, Cleo. This one last favor. How about it? Come on—fifteen minutes. I'll have you back home in less than an hour."

"You say, your sister—Esther's there?"

"Certainly."

"I wish you'd tell me what this is all about, Paul."

"Curious? You'll find out."

Tom Anderson cut his mid-afternoon class in Education, and got an early start for Gulf City. He owned a late model Ford sedan, and driving down from Gainesville he pushed it hard, but it was still a grind, especially when he had the whole weekend with Cleo ahead of him, and couldn't get there fast enough. The full week at school with only the one phone call to her on Wednesday night, wanting badly to see her, to be with her, was rugged.

Tom was a tall, lean, red-haired young man of twenty-one, who had worked very hard for everything he managed out of life, and he considered it a great deal. He had his service time behind him, except for reserve hours, knew everything there was to know about submarines, Key West, Havana,

New London, and a few other places. His folks had died when he was in high
school and he'd been on his own since that time.

He had never discussed it with anyone, but he thought that being on
your own early in life was a good toughening process. He knew he had plenty
to learn, but also figured he had absorbed a good deal.

An acquaintance of his, Al Williams, was on his way to Fort Myers and
had taken a lift as far as Tom was going, so talking helped pass the time.

"You speak of marriage damned seriously," Williams said. "Going to
ask her to marry you?"

"That's right."

"This weekend?"

"Yup."

"Well, all I say is, don't take it so seriously," Williams said with a short
snort of laughter. He rolled down his window and let the wind rake ashes
from his cigar. Williams was a corpulent, sandy-haired fellow, whose
phlegmatic manner would someday possibly endear him to whatever
business associates he managed to incarcerate within the reality of his
dreamed-of mahogany realm. He was an average-to-slow student who liked
to wear white shirts and ties, possibly in preparation for the dream. His face
was round and red, his expression an earnest effort toward cynicism and
wise regret. He had already smoked cigars for over a year, and after drinking
too much beer—which he managed at least twice a week—he was prone to
long speeches concerning his own advent into the world of BIG business.

"Don't know why I'm telling you all these things," Tom said.

"Calm, calm," Williams said. "I wasn't chortling at marriage. Just
thinking how it will be for a luscious bit like her—living up there while you
go to school. Remember, I met her during Homecoming week."

"Others live all right like that."

"I know it, my boy, I know it. And I don't blame you—am I crazy? Who
could blame you?" Williams whistled a large lungful of cigar smoke.

"O. K., Al."

"Har-har-de-har, as the man says," Williams said.

Tom glanced at him, then back to the road. There was quite a bit of
traffic on U. S. 19, but his foot was itchy on the gas pedal. Cleo didn't expect
him for a long while yet. This would be quite a surprise. He came past a
couple of country tourist courts, then began to notice the large red signs
proclaiming the proximity of Ford Lyon's Wild Animal Ranch, Florida's
largest, wildest and most fabulous.

"Any competition?" Williams asked.

Tom looked at him, then away again. "Funny you should ask that."

"Why?"

Tom shrugged. "Matter of fact, I'm not sure. There's a guy—was a guy,
anyway—only she's never mentioned him."

"And you never asked her?" Williams said with immense awe.

"Nope."

"How'd you find out?"

"Queer thing—he wrote me a letter, told me to lay off her. He'd see me in hell. Corny. I tore it up, never did anything about it. Never heard from him again."

"Why the hell didn't you tell her?"

"I don't know. I wanted to tell her—you know how it is? Only finally it just passed by. I kind of thought she should tell me."

Williams grunted, held his cigar out the window, watched the sparks shower. "All I say is, that's the kind to look out for. Sneaky. You know? They can't bear to lose." Williams dropped the half-smoked cigar, lurched back in the seat. "Let's get off this morbid subject. You hear the latest one about Marilyn?"

Tom did not speak.

"Wait," Williams said. "Say—let's stop and have a beer. There's a place. Big Niter Café—wild and woolly—look!"

Tom slowed the car, then speeded up again. Williams hung head and shoulders out the window, flagging his hand at a man and woman violently arguing in the parking area of the roadhouse, beside a dusty maroon, bantam coupé. The thin woman wore a dull red knitted dress and she lurched drunkenly as she beat at the man with a black purse on a long leather strap.

"Not going to stop?" Williams said.

"Sorry, Al—I'm in a hurry."

Williams slumped heavily on the seat. "Ah, youth—ah, love."

"Go to hell," Tom said.

Paul Stapleton drove his newly-washed blue convertible into an alley one block over from Tangerine Avenue, and parked in the shade of stairs leading up to a garage apartment. From where he sat, he could see the mailbox on Tangerine, and Cleo Monohan standing there on the sidewalk in a yellow cotton dress, white moccasins, and holding a small white basket-like handbag.

He waited, his hands tight on the steering wheel, his face oddly strained, his mouth tightly closed, but pulled back at the corners, set. He wore dark blue slacks and a white-ribbed sport shirt, and his crew cut was brushed to perfection. A fine film of moisture showed on his smooth brown brow, giving it the appearance of glazed marble. He had the car in neutral, but kept softly nudging the gas pedal with his toe.

Watching, he saw Cleo Monohan look at each car that passed on the street. Then she moved from his line of vision along the sidewalk. He waited, barely breathing. Cleo returned, gripping her handbag in both hands, and still Stapleton sat there.

A sound caused him to turn his head sharply.

A plump woman in a yellow housecoat, holding a bulging bag of clothespins in her teeth, and carrying a small dishpan full of wet clothes, moved a step at a time down the stairs of the garage apartment. She saw the way Paul looked at her. He grinned and bared his teeth. She scowled and the clothespin bag fell from her mouth, and the wooden pins spilled, bouncing and clattering down the stairs.

Stapleton made an angry sound in his throat, and the car sped down the alley. Cleo Monohan was nowhere in sight. He drove swiftly, hunched over the wheel, skidded for an instant in the dusty sand at the street entrance, then turned the car down Tangerine.

Cleo Monohan was walking determinedly along the sidewalk, her bright auburn pony-tail bobbing prettily in the sunshine.

Paul's mouth sobered. He pulled to the curb, flicked the horn ring, popped open the door on her side.

"Cleo?"

She ceased walking, stood stiffly staring at the car and Paul Stapleton's pleasantly smiling face. Winds from Tampa Bay palmed her yellow dress, molding it along her legs. She lifted the handbag with both hands, then lowered it in a gesture of recognition.

"Come on," he called softly. "Get in."

Cleo glanced up along the street, still gripping the purse in both hands, then ran lightly to the convertible and slid in across the shiny red leather seat.

"Hi."

Paul reached past her, still smiling, and slammed the door before she had a chance to close it herself, and their arms touched.

"M-m-mmmm!" Paul said, driving off. "Smells good. Gosh, it *is* good to see you. Was I late?"

Cleo did not look toward him. "No. I was early." She spoke mildly, staring straight ahead, her shoulders firm against the seat.

Paul took the first corner easily, carefully.

"Paul? What do you have to tell me?"

She held the purse with both hands in her lap, and wind whipped at her pony-tail. Her lips were very red, but unsmiling.

"Let's not try to talk in the car," Paul said. "Let's wait till we get home?"

Cleo said nothing for some moments. She turned surreptitiously toward Paul, whose face shone with obvious happiness now. When he glanced at her, she quickly looked away.

"Have you been out by the mill?" Paul said.

Cleo's even white teeth touched her lower lip. "You told me you wouldn't . . ."

"Sorry. Just asking. The azaleas are in bloom out there. I know how much you like them." He reached back behind the seat with his right hand, and Cleo leaned toward her side of the car as he brought something out. "Here," he said. "For you."

He handed her a yellow, short-stemmed flower. She took it and held it stiffly in her lap, not looking at it.

"There's a bush by my bedroom window," Paul said. "I always think of you when I see it."

Cleo held the azalea and said nothing.

They came through downtown traffic and Paul turned toward the bay. Cleo twisted suddenly in the seat, pulled her left leg up slightly, and looked at him. "Paul, you'd better stop the car. I mean it. I'll walk home."

He reached out quickly and almost, but not quite, patted her knee, then moved his hand back to the steering wheel and swallowed, smiling gently.

He cleared his throat. "Now, come on," he said. "Don't be like that. After all—you promised."

She turned straight on the seat, brushed her dress smoothly down over her knees and watched the street through the windshield.

"After you," Paul said, holding the kitchen door open for her. "Sorry to take you in the back way, but I always use this door. Habit, I guess."

Cleo looked at him and he smiled. She moved through the doorway into the dim, cool interior of the house. Stapleton stepped quickly after her, closed the door and leaned against it. His hands pressed tightly back against the latch and there was a subdued click. Cleo turned and frowned.

Paul spoke loudly. "Come on," he said, moving up beside her, holding the smile against Cleo's accusative eyes.

"You said your sister was here."

"Why, sure. She *is* here." He turned his head away and called out, but he did not move from the girl's side. "Essy? Hey, Essy—where you hiding? We've got company."

There was no answer.

"Be darned," Paul said, frowning. "Must be in her bedroom. Maybe out on the front porch."

"She wasn't out there when we drove in. I don't like this, Paul."

He grinned at her. "Oh, come on, now. None of that. She's here someplace."

He touched his palm gently against her back, pressing her down the hall that led toward the living room. He was beside, but slightly behind her, and his face was like wet stone.

"She's not here, Paul. You told me she was here."

The house was exceptionally still and he did not answer immediately, looking at Cleo where she had ceased walking in the hallway near the open bedroom door that revealed late afternoon sunlight slanting into his room, gleaming on the red box in the center of the blue bed, glowing on the blue curtains, the shiny hardwood floor and colorful throw rugs. From very far away in traffic, a car's horn bleated.

"She must be here," Paul said quietly, watching her.

Cleo moved a pace away and bumped the wall beside the bedroom doorway, looked quickly into the room, then at Paul again.

"She's not, Paul."

"That's not her room—that's my room."

Cleo watched him, standing with her back touching the doorframe, her eyes cautious.

"Just a sec," Paul said. He patted her shoulders with both his hands, grinned, turned and walked smoothly down the hall. "Essy? Say, Essy?" He went to the front door and, with his body shielding him, his fingers twisted the latch. Then he walked across to another closed door, opened it, glanced in, then closed it again. "Not there, either. I'll be darned."

Cleo started toward the kitchen.

"Wait," Paul said.

She hesitated. He moved swiftly down the hall, almost at a run, his feet thumping. "Essy must be at a neighbor's," he said, breathing quickly. "Anyway, she'll be back. Here, this is my room."

Cleo looked in at his room again. Paul stepped through the doorway, turned and smiled. "See?" he said. "There's the azalea bush—right there."

She did not move from the hallway. She looked toward the kitchen.

"For gosh sakes, Cleo."

"You have something to tell me, tell it," Cleo said. "You knew she wasn't here."

"Please, honey—"

"Don't call me that, Paul. I'm leaving."

He rushed to her, touched her arm as she started toward the kitchen. He held her arm firmly, turned her around until she faced him, not roughly, but quite surely.

"I want to show you my room," he said.

She looked at him soberly. His voice had been flat, without any inflection whatever.

"I don't want to see your room."

"I want you to see my room, Cleo."

She was rigid now and he did not release her arm, his fingers biting into the soft ivory flesh. Slowly, he brought her around until she was facing his door and her hand came up, her fingers plucking dreamily at his fingers as she stared into his eyes. His eyes were something like blue mirrors and they were curiously bright.

"Just for a minute," he said.

"No."

But he was already moving her into his room. Inside, he immediately released her, sighed and said, "There," gesturing with his hand. "This is my room."

She watched him, holding her purse, the last low sunlight striking the skirt of her yellow dress, bathing her legs and moccasined feet. There was indecision in her eyes and stance. Already parts of the room were in shadow.

"Sit down," he said. He pressed her back until she moved stiffly across the room, turned her, and sat her on the bed. The shiny red box rested behind her on the bed and it leaned slightly as the mattress sagged with her weight. "Now," Paul said. "Just sit there, and we'll talk."

She lightly cleared her throat. "Really, Paul. I'd better go home. Really. I don't believe you have anything to say at all."

"That's where you're wrong."

He stood before her a moment, then sat on the bed beside her. She began to slip toward him as the mattress and springs sagged, but pushed herself away with her feet slanted hard against the floor.

Paul's voice was blunt. "You ever think about last summer?"

"Yes—I mean, no, Paul. No. We're not going to discuss that."

"What's wrong with it?" he said, obvious irritation revealed in his tone. "I know you don't care for me, Cleo—tossed me away, sure. I told you that. I just wanted to talk with you, that's all. I think about it a lot. Us out there in the country in the sunshine, the summer afternoons—with those banks of flowers, and the old mill." He paused, watching her with angry eyes. "You liked it then—you didn't act like this then."

"Paul, there's something I've got to tell you."

"Yes." He stared at the floor. His face was much paler now, and misted with perspiration. His face looked cold. He began to speak a shade more loudly. "Sure," he said. "You mean about Tom Anderson, don't you? You don't have to tell me, Cleo. I know. I know everything."

She started to rise from the bed. He took her arm and pulled her back with growing intenseness.

"I won't see you again, after today," he said. "I'm going away. That's part of what I wanted to tell you, see?"

She brightened. "Oh? You're going away, Paul?"

"I see you enjoy that."

"No, no—really."

"You're lying. I don't blame you. But—Cleo, I love you. No, wait—listen—" She winced, drawing away from him—"I love you more than anybody will ever love you. Those times last summer at the mill, with the flowers—I'll never forget them." His voice was strained as he held her arm.

"Paul."

"That's the second part," he said, calmer now. "I mean, I wouldn't go away, and we could see each other again, if only you'd even tell me I had a chance with you, Cleo."

She stood up and he did not move. He released her arm.

"I'm sorry, Paul. I should've told you. I'm in love with Tom Anderson. We'll probably even get married, so you leave me alone. That's all there is to it." Her chin began to bunch slightly and she was obviously frightened. "So I don't want to see you. And now I'll just walk home, Paul. You don't have to drive me home."

"I wouldn't think of taking you anyplace," he said. "Didn't you hear me? I said I loved you. Don't you know what that means? I've never loved anybody but you, Cleo—nobody."

He came to his feet as she turned toward the door, and took her arms, not harshly.

"Wait—one more thing," he said. "And you can relax, because Essy won't be home till late tonight."

Cleo's right hand moved slowly up to her mouth and the back of her hand pressed against her teeth. She did not speak and he drew her slowly and intently toward the bed and turned her and forced her down, watching her steadily all the time, his face close to hers, smiling.

"Here," he said. "It's something just for you, darling—a present."

Cleo's hand remained over her mouth as she watched him. He did not cease looking at her as he reached behind them on the bed, picked up the shiny red box and held it out to her. She did not move. He rested the back of his hand on her leg, holding the box, and a single gleaming thread of perspiration moved from the hairline just in front of his ear, down along his jaw.

"It's for you," he said.

"Don't call me that again," she whispered from behind her hand. "I don't want whatever it is."

"Sure, you do. I got it just for you."

She tried to stand. He pressed her down rigidly with his hand on her leg, holding the box, holding her there on the bed.

"Please, Paul."

"If you'd only say there was a chance for me, then I wouldn't even want to give you this present," Paul said.

She swallowed quickly, unobtrusively. "Yes. All right, there *is* a chance, Paul. Really, there is."

He moved his head slowly from side to side, watching her, and he was not smiling now. He seemed very sad. "So," he said. "It's starting already, isn't it? You don't mean that at all. Just squirming."

They watched each other. Neither spoke.

"Here," Paul said. "We'll open your present together. I think it's the best way."

Her gaze dropped to the box. He moved close to her and this time she did not try to move away. She sat stiffly on the bed, staring at the red box with the tiny holes around the sides, and Paul unsnapped a small brass catch, lifting the lid, and the bullet head of the brilliantly colored coral snake wavered out of the box, its long dark red tongue stroking the air in thin lashes.

"Don't scream," Paul said softly. "Just don't scream. I learned how to handle these babies at the wild animal ranch. It's dangerous—but this time it's worth it."

Cleo moaned in her throat, but she did not move. She stared at the snake.

"For you," Paul said. "I got it just for you. Like Cleopatra, see? Isn't he beautiful?"

She did not speak.

Paul's right hand moved in slowly then very fast, caught the snake behind the head. He held it, lashing in the air, and the box fell to the floor. Cleo began making louder noises in her throat and she tried to rise from the bed, but Paul shoved her back. She fell back across the bed, then pulled herself up onto the bed away from Paul, whispering now, "No—no—"

Paul sat beside her and Cleo hunched her shoulders back against the head of the bed and opened her mouth, her throat working.

Paul thrust the snake at her. "Don't," he said. "You make any noise, I'll let him bite you, Cleo."

The scream strangled in her throat as she cut it off with effort, choking. She began crying, without sound, without blinking or even changing expression, the tears oozed from her eyes like oil, dripped on her cheeks.

"That's the way," Paul said.

He moved closer to her, with his back against her, turned, holding the snake close to her. Her white handbag fell to the floor.

"You don't know what to do, do you?" Paul said, his voice rising slightly again. "Now you know how I've felt all this time. How it is to be unable to do anything. Nothing you *can* do—not wanted, trapped—crazy inside. See how it is?"

Cleo nodded, staring at the snake. "Yes—yes."

The snake hung violently rigid and brilliant in Paul's hand, its tiny eyes gleaming in the failing light of the afternoon.

"This is a coral snake," Paul said gently. "You know about them. How completely deadly they are. Everybody lives down here knows about coral snakes. Cleopatra's was an asp, but this one's just as deadly. I caught him just for you, Cleo."

"What do you want?"

Paul shook his head. "It's no use. It's too late now, don't you see? You wouldn't give me a tumble."

"Paul?" Her voice cracked and she shuddered, seeking control, fighting desperately against hysteria. "Paul, listen to me. I didn't know how you felt."

He sighed and stared at the snake. He heard the intake of breath and the first of the scream burst in the room like a shot as his left hand lashed out and clamped over her mouth. The scream was contained in the throat and her face flamed with strain, the eyes wild and urgent above his grip. She struck out at him and he instantly moved the snake toward her throat.

"Stop?" he said.

She shuddered, ceased, and lay quiet, breathing hard. He slowly relaxed his grip on her mouth. She made no further sound. He took his hand away. Her mouth was smeared with lipstick. He wiped his hand on his thigh, but still held the snake close to her throat. Her face was drained of color, gray and tired, the eyes touched with bright terror.

"You see," he said, speaking gently and with a curious sadness. "I can't stand it anymore—I've tried, and I can't. You're going to die, Cleo. There's no other way. But first I want to tell you a few things. If you make any noise, then I'll have to let him bite you. He's very mad. It's up to you."

Her voice was small and faint. "Talk," she said. "Yes," she said. "Talk, Paul—yes . . ."

Tom Anderson's Ford sedan slowed as they came through the business section of town, then drew up to the curb. Winds drew along the streets, raising light dust, folding and unfolding an old newspaper on the sidewalk, and the sun was setting now.

"I turn off here," Tom said.

Al Williams grunted and yawned crackingly, his round face going purplish, eyes watering. "A fine thing," he said hoarsely. "Can't you run me to the edge of town? I'm going to bum to Fort Myers—I'll have to walk blocks."

"Can't you take a bus?"

"Saving my dough, pal."

"I mean to the edge of town."

"The buses are crowded—O. K., you don't want to. But Cleo may not be home. You said she didn't expect you this early. It'll only take you a few minutes."

Tom said nothing, pushed the shift lever into drive, and moved into traffic again.

"Thanks, partner," Williams said. "She'll keep." He turned his head fatly, looking at Anderson. "What'll you two be doing over the weekend?" He chuckled, then went sober, and said, "I mean, of course—"

Tom ignored the remark. "She wants to go on a picnic tomorrow, a place we know. She's crazy about flowers—azaleas. They're in bloom. There's an old mill out in the country. Used to be some kind of show garden, but nobody goes there now. Banks of azaleas."

"Well, well," Williams said. "Love in the azaleas."

"Yeah."

Williams groaned quietly. "I suppose I'll be half the night on the road."

"What are you going down there for?"

"Her name's Nona," Williams said. "A buxom lass, with dark tresses and she administers delicious remedies."

"Seems a long way to go."

"But worth it, my friend."

Tom silently stared at the road and there was a dreamy expression on his face. Williams, too, became quiet. Neither spoke until they reached a corner on the edge of town, where Williams left the car and stood along the curb, waving his thumb.

"Here's hell!" he called.

Tom drove to the Monohans', parked the Ford in the drive and moved rapidly toward the house. He hesitated on the steps as the door opened, and his face brightened, then sobered. It was Mrs. Monohan, wearing a gray cotton housedress with white trim.

"Goodness," Mrs. Monohan said. "You're early. I saw you turn in. Did you see Cleo?"

"Isn't she here?"

Mrs. Monohan looked off up the street, frowning. "She rushed out some time ago. Said she'd only be gone a few minutes." Mrs. Monohan turned to Tom and smiled. "Well, come on in! She'll be along."

Paul Stapleton's bedroom grayed with the last of twilight before dusk. Cleo lay on the bed, hunched back into the pillows, her hands clenched into the twisted spread. She lay perfectly still and stared at the snake in Paul's hand as he talked.

His voice was urgent and contained.

"You understand, Cleo? Nobody else will have you. I couldn't stand that. I tried to work it out another way, but there isn't any other way. I've got to do it." He leaned toward her. "It tears me apart," he said. "See? It's like a bad tooth—it pains you, drives you crazy—so you pull it out and throw it away. Only you've got to suffer like I've suffered, Cleo."

Her eyes were desperate, her face haggard with what was inside her. She tried to speak, but it was only a dry whisper.

"Don't say those things, Paul."

Something came over Paul Stapleton's face, a look of wild urgency, the eyes staring as he reached out, grasped the throat of Cleo's dress and ripped two buttons lose. He began to move his head slowly from side to side.

"You know," he said. "You're so beautiful, and I love you so. We had such good times—don't you see?" He held the snake close to her throat, watching her fixedly. Then he moved still closer, held the snake aside and kissed her, moving his lips on hers. She lay there. Finally he lifted his mouth from hers and she had not changed expression at all, she was exactly the same.

"You don't love me," he shouted. "You don't! So don't pretend—because I'll know." Then he turned his head away, but his eyes still watched her. "Only I can't seem to do it yet," he said, speaking more to himself than to her. He turned violently on her. "You don't believe I love you."

Her mouth opened, eyes wide, but she did not speak.

He again moved the snake close to her throat, his face and arms sheened with perspiration, his hand very steady, and something snapped in Cleo. She cried out, and struck at him, fighting wildly.

"Stop!"

He went at her with direct savageness and his hand with the snake struck the head of the bed. The snake flipped from his hand, bounced off the wall and landed somewhere.

"Now, see—" he said.

He grabbed at Cleo and she strained against him, fighting him. He became furious, dragged her from the bed as she wept, and he whipped his hand around her from behind, clamped it across her jaw and mouth in a vicious lock.

"I'll find him," he whispered, moving toward the bed again. "Don't worry about that. You've got to die, Cleo—don't you see? You've made me this way, Cleo. Because I can't stand knowing . . ." He stopped, listening.

Outside on the street a car door slammed.

Cleo struggled, but he held her easily now, his face crimson, the cords in his arms standing out as he brutally shoved her through the bedroom door into the hall, his hand clamped across her mouth. He forced her at a stumbling run toward the living room.

"It's Essy," he said, and his eyes were vacant.

He squeezed her more tightly and walked and dragged her out through the kitchen. He unlatched the door, then paused, opened a drawer beneath the sink, brought out a bone-handled steak knife. He held it before Cleo's eyes.

"You made me lose him," he whispered.

He jammed her outside and closed the door.

She strained, arching her back, trying to kick at him. His face was wrung as he slammed his arm across her face three fast times, grunting angrily in his throat. He hauled her off the porch and she would not stand now, her legs collapsed. He half carried her to the car, opened the door and forced her in, crawling in with her. She began to fight again.

"We'll go out to the mill," he said calmly. "We won't be disturbed there. You'll like it there. You'll see. Don't cry—please, don't try to fight me."

She struck clumsily at him, trying to claw his arm away, but her blows were weak and flurried now. He got the convertible started, holding his right hand around her mouth, gripping her head into his chest. She kicked at her door. He reached between the steering wheel and shifted the lever and drove the car across a stretch of lawn beyond the garage into an alley, and down the alley toward the street. He slowed the car in the alley and, still holding her, checked her window, then rolled his up. He slammed her over against the far door and headed the car out into the street.

"Go ahead," he said. "Yell your head off."

On the rumpled blue bed in Paul Stapleton's bedroom, the beautiful red-, yellow-, and black-striped coral snake slowly moved, head up, tongue lashing in slow intervals, as it slid soundlessly into a deep furrow of twisted blanket. It rested there, just the tip of its tail showing and there was no further movement.

Esther Stapleton stood reeling on the front sidewalk, listening to the sound of her brother's car behind the house. She wept softly and she was quite drunk, holding the black purse by a long strap in her left hand. Her hair was mussed, and her dress was covered with white powdery dust on the side of her skirt, where she had taken a tumble, getting out of the car at the curb.

She was speaking softly aloud:

"Paul? Where you going, Paul—was that you? Oh, that Gregg!"

She swung the purse, then started up the walk to the porch, veering to the left, then recovering.

"I'm so-o-o-ooo sick," she said aloud. "So awfully—awfully sick."

She moved slowly up the porch steps, finally reached the door and tried it, but it was locked. She leaned back against the door, her head very heavy, eyes snapping closed as she searched in her purse and brought out a key.

After opening the door, she went inside, then fell back against it and it slammed shut.

"Paul?"

There was no answer.

"I heard you, Paul—you in the house?"

She lurched through the dim living room, dropped her purse at a chair, but missed. It clattered behind the chair, spilled open across the floor.

"I'm sick, Paul—I'm sick. I was with Gregg—he was awful. Never see him again. I hate him, Paul—hate him, hate him—do you hear me?"

She paused by his bedroom door. The room was a mass of still shadows now. She began to cry softly to herself, her head hanging down on her breast, her entire body drooping. She entered the room and stood by the window, staring out at the slowly enveloping darkness.

"Gone," she said. "Paul went out."

She turned, hiccupped, lurched backward and fell on the bed.

For a time she sat on the edge of the bed, silently weeping, occasionally cursing the man called Gregg, then she sighed deeply and fell back on the bed and began to snore.

For some time there was no movement in the room; only the lifting of Esther Stapleton's breasts as she slept, and the sound of light snoring.

Then about a foot beyond her head, the coral snake wound up and out of the covers, tiny red tongue stroking the air as it moved toward her hair. The snake did not cease moving. It met her hair and slid right through it, silently parting the hair, moving down around her forehead, and under her chin. Esther Stapleton swallowed a snore, lifted one arm brushing at the snake with her eyes closed and it bit her on the throat, then wound down over her body as she moved blindly. It bit her again and she sat up, reeling on the bed with a sharp cry of pain.

She sat on the bed, then fell sidewards, rubbing her throat, making small cries, and the snake dropped to the floor.

"Paul?"

The snake moved in the darkness of the shadowed floor.

Esther Stapleton pulled herself to her feet, making tiny painful sounds, rubbing her neck. She started for the door and stepped hard on something. It rolled and slid beneath her foot, and she fell on the snake and it bit her again as she saw it in the solution of gray light from the window.

She screamed. She grabbed blindly, dragged the straight chair by the window to the floor, rolling away from the snake, sobbing, and lurched to her knees. She clubbed the chair at the snake, struck its head and it writhed on the floor. She came to her feet, then fell to her knees, trying to get out of the door.

In the hallway, she managed to gain her feet, and turned at a run into the kitchen. She swung at the cupboard doors, reached in and grasped cans and jars that clattered out about her feet. She moaned to herself, tried to find the light switch on the wall by the stove, but she was a good foot out of the way. She whirled and ran down the hall, bumping the wall, and entered her bedroom, panting heavily, and then into the bathroom. In the darkness, she got the light turned on, and tried to inspect her throat in the mirror on the medicine chest over the sink. She could not hold her head up.

For a long time she stood at the sink, gripping the edge, trying to see into the mirror. She clawed the contents of the medicine chest out into the sink.

Her face was red, her eyes wild, and she turned running into her bedroom and fell. She tried to rise, couldn't. She grasped the covers on her bed, seeking a firm hold, but only succeeded in pulling them from the bed out on the floor, and in her struggles she became entangled. She kept muttering to herself in a whisper now, and when she tried to scream it was only a whisper.

"Phone," she breathed. She moved toward the living room and the first of the true reaction from the venom struck. She lay quite still, then finally made another weak and paralyzed attempt to reach the living room.

Mrs. Monohan came out of the kitchen for the fifth time and looked at Tom, seated on the couch by the front window in the Monohan living room. He turned sharply when she stepped through the arch in the hallway.

"I don't understand it," Mrs. Monohan said. "Dinner's all ready. Goodness, it's been ready for nearly an hour."

Tom said nothing. He watched Mrs. Monohan twine her hands in the small frill of red apron she was wearing.

"You're sure she didn't say where she was going?" Tom said finally, leaning forward on the couch. His eyes were worried beneath scowling brows. He had asked her the same thing only a few moments before.

"No. She didn't say. She just said she was running out for a few minutes—she'd be right back. There was that phone call."

"Phone call?" Tom stood up, still scowling. "You didn't mention a phone call before."

"I know." Mrs. Monohan gestured, then rubbed her right hand across her forehead, lifting a wave of damp brown hair. She turned and moved down the hall toward the front door.

"What phone call?" Tom said.

"Oh, it was nothing—just a phone call," Mrs. Monohan said, peering out the window in the front door. She lowered her head, then turned back toward the kitchen. Tom entered the hall. Mrs. Monohan said, "I do wish my husband were home. It's beginning to worry me. He won't be along till at least nine, he had a meeting in Tampa—some directors dinner—"

"Mrs. Monohan, I don't want to pry."

"Cleo told me she didn't want to talk with anybody on the phone," Mrs. Monohan explained. "I thought she should. I suppose if I hadn't done what I did—I called her, you see? Insisted that she answer."

"Oh? Who was it?"

Mrs. Monohan hesitated. "I don't know. It was a man, that's all I know."

Tom turned and went back to the couch and set down. He sat with his elbows on his knees, hands clasped, and stared at the floor. He pursed his lips, then sat back and sighed, fingering the magazines beside him. There was a step on the sidewalk out by the street. He turned quickly and lifted the venetian blinds, looked out. A couple walked past, talking softly, laughing. He let the blinds drop.

Mrs. Monohan watched him from the archway.

"She knew you'd be here by seven," she said. "It's after seven now." She turned toward the kitchen, then looked at Tom again. "Why don't you eat something? I could fix your dinner. You must be starved."

"No," Tom said. "I'm not hungry. I guess I'd rather wait for Cleo."

"Yes," Mrs. Monohan said. She moved slowly out to the kitchen again. She paused, called back, "Why not play some records, look at TV, or something?"

"I'll be all right," Tom said, turning and lifting the venetian blinds again.

Gregg Tillotson stopped the borrowed car he was driving behind Esther's coupé, turned off the ignition, and looked through the window toward the Stapleton cottage. There was a light inside, somewhere in the middle of the house. It shone against the front windows. Sitting there, Tillotson grinned to himself, a brown, dark-haired, medium-sized man, with sharp features, wearing a loud checked sport shirt and light trousers. He found a pocket comb and ran it through his hair, put it away, then climbed out of the car, softly whistling. He closed the car door carefully, then walked up the lawn toward the porch. On the way, he located a stick of gum, popped it into his mouth, and chewed briskly. He stood for a moment at the foot of the porch steps, chewing and swallowing. Then he braced his shoulders, whistled loudly, and tromped up the steps and knocked at the door.

There was no answer.

He ceased whistling and knocked again. "Esther? Hey, baby, come on. I know you're in there. Saw your car outside—still mad?"

The house remained silent. He peered in the front door window, saw light coming through the front bedroom, bathing the living room floor. He saw part of Esther's purse on the floor by the hall behind a chair, and a shoe near the telephone stand.

He knocked again, tried the door, and it swung open, creaking softly. "Baby?"

He stepped inside and started to close the door, then stared at Esther Stapleton, who lay in a curiously contorted position with one knee up under her, her shoulders twisted so she lay half on her back, her face and head arched rigidly, mouth open, and the phone lay tipped over on the floor near her hand.

"Drunk as a lord," Gregg Tillotson said.

For another moment he stood there, looking at her. Then he finished closing the door, stepped over by Esther, stared down at her and shook his head. He kicked one of her feet and it snapped back loosely, her head fell around and she slid further down onto the floor. He leaned and picked up the phone, listened to the dial hum, set it on the table in place again. Immediately he became furtive, glanced quickly around, listening. There was no sound except for his own breathing.

He stepped toward the hall, saw the spilled purse again, behind the chair, knelt down and rapidly pawed around. He found a small, snap-clasp change purse, opened it, withdrew some bills and stuffed them into his pocket. He dropped the change purse on the floor and stood up again, bolder now.

Beside Esther, he stared down at her and began whistling softly. Then he said aloud, "I told you to lay off that hard stuff." He chuckled, started to turn away, then looked at her again, quietly now.

Light from the bathroom spread through the bedroom door across Esther and when he tipped her head up he saw that she was staring at him, the lids of her eyes drooping. He became tense and his expression changed subtly. He straightened with a snap, his face holding the set expression, and backed toward the door.

"Dead," he said. "She's dead for God's sake."

As he left the house, he did not see the tears in Esther Stapleton's eyes and he did not hear her whispered moan.

To Cleo Monohan, seated in the car slowly moving through the night, what was happening was not even a dream; it was simply another early evening with a glare of white headlights out there on macadam, and a humming that was undistinguished, but which she supposed in the latter part of her mind was the sound of the car's engine. She sat there, her legs close together, the yellow dress pulled tightly down over her knees, her hands in her lap, palms up, staring at the windshield. She looked prim and composed except for the torn bodice of her dress which exposed the firm, round tops of her breasts and some white brassiere.

"The sun will shine tomorrow afternoon out by the mill," Paul Stapleton said. "We'll be together again—like last summer." He paused for a time, driving slowly. "I've been thinking, Cleo. I can't let you live. But what good will it be for me to go on living after you're dead?"

She turned her head slowly and looked down at the knife, then up at his face, etched pallidly in the dash-glow, strained forward above the wheel. He held the steak knife with the winking blade toward her on the seat.

"I want to go home," she said. "Home, Paul?"

"You can't, darling. You can never go home again." He did not look at her, his voice persuasive and gentle. Then his lips lifted away from his teeth. "You're not listening to me," he said. He brought the knife up high, still not looking at her, angrily drove the knife into the car seat close to her leg. The blade slipped through the edge of her dress and went in to the hilt. He drew it out slowly with a short laugh, and laid his hand on the seat, gripping the knife, the blade toward her as before. "You've got to listen to me."

Cleo placed both hands against the sides of her face and screamed, the nails digging into her face. She turned, pressed her palms flat against the window on her side of the car and stared out screaming as they passed beneath a streetlight on a corner at the outskirts of town. She ceased screaming and stared at the fat, red-faced young man who stood in the road with his thumb up, calling to them. She kept her face pressed against the window as they moved slowly on into the night.

"He didn't pay any attention to you," Paul said. "He's thumbing the next car. Cleo, it's inevitable. There's nothing to be done. Don't you see that even if I wasn't going to kill you now, I couldn't let you go? You'd run back home with some wild story about me."

"No, Paul—no!" She twisted in the seat, touched his arm. "You'll see, it won't be like that. We could go home, and we could come out here every day. Just the two of us."

"Don't lie to me," he said loudly. "You keep lying. Save it till tomorrow afternoon." He slowed the car still more and they were in the country now, passing beneath the star-studded sky. "We're both going to die," he said. "First you, then me. That's the way it's got to be."

She watched him.

"We'll spend the night together," Paul said, calm again. "Among the flowers—and we can talk, you'll see. You won't hate me so much. I'm going to make you understand me, Cleo. Make you understand just how I feel." He hunched over the wheel, nodding to himself. "It's much better this way—much better than with the snake. It would have hurt you more that way—taken longer, and I really don't want to hurt you."

"I won't scream again," Cleo said.

"Fine," Paul said. "I'm glad of that."

He began to drive faster now. They reached a turn where he took the convertible bouncing along a dirt road banked high on either side with pine trees that hedged the paler sky.

"Nearly there," Paul said. There was a note of excitement now that had not been with him moments before. "Recognize it?"

She did not speak. She knelt on the seat, staring at him, and whenever she moved, he moved the knife toward her along the seat.

He turned the car up a slope, gunning the engine, and they came through a fallen fence among some cedars and oaks, then into a stepped field beside a stream. He drove along the stream past a dam with a bridged walk across the top, and around under some large live oaks that circled the water of the mill pond, and directly into a partially tumbled-down barn. He turned off the ignition and sighed in the darkness.

"We're here, Cleo," he said. "Give me your hand."

They came out of the barn and stood in the white wash of early moonlight. Paul held Cleo's right hand with his left and he still carried the knife. He seemed eager and began tugging her up around the barn, through a sparse woods.

"Paul?"

"Yes, darling?"

He paused, looking at her, and the moonlight struck his face, gleaming on the sheen of perspiration. Cleo swallowed, and spoke with effort.

"I'll just *have* to leave you for a minute, Paul."

"Think," Tom Anderson said. "Think, Mrs. Monohan. Try hard to remember. Are you certain you didn't recognize that voice over the phone?"

Mrs. Monohan sat on the chair across from the couch in the living room. The house was silent save for the slow, reverberant ticking of the china clock on the mantel. She tensed her lips and slowly shook her head, avoiding his eyes. "No. No, I can't remember. Do you think I should call my husband?"

"I don't know," Tom said.

They looked at each other. Tom rose from the couch and walked out into the hall, then came back again.

"You're sure she didn't mention having anything on for tonight? I mean, before I got here—something like that?"

"Oh, no," Mrs. Monohan said. "But she has been acting sort of, well—peculiar. Strange." She ceased, tensed her lips again and stared down into her lap. She had changed her clothes and wore a light tan dress of some smooth material now. She had put on lipstick, carefully combed her hair, and was holding a handkerchief wadded into a ball, peeking from her right fist. She held her hands in her lap, seated on the edge of the chair, with her legs crossed, and stared at her hands.

Tom watched her from the hallway. He ran one hand harshly through his red hair, brought it down around the back of his head and across his neck, brutally, digging at the flesh.

"There anyone else you could call?" He said, bringing the words out one by one as if they held edges. "Anyone might know where she is?"

"I've called all her girl friends. You heard me."

Tom watched her but she did not look at him. She kept staring at her lap, then up toward the clock. Tom stepped toward her, then stopped.

"Mrs. Monohan," he said. "It's getting later all the time and we're both worried." He took another step toward her and she glanced at him, then down into her lap again. She opened her mouth to speak, but did not. She began to touch her teeth across her lower lip, then she quit that as she became conscious of what she was doing.

Suddenly she stood up, turn and looked at Tom, squeezed the handkerchief, and looked away.

"Mrs. Monohan, if there's something you're not telling me—?"

She looked at him quickly. "I didn't want to mention it," she said falteringly. "I don't know—I don't think I should. It's probably nothing."

They watched each other and Tom breathed deeply.

"She went out with someone else? Didn't come back yet?"

"No. She told me just this noon how she really feels about you. She wouldn't do a thing like that, unless—"

"Unless what?"

"The phone call, Tom."

He spoke very slowly. "What about the phone call?"

"I'm sorry, but I think I *do* know who it was."

He did not speak, waiting. The china clock on the mantel chimed eight-thirty, and he glanced at it angrily, then back at Mrs. Monohan.

"I think it was a boy named Stapleton. Paul Stapleton. Cleo went around with him a little last summer."

He still said nothing, his face changing subtly from worry to a kind of impatient excitement.

"I suppose I shouldn't say anything. She acted very funny today. Didn't want to answer the phone, like I said." Mrs. Monohan turned away, then back toward Tom. "I recognized his voice when I answered the phone. I'd told her she should tell him to leave her alone."

"Leave her alone?"

"He's been bothering her. Nothing serious—just calling all the time, calling her friends, asking them strange questions about her. Things like that—he came into church once and sat with her all through service, whispering. He's well—a strange boy."

"You're sure that's who it was?"

"Oh, yes. I'm sure, Tom. She talked with him for a while, then went out right afterwards."

He moved rapidly across to her. "Why didn't you tell me this before?"

She gestured nervously. "I'm sorry. I thought it was Cleo's place to tell you."

"Yes. That's what I thought."

"You know him?"

He was thinking and did not answer immediately. When he did, he spoke more to himself than to her. "Yes, I know him."

"She doesn't like him at all, Tom. Really. I know that."

"Yes." He started toward the hall, then turned again. "I'm going out for a while," he said. "If Cleo comes in, have her wait."

"You think everything's all right?"

"Don't worry."

He went quickly to the telephone at the foot of the stairway, picked up the directory, and flipped it open on his knee, found the page he wanted.

Mrs. Monohan looked as if she wanted to speak. She only nodded and watched him with troubled eyes.

He laid the book down and turned toward the door.

"I won't be long."

She started after him, then paused, one hand out, still clutching the handkerchief. She moved toward the hallway again, but Tom was already out on the porch, closing the door.

Mrs. Monohan stood in the hallway, knotting her handkerchief and listened to the silence of the house.

Gregg Tillotson stood at the bar of the Drink 'Em Up, a tavern on Fifth, and stared through drunken eyes at the phone booth. He was drinking whisky from a tall glass, and three patrons and the barman eyed him with the occasional subtle frowning concern given any strange customer who looks as if he might fuse unwanted action.

Tillotson's lank brown hair hung down over his right eye and he drained his glass, rapped for service. The barman came over and Tillotson pointed to his glass, then stared at the phone booth again and shook his head, then laid his head on his arms on the bar.

"Don't you think you've had enough?" the bartender asked. "You better head for home, fella."

"Fill that damned glass," Tillotson said. "Hear?"

The bartender shrugged, moved to the back bar and reached for a bottle, his lips pursed.

Tillotson stepped away from the bar and stared at the phone booth as if it were animate. He smeared hair off his face with one hand, and reeled down the length of the bar, walking rapidly. He went into the booth, rammed the door shut, and dialed.

The bartender watered Tillotson's whisky liberally.

A coin clanged.

"Hello," Tillotson said. "Police? . . . Woman dead, something wrong . . . No! . . . 777 Hibiscus Court . . . That's all . . . Dum-de-dum-dum!" He hung up and stood there, reeling in the booth, very drunk. Then he slid the door open, stepped out, and began to cry.

Tom Anderson drove fast across town, found Hibiscus Court, and turned down the quiet suburban block. The glow from a streetlight illumined brass numerals on the front porch of the Stapleton cottage, and Tom parked behind the bantam coupé. He climbed from his car, walked around the coupé, looking at it, then moved swiftly up the front lawn to the porch. The front door was slightly ajar.

He stood there, frowning, then knocked on the door and it swung open, revealing Esther Stapleton lying inside on the floor.

She lay flat on her back now, staring at the ceiling, and when he came to her side she moaned faintly.

He knelt, lifted her head. In the light from the bathroom, he could see her swollen, punctured throat, her swollen left arm. She was rather rigid, her eyes unalive, and she was whispering.

"Paul," she said. It was so faint, he could only hear with his ear close to her mouth. "What did you do to that girl, Paul? I know you did something to that girl."

"What girl?" Tom said.

Her voice became still fainter, and there was pain within her, but not enough life to react to the pain.

"Can't move," Esther Stapleton whispered. "Paul—what have you done? Gregg came took couldn't hear me, Paul what have you done? Know you've done something to that girl."

Tom's voice was harsh. He held her up in a sitting position, gripping her shoulders, staring into her face.

"What happened?" he said. "What girl?"

"Snake," she said.

He shook her violently. Her head rolled on her breast.

"Snake," she said. ". . . Paul?"

"What snake?"

"Paul?"

He held her that way for several seconds, almost shouting the harsh questions, before he realized that she had died in his hands. He still held her, staring, holding her stiffly now. Then he carefully laid her on the floor, and knelt beside her. He started to say something, watching her, but he did not speak. Finally he stood up, looked at the phone on the table and started toward it.

He stood by the phone with his hand out, and a slow wind edged the door open still more as it creaked on unoiled hinges. He turned to the door, looked out there at the white wash of streetlights on the lawn and a car hissed past slowly, radio playing. He glanced at the phone again, muttered something, then grabbed the phone book, laid it down, picked up the phone and dialed.

"Operator? Operator, call an ambulance . . . Yes? Have them come to 777 Hibiscus Court, right away." He hung up, stepped away and went into Esther Stapleton's bedroom.

He stumbled on knotted bedclothes strewn in a twisted mass about the floor, and went on through into the bathroom, breathing heavily, almost panting, his movements jerky. He stared at the broken bottles in the sink, returned through the bedroom again and came out past Esther Stapleton's body, glanced at the phone, hesitated, then moved to the front door and closed it. He turned fast, and walked down the hall toward the darkness of the kitchen.

He switched the hall light on midway, and as he came past the bedroom, light angled brightly into the room and he saw the mess it was in, and the snake on the floor.

He entered, turned on the bedroom light and a dark stain of red light illuminated the walls and furnishings. The red bulb was naked in the ceiling. He made a small unpleasant sound in his throat, started toward the snake, then stared at the white basket-like handbag on the floor under the edge of the bed. He grabbed it up, found a thin red wallet, looked inside and then stood there.

"Cleo," he said.

He started toward the door of the room, stopped and looked with repugnance at the snake. It was dead, apparently having been struck with the straight chair that was upended nearby. Again he started for the door and his shoulder knocked against a brown notebook that lay precariously on the edge of the bureau. The notebook fell, open. He picked it up and a pressed red flower fell to the floor from between its leaves. He picked that up. It was an azalea and apparently had been there for some time. He held the flower, his face flushed, eyes drawn together, forehead wrinkled, and flipped through the notebook. There were several girl's names and addresses, some writing here and there. He paused, began reading silently, then gradually read aloud:

"Cleopatra—'Hast thou the pretty worm of Nilus there, that kills and pains not?' Clown—'Truly, I have him; but I would not be the party that should desire you to touch him, for his biting is immortal; those that to die of it do seldom or never recover.'" The last several words were underscored deeply, and Tom began to read again, then stopped.

A siren moaned softly several blocks away. He hurried out of the bedroom and down through the hall into the living room and stood by the front door, holding the notebook. A police cruiser was just stopping with a soft screak of rubber and breaks at the curb. The driver and his partner came running from the prowl car toward the house.

Tom stared, frowning, then turned and ran lightly through the house toward the kitchen. As he let himself out the kitchen door, he heard the front door creak open.

He moved slowly around the side of the house, keeping well in the shadows, the notebook still in his hand.

"I'm awfully sorry," Cleo said. "I can't help it, Paul."

"Damn it," Paul Stapleton said.

They stood up beyond the barn in the stray moonlight that found its way through the woods. He released her hand, staring at her, and she moved a single pace away. He closed in on her, looking into her eyes. The knife winked as he slapped the blade against his leg and cleared his throat.

"I can't trust you for that," he said.

"Yes—you can, too!"

She watched him. She swallowed and glanced once sideways toward the deeper part of the woods. He reached out and caught the side of her face, held it toward him.

"You can," she said. "I couldn't get away from you, Paul. Not now. Besides, I don't want to get away—from you."

He said nothing, staring closely at her.

Finally, he said, "No. That's true. Where could you go?"

"I don't want to go, Paul." She looked at him and smiled and she moved toward him, smiling. The smile was on her lips, but it was not in her eyes, though she wrinkled her eyes up, looking at him, and moved closer to him. She touched his arm with her fingers.

"I'll only be gone for a minute."

"How can I know?"

There was quiet agitation in his voice, but he spoke softly. He slapped the knife against his leg.

"Paul—I *mean* it."

"Please," he said.

The night was very still save for the wind on the tops of the trees and the moonlight was like snow on the hill; the moonlight like ice on top of the barn and the smooth surface of the water in the pond.

"Really, Paul."

"All right," he said. "But we'll talk. You'll keep talking to me."

"Yes. That's a good way, Paul. Only I do wish you'd trust me."

"God," he said. "Don't say that."

She started to speak, but did not. She moved a little away from him and said, "See, Paul? We can talk."

"Hurry up," he said with sudden viciousness.

She turned and ran swiftly toward the deeper shadows of the woods.

"Cleo?"

"Yes?"

"Keep talking to me," he said loudly.

"Yes, Paul."

"Don't go too far away—you hear me?"

"Yes. I won't."

"Cleo?"

"Yes?"

"Wait. That's far enough."

She did not answer.

"Cleo!" he shouted.

"Yes, Paul," she called softly.

"Right there. No farther. That's far enough." He could not see her. He waited a moment, beating the blade of the knife against his leg. "Cleo?"

She did not answer.

"Stop, Cleo—didn't you hear me!" He began moving toward her. "Cleo!"

She did not answer. He cursed savagely and ran headlong toward the dark area of the woods where she had vanished.

"Cleo!" he shouted. His voice echoed and then was muffled among the trees and there was loud agony in the sound. "Cleo—!"

He ran violently, stumbling, holding the knife.

As soon as she was in the shadows, she turned and ran. She grabbed her skirts up and pumped at the ground, running with all her might over toward the slant of the hill through the thicker woods. It was young pine and oak scrub for the most part in this area beyond the stepped ground where the flower bushes were. Her body flashed running in the snowy moonlight, her moccasined feet light against the slippery-needled ground.

"Cleo!"

She did not pause, gasping and sobbing, her eyes stricken with fear and the possibility of escape. It had been an only chance and she had taken it, and for the moment she had won over him.

She tripped and fell sliding on her face among the smooth brown needles, started to scramble to her feet, then lay still, listening.

He crashed through brush a bit above and to the left, yelling her name so it echoed and rebounded against the night, screaming her name. He ran in short violent bursts, pausing between for the sound of her running. Then it was silent and there was no sound at all save for her restricted, choking breath and the angry sobs in her throat. She pressed her face against the ground, covered her mouth with her hands, trying to muffle even her breathing.

"Cleo?" he said from not very far away. "I'll find you—believe me— I'll find you." His voice was more than just calm; it was wrung dead. There was no sound at all of his moving now, yet the voice came nearer. "And when I do, we won't wait, Cleo. I knew I couldn't trust you. Cleo!" he shouted, cursing her, shouting obscenely into the moon-washed woods.

Cleo's shoulders heaved above the ground, her mouth wide with an attempt for silent air. She clutched at the front of her dress, listening.

"We'll bleed together," Paul Stapleton said, still nearer now, but above and to the left in the woods, moving absolutely without any noise whatever. "I'm glad I didn't let the snake bite you," he went on, speaking in that wrung and dead tone. "You aren't worthy of the snake. What was I thinking, to bring you out here—soil the only thing we had? Do you hear me, Cleo? Do you think you're going to get away—do you?" He laughed softly, then shouted again, wild with it. "Cleo! When I find you, I'm going to kill you."

She sprang to her feet, running with the sound of his shout still upon the cooling air, and instantly he burst upon the narrow clearing where she had lain. He whirled, glared around, then ran at the sound of her feet.

She came out of the woods, gripping her skirts up, sobbing without restraint now. For a second she stood utterly still in a flash of futility, the moonlight coldly bathing her, and he was loud behind her now, running. She ran. She came along the edge of the woods, the dark soft pine boughs brushing her arms, then she plunged into it again and stood still, then began to walk very softly toward the downward slope of the gentle hill, felt rather than seen in the dark thickness of the pines.

"Cleo?"

Again he was near, calling softly, his tone almost musical now, singing the name out upon the night earnestly, but somehow tragically.

She kept moving down the slope. The woods became thicker and she moved among pines planted closer together, and the boughs waved and brushed and palmed her. She trembled all over at intervals between her choked breathing, and once a moan escaped her throat before she could prevent it.

"I heard you, Cleo."

She began to run again. The sound of his voice had frightened her with its nearness. He moved silently and seemed to sense where she was.

"You know you can't drive a car, Cleo," he called. "So that won't do you any good—" and she fell again. And again she lay still.

He laughed from back there. Quick, short, soft laughter—flat and cold. "The only thing is," he said. "I still love you. I still want you, just like always. I tried to find other girls like you, only it's no good. What's the use of running?" he said, standing silently, or perhaps moving slowly toward her from someplace in the woods, his voice not loud now, just speaking conversationally. "I am going to kill you, Cleo. *You know that.* You must know it. How else can it be? Don't you understand that I can't let you go? I can't live knowing you're alive—with other men." His voice ceased painfully, then he spoke again. "And I don't want to live after you're dead." He paused for some time, waiting, and she lay there on the ground, not even sobbing now, just holding her mouth open, drawing air into her lungs. She kept trying to see down past the trees, but she could only see the frost of moonlight on the boughs.

"So," Paul said. "We'll die together. By the knife. It's a clean way, Cleo. The cleanest, really. Do you understand now?"

Silence.

Very carefully she rose to her hands and knees, looking off down the slope between the trees. She saw a flash of the barn roof down there, ice-white in the night, smooth and flat, and a reflection of water from the pond, no larger than a fly's wing. She began very slowly to creep down the slope, her hands and knees sliding among the smooth needles.

"Cleo?"

She did not pause. She moved very slowly down the slope, a foot at a time, putting first one hand out and feeling for solid ground, then setting it, then one knee, carefully, and then another hand . . . moving in a solid pool of fear down the slope toward more of the same nothing she crept through right now.

He called her name again, but there was something new in his voice; a note of warmth, of love, even. She looked back once over her shoulder, her face wild in the moonlight, her hair fallen down across her arms.

"Cleo? When I find you, I'll have to kill you—but if you'd come to me now, we'll wait." He ceased and laughed. It was high, tight laughter that was close to hysteria, drawn with agony.

She came to the sparse woods and rose carefully to her feet, looking down the slope at the old mill, the barn and the pond. Beyond the pond, across the bridge on the dam, the woods were thick again. The only way she could get over there was to cross the dam and that would show her full in the bright white moonlight.

"Cleo?"

He was running toward her. His feet pounded down the slope, and with every step he grunted softly.

She ran again. She came through the woods past some of the sleeping azalea bushes, and turned toward the barn.

"I see you," he called.

She looked back, running toward the barn, and saw him come out of the woods, holding the knife high, the blade flashing.

She stumbled now, exhausted. She weaved from one side to the other, panting as she reached the side of the barn. He came running very fast and she looked at the barn, moved quickly around to the front, then past the opening and over toward the pond. She leaped down the bank into waist-high grass and mud, and stood silent below the cover of the bank, gasping into her hands, her eyes turned up, watching as he came down the slope and around the corner of the barn.

Turning, she ran toward the dam along the soggy bank. He came toward her from the barn, not even running, lurching and crashing with the knife, and he saw her fall into thick weeds and heard her cry.

"I've got you now, Cleo," he said.

On her feet again, she kept moving, and reached the bridge that crossed the top of the dam. The water was perhaps fifteen feet deep in the damned-up pond, a shallow trickle on the other side. She ran heavily, staggering across the bridge, past the wheel that operated the dam openings, and came to the other side.

Paul crossed the dam, walking heavily, the knife gleaming at his side.

"No use running," he called. "Really—can't you see that? There's no place for you to go."

She was in the edge of the woods on the other side, but she could no longer move. She lay back against the slope of a large scrub oak and stared at him as he came closer to her. She was panting like an animal, and she slowly slipped down the tree until she was on the ground, her yellow dress stained and splotched with mud now, her pale face turned up toward him as he silently approached.

"We were going to wait until tomorrow afternoon," he said. "In the sunshine. But now we're not. Only first," he said softly. "You've got to learn to understand how much I love you. There's only one way to show you that."

"Paul."

He did not speak.

She tried to move, but could not. She watched him come up to her, the moonlight cold and white across his shoulders.

Tom came slowly around the side of the Stapleton cottage, pressed in among the bushes, and he could hear them talking in the living room.

"Get on the phone, Stew—she's dead."

"What killed her?"

"Looks like snakebite to me. Throat, arm, and just above the right knee."

Tom heard one of them walk through the house.

"Better call homicide."

"What?"

"This place's a mess. It was a coral snake, Stew. Man, three times—it's no wonder. Better get a doc out here fast, though—just in case we're wrong. Hey, the back door's open."

He ran along the side of the house, reaching with his feet for whatever silence he could find. He ran for his car at the curb, opened the door, slammed behind the wheel and looked once toward the cottage as he started the engine. There was no sign of them. He threw it into gear, jammed the accelerator, and sped down the street. In the rear view mirror, he saw one of them run down across the lawn, but there were no shots.

He drove fast along back streets and after a time slowed. No car was in sight behind him. He parked near a streetlight, shut off lights and engine, and sat there. Finally, he opened the notebook again, and read some more in the light from the streetlight, his face a deep scowl as he gnawed the inside of his cheek.

"... I tell you, what have I ever done that you should do this to me? God, God, I can't stand it! There is only the one simple thing to do, and I am going to do it, because there is no other way. She laughed at me—*laughed!* Sometimes the walls of the room come in at me, folding down upon me, and there is laughter in everything I see, her laughter, as she laughs at me . . . last summer out there among her flowers that she loves more than she even *likes* the thought of me. We must go there once more before I do it. Why won't she listen? . . . and sometimes it's all I can do to keep from telling Esther, but I'll have to kill her, there is no other way."

He turned pages rapidly, came to the list of names and addresses: Angela Marrs, 69 Port Terrace. He stared at the first name on the list, his face pale, threw the notebook aside, started the car and drove off.

Port Terrace was down by the bay, a street that wound on old brick between large homes in tall lanes of royal palms. The air from the bay was warm, soft, sulphurous and not unpleasant, as he parked the car in the winding drive of the Marrs home.

A portly, middle-aged man with an empty martini glass in his hand answered Tom's ring.

"Is Angela home?"

"Yes? Who—?"

"A friend—could you tell her?"

The man stared, gestured with the glass, raised bristly gray eyebrows, turned and walked away calling the girl's name.

Tom waited, just inside the doorway, in a large marble-floored hall. Saffron light exploded in small bursts on glazed columns, and he heard quick, light footfalls, then stared at the tall, slim girl who moved toward him, auburn hair full about her oval face, the hair drawn back into a pony tail. The girl wore a pale blue sheath dress, with a black belt, and slippers.

"Yes?" she said lightly, frowning.

He stared, not speaking.

She halted a few feet from him, smiled, then tipped her head to one side. "I'm afraid I don't know you," she said. "What is it?"

"You're Angela Marrs?"

"Yes?"

"I'm sorry," Tom said. "I didn't mean to stare. You look like someone I know."

"Oh?"

He rammed his hands nervously into his trousers pockets, then removed them. "Do you know Paul Stapleton?"

She straightened and her face was quite sober.

Her voice was stiff. "Are you a friend of Paul's?"

"I just wondered—?"

"You'd better go." She moved quickly to the door, opened it and stood aside, regarding him coldly.

He stepped over to her. "I'm no friend of his, Miss Marrs. I just wondered if you've maybe seen him?"

"I'm sorry, no. Goodnight."

"Please, Miss Marrs, it's very important."

She started to say something, then did not. She looked at Tom, then said, "The person I look like—is her name Cleo?"

"Yes."

"You'd better go," she said. "I mean it."

"Please, Miss Marrs, look—"

She shook her head, holding the door. "I'll call Father," she said. "I mean it—I had all I can stand of that guy—he's crazy, and I mean crazy!"

He did not move. She turned from the door and began walking rapidly along the hall.

"Miss Marrs?"

She paused, turned to him again.

"Have you any idea where he might be?"

"If I know Paul, he's probably out among his damned azaleas!" Again she whirled and walked off.

Tom returned to the car, drove down the block and parked again. He opened the notebook, his hands nervous and rough with the pages, breathing sharply now, and checked the second name on the list. Ruby Gallant, 5130 Rose Park. He drove off, hunched up over the wheel, giving the car everything it had.

In the steep twist of hills and streets of Rose Park, he stopped the car at the Gallant address, and was already out on the curb when he stopped. He climbed back in, slammed the door, and drove off. He struck one of the main streets in town, and pulled in at a gas station. The attendant moved toward him.

"Use your phone?" Tom said.

"Inside."

He dialed and waited, his face drawn and white now.

"Mr. Monohan? . . . Yes, I see—listen. I took a chance you'd be home by now, this is Tom—Tom Anderson. Don't let on to Mrs. Monohan—I think I know where Cleo is . . . yes. Listen, you've got to contact the police . . . No—listen, Mr. Monohan, you've got to listen. Damn it, I don't give a damn what you think, you've got to listen . . . yes! Listen, there's an old mill outside of town." He gave directions, his voice cut fine with tension and excitement now, not quite shouting into the phone. The attendant watched him from just outside the plate glass window of the station office. "I would go to the police, but I can't waste time," Tom said. "I've wasted too much already, and they wouldn't mean to, but they'd slow me down. I've got to get out there. It's this Stapleton—Paul Stapleton . . . No, Mr. Monohan—yes, I think he's flipped, or something . . . I'm sorry, do you think *I* wanted this to happen? . . . no, it's something he wrote, something in a notebook of his . . . For God's sake!"

Tom hung up, and turned running for his car.

"Say," the attendant said. "You'd better wait a minute."

Tom reached the car, flung open the door, got behind the wheel and drove off. He headed on out of town, and as he passed the corner where he'd let Williams out, he saw that there was no one standing beneath the streetlight.

He spoke half aloud, muttering above the steering wheel. "She's got to be there—*she's got to.*"

Once out of town, he stepped the engine up still more, and he held to the wheel with a kind of subdued patience, watching the white glare of the headlights on the road. The night swept past, his expression intensely patient.

He drove past the turn-off that led to the mill. He was nearly a quarter of a mile down the road, before he realized his mistake and, using the brakes harshly, he made a swift U-turn and approached from the opposite direction. He took the car up into the dirt road, between the hedge of pines, and began to drive more slowly, searching up ahead in the shadowed, wooded country.

Finally he stopped the sedan, turned off the ignition and lights, and got out. He did not close the door, but immediately began running along the road, breathing heavily.

There was no sound. His feet drummed rhythmically against the hard-packed sand and clay of the road, and he stopped, listening, then took to the grassy shoulder.

His feet hissed in the grass and he ran still harder as he came up a slope and rounded the curve that led into the mill area. He saw the gleam of the car's bumper in the shadows of the barn. He paused, looking around. He moved quickly and cautiously to the barn and there was no sound as he inspected the car.

He came out of the barn and stood in the moonlight. He turned up around the corner of the barn, running softly toward the sparse woods, then stopped. He leaned, listening intently and heard Cleo's voice from somewhere off to the left, in the darkness.

"Please, Paul—" she was speaking rapidly, in a tight undertone and there was a high note of leashed hysteria in her voice.

Tom ran lightly down along the road to the barn, past the dam and on down the stream, along the road again. Then he paused. Again he heard her, this time behind him, somewhere over there across the stream.

"I'll do anything you say, Paul—only let's wait and talk a minute, Paul. I didn't really know how you felt—no, Paul!"

"You heard me, Cleo."

"Wait—!"

Tom was already running toward the stream below the dam, and he saw them in the moonlight over there, saw Stapleton struggling with the girl, and he saw the flash of the knife and heard her scream again, not with hope, either—with futility and despair and pain.

"I love you," Paul Stapleton cried.

"Stapleton," Tom called, leaping down the bank into the broad stream bed. He started up toward the dam, heard Stapleton's cry, saw him dragging the girl toward the dam. Cleo stumbled and fell but he continued to drag her.

Tom ran directly up the bed of the stream, searching for a place to cross, and he saw Stapleton pause on top of the dam, saw her fall back on the network of cement and wood that formed the bridge.

Stapleton was at the wheel that opened the dam, working it rapidly in swift rotation by the handle. Tom saw it and leaped for the opposite side, but already a roaring wall of foaming water burst out and up and down, the froth of suddenly formed waves fingering the moonlight like a giant's descending hand.

He heard Cleo scream his name. The thundering mass of water flew toward him, pounding in the bed of the stream, and he dove headlong for the opposite bank, clutching to a rooted mass of trees and roots and brush and the enormous mass of water sucked past, dragging at his legs. He tangled his body into the roots and the water was cold, and for a single instant he was under, holding his breath. Then he clutched roots above a small stream again. The pond had emptied. The mass of water thundered away toward the far main road.

They could not see him from the dam.

"Now, you see?" Stapleton said to her. "See what you've done? I didn't want to kill *him*. I have nothing against *him*. Only you. You've made me kill him, too." Stapleton spoke harshly, grasped her hands and dragged her off the top of the dam toward the barn. "We'll go to the flowers, darling," he said. "That's where we'll die."

Tom let himself down into the wet stream bed and ran lightly up toward the hovering shadow of the dam, and crossed underneath, listening to them. Cleo said nothing.

Paul and Cleo rounded the corner of the barn. Tom reached the far bank of the stream and came up, dripping wet, over the ridge of grassy bank, and ran toward the barn. He reached the corner and looked around.

Cleo called his name.

He ran at them and saw Paul Stapleton turn, knife in hand, to face him. Cleo lay on the ground, watching.

Stapleton yelled something.

Tom reached him, but the other looked wild, holding the knife point-down toward Cleo on the ground at his feet.

"Another step," Paul said. "And you'll watch her die."

Tom stood there.

"Don't try to move, Cleo," Paul said. "If you do, I'll kill you."

"Is that all you've got on your mind?" Tom said.

Stapleton did not answer. He stood there in the frost of moonlight, holding the knife down toward Cleo, his face pale, his teeth showing in a thin white line between dark lips.

"Cleo?" Tom said. "Are you all right?"

She did not answer. Her face was turned up to Stapleton, the blade of the knife not three inches from her breast. She lay on her elbows in a strained position, her shoulders shaking. There was only the sound of their breathing.

"You took her away from me," Stapleton said.

"You're wrong, man."

"No. I'm not wrong."

"Did you know your sister is dead?"

"Esther?" Stapleton straightened slightly. "What do you mean, dead?" His voice was even-toned behind the labored breathing.

"A snake killed her, Paul."

Paul Stapleton said nothing, standing there, holding the knife, and his shoulders sagged faintly. When he spoke, his voice was a bark.

"She's not dead! She's not!"

"I'm sorry," Tom said. He moved a scant inch toward the other, watching his eyes. Stapleton moved his head slowly from side to side. "Esther?" he repeated. "Essy? She's not—you're lying."

"Why would I lie?"

Paul did not answer. He looked down at Cleo and Tom moved another step toward him. Paul snapped his head up.

"Don't come any closer," he said. "I'm warning you."

"You're finished," Tom said. "Don't you know that?"

"You're lying—"

"You didn't want Esther dead, did you?"

Paul leaned down closer to Cleo, panting now, his eyes crazed. Still he said nothing.

"If you'll give me the knife," Tom said, "I'll try and help you. Otherwise, you'll only cause trouble for yourself."

"Nothing's the matter with me," Paul said. "Nothing. Why did you come out here to bother us? We don't want you around. We don't want anybody around. Can't you see that? Don't you understand? This is our place," he said, his voice rising. Then he spoke softly. "How did you know where to come, Anderson."

"Cleo and I sometimes come here, too, Paul." Tom hesitated, looked up on the hill and saw movement among the trees. "I figured this was where you would be—feeling the way you do. I talked with Angela, too, Paul. Did all the others resemble Cleo in some way, Paul?"

Paul turned on Cleo. "You lied to me. You said this was *our* place," he said softly. "It *was* our place, only now I have to kill you anyway."

The knife swung up and Tom came at him fast. He caught the knife arm, and they staggered together as Cleo scrabbled off and knelt watching. She kept trying to speak, but she said nothing.

Suddenly a bright white light splashed across them as they fought. Paul broke and whirled toward the light.

"Drop the knife, Stapleton!" somebody called.

"You'd better," Tom said.

Stapleton turned on him, lunged with the knife, and the blade raked deep along Tom's right forearm. He tried to grab him, but Stapleton ran at the girl and there was a shot. Then another. Stapleton staggered, went to one knee, started crawling toward Cleo.

"Run, honey," Tom said. "He can't get you now."

She got to her feet and ran back a few paces. Stapleton stood up and fell again, then crept toward her, making angry sounds in his throat.

"Get his knife, you," somebody called.

Tom went over to Stapleton. Dark shadows moved down from the woods, the bright cone of light circling Paul Stapleton as he turned, arm up, waiting for Tom.

Tom kicked sharply, caught Paul's arm, and the knife twinkled off into the grass. Stapleton got to his feet and ran blindly at Cleo. She dodged him and he sprawled on the ground.

A uniformed officer ran up to him breathing hard, and said, "Lie quiet, there."

Another officer came over to Tom.

"Who are you?" he said.

Tom did not reply. He went over to Cleo and she looked at him, and smiled. He took both her hands and drew her to him and she lay her head on his chest.

"Your arm," she said.

"It'll be all right."

"Didn't you hear me?" the cop said.

"I'm nobody in particular," Tom said. "Leave us be."

Men grouped around Stapleton. They treated him with rough disregard. "Got him in the leg, Arch. Needs some first aid."

"All right."

"Bring that first-aid kit over here, Kirkham."

A tall, sober-faced man in plain clothes stepped up to Cleo and Tom.

"You're Cleo Monohan?"

She nodded and Tom held her tightly.

"All right, you two come along with me. You're Anderson, I take it?"

"Yes."

The man turned to Cleo. "We were at your home, Miss, when Anderson called. Found a handbag and some identification of yours at Stapleton's home. If Anderson hadn't called—"

"Is Esther really dead?" Cleo asked softly.

"Yes," the man said. He cleared his throat, looked at the ground, then at Cleo again. "Her boyfriend, fellow named Tillotson, turned himself in. Couldn't stand the strain. Drunk. He'd robbed her, found he had a conscience after thinking he didn't have one for years." He turned to Tom, then. "We sort of almost had something just before you called. Seems a friend of yours went broke trying to bum to Fort Myers. He came to Monohan's hoping to borrow some money from you. He mentioned the fact that he thought he'd seen your girl riding past him earlier and she looked bad off. Almost didn't say anything about it at all." The man shook his head. "Name's Williams. Mrs. Monohan knew about this spot, too—Cleo'd told her." He touched Anderson on the shoulder. "We thought we'd be too late," he said, then turned away toward Stapleton again.

Cleo looked at Tom. "You almost were too late."

"Yes."

Her voice was gentle. "I couldn't bring myself to tell you about Paul. I'm a fool, I guess. I thought you wouldn't understand—about us coming here, before you and I came here. I thought he'd just stop, I guess."

"It's all right," Tom said. He held her a little away from him and looked at her and tightened his hands on her shoulders. "It's all right," he said again, and drew her to him and kissed her on the mouth.

The man in the plain clothes tapped him on the shoulder. "Come on fella, let's go. The Monohans are worried, too, you know?"

They looked at him, then began walking down the hill.

The Peeper

late 1960s

Jason Wainright knew for certain exactly what he was going to do about his stepson, Daniel, long before the front doorbell chimed that evening. The subject of Daniel was a festering sore that threatened to engulf Wainright; either that or drive him mad. He was nervous, thinking about what he had to do, so when he heard the bell, he leaped from his chair in the living room, dropping his copy of "The India-Rubber Men," by Edgar Wallace—he collected the works of the famous mystery writer—and stumbling on the hearth rug.

"Are you all right, darling?" Danella, his well-rounded wife asked. She was watching TV, and turned her pretty head to look at him. "I'll get the door, if you like."

"I've got it," Wainright said.

He set down his half-finished rye highball, and crossed the sprawling, richly furnished sunken living room, then hurried up the flagstone steps to the foyer. The chimes sounded again, and there was a loud knocking on the door.

He flung it open.

"Oh, Mr. Wainright, it's happened again!" It was Janie Northe, from two houses down, slimly built, with short blonde hair, dressed as usual in a shirt with the tails out, and pale-washed blue denims. "Robert isn't home"— "Robert" was her husband, a well-fixed lawyer—"and I didn't know where else to come." Her pale blue eyes were wide. "Somebody's been sneaking around the house again, looking in the windows. I heard him. I'm sure it's a man. I saw a face at the library window. It's awful. I don't know what to do. I won't call the police again, they just drive around the block. They don't *do* anything. It scares me."

"Now, now—" Patting her arm, drawing her inside, closing the door, Wainright tried to swallow the bitterness he felt. Damn the stupid kid. He'd done it again. It was only a matter of time before he was caught at it, and it would make headlines on the front page. Wainright knew he and his wife would be the talk of the town. It would be positively ruinous to his social position. Because he knew very well it was Daniel who had been prowling and peeping again. Wainright felt a sharp wring of satisfaction, knowing what he was going to do about it. "Just be calm, Janie," he said.

"But it's terrible."

The light click of high heels sounded on the hardwood floor. It was Danella approaching them, one well-shaped hand touching the rich mass of black hair that foamed about her shoulders. She wore an orange knit dress that revealed her marvelous shape, the shape that made Wainright so happy.

"Janie," Danella said. "Whatever's the matter?"

"It's that peeper again, Mrs. Wainright."

Danella cast a quick glance at her husband, then took on a shocked expression.

"I told her to be calm," Wainright said, knowing his wife knew. "She mustn't let it trouble her. I'm sure whoever it is means no harm."

Danella bit her plump lower lip and made small ineffectual motions with one hand.

"Means no harm?" Janie said. "How can you say that, Mr. Wainright? There's no telling about people like that. They're apt to do anything. You *know* that."

Again he patted her arm, secretly pleased with her attitude; it fitted perfectly into his plans. He wished he had done it tonight. Well, no matter. Tomorrow night would work all right. But he must keep her from calling in the police. That could ruin things.

"I agree with you that phoning the law doesn't seem to help," Wainright said. "Tell you what. I'll keep an eye out myself. How's that?"

"*Would* you, Mr. Wainright? Just till Robert gets home. With the Pearsons away, and everything, I feel so *alone*." The Pearsons lived in the house between the Wainrights and the Northes. They were still in Florida, and probably wouldn't return for another month.

"Be glad to, Janie," Wainright said. He eyed Danella. "Maybe Janie would like a drink, something?"

"Oh, yes," his wife said, her voice shaky. "By all means."

Janie swallowed. "Thanks," she said. "I'll just run back home. I had to tell *somebody*."

"I'm sure you won't be bothered again tonight," Wainright said. "You probably scared him off, running from the house and all."

"Sure hope you're right." Janie Northe grinned boyishly. "Anyway, I feel better now, just talking with you."

"Certainly," Wainright said. He hesitated. "Of course, I'll phone the police, if you really want me to."

"Nah," Janie said. "They make a big production, but they never really *do* anything." She grinned again. "Thing to do is catch this guy, then call the cops. Robert's boiling over it. He ever lays his hand on him, it'll end right now."

"Yes," Wainright said. "And I'll keep my eyes peeled. You can depend on it." He looked at his wife. "Don't you think she's right about not calling the police, honey?"

"Oh, yes. I'm sure she's right."

They all looked at each other.

Janie sighed. "Well, I'll be going. And, thanks, you two."

The door closed after her. He and Danella stared at each other. Danella wrung her hands.

"Well," she said. "Go ahead. Say it!"

"I'm not saying anything. It's all been said a hundred times."

The fact was, he knew he needn't say anything anymore. Tomorrow it would be finished, if Daniel ran true to form, and the subject would be closed forever. He would give her some peace tonight.

"Daniel's my son," his wife said. "I love him. He does no harm, no harm at all. He wouldn't hurt a fly and you know it. Just because he's slow is no reason to hate him."

Slow. He was slow, all right. My God.

"Don't be on the defensive," Wainright said. "Forget it. I don't want to pursue the subject. Go watch TV, read a book, have a drink." They moved to the stairs leading down into the living room. "Oh," Wainright said. "Here's our boy, now."

"I didn't like the way you said that," his wife said.

"Sorry, dear."

They looked across the room at the slim, gangling, pale-faced youth standing in front of a red sofa. A large moon-face, with large luminous eyes regarded them without expression. The eyes were brown, patient, bovine. Slack lips hung open revealing gleaming white teeth. He wore a grass-stained white shirt, and narrow gray trousers, crepe-soled canvas shoes.

Wainright watched grimly as his wife hurried down the steps, and moved swiftly across the living room. She took her son's hand.

"Are you all right, dear?" she asked him. "I told you, you really should stay in your room. If you go out, dear, you must remain near the house. I couldn't bear it if you got lost."

"Lost?" Daniel said. "Lost?" He had a strange, high-pitched voice. Abruptly, he opened his mouth wide, his upper lip lifting over his teeth. He cocked his head back and burst into loud guffaws. He put both hands on his mother's shoulders, and began to jog back and forth, from one foot to the other, all the time laughing loudly. "I wasn't lost, Mommy-dear," he shouted, baring his teeth. "I won't get lost, I won't get lost."

"Yes, darling, I know, but you must be careful—you simply must."

Wainright could not stand it. He hurried down the steps, crossed the room without looking at them, and went rapidly down a hall, into his book-lined study. He closed the door, switched on a light, and stood there, breathing heavily, rapidly.

Somehow he had to stand it—until it was over.

A seventeen-year-old boy, acting the way Daniel did. It was horrible to even consider. Daniel looked no age at all, but, if anything, older than his age. But his mind, his mind . . . Wainright shook his head, moved across the room to the small glass bar against the wall, poured himself a straight Scotch, stood there sipping it.

Daniel had been a problem from the very first, but at the first he'd thought he would be able to solve it easily.

Jason Wainright's first wife, whom he had hated with a terrible vengeance for her drinking, her carrying on, her spending of his money, had conveniently died due to diving into an empty pool at a party. He had already known the widowed Danella, and lusted for her mightily. He knew about her son, Daniel, who had been born when she was eighteen after a youthful marriage. She was thirty-five, now. Jason Wainright was forty-two, retired from pursuing any career, living fatly on a large inheritance. His father had made a million on Wall Street, died decently young, and left everything to Jason. Jason's mother had committed suicide a year before his father's demise.

Jason Wainright hooked Danella with his immense charm and his wealth. His love for her was overwhelming, and it never diminished. But Daniel, her son, was the centipede in the stew. Daniel, mentally unequipped to face even the most elementary matter, let alone the world, home-nurtured and -tutored, loved violently by his mother, trotted about like a foolish dog, forever into one mess or another. He wasn't actually retarded, he was just nutty, with overtones. Something had happened at birth. He grew up bumbling and bungling. Revealing little or no memory, he could, on the other hand, whiz through taxing mathematical problems with awesome ease. Anything else was a blubber of sound.

And lately he prowled nights, escaping from his room by both window and door, and vanishing into the night. There was no point remonstrating with him. He did not understand what was meant.

When Jason had first married Danella, he had planned to commit the boy as immediately as was decent after the wedding ceremony. He would talk Danella into it.

It never worked. She would not listen. Even after he began prowling, peeking into windows, startling people, and getting away with it, she would not listen.

"If he's picked up, what will happen to us?" Wainright asked her. He was terribly conscious of his social appeal. "I couldn't face it, I tell you."

"You'll have to face it, if it ever happens. I love Daniel. No harm must ever come to him. In my life, Daniel comes first. You'll have to get used to that, Jason."

He was deathly jealous of Daniel. Over the year and a half since they married, his furious feelings had driven him to the contemplation of the final act.

He had pled with her. He had gone on bended knee. He had talked calmly, while berserk inside. He had ranted and he had raved. It was all to no avail, she would listen to nobody where Daniel was concerned.

"Yes," he muttered, draining the glass of Scotch and pouring another. "But now she won't have to listen. Not anymore."

He would kill Daniel.

It was the only way out.

They could go no place. He wanted to travel. He wanted to enjoy his wealth, as well as his wife. He wanted to live, love and be happy.

He was sick of going someplace among people, on some rare occasion, and every moment be on the defensive, hoping he could parry some questive soul who inquired about their son.

He could not stand it. Not any longer.

He knew exactly how he would to it. He raged inside, thinking about it. He would do it with a knife. His mind was made up.

Daniel prowled and peeped nights. He was given to wandering around Janie Northe's home a lot. He liked Janie, and sometimes in the daytime, followed her about in her garden, giggling and carrying on.

Wainright planned to follow Daniel, he hoped tomorrow night. It was the only way. He had been driven to the brink of madness with worry and fear. He couldn't last. He had to have his freedom from this rusty-linked chain.

There would be weeping and wailing. But it would die, gradually. He knew Danella loved him as he loved her. He wanted that love to bloom. He wanted to travel with her, show her off, enjoy their life together.

God, to think of what he put up with.

It was outrageous.

When the first thought struck him, of killing Daniel, he hadn't even been shocked. It was the solution, and he had shivered with content.

On his East wall, along with his collection of Edgar Wallace, was an extensive display of knives and daggers from all over the world. He had picked them up in far places, before meeting Danella. He moved over there now. He stared at them for a long time, then selected an Ethiopian pig-sticker, with a slim, gleaming blade and a carved horn handle. He took it over to his desk, laid it down. This was the one he would use.

He heard a noise, whirled.

Daniel was standing there, staring at him with his mouth open. He held the door ajar. Wainright almost screamed. The boy was always sneaking up on him, staring at him, just staring, with those patient, blank eyes, that pale moon face.

"Go away," Wainright said.

Daniel began to laugh. He screamed with laughter, standing there, eyes like mirrors now, his mouth gaping, his curiously white teeth gleaming.

"Go away!" Wainright shouted.

Daniel ceased laughing, turned and vanished, closing the door behind him.

That night Wainright slept with anxiety. Would he get the chance to take care of Daniel? Would it work out?

It had to. *It damned well must.*

All the following day he waited. Would Daniel surprise him and remain in his room, or wandering about the house? Or would he sneak out, as usual?

At seven o'clock that evening, Danella was watching TV. Wainright was on the edge of his chair, in deep meditation about how it would be once he was free. They would do so many things. Freedom. Above all he desired that. Complete freedom, and a long life ahead of him with shapely Danella, luscious Danella.

He jerked to his feet. Had he heard a noise? Was it the rear door closing?

"Get some ice," he said, excusing himself for the fifth time to go to the kitchen.

"All right, honey," Danella said, deep in "I Spy."

He moved rapidly down the hall to the large, shining kitchen. He opened a door, ran soundlessly upstairs, and down that hall to Daniel's door. He opened it. The room was empty, a light glowing over the bed, toy animals jumbled on the spread.

"He's gone out," Wainright whispered, satisfied.

He rushed downstairs, through the kitchen, over to the rear door. Opening it, he stepped out on the porch and peered into the darkness. He immediately saw a black shape moving slowly, detaching itself from the side of the house. It was Daniel.

Back in the living room, he said, "I'm going for a walk. I need some air. Be back in a while."

"All right, darling. Better wear a sweater. It's chilly."

"I'm fine."

"I insist you put on a sweater, Jason."

"All right."

He did. Then he went quickly to his study, picked up the Ethiopian dagger, thrust it into his belt beneath the sweater, and hurried to the front door.

"Won't be long," he called.

"Yes, darling—all right," Danella called back.

He went out.

Immediately he ran as fast as he could around the house, running between the pines and elms. No light from the streetlamps glowed back here. It was very dark. He moved rapidly in the direction Daniel had taken.

His breath surged in his throat. His heart hammered. This was the night. He would do it. It would be all over. They would miss Daniel, and he would be discovered tomorrow, lying somewhere. He would face the news of his son's death, which would be everywhere. He would be able to face it, with Daniel dead, unable to act the jackass in front of reporters.

He hurried past the dark home of the Pearsons, running lightly between the trees, staying close to thick shrubbery. Then he saw Daniel. The boy was just beyond a thick hedge, in Janie Northe's garden. The garden was huge, traversed by grassed paths that wound among the beds. The flowers where slain by winter, now, and Wainright heard the sere crisping as Daniel crossed a wide bed, making his way toward the large brick house, where lights shone.

Wainright waited by the hedge, then broke through, and cut along the edge of the garden. He reached a low stone wall, stepped over it, and hid by a pear tree.

He was wild with it, now. He saw Daniel going around the side of the house. He ran desperately after him, hate and vicious anger rising within him as he drew the knife. He would do it, now, right here, in the velvet darkness.

Just as he reached the corner of the house, a figure, Daniel, came back around, bumped directly into him, gave a sharp gasp.

Wainright did not pause. He whipped his arm back, then buried the knife in Daniel's chest. He withdrew it as Daniel screamed in that high voice of his. Again, and yet again, he sank the slim blade. The body sagged to the ground at his feet.

He was panting, almost ill with the energy he'd been using. He stood there over the thin, inert shadow on the ground, still gripping the hilt of the dagger.

It was done. *He was free!*

He gulped at the air, trying to still the remnants of rage inside him.

"Here—what the hell?"

A white light speared the darkness, focused straight into his eyes, glaring.

"What?" a man said. "What is this?"

Wainright turned to run.

"Jason Wainright."

It was Robert Northe, Janie's husband.

"What's that—Janie! Janie!" Robert Northe shouted the words, the light bright on the dead body on the ground. Wainright turned back, staring. He saw the pale blonde hair, cut short, the red lips, the shirt, the pale dungarees. It was Janie Northe. He had killed her. It wasn't Daniel—it wasn't. . . .

Again he turned to run.

Robert Northe leaped at him, cursing. Wainright tried to duck, but the flashlight struck him over and over, slamming against his head. He sank to the ground, still clutching the bloody dagger.

In a daze, he realized he was being dragged through a door, down a short carpeted hall, into a lighted room.

"Killed her, killed my Janie," Robert Northe was saying. "And we finally got you. Damn you. We were searching around the house. Thought we heard something. Janie, my Janie."

Still dazed, Wainright sat half up, the room whirling, his head bleeding. Robert Northe was telephoning. Soon he had the police on the line, and began telling them about it. "Jason Wainright, yeah—Jason Wainright. He killed her. He's the peeper I called you about last night."

Wainright glanced toward a window where he heard a light scratching. He saw a bobbing head, and went utterly sick inside. It was Daniel outside, staring in at him through the window. He was making faces at Wainright, his pale features gleaming as he opened his mouth, bared his teeth, rolled his eyes.

"Don't worry," Robert Northe said into the phone. "I won't let him get away. He'll be here, all right."

Number One

He looked at me with those frogs' eyes of his.

"So you're Hudson Simcoke?"

"Yes, Mr. Ferdon. I've looked forward to meeting you. You're big in the business."

"Where'd you pick up a name like that?"

"Like what?"

"Simcoke. For God's sake, Hudson Simcoke." He leaned his big head back and gargled. I suddenly realized he was laughing. It was some sound. It went with what he looked like. He was like a frog, all over, squatting there, behind the enormous glass-topped desk; a frog in a charcoal gray suit, with a red carnation in his lapel. I had expected something more sinister. Curious how things work out.

"Sorry about my name," I said.

"You should be. For God's sake, your parents should have been shot, slipping you a handle like that."

"It's all they had, I guess."

He pudgily selected an expensive cigar from the ornate box on the desk, chewed the end off and spit it on the floor, then lit it carefully with a heavy gold filigreed lighter. When he had it going good, he stared at me with those eyes some more.

"You know why you're here, Simcoke?"

"Yes."

He was gargling again. "Jesus," he said. "Simcoke."

I watched him.

"All right," he said, holding the cigar out and giving it a loving glance. "You're here because they're all sent here first. I have to pass on you guys."

"I see."

"No, you don't see. You see from nothing, Simcoke. How could you?"

"I don't know."

"You don't know. That's about what I expected."

I didn't say anything.

"You birds are all the same. You think it's easy pickings. Don't you? Don't you think that, Simcoke?"

"Not exactly. No. It's just a job, I guess. That's how I look at it, anyway."

"It's not just a job," Ferdon said. He had raised his voice, and with it the color in his face altered, crimson flushing his cheeks. He raised his voice still more. "It's a professional undertaking, Simcoke. By professionals, for professionals. Understand?"

"Yeah."

"Don't get flash with me."

"Sorry."

"That's better. A little damned respect. How long you think I've been in this business?"

"A long time. I've heard . . ."

"You've heard nothing, Simcoke." He shook his head and gave a little smile. "Jesus." He cleared his throat. "I have to pass on you guys. I said that, didn't I?"

"Yes."

"Professionals. That's what you're supposed to be. And you haven't even done number one yet."

"You have to begin somewhere."

"Arnie claims you're pretty hot with a gun."

"I try to be as good as I can."

"Sometimes situations won't call for a gun. Are you prepared for other ways? Arnie claims you use your noodle."

I just stood there.

"I don't know," Ferdon said. "I just don't know."

"I can do the job," I said.

"What job?"

"Whatever it is."

"I don't have a job for you. Yet."

"Oh."

"That hurts, doesn't it?"

I tightened my lips.

"I've seen them come and I've seen them go," he said. "But never with a name like Simcoke. Cripes." He paused, waved the cigar. "You have to be good. Of course, the reports on you are good. But I'm here to size you up."

"I understand. An oral test, sort of."

"Yeah." He smiled. "Oral test. Well, I don't know, Simcoke. I just don't know. I've been watching you."

"Watching me?"

"Yes." He flagged his hand toward a mirror on the wall. "Two way," he said. "I watched you while you were waiting outside, in the other room. I don't much admire the way you carry yourself, Simcoke. You got a gun?"

"Sure."

"What kind?"

"Luger."

"Christ, Simcoke. It might get caught in your clothes, something like that. Whyn't you carry a revolver?"

"I like the Luger. I'm used to it."

"But you've never really used it."

"Well, I think—"

"I don't really care what you think," he said. He wiped some of the white ash off the cigar into a gold tray, and blinked at me. "I'm here to judge. I been judging them for years. You know who I am, don't you?"

"Of course."

"Don't forget it, then."

"Arnie said—"

"I don't give a damn what Arnie said."

"I see."

"You see nothing, Simcoke. You're still wet behind the ears. You're a baby. That's what they send up here these days, babies. Didn't used to be that way."

My legs were beginning to ache. They always got like that if I stood in one position too long. I sure didn't care much for Newell Ferdon.

"How do you operate?" he asked.

"Well, I like to get right in there, fast," I said. "Day or night. It's all the same to me."

"Consider yourself lucky, eh?"

"I suppose luck plays a part."

"You'll never make it, kid."

I stood there watching him blink at me. He pointed with the cigar and his voice was nasty.

"You just haven't got it, Simcoke," he said. "I can tell. I've seen them come, and I've seen them go. I suppose it's the big turnover they're all talking about, the big change. Well, you're a baby, get that?"

I said nothing.

"Okay," he said with a sigh. "What the hell can I do? Arnie likes you." He paused, holding the cigar in the air. "I had my way, I'd kick you into the street. Get that? Into the street. Because you just haven't got it."

"I kind of lied to you," I said.

"What?"

"When you asked how I operate. Actually, I like to get to know them a little first."

"Get to know them? You *are* cracked, Simcoke."

"Yeah," I said. "Like right now, Mr. Ferdon. You see, Arnie gave me the word. And I know as much as I want to know."

"Arnie—what?"

I took the Luger out and held it steady.

"It's the big turnover, Mr. Ferdon. Like you said. The big change."

He stared and said, "Simcoke. What the hell are you doing?"

"This," I said. I shot him, just once, and for an instant he sat there with his cigar and those frogs' eyes, and he had a matching red flower right in the center of his forehead. Then he collapsed.

I got out of there. Number one, I thought. Wonder who's next on the list?

Southbound

They had only been married a month, and were on their way to Key West. It was a delayed honeymoon, and they had stopped at this motel on the Gulf Beaches. In the room, her husband lay on the bed, with his head propped on two pillows, reading. She moved around the room, occasionally looking at him, but more often out the large window. Beyond the window were palm trees and white sand and the green of the Gulf, slowly changing color with the red wash of the setting sun. A wind tugged at the palm fronds, and she stood by the window, staring out there.

"It's so beautiful," she said. She was a very young girl, slim, and with straight blonde hair. She wore a white shorty nightgown, with red trim. They had already eaten, and were just taking it easy. "Don't you think it's beautiful?"

Her husband was reading a book. He apparently didn't hear her.

She turned toward him, watching him. He went on reading. She slowly crossed the room, and sat on the edge of the bed by his feet. He was barefoot in his blue- and white-striped pajamas. She touched his right foot.

"Uh," he said, reading.

She squeezed his ankle. He thrust at her hand with his other foot, then looked at her.

"I'm excited," she said. "We'll be there tomorrow."

"Yes. That's right. Say, Jean, would you mind drawing the drapes? I like it dark in a motel room."

She jumped up, hurried across the room, drew the drapes, then returned to the bed. She sat on the edge of the bed again.

He had the bedlight on, reading.

"I drew the drapes," she said.

"Yes. Thanks. That's how I like it. It's cozier, somehow."

"How can you say it's cozy with air-conditioning? I always associate coziness with warmth."

"It's all a matter of degree."

She watched him.

"Personal taste," he said.

She sat there. He returned to his book, frowning in the glare of light above his head. She sat there a while, watching him, then suddenly she got up and began to move around the room. She paced back and forth aimlessly.

Finally she went into the bathroom and stood in front of the sink. She made faces at herself. She smoothed her hair with both hands. Then she inspected the toilet articles on the gleaming bar beside the sink. There were her things, a small assortment of bottles and jars, brush, comb, toothbrush, toothpaste.

She looked at his toothbrush. Then at his straight razor, in the black case. He always used a straight razor. His father had told him the only way to get a decent shave was with a straight razor.

She returned to the bedroom again. He was still reading. She moved over close beside him, and touched the top of his head. She ruffled his black hair, smiling down at him.

He looked up at her, grinned, then went on reading. She leaned down and kissed his ear. He reached up and patted her hand.

"Why don't we go outside, by the Gulf?" she asked. "It's so beautiful out there."

"Plenty of time later on," he said. "We'll be in Key West tomorrow. Plenty of fishing. Plenty of everything."

"Yes, but this is right now."

He was reading.

"You didn't hear me."

"What?"

"Nothing."

She kissed his cheek. He patted her hand.

She went to the other bed, sat on the edge, and watched him. Her right hand was clenched beside her, and she was unconsciously biting her lip.

"Couldn't we take a walk down the beach, or something?" she asked.

He grunted.

"Please?" she said.

"I'm tired," he said. "That long drive. There's plenty of time."

She sat there and they did not speak for a long time. There was only the rushing sound of the air conditioner in the room. And she could hear her own breathing. Sometimes she thought she could hear her heart, but she knew that was stupid. You couldn't hear your heart if you were sitting up. If you were lying down, your head on your arm, or your ear on a pillow, then sometimes you could hear your heart. But not sitting up, like she was.

She watched him. He went on reading, methodically turning pages. Both of her hands were clenched now, and she sat there rigidly, watching him.

"Well," he said, closing the book.

She leaped to her feet, moving toward him. He swung his feet to the floor, walked past her, and went into the bathroom. He closed the door.

She stood there staring at the bathroom door.

Presently he returned. He grinned at her.

"We'd better catch some shut-eye," he said. "Long drive tomorrow."

"Yes."

He kissed her lightly, slapped her rump, and moved over to his bed. He threw back the covers, stretched out on the mattress. He looked at her and grinned. Then he reached up and shut off the bedlight.

"'Night," he said.

"Sleep tight," she said.

"You bet."

She was still standing there in the dark. A thin strip of light showed between the drapes, but it was very dim, just a shadow, really.

She moved over to the drapes, peeked through. The sky was purple now.

"Better get to bed," he said.

"Yes."

She went to her bed, drew back the covers, and crawled in. For a long time she lay there, listening to him breathe. Gradually his breathing became very even, and she knew he was asleep.

She lay there staring into the darkness. There was no light showing between the drapes, now.

Slowly, she got out of bed, and went over to the window. She opened the drapes. There was a yellow light on one of the palm trees out there. It shone dimly into the room. She stood there staring outside, listening to the rushing sound of the air conditioner.

She returned to her bed, lay down, covered up to her chin, and stared at the ceiling. Then she rolled on her side and stared at him. She could make him out, a gray shadow on the bed, sound asleep.

She began to breathe raggedly, her hands clenching and unclenching, her teeth tight together.

Abruptly, she sat up. For a very long time she sat there like that. She put her hands to her face, pressing the fingers into her forehead, breathing rapidly.

She got out of bed and moved slowly across the room to the bathroom. She stood by the sink in the pale darkness, then began to feel around on the bar. She found what she wanted, the straight-razor. She took it out of the case, and carried it back into the bedroom.

Standing there, staring at him in the bed, she opened the razor. The keen blade gleamed in the dim yellow light from outside, and a reflection of light flashed around the walls of the room from the shining blade.

She was nearly panting now. She crossed the room and stood beside the bed where her husband slept. He slept on his back, and he seemed to be smiling.

She stood there for some time. Then she held the razor out, the blade close to his throat. Her hand trembled and she was breathing loudly, panting, her breasts rising and falling sharply beneath the thin nightgown. The blade flashed and gleamed just above his throat, her white hand gripping the razor tightly.

She gave a sharp gasp, and drew the razor away.

Whirling, she ran sobbing across the room, into the bathroom. She was sobbing wildly, tears flooding her eyes. Shaking all over, she folded the razor, and jerkily put it back into its case and laid it on the bar.

She turned, and ran to her bed, lay down, and wept silently into the pillow, smothering all sound.

In the morning, he got up and stretched. She watched him, her eyes slightly red-rimmed. She got out of bed and moved up to him.

"Do you love me?" she said.

"You know it."

"I mean," she said, her voice desperate. "Do you really love me. *Really, really!*"

"I love you," he said. "I really, really do."

He kissed her lightly, slapped her rump, and headed for the bathroom.

The Milkman

"The fact remains, Harvey, that you're just a lousy milkman. That's all you'll ever be." His wife grimaced, then tightened her full lips. "I thought when I married you that you'd make all those promises come true."

Harvey Stone regarded her with as much patience as he could summon. He loved her, he needed her, and he would do anything for her. But, it was true—the years had rolled by and he was still just a milkman. All the hopes were down the drain. He would never have enough money, the kind of money he dreamed of, the money Virginia deserved—unless . . .

Unless he put into immediate operation the scheme he'd been musing upon for days. It was a mad idea, and he had only played with it.

Now, this afternoon, after returning from his milk route to face the outright argumentative Virginia, he began to know he was going to do it.

"There'll be some money," he said. "I'll get some money, somehow."

She laughed at him. The fine blue eyes crinkled, and the normally pale-skinned face that he loved so much flushed. The laughter ceased. "I'd just like to know how, Harvey. How you going to get any money? You. If you tripped over a windfall, you'd never see it."

"I tell you, Virginia—I just have a feeling. In the old days you used to say I was kind of psychic. Well, it's true. I keep getting these dreams. It's money, every time. Lots of money. It's coming to us from somewhere. I'm sure of it."

Her slim figure in the short pink dress straightened. She gave a quick meaningful sigh. "Honestly," she said. "You make me laugh. I can't help it. Lucille was right. She warned me years ago. She told me you'd never amount to a hill of beans." Virginia paused, her lips tight again.

Lucille was her older sister who lived on the other side of town. Lucille Waters, spinster, alone in the world, always bitterly spiteful on their seldom visits. Harvey delivered her milk, every day. He had tried to get his route changed, because he did not like seeing her when it was time to collect. His boss refused.

Virginia's voice cut in. "For the rest of your lousy life, you'll get up at two-thirty in the morning, and rush out to your lousy milk truck. All the skimping and saving in this world won't help us." Tears welled in her eyes. "You make me sick, Harvey Stone!"

She left the room. He watched her go helplessly. Every day she was at him. She seldom spoke anymore, unless pressing the fact of his inadequacies.

Yet, he loved her. The worst possible thought he could have, was that of facing the rest of his life without her. Attendant to her, even against her bitterness, he swallowed what little pride there was left, living with hopes of what might have been.

He slumped on the couch. There was a sick feeling in his solar-plexus. Not about Virginia. He was used to that, and he could overcome it. It was because of what he planned. He was going to murder Lucille Waters, Virginia's sister—because it was the only thing he could do.

The thought of killing was repugnant. He drew a deep breath, blew it out. Lucille kept up an enormous life insurance policy, and Virginia was the lone beneficiary. It was that simple.

Lucille had no life, so why in the world she had wanted to insure it was beyond him. Maybe she was actually thinking of Virginia. Certainly not of him. Lucille had no redeeming qualities. She possessed none of her sister's beauty. She was a wretched, bitter woman, filled with malcontent, living out her days in a run-down house that stank of ancient cabbage and fried onions, situated on a weedy lot. Harvey was always frightened of snakes when he took her daily quart of milk to the back porch steps. Flies bombarded the screen door. And from the dark hollows of the hall, she would peer out at him, eyes glinting, silent.

Even so, he did not *want* to do it.

He *had* to do it. Finally, for once, Virginia must look up to him, love him again as she had loved him in the beginning. It was vile to think money could buy love. He did not care. Not anymore.

There was a kind of desperation inside him now.

His life had never been anything but a series of minor disasters. Nothing big, ever. He had gone from one job to another, failing each time. Until he managed to land the milk route. This was his security. Lord, how he knew theirs was a gray existence. He knew he could never earn enough money to change the look in Virginia's eyes.

The desperation grew as he sat there. It was the only way out. Little enough to do for her—small quotient of chance to spend in an effort to bring her back.

He ate alone. Virginia kept to her room. He watched some TV, not seeing it. He went to bed with the knowledge of what he must do in the dark hours of the morning. Her silent hulk beside him in the bed, was a cruel reproach.

He rose a little after two, his ingrained mental alarm clock having awakened him. He stood by the bed, looking down at Virginia, asleep.

"For you," he whispered, and a rustling of the late night whispered back.

A half hour later, working his way to the south side of town in the milk truck with sides emblazoned: BROCKMAN'S DAIRY, Harvey tried to quell the anxiety. It was no use. He gave up. He would have to live with the horrible feeling.

But mixed in with worry, was a growing sensation of elation. There was the promise to consider.

He would go immediately to Lucille's house, take care of it, then return to his route. He had to get it off his mind. He knew he would do it. He knew how chancy it was.

He parked in an alley a half block away, ran lightly to her overgrown lot, and through the knee-deep weeds to her back door.

He paused. The early morning was silent, and back here no streetlight glowed. He tried the door. Locked, of course. He moved quietly alongside the house, trying windows. The bathroom window was open a crack.

It was narrow, and screened, but it would have to do. The house was at the end of the block, with two vacant lots on one side, the street on the other. No one would hear, even if she cried out.

He opened the window. It creaked. Then a warm fury touched him. He tore at the screen, and it ripped like old cloth, showering dust in his eyes. In moments, he was through the window, standing in the thready darkness.

He knew the lay-out of the rooms. He knew where she slept, went through the hall, up the stairs, and straight into her bedroom.

A flashlight glared in his eyes from the bed.

"Hello, Lucille."

"Harvey!"

"Yes."

He advanced on the bed. He could see her now, hunched against the pillows, clutching a sheet to her breasts. Her hair was in pin curls.

"What do you want?"

"I'm going to kill you, Lucille," he said. "It's for Virginia."

The flashlight wavered and he saw her mouth come open to scream. But he was on her then. He had thought of strangling her. Instead, he snatched the flashlight, and beat her on the head. A voice cried within him: "Virginia! Virginia!"

Breathing fast, he dropped the flashlight on the floor. Lucille was dead.

He acted quickly, emptying drawers, working his way through the house, leaving it a shambles. He did not fear leaving fingerprints. He and Virginia sometimes visited Lucille, and he could have left his prints anywhere.

He was terribly excited, and sweating profusely. As he finished tearing the living room downstairs apart, it suddenly occurred to him that someone might see him returning to his truck. It was then the full realization of what he'd done touched him.

He left the way he'd come, by the bathroom window. Hurrying, frightened, he ran for his truck. He saw no one. Once behind the wheel, he got out of there.

Gradually, as he drove along his milk route, he talked himself into a semblance of humanness. It had been a heavy flashlight. He kept remembering the sound of it striking Lucille's skull. He kept hearing the tiny whimpers.

It was a little past noon when he started for home.

The days passed and Harvey Stone waited. He had expected Lucille's body to be found immediately. But four days went by and there was nothing in the papers. Virginia had not been notified.

Lucille had had few friends. She was something of a recluse, actually. This accounted for the fact that nothing had been noticed.

Virginia was the same as always, nagging, pestering him, or leaving him entirely alone. He endured it with anxious hope. Each morning he left on his milk route, and when he drove past Lucille's house in the truck, pale darkness shrouding the street, he would stare, swallowing fear. He could not really rid himself of the fear. Would it always be like this?

A week went by. He bought an early morning paper, as usual, quickly tore through the limp sheets in the light of the truck cab.

There it was . . .

She had been found. A neighbor noticed an odor. There were questions. Somebody else saw the bathroom window, the torn screen.

He threw the paper away, and went through the route fast, so he could get home. He was there before noon. Virginia greeted him at the door.

"Oh, Harvey—Lucille—Lucille's dead."

Virginia's nose and eyes were red from crying. He tried hard to comfort her, murmuring bits of understanding.

Somehow the anxiety left him now. It was over with. There was a strange relief.

He knew he had to ask. "Died in her sleep?"

"No. She was murdered."

He pretended shock. "How?"

"Someone broke in—it's awful."

He patted her shoulder, thinking of how their life would change now. Virginia would have the things she wanted. True, he would not, so far as she knew, have given her this new life. But it was enough to know inside that he actually had. And there would be a return of the old loving. He could feel it already.

Was Virginia thinking of the insurance money?

It was possible. Even in the face of death, people could not help being human.

Two days went by. Virginia was notified by phone that she must visit The Southern Life Insurance Company. A date was set. She seemed to brighten, taking care of funeral formalities. A Detective Connely stopped by and questioned them. It was purely routine, and now Harvey felt quietly secure.

On the third afternoon, he had just returned home, when the doorbell rang and Virginia went to answer.

"It's Sergeant Connely again," she said. "He wants to see you, Harvey."

Harvey came from the living room into the hall.

"Well," he said. "More questions?"

The sergeant was a medium-sized, pale-haired fellow, with very neat clothes. There was something grim about his mouth that Harvey did not like.

"I'm afraid it's more than that," Connely said. "Of course, there are some questions. But I'm here to arrest you on suspicion of murdering your sister-in-law, Mr. Stone."

Harvey stared, unable to speak. There was a tumbling of violent emotion in his solar-plexus.

Virginia said, "What do you mean?" Her gaze danced from the detective to her husband.

Connely was stern. "I'd better warn you," he said. "Anything you say now can be held against you. Actually, Mr. Stone, it's pretty pat. Only need your confession, and I'm sure will get that. It would make it a lot simpler if you'd just—"

Harvey's voice was loud. "What are you trying to say?"

Connely sighed. "You do work for Brockman's Dairy, right?"

"Yes. Of course." Harvey swallowed and tried to grip the remnants of his calm. It was fast dissipating.

"You delivered milk to your wife's sister, Lucille Waters. Is that correct?"

"Certainly, I—" And then he knew. But it was too late now.

The sergeant was speaking.

"It's a pity you didn't stop to think, Mr. Stone. But, believe me, with every crime, there's a loophole—something the criminal forgets—"

"You're wrong!" Harvey said. "I didn't do this. I don't care what you think."

Sergeant Connely smiled bleakly. "Then why is it you quit leaving milk for Lucille Waters?"

Memento

He could see the girl from inside the jewelry store window, if he stood far to the left, by the wall behind the counter. He had not noticed her at first. She was suddenly just there, standing half under the awning of the store next door.

It was a small jewelry store, but well kept, with meagre, obviously expensive displays of necklaces, bracelets, pins, rings. Diamonds glittered on purple velvet. Glass cases shone. The air inside the store was subdued, cool with air-conditioning, the aroma quite impersonal.

He did not know why he should be concerned about the girl. But he could not stop going behind the counter at the left wall, and looking at her.

He would stand there for some moments, then, with a sigh, walk to the other side of the store. In minutes he was back again, looking.

She was really rather pretty, in a pale sort of way. But he knew this was not why he kept looking at her. She wore a saffron-colored skirt, and Italian sandals, and a crisp white blouse with a long-winged collar. Tumbles of corn-hued hair fell about her shoulders.

Natural curls, he thought. You don't see much of that these days. Mostly it just hangs. Even if it does curl, they iron it, or something, and it just hangs. Either that, or it's one of these bee-hives, or else it's all cut off.

He shrugged and left the window. But the impression of the girl's face stuck with him, pale, with large brown eyes, what he could see of them, and that patient look to her mouth. A broad mouth, with little, if any, lipstick. Maybe it was that off-white lipstick they wore. Still, the lips looked very good, appealing somehow. Yes.

He stood behind the counter on the right-hand side of the store, by the gleaming mahogany cash register. He rocked on his heels. He lit a cigarette, took a deep inhalation, then found himself rather abstractedly moving over behind the left counter again.

She was still there.

It made him feel better, somehow, that she was still there. Could she be waiting for somebody?

Now and again she would look first one way up the street, then back down his way. People passed, talking together, or singly, grimly silent. Most moved rapidly. Women's heels clicked. There were sun-touched attaché cases and flipped cigarettes. When she looked down the street, his way, he saw that her eyes seemed empty. Or maybe it wasn't quite that. There was the tiniest of quirks at the right corner of her mouth, as if she were prepared to smile, but had not been able to make up her mind.

Her hands were pale, too, and long-fingered. She kept fiddling her hands together. He could not tell what she was doing, exactly. It interested him, and then he realized she was fussing with a ring on the forefinger of her left hand. He tried to see the ring, but could not make it out. Professionalism.

He stared at her forefinger. That's where they wear them these days, he thought. He considered it an affectation.

A long-strapped fringed suede purse hung from her left wrist. It almost touched the sidewalk. Then, even as he watched, she suddenly shrugged the purse strap up around her shoulder.

She's leaving . . .

No, she wasn't leaving.

He lit another cigarette, prepared to wait right here by the left counter, now. He glanced at his wrist where gold gleamed, and realized an hour and a half had passed since he first noticed her. It was early afternoon, now, the sun boring over the tops of buildings across the street, blazing against the blue glass at the front of his store.

He watched her, smoking. Suddenly she made an obvious exclamation. He did not hear it, but he saw her frustration, the parted lips. She clutched her hands together and ran toward the curb. She put one hand to her head, pressing her hair, staring down into a gleaming, steel grating. Abruptly, she knelt, staring at the grating.

Somehow it troubled him to see her kneeling on the hot pavement. What had happened? She continued to kneel there, staring at the grating, poking at the grating with her finger, shoulders hunched, the suede purse lying on the sidewalk.

He laid his cigarette in a silver ash-tray, and walked around the counter, and over to the front door. He stood there, anxiously watching the girl.

Few people passed now, the remnants of the lunch-hour crowd dispersed. The street looked vacant and hot, almost deserted. Cars hissed and honked along, but they were so frequent as to have long since become invisible.

Anyway, he saw only the girl. And he abruptly knew what had happened. Her ring and come off, and rolled down the grating.

He pushed the door open, and walked over to where she knelt.

"Could I help you?"

She turned with a kind of wildness, looked up at him. This close, he could see that she was really terribly pale. The skin looked like silk, and the eyes were even larger and browner than he had thought.

"Oh," she said.

"What's the matter?"

"My ring jumped right off and fell down there."

Her voice was soft, almost like a breath. It was a most curious voice. He had never heard one exactly like it. Not that all voices were not different, but there was a peculiar quality of sweetness to this voice.

"Well, that's the dickens," he said. "Where is it?"

"Right down there."

She pointed at the grating.

The sun was bright, and he couldn't see past the grating itself.

"Can you see it?"

"Yes. It's right there. But how will I ever get it back?"

He leaned low, but still could not see. He looked at the girl. Then, abruptly, he knelt on the hot pavement and put his eye close to the grating.

"You'll soil your clothes," she said.

He grunted. He saw dirt, and flecks of this and that, burnt matches, chips of paper. Cigarette butts. A bottle top.

"I don't see it."

"Right there." She leaned close to him and her hair brushed his cheek. She was pointing with one of those immoderately long fingers. "Don't you see?"

"Ah, yes. Damned. Sure, I see it."

"What will I do?"

"It means a lot to you?"

"Oh, yes." That breathing voice again. "A great deal." She squatted back on the pavement, looking at him with those enormous brown eyes, that mouth.

"It's probably expensive, too," he said.

"I've simply got to have it back. But how?"

He heaved himself to his feet. "The grating comes up."

"Huh?"

"You can pull it up. I'm sure of it. I never did it, but look. See? It's just resting there, on those nubs—"

"D'you suppose?"

He knelt down again and looked. He saw the ring, twinkling beside a cigarette butt. It looked terribly dirty down there.

"Why ever do they have them?"

"Have what?"

"These grates, whatever they are?"

"I never knew. Ventilation, or something. Of course, some of them open into cellars. But this one doesn't."

"You mean, just a silly hole in the sidewalk?"

"There are some pipes down there."

They knelt on the hot sidewalk, looking at each other.

She said, "D'you think it can be done?"

He came heavily to his feet, sweating, scratched his jaw, looked at the girl. He leaned down, took hold of the grating, and lifted with all his might. It was heavy, but it moved. He heaved again, managed to get one edge up. He quickly slipped his fingers beneath the edge, sweat in his eyes now, and lifted and got one knee beneath the grating. The girl took a grip on the grating too. They both lifted, grunting and breathing heavily.

"Slide it over," he gasped.

They managed to slide the grating over to one side. It scraped the pavement, leaving a white mark. A man in a light-colored shirt, smoking a cigar, paused to watch.

"There," he said. "That'll do it."

"You're all mussed and dirty," she said.

He stared down into the shadowed cavity. It was about five feet deep.

"I've read maybe taking a stick with gum on it," the girl said.

He looked at her, that pale face, the dreamy eyes.

The man with the cigar, tired, moved on.

"Can you?" the girl ask.

He turned abruptly, knelt down, then slid his legs over the edge of the cavity, and sat there a moment. Two women passing by, stared at him.

The girl watched him. She seemed to be holding her breath. The corner of her mouth lifted in a very faint smile, but her eyes were serious. But the dreamy look was still there. She licked her lips nervously.

He thrust himself off the edge and dropped. His feet sank into deep filth, and a thick cloud of dust rose about him. He coughed lightly, tasting the dirty tastes of the street.

"Are you all right?"

"Sure."

He looked for the ring, spotted it, picked it up and put it in his jacket pocket. Then he thought about getting out of this. The clouds of choking dust thickened, and he coughed again. His eyes watered. The girl was watching him. Through the dust he thought she had very good legs.

He braced one foot on a pipe, lifted, and his foot slid off and went ankle deep in the filth. He tried again, and this time his foot held. He got his elbows over the edge, on the sidewalk, and leaped up, swinging one leg over the top. He strained, and pulled, and managed to haul himself up on the edge. He rolled over on the sidewalk, and came to his knees, then to his feet.

She watched him, unsmiling, patient.

"Help me get that grating back," he said.

Between them, they dragged the grating back into place.

He smiled at her. He took the ring from his pocket, was about to hand it to her, when he happened to look at it. "Christ," he said.

"Oh, you got it," she said. "I had to have it. You're wonderful."

He looked at her, thinking she was making fun of him, putting him on. She wasn't. There was actually a film of tears in her eyes. He had been going to say something about the ring. It was something you got out of a Cracker-Jack box, a tiny ribbon of lead, with a chip of glass. He said nothing. He handed her the ring.

She took it with almost a desperation, and slipped it on her forefinger. "Thank you," she said, with that curious voice.

They watched each other for a moment.

"Okay?" he asked.

"Yes," she said.

"Well, I'd better get inside. Somebody might—"

"How can I thank you? It means so—"

"That's all right." He had cut her off sharply.

He left her standing there and went into the store, closed the door. The air-conditioning was heaven. He walked immediately to the rear, and into the wash room. He took a brush and brushed himself all over. He had torn a slight place in the knee of his trousers. He brushed harshly, then washed at the tiny sink with a kind of brutal energy. He kept saying, "Christ. Christ. Junk. Not even junk."

Deliberately, he remained at the right hand side of the store during the last of the afternoon. He muttered to himself. He could taste the filth, the vile dust of the street. He blew his nose several times.

At five, he locked up, started off along the street for his car.

She was still standing there. She gave him a brief sad smile as he passed. He flapped his hand. As he rounded the corner, he had an urge to go back there. The urge was strong. He felt sure she was waiting for somebody who would never come. He could still hear her voice, the gentle sound. He did not go back.

Window of Deceit

"Come, Derek . . . wake up now!"

He felt cool fingers stroke his forehead, luxuriated in the hazy interim, and thought of Isobelle. But that hadn't been Isobelle. He awakened, startled, and stared at Brenda, his wife, beside the bed. She watched him, her lips parted, as always, revealing the buck teeth, the round-lipped mouth devoid of lipstick, the owl eyes behind those thick-lensed glasses, and the flat, black, pulled-back Mexican hair-do of an Indian; something he'd never been able to stand. She wore a heavily brocaded silver and green robe, with a Singapore collar. Even that did not conceal the way her stomach protruded.

Even in the dim state of awakening, he hated her with a profound disgust.

"You awake now?"

"Hello," he said.

"Breakfast in bed this morning?"

"Yeah." He said it without thinking, because his mind was already thronged with the details of his wife's death. The murder plan had been formulating for three months.

He lay there between the pure silk lavender sheets, watching her with the forced smile. It sure would be something if there were such a thing as thought transference. The agonies Brenda Llewellyn Fox Cameron put him through were anything but just desert. Even now, under her brilliant, staring, blue-eyed gaze, he longed for freedom with a passion that was disconcerting.

He was awake now, shocked at her intrusion, startled at the momentary guilt of thinking she had been Isobelle.

"What'll you have this morning?" Brenda asked.

"Eggs Benedict. Coffee."

"You're getting to be a cliché. Why not pressed guinea hen, under glass?"

"Tell Dora heavy on the Hollandaise." He reached up and touched her cold hand; might as well keep up appearances. "What time is it?"

"Not that you could turn your head to see the clock."

He chuckled.

"Eight-fifteen," she said.

He lurched to a sitting position. "My God. You know I like to sleep late, Brenda. How come?"

"Thought you'd like to know. Rudy's flying me to San Francisco today. I've got to check out Consolidated Pre-Fab, and that new mini-computer company. Leck-Tec. You know we hired that man, Rodell. He's positive about his circuitry design—everything else'll be obsolete. Glad I retained interest. Come to think of it, that was your idea, Derek."

"I suppose as soon as it's working, you'll cash it in, like all the rest. I'll never understand you selling out everything you inherited from your father."

"Who in the world wants Texas cattle and oil? I was sick of it. I'd had it all my life. Don't you understand?"

"Yeah, sure. Rudy sober?"

Rudy Fellene was the salaried pilot of Brenda's Lear jet, kept in a hanger on the private air-strip here at Rancho Rojo, just outside of Albuquerque, New Mexico.

"We're leaving as soon as I dress," she pointed out. "Think you can find things to do while I'm gone?"

He was immediately guilty. He wished he weren't like that, but there it was. Isobelle was like some kind of special cell in his bloodstream. The very thought of her set up a tingling. The tingling only increased the hate and detestation he felt for his wife, Brenda. Staring at her, he scratched his neatly haired chest, in the open flare of his black silk pajama top. He was excited, but somehow keeping a grave face was simple. Possibly it was how she looked, how she behaved. Her strident voice, the thought of the weekly allowance he had to beg for. Well, she would soon be dead, and he would come into over two hundred million dollars, not counting the companies, and foundations, she controlled. He smiled inwardly, without moving his lips. Hell, he would sell out too. Or, maybe not—it might be fun, spinning about the country in the jet, heading board meetings, conferences. Some drastic change from the old life. The vagrant strains of a dim tune sounded at the back of his head: "Just a Gigolo." Well, that's what he was, had always been; he'd played hard and he'd won. But there had been a price tag, what Brenda was. She knew what he was and put up with him. He had confessed to her, rather more than that, really. And, one night, while drinking, she had told him what she was—but she'd also told him she loved him, would endure him. But he had to face the facts of her regime. And regime it was. Good clothes, fine food, and luxurious quarters at all times, but with a stipend for an allowance, and drastic measures to procure that, even: a curtailment of the activities he was so used to, especially that lack of covetous female pulchritude that had always fawned over his handsome manliness . . .

Brenda had told him just once, but he remembered clearly: *"I've got you and I'm going to keep you. But you'll live up to my rules. You'll live and you'll love it. Really, you do like it, don't you, darling?"*

"Well, I'll leave you to your thoughts, Derek."

"You staying over in San Francisco?"

Her buck teeth flashed. Well, they were clean, anyway. But she did not answer. For over a year of their two-year marriage he had not attended to the extremities of the marital bed. They had attained an understanding.

Sitting there on the bed, he envisioned Isobelle in Brenda's place, in this big house, or maybe at the chateau in Lucerne, The Fox Den; or the penthouse in San Francisco; the apartment in New York. It would all be theirs, and if, so-be-it, he ever tired of Isobelle, that could be taken care of, too. In a different manner, of course. Rigid dismissal. He wouldn't have to resort to murder with Isobelle. There would be no reason.

He looked Brenda straight in the eyes and thought coldly: "You're a dead pigeon, baby."

She continued looking at him, frowning slightly, and her eyes seemed to change as if she had read his mind. It jarred him some, but he dismissed it. That sure as hell wasn't possible. He was getting paranoid.

Abruptly, she turned and drifted from the room, calling over her shoulder. "Have fun, Derek."

He had almost missed her usual verbal display over what he termed the petty trifles of her existence. As a rule she outlined every move she made, to him, explaining incessantly, until he thought he'd go mad. He detested these moments; one of the strong points that made her life worthless in his view. And now he found himself missing that . . . ?

He laughed aloud and, stripping off his pajamas, headed for the immense bathroom and the sunken black marble tub that awaited him. . . .

Back in the bedroom, he ignored the tray on his bed, except for a swallow of black coffee. He dressed quickly in coal silk slacks, an off-white Shantung shirt, hand-sewn, stitched, with a shadowy black-and-red abstract design, one of a dozen Brenda had picked up for him in L.A. He enjoyed the feel of silk.

Brushing his thick, dark hair, he hurried from the room, downstairs, and through the large-areaed, luxurious dwelling, to the kitchen.

Dora was in the hall, a dumpling in pale blue.

"Where's Rudy?" It was imperative that he know if they would return tonight or tomorrow . . .

"At the fridge," Dora told him, smiling plumply.

He entered the kitchen. Rudy was by the open door of the refrigerator with a can of beer, tall, slim, slightly disoriented looking, in a flyer's uniform, with a cap on his blond head. Rudy Fellene was of indeterminate origin, with an accent that might have been Portuguese or Spanish. He was a loner. He was also Derek's closest friend. They confided in each other, up to a point. Rudy seemed to bare his secrets well, but Derek always shielded his true relationship with Brenda. Rudy's single concern was where his next drink would come from and when. He did not drink when flying, except for the occasional beer. But in between, on the ground, he was usually in a comfortable coma. The curious thing was his complete dependability. This was why Brenda continued to employ him. He had quarters of his own at the rear of the house, was well paid, and seemed to have no acquaintances, his seldom companion being Derek himself.

"Hear you're headed for San Francisco?" Derek said.

Rudy nodded, took a swallow of beer. "Don't even have time for this, but I'm taking it."

"Don't let Brenda catch you."

"She doesn't mind beer."

"Good thing. Plane stocked?"

"You bet. Have to keep the fuel up somehow. What you into while we're gone?"

Derek grinned. "I'll get by. Running into town—picking up some books."

"We'll return sometime tonight. Depends how long it takes her."

The relief was heavy, like taking off a wet overcoat. He said, "What d'you do on trips like this, Rudy?"

"I sleep while I wait—in the plane."

There was a sharp smack of high heels. Derek turned. Brenda was there, carrying a purse with a coat over her arm, an attaché case in her other hand. She wore severe black, her buck teeth and owlish gaze behind thick glasses giving her the appearance of a medical chipmunk.

"You didn't eat your breakfast."

"It was cold."

She brushed past him into the hallway. "C'mon, Rudy—the plane ready?"

"All set, Mrs. Cameron."

Isobelle Lang lived in a decent hotel in Albuquerque's business section, not far from Old Town. But the cramped quarters were distasteful to Derek. He could afford nothing better at the moment. Isobelle refused to take a job. She knew of his plan, and was as eager as he.

Death was very much on Derek's mind as he came down the hotel hall toward Isobelle's door. Death had been foremost for some time, eyeing him in the darkness of his midnight bedroom, reminding him that he would be the instigator of doom. But it was a cold Death that Derek lived with, Death without emotion, without fear; a Thing of hoped-for release and relief and gain. Death was a sensation of excitement, impending fortune; the life of creatured ease Derek envisioned, was but a short while away . . .

He touched Isobelle's door-buzzer, heard the chime from inside. The door opened and there she was.

They clinched in the hallway, then walked into the small sitting room. She closed the door, leaned against it.

"She's gone to San Francisco," Derek said.

"But tomorrow morning's when it's supposed to happen!" Isobelle was as excited as he. Where Brenda might have been complex mentally, a sick example of womanhood physically, the opposite was true of Isobelle:

Her flowing golden hair was brushed to a sheen, her heart-shaped face piquant, with a broad, tenderly shaped pink-lipped mouth, and dark eyes that just escaped the look of pure sin. Right now she wore thigh-tight linen pants of white, and a flame-colored blouse, sashed at her slim waist. Derek knew she was as determined as Brenda, in her own way. She was his breed; they were of the same mold, and he was more than ready to succumb to her determination, with the awareness of practiced resignation to the fact that he could possibly tire of her in the future. At the moment this did not deter him from holding her close, tangling his fingers in her rich, luxuriant hair, kissing her on the mouth.

Isobelle was happy, too. They broke free. She stepped away. "Right about tomorrow morning?" She was anxious.

"You know it."

"Any reservations."

"Why should I have? We go out riding, it's quite regular with us. She loves horseback. All I have to do is mention it . . . I hit her on the head, knock her off her horse, then finish her off on the ground if it's needed. Simplicity. It's the best way. There'll be no questions. She isn't a top horsewoman to begin with, everyone knows that. We raced at her suggestion . . . the horse threw her—"

"Don't forget to run her horse. They can tell, y'know?"

Derek grinned. "Think you can stand the waiting?"

She touched his arm. "I can't wait, really. It won't be long before we'll be able to be seen together, live together . . . but I still can't believe it, Derek."

"You'd better . . . it's true. I love you and you're going to be Mrs. Cameron the second, and rich as all get-out."

She stared at him. Her allure was devastating. "Rich," she said softly. She stepped close to him, put her wrists around the back of his head. She drew his head down. "I can't wait. I want to be with you for always, Derek— always, as we were meant to be . . ."

Abruptly, the room door slammed wide, rattling against the wall, and lights flashed. The glares were automatic, persistent.

Isobelle clung to his neck, her mouth open in a husky scream. Derek whirled, and stared . . . knowing immediately what it was. The surge of wild anger, guilt, frustration, was extreme—he wanted to hurl Isobelle away from him, but she clung . . . he thrust at her . . . it did no good . . .

"That enough, Mrs. Cameron?"

It was a sharp question, voiced by a lean, tall, bald-headed fellow, who carried the camera. A bellhop and two uniformed policeman crowded the door, but Derek's gaze was riveted to the buck-toothed, owlish face of Brenda, his wife; black-suited, still carrying the attaché case, she watched him without expression. The cameraman backed from the room and started off down the hall. The two policeman stood stolidly, peering in at him with straight, young mouths.

Brenda took two swift strides into the room. "Hello, Derek—Hi, Isobelle Lang . . ."

Derek couldn't speak. He just stood there, wild and empty in the midst of total collapse. Isobelle continued to cling to him. He was frantically repelled by her touch, the sight of her open mouth, but there was nothing he could do.

"My lawyers will contact you," Brenda said. "I've known about it for some time, Derek, dear. Divorce proceedings will commence immediately. I don't think I need say anything more, but I will let you know . . . I tired of you, after all. There are better fish in the sea, Derek. You may come home and collect a change of clothes. I want you out of the house within the hour." She paused, turned to Isobelle. "Did I startle you, honey?"

Isobelle's lips were still parted. She breathed sharply.

"It is rather abrupt, isn't it?" Brenda said softly. "Good-by, you two— and may your lives be interesting."

Due to the nature of events, collated documents with signed witnesses as to Derek Cameron's background, the photographs, further signed statements by witnesses at the hotel who vouched for Derek's comings and goings, the signed and witnessed records of a private investigator who'd been hired by Brenda to report on Derek's whereabouts, and because of Brenda's own avowed statements about their marriage, the divorce decree was handed down less than a month later.

Derek found himself in the small hotel room, with Isobelle, no money and no prospects. He was a beaten man. He saw no way out. He still desired Isobelle, but could see no way to keep her. He had failed in life and his misery kept him from even sleeping. He had become accustomed to a life of luxury. This step back down to worries of money, disgraced him to the extent that he considered suicide.

He told Isobelle about this.

"Baby, we'll work it out somehow. At least, we have us."

Derek said nothing, but felt the stillness of disgust. He took the Albuquerque newspaper that Isobelle had just brought up from the lobby. He unfolded it on the bed.

He stared in shock, disbelief, at a photo on the front page. It was Brenda and Rudy, arm in arm, standing by the jet. They were man and wife, the photograph taken just prior to their flying to Lucerne, Switzerland, where they would make their home at The Fox Den, Brenda's chateau, overlooking the lake. "Rudy and I are very happy," Brenda was quoted as saying.

That night Derek got drunk. He raved. Isobelle could do nothing with him. Exhausted, he finally slept on the floor. Deceit, deceit—Brenda had deceived him. It was all he could think through the alcoholic blur. He felt he'd been harmed, that there was no recompense in this life. He had been robbed of his due. Yes. By his best friend. More deceit. Lies and cold-hearted finesse . . .

Derek Cameron awakened the next morning, clear-headed, with the bright fire of vengeance streaming through him. He told Isobelle nothing, but knew clearly what he would do.

He had to do it. His life was an arena of defeat. It had collapsed in mid-stride. The thought of that horrible woman made him nauseous, and he had but one aim . . . he would defeat her. The plan was death . . .

He did not know how he would kill her. He only knew that he would, that he must. He had Isobelle, and he would keep her as long as he was able.

Suiting action to thought, without breakfast, without telling Isobelle, he went to the bank, withdrew his small savings, $2346.00. At the airport, he made reservations for two on the next flight to Zurich, Switzerland, by way of Kennedy, in New York. At the hotel he told Isobelle where they were going, but nothing of why.

On the plane she questioned him incessantly—

"It's something I must do," he told her. There was a cold quality to his voice, a steel in his being.

"You've changed, Derek—you've changed."

"No change as far as you're concerned, Isobelle."

It was while over the Channel, after leaving London for the Zurich hop, that Isobelle caught on:

"You're going to see her . . ."

"Don't talk about it, Isobelle."

"But, why—what can you do—there's nothing . . . you're blowing all our money."

"It's nearly gone, true. But enough for a hotel for a time, in Lucerne."

"Lucerne. I knew it. Brenda—What're you planning, Derek? What're you going to do?"

He smiled coolly and sipped his drink. Inside he was a sick man and only one thing could make him well—Brenda's death, in as fitting a way as possible. He would contact Rudy, explain a visit to Switzerland, insist he convey best wishes, and abjure any hard feelings . . . winner take all. He

knew he stood no chance with the money, now. There was no way to re-
coup. But he could avenge his pride. He knew he walked a thin edge, and
the balance was precarious: Brenda's death at his hands, would bring a
return to sanity. He had never realized life could be so complex, such an
ignominious defeat. He never knew that despair was a cloak one wore like
a second skin.

Flying over France, approaching Switzerland, his heart began to
hammer tightly. He knew he was what they called a monomaniac, now. He
did not care. All reason had deserted him. He refused himself the pleasure
of making any plans. Her death would come about naturally . . . in some
way he was as yet to understand. But he would do it—he would be the
instigator . . . she would not, could not escape. He was the demon of the
inevitable. Somehow she would pay with her life for what she had done to
him.

This was his vengeance. It was all he considered.

". . . I've been talking to you for five minutes, Derek! You haven't heard
a word I've said."

"Sorry. I was thinking."

And he thought more in Zurich, where they spent a week cooped up in
a hotel room, sipping Kirsch. He brooded. He wanted to feed the fires of his
personal temptation.

Isobelle watched and waited.

A week and a half later, in the evening, he was in the lobby of the Hotel
Lucerne. Isobelle was up in the room, probably weeping, he thought wryly.
He didn't want her to overhear his phone call. He knew the number of The
Fox Den, well enough, dialed it, and waited.

Rudy answered with a jovial, "Hello?"

Derek explained that he was in Lucerne and wanted to pay a visit for
old time's sake. He did not mention Brenda, thinking it best to wait till he
was at the chateau, able to confront her.

"Why not come over now?" Rudy said pleasantly. "We'll knock down a
few. The cellar here's a marvel. I'm happy you're not irritated with me, pal."

Derek could not discuss it further. "I have a rented Fiat—be there
within the hour." He hung up with a sensation of elation.

He did not check with Isobelle. He left immediately, driving through the
crisp night, across snow-dusted streets, on to the country road, until he
turned in at the gates of The Fox Den.

Rudy met him at the door. The jet pilot was a changed man, the thick
blond hair gleaming in the light from a chandelier. His eyes were bright, his
greeting warm. He seemed taller than usual, the dark cut of his suit rather
extreme, Derek thought.

"Come in, come in."

Derek entered the familiar hall. He noticed a statuesque brunette, standing to the left of the drawing room entrance. She wore pale green, a clinging evening gown. Her gaze followed him as Rudy led Derek to the study.

"A guest," Rudy murmured as they entered the study.

A lithe blonde, with flashing dark eyes and silver lips, slithered past the study door, wearing icy lamé.

"Another guest?" Derek asked.

"Yes," Rudy said. "Here, a chair—sit."

Derek lowered himself into a comfortable wing-chair he recalled. Rudy mixed drinks, handed him a tall glass.

"I seem to remember this whisky," Derek said.

"Well you might, pal."

Rudy sat in a leather chair beside a broad desk. The room was lined with books, dimly lighted. Fine oil paintings glistened in the light.

For a moment, Derek was overcome with the sudden return to luxury that he'd been forced to bid good-by to.

"I didn't mean to interrupt a party," Derek said.

"No, no." Rudy was sharp. He had finished half his drink. "Not really a party—just sort of a gathering. Old friends, you know?"

"I don't understand. Where's Brenda—I haven't seen her, Rudy."

Rudy's brows lifted. He set his glass on the desk, leaned forward in the chair. "Surely, you've heard."

"Heard what?"

"Why, Brenda . . . Brenda is dead."

Derek heard his own voice, echoing in the room. "Dead? Dead . . . *dead?*"

Rudy was talking about their visit to St. Moritz, their first time on the ski slope together. Brenda had inadvertently gone over the edge of a drift, but it had, surprisingly, been the side of a mountain. It took a rescue team two days to recover the body from deep snow.

Derek sat there. His glass dropped from his hand, shattered against a standing ash-tray.

"My God, man," Rudy said, "you didn't know . . ."

In a fog, Derek was led to the private cemetery in the woods on the hill beyond the chateau. "You know of the mausoleum, of course?"

Derek said nothing.

They entered the cold, vaulted chamber, and Rudy switched on a silent, saffron light.

"It's in memoriam," Rudy said, his tone a vibrant whisper. "An idea I picked up from a friend. Brenda had so many friends, acquaintances. They didn't have a chance to say good-by. Now, they can."

"What . . . what d'you mean?" Derek said, his voice hollow, empty.

"Here—look . . ."

Rudy gestured toward a marble plinth, upon which rested an ornate limestone sarcophagus. Derek stepped forward. He looked down at the glass-fronted coffin.

There she lay. Brenda. Sleeping, her lips closed firmly over the buck teeth, the thick-lensed glasses held glinting in folded hands, her black hair sleekly drawn to the back of her head, glistening in the shadowed ochre light.

She was smiling, ever so faintly.

Derek stood in secret darkness, feeling the first worm of bleak despair.

From the open door of the shadowed vault came a girl's haunting call: "Rudy, baby . . . we're lonely! When are you coming out of there . . . ?"

Rudy cleared his throat softly and glanced at Derek, and Derek knew what had really happened on the high ski-slope at St. Moritz, out of sight of everyone.

He turned his sick gaze down to Brenda's face again. Life itself had deceived him . . . and in that moment, he knew the finality of real defeat.

Whittle Whittle

Clarence Klutts stared out his bedroom window at the ice storm. The trees were heavy laden with white, dripping, sagging. Branches cracked like gunshots, fell to the icy ground. Clarence watched the seasons, Spring, Summer, Autumn, Winter. He remained in his room and watched, his big, watery blue eyes behind thick-lensed glasses, like an owl's. He breathed rapidly now, looking out there in the early night. The huge oak in George Thornton's yard, next door, was splitting, tilting. The ice would smash it. Clarence breathed faster.

He hated George Thornton. George Thornton laughed at him, pointed his finger, made remarks about how fat Clarence was.

Oh, he was fat. He was like a balloon, and he moved carefully about his room, his swelling stomach floating and bouncing.

Outside the window sometimes, George Thornton would look up, and point and shout:

"You getting enough to eat, Clarence? Hey, Clarence! I got just the girl for you. She works in a side-show. The two of you oughta get an act together. Hey, Clarence! You don't like me, do you? Whyn't you come down here and fight?" Then George Thornton would laugh. "I'll prick you with a pin, Clarence, and you'll explode."

George Thornton had a heart condition. Sometimes Clarence wished the man's heart would just stop, like a clock. Sometimes sounds of laughter, like nuts cracking, burst from his lips when he thought of George Thornton's heart quitting on him.

Lord, how he hated George Thornton.

And Henry Klutts, Clarence's father, never said a word to George Thornton, either. He tolerated whatever George Thornton did, because George Thornton was a big man in the town. Henry Klutts looked up to him.

"He don't mean nothing, Clarence. You got to understand. Henry's a big man. He's just making fun."

And Clarence's mother, Nellie Klutts, felt the same way about George Thornton.

"He's a big man, Clarence. And you're just a little man, even if you are big to look at. And anyway, you can't really say anything. You can just sit here in your room with your books, and read, and whittle on pieces of wood." Then she would give a sob. "All those shavings. Whittling." And she would begin to cry. "My son, my son. What has the Lord done to me? Why am I paying?"

Clarence couldn't say anything. He would just look, and make noises with his lips. The doctors had explained something to the effect that certain wires were crossed in his brain. He couldn't make out like other people.

So he just remained in his room, reading, whittling. He read a great deal. He was a wizard with electricity. There was all sorts of junk in his room, to the eternal dismay of Nellie Klutts. Wires, and transformers, and train tracks, and engines, and chemistry sets. He was a great one for making stink bombs in the dark of the night, and dropping them down into the driveway, so maybe some of the smell would drift over George Thornton's way.

It never did.

Sometimes, even, Henry Klutts would bring George Thornton into the house, and upstairs into Clarence's room. George Thornton would come right into the room, and parade around, and make remarks.

"Clarence," he would say. "You're a sight for sore eyes, that's what. Why don't you eat a little more?" Then he would laugh. "You have your breakfast yet, Clarence? Henry," he would say, turning to Clarence's father. "You've got a real son in Clarence. Look at all those books. And, boy, can he whittle."

So when the ice storm came in February, Clarence was glad, because it was ruining George Thornton's big old oak tree.

He sat by the window and watched out there.

In the morning, the tree was a mess. It was split, and the limbs were broken. It was just a tremendous skeleton, completely destroyed by the thick, terribly heavy layers of ice that had formed.

By noon, George Thornton had men out there with saws, and a huge truck. They were cutting away at the oak tree, clearing the yard.

Clarence began to make weird noises. He banged on the floor of his room. Nellie Klutts finally came upstairs. "What's the matter, Clarence?"

Through gesture and careful patience, he finally explained that he must see his father, Henry Klutts. Henry Klutts was emptying the garbage, but as soon as he finished, he came to Clarence's room.

Again, Clarence patiently explained, and finally Henry understood.

"Well, I dunno, Clarence. You know how George Thornton is."

Clarence rumbled and his stomach shook. He made wet noises with his lips.

"See what I can do," Henry Klutts promised, and left the room.

Clarence waited at the window. Pretty soon, his father was out there talking with George Thornton. George Thornton kept waving his skinny arms, and shaking his head, saying things that Clarence couldn't hear. Finally George Thornton came into the driveway, and hollered up at Clarence's window.

"You want a hunk of my oak?"

Clarence stared down at him from the open window.

"You wanta whittle something from my oak?"

Clarence nodded. He was very pale.

George Thornton suddenly laughed. "Okay, you big blimp. You can
have a hunk. Your father says you want a hunk right out of the heart of the
trunk. How'll we get it up to you?"

Henry Klutts was beside George Thornton now.

Clarence made frantic motions at the window.

"Clarence says you could rig a hoist. There's a derrick on that truck.
You could slide the wood right through his bedroom window. Block and
tackle, you know."

George Thornton thought about it. He kept laughing to himself, looking
up at Clarence, and laughing and shaking his head.

Clarence drooled a little on the window-sill, he was so worried.

"All right, you big blimp, I'll do it," George Thornton said.

Clarence nodded and nodded, drooling on the window-sill.

He waited in his room. The men cut a big piece of the trunk with
machine saws, and then the truck moved into the driveway, and it wasn't
long before the huge piece of oak trunk swung into Clarence's window. He
was quite strong, and he helped all he could. In about fifteen minutes, he
was sitting there in his room with the big chunk of wood, admiring it.

Henry Klutts stood in the doorway.

"Don't never say George Thornton isn't good to you, Clarence. Look
what he went and done. You can whittle your arms off, now."

Clarence was happy. But behind the thick-lensed glasses, his watery
blue eyes were somehow sly.

Days passed, and Clarence sawed and cut and sliced and chiseled. When
his hands got sore, he would play with his electric trains, working the
transformers, or maybe read, eat whatever Nellie Klutts would supply him
with. He was extra hungry these days.

"Clarence is happy," Henry told Nellie.

"I hope so," Nellie Klutts said. "It takes a lot of happiness to get to
Clarence. He's so big."

"Now, don't you be like George Thornton," Henry Klutts said. "George
Thornton just stands out there in the driveway, shouting things up at
Clarence."

"Yes, but he's a big man," Nellie Klutts said.

And Clarence cut and chiseled and whittled. And one day they knew
what it was. It was a chair. A big chair, and as it took form, Henry Klutts
marveled at it. It was a beautiful chair, with filigree work on it, and it was
all cut from the one piece of oak tree.

Time after time they carted wood chips from Clarence's room. He
worked feverishly now, sweat coursing down his huge, fat body. There was
a kind of heavy determination on his face. He worked mostly with a knife,
now, whittling and carving on the chair.

People came from all up and down the block to see what Clarence was carving. He whittled and he whittled. They stood in his doorway, staring at the chair.

But not George Thornton. He would stand down there in the driveway and shout up at Clarence, and wave his arms, but when Henry Klutts asked him to come and see the chair, he just spat, and shook his head.

"I've seen lots of chairs, Henry."

It worried Clarence some, the way George Thornton acted. But he went right on whittling. And when he got tired, he would read, or play with his trains, working the transformers.

As he worked, he thought dizzily of how the wood was George Thornton, and he was whittling George Thornton. He hated him so much it made him sob, sometimes. He worked fast, though, even with the blisters, and the cramps, and presently the chair was finished.

It was a sunny May afternoon. He called to Henry Klutts, and waved his arms, and made weird noises.

"It's a beautiful chair, Clarence."

It was a gorgeous chair. It was huge, and fresh-cut white, with filigree work. It had been carved with care and love. You could see that. It sat in the exact center of Clarence's bedroom. Clarence lowered himself into the chair. It was just right for him. Then he began trying to explain.

"Oh, I get it," Henry Klutts finally said. "You want George Thornton to come up and see your chair?"

Clarence nodded, his eyes excited behind the thick-lensed glasses. He was very pale. He beat his hands against his elephantine thighs.

"I'll see what I can do," Henry Klutts said. "But I won't promise anything."

Clarence nodded with excitement.

Henry Klutts went downstairs. Clarence watched from the window, drooling a little.

He could see his father at George Thornton's front door. The door opened, and there was George Thornton. Henry Klutts was talking.

Clarence held his breath, watching.

Pretty soon the two men walked over across the driveway together. George Thornton was laughing.

Clarence waited. Henry Klutts brought George Thornton to Clarence's bedroom doorway.

"There it is, George," Henry Klutts said. "Clarence just insisted you come and see it."

"Well, well," George Thornton said. "It sure is big enough, isn't it, now? Reckon it'll hold you, Clarence?" He laughed, and winked at Henry Klutts. "It sure is big enough, now."

Clarence made some quick burbling noises, and waved his arms, bobbing his head at his father.

Henry Klutts said, "He wants me to go downstairs and make some coffee. He wants you to come into his room, and have some coffee with him."

Clarence nodded, burbling.

"Well, well," George Thornton said. He laughed, and pointed at Clarence. "Me and you, eh? Having coffee together. That's a hot one, all right. Coffee with the blimp."

He said all of this right in front of Henry Klutts, Clarence's father, but Henry Klutts thought of George Thornton as a big man. So he went downstairs to make coffee.

The room was silent.

Clarence motioned to George Thornton.

"What you want, you big, fat ignoramus?" George Thornton said. "You getting enough to eat?" He laughed.

Clarence motioned to him, and to the chair.

"You want me to try it, you big ape?" George Thornton said. "That what you want?" He laughed again, and entered the room, and stepped over to the chair, looking at Clarence. "You know?" he said. "It'd be a big load off your daddy's mind if you'd just die, Clarence. You ain't fit to live. You eat too much, and all you do is mess things up, whittling."

Clarence motioned to the chair, burbling.

"All right, all right. So I sit down." George Thornton sat in the chair. "It's damned hard, that's what it is. You just wasted your time, Clarence. Whittling a chair."

Clarence watched him a moment, then stepped over to his trains on the floor, and touched the transformer, all the time watching George Thornton.

George Thornton's mouth flew open. He bucked up and down in the chair, and his arms flew around. He tried to say something, you could tell that, but only gagging sounds came from his mouth. It was as if somebody was stabbing him in the back or something. Then, very suddenly, he just sagged in the chair, his eyes wide open, staring at his lap.

Clarence turned off the transformer. Then, working swiftly, he detached all the wires from the chair, and disconnected the circuit from the wall fixture. By the time Henry Klutts returned to the room carrying a tray with coffee, Clarence was just standing there, looking at George Thornton's body.

"Clarence! He's dead."

Clarence burbled a bit.

"Must've had a heart attack," Henry Klutts said. And that was what the doctor, Orwin Caswell, said when he confronted what was left of George Thornton in Clarence's room.

"He had a bad heart," Orwin Caswell said. "It finally carried him off. Must've got excited, something like that."

Clarence watched.

They took George Thornton away.

That same day, Clarence made such a fuss about the chair, that Henry Klutts hired men to move it away.

"Can't stand the thought of what happened, I guess," Henry Klutts told Nellie Klutts.

It was sold for ten dollars to a man who owned a second-hand store.

Nobody wanted to buy the chair, because it was much too large and cumbersome for most people.

And Clarence Klutts sat by his bedroom window, watching the seasons come and go. He would look down into the driveway, and smile, and then he would feel sad.

Lying stretched flat out on the sand, with water lapping at his feet, he thoughtfully considered his next move. His fingers circled her left ankle and now and again he squeezed.

"Don't do-o-o-o *that!* I can't stand it."

He would relax his fingers then, knowing. He could hear her breathe. Her ankle was smooth and firm. It was strange, what it did to her, when he squeezed. He loved the feeling this imparted to her. He knew what it was and that she wanted him to squeeze her that way.

The sun shone through a mist of heat, coating them with the fluorescence of life, and the clear, clean smell of salt and water and sand and body heat was in the small wind that drew through the Australian pines above the dunes.

"Don't—please, don't . . ."

A gull screamed.

He lay on his chest, the sand like a vast endless plain, a Daliesque—don't think, he thought, don't think. A Daliesque—no, it was more than that.

He wanted to squeeze her ankle . . .

The plain was white, an indescribable dream, endless: an infinitude of incomprehensibility, and he lay there, near a smooth white boulder. He could feel the plain in his mouth, his throat; memory flung him back and back.

"Please!"

"You like it."

"I can't stand it."

"But you like it."

"Oh, God."

The plain was indescribable, yet he saw it, felt it, like air with humps in his mouth, smooth and marvelous against his body. He was alone and lost. He could not move.

Water searched about his feet. A sand-fly lit near his nose and he watched it. The sand-fly did not touch him.

"You can squeeze my other ankle. That one doesn't do it."

He did not want to squeeze her other ankle. He wanted to squeeze her left ankle. Knowing.

The plain was an infinity, a complete foreverness, upon which he lay, alone.

The plain was in his mouth, yet pressed magnetically against his entire body. He was the weight. He could not move. Nothing moved. Light came from somewhere, suffusing all with a steady glow which was also in his mouth, against his cheekbones, his teeth, his body. He was naked, the wonder all around; sometimes he thought it was bed, the sheets—it was not. It was all through him, so smooth, so filled with silent power. He could feel the immense power.

He fought with all his energy to move, but he was frozen in warmth.

Where did the light come from?

It was pale light, a glow, as complete as the plain.

For a long time he lay there.

Then he drew his feet from the water and wriggled up, close to her.

It was twilight, not quite dusk—

He could smell her lotion and her.

She watched him patiently.

He knelt and rolled her to her side and unfastened her bra. He removed it and kissed the smooth breasts, savoring.

She watched him.

He reached down and slowly removed her bikini bottom.

She watched him through closed lids. She did not stir.

He caressed her. He kissed her smooth belly.

She did not stir. She was breathing evenly.

He sighed and pulled her bikini bottom back on her beautiful body. Then he covered her breasts and fastened her bra.

He slid down until his feet were in the water. Then he squeezed her left ankle.

"Don't," she said. "Please, don't."

He lay on the plain.

The smoothness was infinity.

He could see it in the glow. He could feel it in his mouth, against his cheekbones, his entire lost naked body.

Water lapped at his feet.

Lapse

He came upon the hanging body in the woods, at three-thirty that afternoon. The body was that of a young man, and it hung by the neck from a long hempen rope, knotted to a hickory branch high in the tree. The body swung slightly, and rotated gently, eyes bugged wide, mouth gaping, and head awry, the neckbone obviously cracked from what looked like a professional hangman's knot.

The dead man wore a red silk shirt, and sky-blue flared pants, with gleaming tan boots, brass-buckled. The palms of his hands, at his thighs, were turned outward, as if in supplication. The feet were perhaps a yard off the ground.

Almost at the same moment that Martens came upon the body in the hickory tree, he heard a girl, or woman, sobbing. He looked around. He saw nothing at first, but the sobbing was distinct.

He stepped over by some chest-high, thick fern, and glimpsed a bare leg, a foot wearing a sneaker that had once been white, but which was now dirt-stained.

"Hello?"

The sobbing ceased, cut off sharply. Then it resumed, more wildly uncontained than before.

Martens smelled an elusive perfume, and noted that the bare length of ankle and calf was clean and white, foreign to the dirty sneaker.

He thrust around the fernery.

It was a girl, young, perhaps nineteen. She lay flat out on the brown-leafed ground, her hands at her sides, sobbing.

She was completely naked, except for the sneakers.

Her body was willowy, vital looking. A wealth of tangled, bright blonde hair sprung about her shoulders.

She stopped sobbing sharply, and said, "You're—you're the artist. Your name's Race Martens."

Martens didn't know what to say, and did not know where to look. He wanted to stare at the girl. It was a strong desire. But he gazed instead at an ash sapling nearby.

"Yes," he said, "my name's Martens. I live just down the road. I was—I walk every day here in the woods."

"This—this—" Her voice was a half sob.

"I know," Martens said.

"It's Johnny."

"But where are your clothes?"

She sat half up, as if just now realizing she was nude. She covered her breasts with her palms. She stared at Martens. Her eyes were very pale blue, with tiny spokes in them. As he regarded her, those eyes seemed to be almost spinning in her head. The eyes were damp.

She said, "I was taking a sun-bath—on the roof, the terrace, rather. I happened to glance through the railing. I saw some men, taking Johnny into the woods. He was supposed to meet me—"

"Taking him into the woods?"

"Forcing him, pulling him, knocking him."

She leaned to one side on an elbow, and her body throbbed with sobs again. Martens wanted to help her, but he didn't know what to do.

He knelt and gently touched her shoulder. The lush, curved bareness of her body seemed to thrust at his gaze, magnetizing.

"Believe me," he said. "I want to help."

She turned back to him, sitting up again. Her breasts were uncovered now. They were firm and pointed.

"Your clothes," he said softly.

"I told you," she said. Her tone was broken. "I knew something was happening. Johnny was acting strangely lately. Fearful, sort of. I watched them go into the woods, and I waited. Then I even heard them laugh. It echoed up across the hill. I knew something was wrong. I heard a yell. I thought it was Johnny."

Her shoulders trembled and he wanted to hold her, but refrained.

She went on jerkily. "I just ran, that's all. I ran down across the field and came into the woods. This is what I found, just like you. There was nobody here—just—just—"

"Never mind," Martens said. "We've got to call the police."

"Yes," she said.

"Would you like my shirt?" Martens asked, proceeding to loosen the buttons.

"Yes."

He took off the gray gabardine shirt, and put it about her shoulders. She buttoned it down the front. It touched the tops of her thighs.

She stood up now. The bright blonde hair was quite tangled, and pine needles, small pieces of leaves stuck to it.

"I walk here every afternoon," Martens said.

"I know," she said. "I've seen you."

"We'd better get to it—maybe I'd best—cut him down?"

"No. Leave him for the police. You know that's how it's done. Never touch anything."

She turned and started walking rapidly off through the woods. He heard her sob again. Her white buttocks flashed in a slant of yellow sunlight. Shadowy freckles from overhead leafed branches touched her.

She whirled. "I'll go ahead. You come along, then. You know where I live?"

Martens did know where she lived. He had often seen her. He also knew her name. It was Julia. Julia Simmons. He had day-dreamed about her, as he did many things. From his studio window, he could see her often, running down through the field to the woods. He had painted her. He had never been this close to her before. He had never really known what her features were like. But now he knew they resembled the face in his imagination.

Usually she wore tattered denim shorts, some skimpy, colorful scarf across her breasts. The blonde hair always flowed tangled and long about her shoulders, and down her back.

"You come along," she said.

Then she was running like a deer, off through the woods. Almost immediately, he lost sight of her.

He started to run, then slowed to a walk.

He wondered who Johnny was, what the man had meant to her. Without a doubt they were very close, though he could not recall seeing him with her at any time. Perhaps they only met at night.

When he entered the gate on the railinged terrace of her home, he saw the blanket, the pillow, the book, the drink. This was where she had been sun bathing. Why did the thought of the sneakers bother him?

"Hi," she said..

She stood by some glass doors, leaning. She held his shirt up. He took it and slipped it on, buttoned it, watching her.

It was cool now, and a wind drew over the tops of the woods, across the field onto the terrace, and ruffled her blonde hair. Her eyes were red, but otherwise she was quite beautiful. She wore a thin red peignoir that came to just above her knees, and tied at her throat with a pink bow. There were ruffles and silk underneath.

The sneakers were gone now, and she was barefoot. Her toenails gleamed.

"I've called the police," she said. "Come in, come in—won't you have a drink?"

"I could do with one."

"I just gulped from the bottle. Believe me, I couldn't help it."

He followed her through the glass doors into a broad living room, with a gray fieldstone fireplace at the right side. It reached to the ceiling. She was already at a bar to the left, pouring drinks.

"Is bourbon all right?"

"Yes."

"I'll make it a big one."

"Thanks."

He watched her back. For a moment she stood still, then turned, and with what he thought was a brave smile, walked across and handed him a glass. They both drank.

She cupped her glass with two hands, took the rim from her lips and said, "Oh, God. Johnny. Johnny." Her eyes were pained. "What could've happened? Why did they do it? I don't understand! I don't—"

He did not know what to say.

She stood close to him. "Can we go to your place? Can we? Can we?"

"My place?"

"Yes. I don't like being here. I live alone. I don't want to be here when they come. I told them where he is. If they want me, they can find me." She looked at him that way, then said, "I can't believe it. He was an acrobat, he even worked in a circus. He was strong. He was so strong!"

Martens thought she might break down. He didn't want that. It was a bit unusual, asking to go to his place, but she was very distraught. It was in her eyes, the twist of her mouth.

"I'll bring a bottle," she said, pleading.

"Don't bother," he told her. "I have plenty."

"Then, let's go—let's go—I can't bear it, to stand here . . ."

Martens' place was a single overly large room he had rented for the summer, a barn done over into a studio. The entire north wall was a window. Paintings were everywhere. He was a successful painter and magazine illustrator. Summers he like to spend in different spots, just doing his own personal work. Rather parts of summers; no more than a month, ever. The rest of the time was spent hacking.

They entered the studio.

Immediately he realized there were paintings of this girl, Julia, everywhere.

She ran across the room and stood by the one that sat on the easel. It revealed her running across a field, chasing an English Setter. She wore only a billowing scarf of pale green, her nearly white blonde hair flowing back about her shoulders, capturing glints from the sunlight.

"Why!" she said. "That's me—me!"

Martens said nothing.

Finally, he said, "Would you care for another drink?"

"Yes—yes!" She whirled and looked at him. "But that's me—that's me—"

"Yes."

She turned and looked around the room. There were other paintings. Most of them were of her. He realized this now. Others were turned to the walls. But the ones of Julia Simmons all stared out at them. He felt embarrassed. A flush crept into his face. Warmth bathed his shoulders.

"The drink," he said.

He entered the small kitchen area and quickly fixed two drinks.

Back in the studio proper, he handed her one, and tried to smile. He knew it was forced and that it looked forced.

"I would see you out there," he said, trying to explain. "You looked so alive. It was a feeling. I couldn't help painting you. I had to do it."

"But—this one—" She pointed to one over against the wall. It was in imaginary close-up of her face, curiously resembling her to a near amazing exactness. "It looks just like me, just like me. When did you see me? When were you this close to me?"

Martens took a swallow of his drink to cover more embarrassment. Then he shook his head. "Never," he said. "Never. It all came from my head."

She moved swiftly up to him. "The police should be coming. We'd better watch for them."

"Yes."

For some reason there was turmoil in Martens' stomach, his chest, and he could actually feel the beating of his heart. The heat had not left his shoulders. There was a thrust of burgeoning energy in his loins. He knew what was beneath that crimson peignoir. He kept picturing her by the ferns, naked, lying on the leafy ground, her hair tangled, sobbing.

She was staring at him, sipping from her glass, and it was now he realized that she had put on lipstick. As she took the glass away, he saw that the corners of her mouth turned up, just as he had imagined. It truly was all rather amazing.

Then he remembered, sharply, the body hanging in the woods. Johnny. Who was Johnny?

"Who was Johnny?" he asked softly.

Her chin bunched. "We were going to be married."

"I'm sorry," Martens said.

Then she exclaimed, "Oh, Johnny," and ran past Martens to the left. Martens turned.

The man who had been hanging in the hickory tree, with the red silk shirt, and the sky blue trousers, and the gleaming tan boots with the brass buckles, stood there grinning at them both.

"Johnny, Johnny!" she said. "It worked. It worked."

Martens did not know what to say. Apprehension swallowed him.

"Let's get with it," the young man said. He was looking around the room. He walked over to the painting on the easel, took it in both hands, and hurled it to the floor. He stomped on it, slashing it with his sharp, cutting heels. "The rest of them," he said. "Get 'em up! Get 'em!" He was wild. There was a craziness in his eyes.

Martens had never seen anything like this. "Don't—don't," he said.

Julia Simmons threw her head back and laughed. The laughter was catching, and the young man called Johnny began laughing, too, as he ran around the room, snatching up the paintings Martens had done of Julia Simmons, throwing them to the floor, cutting them with his wicked boots. Even during this wild scene, stunned, Martens felt bursting anger and disbelief. Those paintings were precious to him; more precious now than ever before.

He ran toward the young man and grasped his arm. Johnny turned and swung at Martens' face, striking him in the left eye.

Martens stepped back. "What are you doing?" he asked. "What're you doing?"

The girl was helping. She, too, was running about the room, throwing paintings, upsetting tables covered with palettes and bottles of turpentine and linseed oil.

Then Johnny ran to the door. As he ran, he called out, "He had it coming to him—I told you I'd never stand for this, Julie."

"I know—I know!" the girl cried.

Johnny swung the door back open and re-entered with a large five-gallon can. He uncapped the can and began sloshing the contents over the floor of the studio.

Martens rushed at him, but Johnny swung a red-shirted arm, holding the can, and struck Martens full across the face. Martens sprawled on the floor. He didn't know what was happening. It was all too swift. He knew he could not fight this man. He had felt the wiry muscle, experienced the near-crazed anger behind those eyes; they were crazy, both of them. The girl was kicking at him now, with her bare foot.

"C'mon," Johnny said. "Let's get him out of here."

The girl took one of his wrists. The young man grabbed the other, and hauled Martens to his feet. The next moment, they were spinning through the doorway, and then they were crossing the field toward the woods, and his studio was a flaming pyre. Smoke billowed from the north window, and the edge of the roof seethed with crisp yellow flame. The can had held gasoline.

Then they were in the woods.

Martens still didn't know what to do. Both the young man and the girl laughed hysterically.

"We planned it," she said in a whisper. "I told you Johnny was with a circus. He ran a magic show—he can do anything—anything at all. But he's jealous, get it. Jealous of you. He knew about you. We saw your paintings before. We sneaked in when you went for walks in the woods. When Johnny saw them, he knew what he had to do. Do you know what jealousy is?"

Martens looked at the young man and he saw the wild, laughing face, the torn eyes, and he did know. And as he walked along between them, he realized for the first time that this girl had become an obsession with him. That was why he had painted her so often. She had lived in his dreams, dreams that were almost nightmares. He knew now what Johnny planned to do. He knew that they were crazed youth, both of them, wild and unfettered.

But—he, too, felt an insanity.

Yes, it was an obsession, but secretly he knew it was still more than that, even. The girl kept brushing against him as he walked. The youth yanked at his arm as they moved toward that same hickory tree, on the path that Martens took every afternoon. They had known he would follow this path. They had planned the whole thing.

The youth's grasp was loose on his arm. Both Johnny and the girl were babbling together, and though there was rage behind the young man's words, he laughed with scorn as he spoke.

Afterward, Martens did not now how he accomplished it. It all happened so fast, it was almost like one of his dreams.

He spotted the heavy chunk of flint in the pathway; the sharp, scalped edges of the gleaming black stone. The girl was to his right, with her hand on his wrist.

He broke free, reached down, grabbed up the piece of rock, and whirled directly into Johnny's face.

He struck with an abrupt maniacal force. They had ruined and burned his paintings. They had done away with something that had become terribly precious to him; more precious than he had ever realized, until now.

The girl screamed.

He kept striking Johnny's head. The sharp flint bit into the young man's forehead, his nose, his lips, and cheek. Blood spurted. Johnny was on his knees, with Martens standing over him, hammering at his skull.

The girl tore at Martens' back. He whirled toward her. She backed off.

Reaching down, Martens grabbed Johnny's wrist, and yanked him along the pathway. The girl watched with a kind of awe, moving along some distance away.

The hemp rope was by the hickory tree.

He loosened the hangman's knot, and saw how it had prevented the young man being throttled with an extra knot. He untied the knot, and fastened a true hangman's noose. He placed it around the unconscious man's neck.

Then he climbed the tree with the other end of the rope, and, breathing heavily, working slowly, lifted the body until the brass-buckled boots were at least a yard from the ground. He knotted the hempen rope.

Panting through tightly clenched teeth, he descended to the ground, working himself limb from limb.

The girl stood by the green fern, in her crimson peignoir.

Martens said nothing. He just stood there a long moment, staring at her—then he moved toward her.

Southern Comfort

Baxter Beatty tooled the rented Ford sedan around the corner, and cruised slowly down the dark street on the edge of the business section in the small Florida town of Gulfport. With robbery in mind, he should have been slightly nervous. He wasn't. This was a sure thing, one of those seldom jobs that fell into your lap, and promised a good take.

Money was low. Florine and he had covered the entire Eastern seaboard, knocking off gas stations, and small stores, and they had done quite well. But Baxter Beatty spent what he earned. True, he envisioned mighty things, dreamed of knockovers that would set him for life behind low ivy-covered walls, in a home of splendor—and, true, he had never attained his goal, but just the same, money came and money went, and he had never truly had to grub. Florine admired pretty things, and Baxter saw that she got them. They lived well, they ate high, they drank the best, and to date Baxter had managed to stall Florine on her marriage inclinations.

Florine was a South Carolina girl, a country girl, and her man could do no wrong. She wanted Baxter as her husband. She was at him every minute. Probably, in time, she would land him. He knew this. Nevertheless, he still hearkened to the small voice, and artfully kept her at bay.

Why marriage, anyway? Didn't they spend every moment together—wasn't it just as good as marriage? To Baxter, it was. Florine found it wanting.

Slowing the car in front of a small shadowed building, Baxter thought of Florine's heritage, of her family, her Ma and her Pa, and her four big brothers, one of whom was a minister. She had been brought up in close to poverty. He could not blame her for wanting security. She was more than just pretty, she was loaded with love, utterly devoted, but marriage was a bit too much.

After all, Baxter Beatty had a certain code.

He stopped the car, took out a cigarette, lit up, and sat there, musing. The sharp red glow from the ember revealed finely chiseled features, dark hair, a well-shaped mouth. He was a handsome man, and he knew it. Didn't Florine tell him so, every hour on the hour? Satisfaction quirked the corners of deep-set dark eyes.

Her family should be proud of her. She had done well.

Just like Bonnie and Clyde. In a small way, of course.

Baxter prided himself on one thing. He had never done the big picture . . . he had never killed anyone. He had come close. He carried a .32 revolver. But he had never used it except to frighten an obnoxious mark.

He turned his mind to the job at hand.

Alice Harrod's Antiques.

A shop larger than most, just waiting to be robbed. He couldn't get over it, really. It was almost like a plant, the way the news was in town.

Alice Harrod was a wealthy spinster who owned an enormous home on the edge of town, and ran her store for something to do. It was stocked with collector's items of all kinds. Her mail order business was large, and buyers visited her from great distance.

But that wasn't it.

The loud voice in town was that Alice Harrod kept the earnings of the store in a tin box *at the store*. She never took it home and she visited the bank only monthly. She was trusting. There was no crime in Gulfport, nothing to fear. Everybody talked of it. Baxter had heard the talk in six different places.

Ordinarily, Florine worked with him. This time, he planned the job alone, as he sometimes did. There was no need for the two of them.

"But I could hold the flashlight, Baxter."

"You just sit here and do your nails, honey. It won't take an hour."

"Well, if you insist, Baxter, darling."

So here he was. He had never laid eyes on Alice Harrod. All he knew was that she rolled in wealth. Imagine, he thought. All that loot, and wasting time running an antique store.

But—thanks be to God for little Alice Harrod.

He left the car, walked across the silent, deserted sidewalk, up to the front door. No one was in sight anywhere. He bent to the latch. It took him a full minute with the right-sized pick, and he was inside, breathing darkness, furniture oil, hearing the slow tick of a clock.

He closed the door.

He had no idea where the tin box would be. He only knew it existed. It was black, from all reports, and fairly large, too.

Not wanting to flash his light this close to the door, he waited till his eyes became accustomed to the dark. Then, gradually, he saw the shadowed room. It was small, smaller than he had imagined, stocked with furniture, walled with racks.

Then he saw the partition, a door. He walked softly toward the door. There was no counter in the front room, only the bulking antiques. A curtain covered the door, thick brocade. He stepped through.

Darkness. He couldn't see a thing.

He blinked on the flashlight, thinking about that tin box, and an old man rose from a chair and ran at him full tilt.

Baxter hadn't time to think. He grabbed for his revolver, whipped it out.

"Hold it!" he said.

The man paused, gray-haired, burly-shouldered, a face carved from old oak with a scarred blade. The man wore a blue work shirt, once-blue overalls.

"Just stand still," Baxter said.

"Won't stand still," the man said. "What you want in here?"

"Who the hell are you?" Baxter asked.

"The night-watchman, that's who. Now, you git!" The man advanced two steps, bent over slightly, brandishing his arm.

"Stay back," Baxter said loudly.

"You crazy punk," the man shouted. "Think you can come in here—"

"Back!"

The man was striking at him, crowding him. Baxter experienced a wild, smothering fear. He brushed at the old man. But the man was strong, clinging to his gun arm.

"I'll git the law on ye!"

Baxter heaved and broke his arm loose, struck savagely at the old man's head. It was like hitting rock, with as much results.

"Ayeiii!" the old man yelled, suddenly berserk, fighting like a maddened ape.

The gun went off. Baxter did not recall touching the trigger. But there it was.

One moment the old man was raising hell. The next, he stood there like a tree, his face registering shock, mouth open revealing toothless gums, eyes wide and red.

Then he fell. Baxter had seen the hole in the front of the blue work shirt. He played the flashlight beam on the old man. He leaned and touched him. He shook him.

"Wake up, old man," he said. "Snap out of it!"

The burly figure rolled over on its back. The old man was dead.

Baxter stood there. No noise reached him from the street. There was every chance that the sound of the shot had gone unnoticed. But he could take no chances. He would have to let the tin box, the money, go hang. He had to get out of here.

He had killed.

All his life, Baxter had dreamed of this moment. In his dreams he had done the big thing, killed a man, from which there was never any escape. Wherever he went in his dreams, he was continually fearful. The dead eyes always leered back at him. "I'll get you—I'll get you!" And, eventually, they always did.

And now, it was reality.

He turned toward the curtained door and the room flooded with light.

"Drop the gun."

It was a woman's voice, from behind.

"Drop it, I say, or I'll shoot. I mean it, that's a promise."

Baxter dropped his revolver. It bounced slightly on a Persian rug. The room was bright.

"Now, turn around. Slowly, please."

There was something almost prim about the voice.

He turned and stared at the ugliest specimen of womanhood he had ever seen in his life. She was beyond imagination.

"Take a good long look," the woman said in that prim, musical voice. "Satisfy your curiosity."

She was paper pale, the color of old death, with bulging black eyes, no eyebrows, thin red hair in a kind of floating nest over gleams of pale skull, a nose like knotted rope, a bloody slash of mouth, and three chins. She wore black, with lace at throat and cuffs. Pale hands gripped a rifle that was stolidly aimed at his middle. The nails of the woman's hands were purple.

"Who are you?" Baxter managed.

"Alice Harrod, that's who."

They stood there like that, staring at each other. She was at the end of a gleaming wooden counter, by some stairs that led down to darkness. Furniture was stacked about the room; tables, chairs, bookcases, old secretaries.

"Over there," Alice Harrod said in that curiously prim and musical voice. "Over to that rocking chair. Go there and sit. Now. Get a move on."

He did as she asked. She might become nervous and shoot. It was an old Boston rocker, quite comfortable. She stepped away from the counter, crossed the room to a straight chair, dragged it in front of Baxter, and sat down. She sat with her lumpy knees close together, her thick ankles touching, the high, laced black shoes shining in the overhead light.

"Don't say a word," Alice Harrod said, the rifle pointed straight at him, her finger crooked at the trigger.

They sat there. Long dragging moments passed, and Baxter began to wonder what she was up to? She stared at him. For a time he returned her stare, then he was forced to look away from those protruding black eyes. They seemed to search straight through him. He was subtly fearful of them. He turned his gaze to the dead man, lying on the Persian rug, near the door to the partition.

They sat that way, with Alice Harrod staring at him, for a quarter of an hour. The clock in the other room ticked loudly. Occasionally a car passed out on the street.

Suddenly, she spoke. "Perhaps you will do. What is your name?"

"Baxter Beatty. What d'you mean?"

"Well, Baxter. I suppose you've heard plenty about me. Own up. True?"

"Well—"

She laughed abruptly. "It's finally paid off. I know you'll do. I can tell."

"I don't get you. You hold all the cards. You might at least tell me what the joke is."

"It is and it isn't. A joke, that is. Baxter," she said. "You've been trapped by greed." She smiled, and it was horrible to see; the crimson lips wrinkling up over a set of winking chins, the eyes protruding even more than before. "I'll tell you, Baxter. You wanted my money. You shall have it. Not just the money in the tin box, but all of it, Baxter. And let me tell you, I'm rich—so rich you could hardly count it all."

"You miss me in the fog."

"Yes," she said. "The fog. I'm ugly, ridiculous to look at, aren't I? But I'm rich. Think that over."

Baxter said nothing.

"You're going to marry me, Baxter."

He came half out of his chair. She lifted the rifle, smiling at him, her gaze wanton, hawklike.

"It's what you would call a set-up," she said. "I've been noising it around for months that I keep money here at the store. But nobody knew till now that I've been here every night, waiting."

Baxter began to experience a sick feeling.

He said, "Who's that?" gesturing toward the dead man.

"My gardener, Bill Doxy. He was the only one who knew I was here, and he'd never tell, because I made him promise. He brought me a sandwich tonight. We were talking in the dark. I just told him I was guarding my store. Old Bill was sort of feeble-minded." She paused. "I'd just planned on robbery. But you've killed him. Now you're really mine."

He stared at her. She was mad.

"Oh, yes, Baxter," she said. "You'll do as I say. My brother's the Chief of Police here in Gulfport. My cousin, Albert, is the judge. Another cousin, Norris, is the Sheriff. You'll do exactly as I say. You're going to marry me, Baxter. You understand?"

"You're crazy as hell."

"Then I call my brother. Right now."

Baxter chewed the inside of his cheek. He tried to look at her, but it was difficult. Sure, she was mad. But could she do this thing?

"I'm ugly. Rich, but ugly. Nobody'd ever marry me, even for my money. It was too much to ask, living with somebody like me. So I had to get a husband. I couldn't get one any conventional way. So I am a bit unconventional. I've waited for this moment, and here it is, and, really, Baxter—you're not half bad."

Baxter's mind worked overtime.

"I have strong lusts, Baxter. And you look like a resilient fellow. You'll do smartly."

Baxter saw her game. And he did want her money. He knew he would swing with her wild notion. But at the back of his mind he already had her dead and buried; he would work it somehow, he knew. He would have the money. He would finally live the high life. Somehow he contained an abrupt exuberance. He had always been quick with personal decisions. He could wait. So what if he did have to live with the old bag for a time? He could do it. Because there would come a day when . . .

"You're liking the idea, aren't you, Baxter? You have no morals, no ethics. You just *want*, don't you—and we're alike in that."

He tightened his lips. He mustn't give in too readily.

They talked. He refused. She urged, promised, painted glowing pictures of her wealth. Gradually, he gave in. He told her she wasn't as bad looking as she surmised. She scoffed. He was adamant. They came to the ultimate conclusion. He would court her, like any man, coming to her home on the edge of town. Subsequently, they would announce their engagement—then marriage. All quite aboveboard.

She pointed toward the dead man. "His grave will be in the cellar. We'll dig it. Down there." She looked at the descending stairway. "And then, we'll carry on. We'll make it all as quick as possible."

"Yes, Alice—I'm agreed."

"Baxter, one thing. If you try anything, anything at all, I promise you'll regret it. I'll turn you in as a thief and murderer. I'll produce the body. I'll tell them you threatened my death, but that I finally had to take the chance and turn you in. They will believe me, Baxter. You could rave forever, but they will believe me. I promise you that. You marry me, or you die in Raiford—as sure as my name is Alice Herrod."

"It'll never be like that, Alice."

"I believe you. Now, let's get old Bill down into the cellar."

The pact was made.

During the next week, Baxter soft-soaped Florine. She was a willowy young thing, a blonde, with pouting red lips, and eager blue eyes. Baxter explained that he was planning big things in this town, had something good lined up. He knew he had to tell her he was through with her. He had to get her on the way back to South Carolina. But how? She was loving, and she clung like old ivy. She adored him.

"When're we going to get married, Baxter, honey?"

And every afternoon he was out at Alice's, sitting in her dim parlor, drinking iced tea, hoping he would be a winner, overcome with the obvious wealth of her home, her large gardens, her cars—everything.

He could stand her ugliness. For a time.

On Thursday afternoon, they were in the summerhouse, gazing out across the gardens, talking, when something Alice said jarred him to the bone.

"I know all about you, now, Baxter. I've had you investigated. I know everything, all the sordid facts. But you're really not so bad. Except—" She paused. "That girl, Florine. You must get rid of her. Today, Baxter. I want no more of her. You're to get her out of town. Understand?"

"Yes."

"I wonder if you do? We're going to announce our engagement next week. I want nothing to interfere. Least of all a silly girl. Besides, Baxter," she said, leaning close, speaking in a whisper. "I really don't like you going home to somebody else."

"All right, Alice. I'll take care of it."

"See that you do, Baxter. And remember exactly what I told you that first night we met."

He remembered, all right. He knew he had to send Florine away.

"You go, now, and take care of her, Baxter. I want to see you early in the morning. We'll have breakfast together, and plan things."

"Yes, Alice."

He returned to the hotel and faced Florine. He was ready. He was abrupt, cold, cruel.

"That's all there is to it, Flo, baby. We're through. I'm sending you home on the bus tonight. Here's your ticket."

"But—Baxter!"

He was closed to pity. She pled, she begged, she cajoled. All to no avail. Then, curiously, she suddenly packed her bags, took the ticket, pecked him on the cheek, wiped away a tear, and left.

Somehow it made him uncomfortable.

He thought of her family, after she had gone. They were closely knit. They would welcome her home. Her four brothers would enfold her in their arms. He was almost happy for her. And he was entirely overcome with excitement for himself.

He wondered how long he could stand it with Alice Harrod, before he wrung her miserable neck? Because he knew he would eventually do just that. He had finally made it into God's sweet lettuce patch.

That night he slept well, rose early, bathed, shaved, and dressed carefully. It seemed slightly strange, not having Florine around, making her off-beat comments. But he could bear it.

He thought of Alice. He would woo her for real today, tickle her ribs, make her happy, show some honest affection. He would forcefully explain that money wasn't all he desired; that he, too, understood loneliness.

They were a surprising pair, Alice and himself.

He left the room, started down the hall for the elevator. The doors slid open with a hiss. He caught a brief glimpse of something steely swinging viciously for his head, but he was much too slow to stop it.

". . . and do you, Florine, take this man?"

"I surely do."

"I now pronounce you man and wife."

Baxter heaved himself up, head swimming, aching.

He was in a room.

It was his hotel room.

He saw Florine, smiling, dressed in white. Four large men were in the room, all beaming. One held a black book. As he moved to get off the bed, reeling, one of them stepped close and gave him a shove. He sprawled back. The man grinned at him.

"He's awake, Flo. Kiss him—kiss your husband!"

"What?" Baxter said. "What's this?"

Florine snuggled close. "We're married. Baxter, honey—don't you see?" she whispered. "Kiss me, now—you simply *must* kiss me." Her soft lips thrust against his mouth. He struggled free, leaped to the floor.

"Just hold it, brother," the largest of the men said. "We're Flo's brothers, and you're our brother now. We came as soon as she wired, last night. Everett, here, has married you up, right and proper."

"I know you've been seeing another woman," Florine said, looking almost timid, and very pretty in wedding white. "That awful Miss Harrod. I followed you. You should be ashamed. Don't you know, Baxter, that—that a southern girl always gets her man? Especially one like me. And *always* when they've been living together like we have? You'll see it's the only way, Baxter, honey."

He thought dizzily of Alice Harrod, of the promise she'd made him. He could almost hear the sirens of police cars.

"You're going to live right here in this pretty town," one of the brothers said. "Flo likes it here. And we're going to take turns seeing you do right by our little sister." His voice turned grim. "Isn't that nice, Baxter?"

They were all grinning now.

Florine was excited. "Let's all go out and celebrate. You feel up to it, Baxter, honey?"

He knew he had to escape. But he could never escape. He wanted rest. And then he knew where his final resting place would be—at Raiford Penitentiary, in an extremely uncomfortable chair.

Hell House

He whispered to her in the fragrant darkness of their bedroom.

"Helen?"

She turned over in bed, the sound a silken rustle. He staggered slightly and sat down heavily beside her.

"You positively reek," she said.

"I've been thinking."

"Oh, wow! The great man's been thinking. You call drinking *thinking*, then that's a brand new one on me."

"Shut up and listen, Helen. I've got every right to drink. A bloody wonder I'm not in a hospital. Uncle Alvin's finally got to me. I can't stand it anymore. I tell you, the old galoot's insane. And I know what I'm going to do . . ."

"Insane, huh? Well, so he's wobbly. He's been good enough to take us into his home, here. We were flat broke, remember? And what the devil d'you do now? Lay around all day in the Florida sun and guzzle his liquor. You haven't lifted a hand to get a job in over four years—"

He hiccupped. "So, why should I? Uncle Alvin's rich. He's got enough to keep us for the rest of our lives. That's what I'm trying to tell you."

Helen Brinkerhoff sat half up in bed, a blurry shape against the white pillows. Through partially open French windows washed the cloying scent of night-blooming Jasmine, and black cut-outs of royal palm fronds drooped motionless on a paler sky. A whippoorwill sang.

"Thank your lucky stars," she said.

"Come off it, Helen. Thanks for what? We're tied here forever. That what you want? When we could be traveling all over the world? Tokyo, Bombay, Paris, Rome? Yeah, we could be in Europe, having a ball. This is fine, all right, just dandy—"

"It is fine. Except for you. You're just a damned drunk, is all. That's what you are. Taking out your frustrations on me. A slob. I'm sick of you, Herb."

His words were barely audible. "I'm going to kill him."

The whippoorwill sang again. It was somehow mournful.

"Kill Uncle Alvin?"

"Yes, Helen."

She laughed softly.

"Shut your damned mouth," Herb said in a harsh whisper. "He'll hear you. He's got ears like a cat, you know that."

"I can't help it, Herb. So help me. You're such a fool! Kill Uncle Alvin—you haven't got the nerve, you spineless idiot."

"Haven't I?" He hiccupped again.

"No. You're a weak, meek, wishy-washy lush. I don't know why I married you—"

"You love me, that's why."

She did not answer.

He said thickly, "I'm going to kill my uncle, and that's final. I've got it all planned. Afterward, we'll have his money. You know we inherit. The crazy thing is all these years I never thought of it before."

"Herb, go to bed. You're drunker than I figured."

"I mean it, Helen! Don't make fun of me."

"And just what the hell will Uncle Alvin be doing all this time?"

"Nothing. Plain nothing. I'm going to do it tomorrow night. There's no risk, and there's a perfect time for it, too." He paused, breathing loudly through his nose. She said nothing. He went on. "You know how many beach houses been broken into along here the past month? Five, Helen—" He waved his fingers—"five places. An' Bill Burdock got beaten within an inch of his life. A perfect time, I tell you." He leaned closer.

She averted her head. "You stink."

"Shut up, or I'll hit you!" He was still for a moment. "We'll find Uncle Alvin dead in the morning and some junk stolen. We'll call the cops an' tell 'em we slept through it. We'll be all broken up . . ."

"Good Lord. I think you're actually serious."

"Of course I'm serious, lame-brain. I've even bought a knife. That's why I went to town this afternoon."

"A wonder you could see to drive."

"Keep it up, Helen. You're asking for it."

"So you plan to use a knife?"

"Yeah. Right. A gun'd make too much noise—might 'rouse somebody. An' we couldn't 'splain sleeping through it. Too chancy. Knife's perfect. I been thinking 'bout it for a long time. He's driving me up the wall, always talking about his damned idiotic Army career—"

"He was famous, Herb—a detonations expert. Did all sorts of weird things with bombs and stuff. Built a real rep for himself. All sorts of medals for bravery in action. You've seen them."

"Yeah."

"Look what he did in Berlin, blowing up that Nazi headquarters by some sort of remote control. I've read about it—all those books and citations—"

"Yeah! His damned library. Always reading to me about dynamite an' nitroglycerin, plastic explosives on his back—I can't stand it, I tell you! I'm fed to the teeth."

"You really mean it."

"You're damned right."

"You might've consulted me."

"Consider yourself consulted."

"You better go to bed."

"I'll have a little nightcap, first."

"You've drunk up almost everything in the house."

"I should give a bloody—"

The whippoorwill sang.

Herb stood before his shaving mirror in the morning, and winked at himself. He was pleased and pent-up inside. So used to drinking, long past the stage of hangovers, he looked forward to his first nip. And he knew it would be a long day, waiting for the night.

Helen had already gone down to breakfast with Uncle Alvin. Herb knew he would have to spend another hellish day humoring the old fool. This close to the promised end, it would be even more difficult to pretend interest in the old man's boring accounts of heroism during the wars. Oh, for tomorrow when it would be all over, and he and Helen would be well on their way to a new-found paradise.

True, there were some misgivings, not about the deed itself, but about the chance of being caught. He thrust such thoughts from his mind, but they continued to gnaw at the edges of his consciousness.

Herb knew police had been posted around the perimeter of this Gulf beach area, hoping to catch the nocturnal prowler who had been in evidence the past few months. But that prowler was himself Herb's alibi.

Dressed in a flowered red-and-blue sports shirt, and gray flannel slacks, Herb stood before his bureau. He thrust his protruding chin even further out, blinked his pale blue eyes, and opened the top drawer.

There lay the knife, partially covered by a green sock. He lifted it out, unsheathed it, and tested the blade on a thumbnail. Real sharp. He sucked a breath, laid the knife to rest, pushed more socks aside, and came up with a partly filled bottle of brandy.

Precious little left. But enough to start the worms crawling before going down to breakfast and facing Uncle Alvin, the old coot.

Herb tilted the bottle to his lips, and gulped the cognac. Moments later, the bottle was empty and he felt a pleasant warmth creeping through his vitals. His head whirled lightly.

He tossed the bottle into a wastebasket and headed for the stairs. There was little he enjoyed more than that morning eye-opener.

Uncle Alvin was holding forth at the breakfast table, while Helen leaned forward, revealing interest. The old man held a slice of half-eaten toast in one hand, a cup of coffee in the other. His mouth was half full, and he talked around the food, his shiny black eyes tight with eagerness, gray hair combed back in a pompadour, Van Dyke beard bobbing.

He was a wiry looking old bird, wearing his ubiquitous white linen suit, with a black string tie.

Uncle Alvin swallowed a lump of toast and continued speaking, after a quick nod to Herb. "Just telling Helen about this Nazi sub I blew up in the Arctic straits off the Norway coast. Just nosing into a fiord, you know. And I swum out there with a back pack, the water cold as a witch's you-know-what, and I used plastic. You got to be careful of plastic in cold water—"

"But why, Uncle Alvin," Helen asked.

Herb winked at her over the old man's shoulder, and helped himself to ham and eggs from the buffet. Maria, the fat Spanish cook, poked her red face around the door of the butler's pantry, and stared at Herb. She scowled as he forked more eggs onto his already overladen plate.

Herb stuck his tongue out at her. She made a twisted face, and let the pantry door fall to.

Herb sat and began to eat.

Uncle Alvin was talking about the cold waters of the fiord, and of how deep he had to swim, and of the plastic explosive. "It gets hard an' cracks," Uncle Alvin said. "That's what I was worried about this time. It had to stick to the sub so I could attach the detonating device, or the whole thing would fail. Everything depended on me. An' there was a time element, too—"

"My God," Helen said. "Weren't you scared?" She clutched at the breastline of her blue housecoat, then tugged at a wisp of dark auburn hair. Her brown eyes were round.

"Of course he was scared," Herb said, chewing on a mouthful of ham and egg. "Anybody'd be scared."

Uncle Alvin fixed him with a steady calm. "Oddly, Herb, I wasn't frightened at all. You get that way from experience, you know."

"You trying to say you weren't even a little bit afraid?" Herb said, still chewing. "Down there in all that freezing water, alone, in the darkness with a Nazi submarine? Don't try to kid me, Uncle Alvin."

"He's not trying to kid you, Herb," Helen said sharply. "He's a brave man. Just pay attention—"

"Well, *I'd* damn well be scared," Herb said.

"You an' me, we're different," Uncle Alvin said, his tanned, knobby fingers fussing with a silver spoon. "You place too high a premium on life, Herb. Not that I don't admire life, now—don't get me wrong. But, Herb, everybody's got to die. That's how I always figured it. Like the bard said, 'Die today an' be quit for tomorrow,' something like that, anyways."

Herb swallowed, unable to speak. The old coot didn't know the truth of his own words.

"Anyways," Uncle Alvin continued, nodding, his beard bobbling, eyes bright with memory, "I finally got that cussed plastic stuck to the stern side of the sub, an' that's when I spotted the shark . . ."

Herb groaned, wiped his mouth with a napkin, excused himself and wandered into the living room. He went directly to the small ebony bar in the corner by the fireplace, and proceeded to check the liquor supply for today's libations. It was getting low. He poured himself a healthy drink . . .

From the dining room came the steady drone of Uncle Alvin's voice, accompanied by sharp "Oh's," and "Ah's," from Helen. How could she stand it, Herb wondered, emptying his glass and immediately pouring another drink.

The rest of the day was more of the same, the weary procedure to Uncle Alvin's study, where the old man held forth on his exploits of blowing up ships, armament depots, railroad bridges, airplanes. To hear him tell it, Herb thought, Uncle Alvin had won every war from the beginning of time. Won them himself, alone, single-handed.

"I received the *Croix-de-guerre* for that one, bestowed by France—and, you know, I didn't really want to take it?"

"Could I see it?" Helen asked.

"Of course, my dear—it's right here in the safe—"

The old man tottered to the huge black steel safe at the far side of the room. The enormous safe dwarfed Uncle Alvin, and Herb unconsciously licked his lips. He had never looked into that safe. He saw, to his mild surprise, that Helen seemed overly interested, too, and smiled to himself. He knew Uncle Alvin's wealth was kept in the bank, the First National, but Herb suspected that more things of monetary value were in this big old safe.

Herb watched closely as Uncle Alvin turned the big knob for the combination, and managed to memorize each number.

Then the huge black door swung open.

"There," Uncle Alvin said, reaching inside.

Herb grunted involuntarily. What he saw were trays and trays of papers, gleaming medals and ribbons, packets of currency all neatly stacked, and other trays of glittering jewels. The latter would of course be Martha's, Uncle Alvin's wife's. Martha had died ten years before.

"Someday, Helen," Uncle Alvin said, "I'll let you go through Martha's jewels. I keep them for sentimental value. I'll let you select something to keep as your own."

"My goodness!" Helen said, one hand at her lips. "Aren't you afraid, keeping all those valuables in your home? I should think you'd—"

Herb cursed his wife inwardly.

Uncle Alvin gave a dry cackle. "I'm an old man, and this safe is strong and sturdy." He withdrew a black velvet tray. "Besides," he said, turning and winking at Helen. "I take precautions." He lifted a bronze, be-ribboned medal from the tray. "Here it is, dear." He smiled. "The *Croix-de-guerre.*

The president of France hung it on my chest himself. But of course, as I say,
I didn't really want it—"

You old liar, Herb thought, his heart thudding against his ribs at the
sight of so much near wealth.

"Oh, Uncle Alvin!" Helen said. "You've got more medals than I ever
thought. You've simply got to tell me about all of them."

"I'll do that, my dear—I didn't know you were so interested."

"This afternoon?"

"Certainly."

It better be this afternoon, Herb thought. But he felt sickened at the way
these two went on. He could stand it no longer . . .

"You'll have to excuse me," he said. "I have something important to
do."

Uncle Alvin, tray of medals in hand, looked at Herb.

Herb turned sharply and left the room. He headed immediately for the
living-room bar, the rapidly diminishing supply of liquor.

Helen spent the remainder of the day with Uncle Alvin.

Herb drank away the hours, anticipating the night.

The old man was snoring fitfully, probably dreaming about some stupid
Nazi submarine, Herb thought.

Herb Brinkerhoff stood about Uncle Alvin's bed, knife in hand. Winds
softly gusted at the curtains, and the whippoorwill sang just once, lyrically
stroking the night.

Helen had pled with him to reconsider, but Herb knew she had
weakened toward the last, what with his descriptions of the wealth they
would have. He knew that deep in Helen's heart, she was as avaricious as
he.

The room moved giddily, and he knew he had put away a prodigious
amount of Uncle Alvin's liquor. Well, he could buy more—all he wanted, in
fact—just as soon as—

He gritted his teeth and admonished himself. What the hell are you
waiting for?

He hunched above Uncle Alvin's prostrate figure under the thin blanket.

Abruptly a fury came over Herb. He saw what he could have, and what
stood in his way. He choked with it, and was suddenly savage. His arm
flashed up, the knife blade flashed down.

Uncle Alvin jumped and gasped in bed.

This was the last sound the old man ever uttered.

"Well, I did it."

"Now what?" Helen asked from her bed.

"We wait till morning, then when he doesn't come down for breakfast, we investigate. That's all there is to it."

"What'd you do with the knife?"

"I buried it in the back yard, along with a bunch of silverware and stuff. Some paintings, just junk we'll never want. I messed up the place a little, too—just to make it look good. The prowler, y'know?"

"You're blind drunk—"

"I'll be blinder, old girl—we're rich, now, rich!"

A long silence filled the darkness, broken only by their breathing.

"Well, what've you got to say?" Herb asked.

"Poor Uncle Alvin," Helen said. "Poor, poor old Uncle Alvin." She sat up in bed, a black shadow. "You're terrible, Herb—just plain awful!"

He strode toward her with a wild lurch, grabbed her by the shoulder, and struck her three times in the face. She fell sobbing back on the bed.

"You watch what you say to me!" he told her viciously. "Just watch it, hear?"

Her sobs filled the darkness.

Herb chuckled and staggered toward the bedroom doorway.

The police were thorough, but it seemed as though they had hardly come after Herb put in the phone call, then they were gone again.

"We're sorry," a Lieutenant Adams, large and beefy-faced, said. "And we'll do everything we can to catch the person who did this. We've posted men everywhere. I know how you must feel."

"You'll never know," Helen said. "He was such a wonderful, kind, gentle old man. We loved him."

"He was thought of highly in these parts," the lieutenant said. "You just rest easy, now."

"I'm sure, with you taking charge and all—" Helen said.

The lieutenant shook his big head. "Damned odd you didn't hear anything. If only—"

Herb inwardly cursed the man. If he would only go away, and leave them alone.

Helen was smiling.

Lieutenant Adams glanced at Herb, then left abruptly.

"Well?" Herb said to Helen. He rubbed his palms together.

"I gave Maria the day off. We've got to eat. I'll have to run to the store for some groceries, there's nothing in the house."

"There's no booze, either," Herb said. "Pick up a couple jugs of bourbon, okay?"

"All right. But I really don't think you should drink so much now. We've got to be circumspect, Herb."

"Circumspect?" He made a mouth noise. "I'll show you circumspect at the funeral. Right now I'm going to get loaded, see? Now you go ahead—get that booze!"

"All right, Herb."

He watched her from the side window as she went to the garage. He watched the silver Porsche back out and swoop off through the drive. It was his car, now—his, all *his* . . .

Helen was gone some time, and Herb chewed his nails, wishing for a drink, drowning in the swoop of happy thoughts that swarmed through his mind. Paris. Rome. Everything he'd ever dreamed of.

Then he heard the car bubble into the garage. Moments later Helen came to the house, loaded down with sacks of groceries.

"You get the booze?" Herb said, running up to her. "I'm half nuts for a drink."

"Booze?" She seemed rather abstracted as she set the sacks of groceries on the kitchen table.

"Yes, damn it," Herb said nastily. "Booze. What you went after—in bottles, remember?"

She stared at him. "Oh, darling—I forgot. I was thinking of everything, and I simply forgot."

"Damn you!" He lunged at her, and smashed her across the face savagely twice. She sprawled back across the table, and fell to the floor. Red welts appeared on her cheek. "I'll go myself," he said. "You'd better do some thinking, hear?"

She groaned and he left the house, slamming the back door.

Immediately, Helen was on her feet. She ran through the kitchen into the butler's pantry, then into the dining room, and across to the side window which commanded a view of the garage. She saw Herb hurrying through the doors.

Seconds later a thunderous roar knifed the peaceful Florida day. The garage split wide open, and cement, loose boards, rubble exploded into the air. The rear end of the Porsche flew across the back yard and struck the house. There came a raining rattle of falling things.

Helen didn't move a muscle.

Uncle Alvin, with her careful prompting, had taught her a great deal about demolition; enough to wire dynamite to the ignition of the car. It had paid off. She was rid of her husband, and Uncle Alvin was gone, too.

She would have everything she'd always wanted. She knew she was as greedy as Herb had been. She had planned everything well, and she was in the clear. Who would ever consider that she'd been able to blow up a car?

Then she remembered Martha's jewels, the safe in Uncle Alvin's study.

She ran through the house. She wanted those jewels, and whatever else was of value in that safe. And she knew she had to get it now. The police might want to go through everything, what with all that had happened.

She too had watched as Uncle Alvin opened the safe, and she knew the combination.

She knelt before the safe, and spun the dial left and right. There was a metallic click. She grabbed the handle, thinking, Good-by, Herb—good-by everything—hello, fun!

She yanked on the door.

Good-by was right. The explosion was a white, almost soundless blast, and just before Helen flew apart, in that interim of inertia split-seconds before death, she remembered how Uncle Alvin had said he "took precautions."

Leave it to Uncle Alvin . . .

It was quiet for a moment. Dust settled. Sparkling jewels of all kinds littered the demolished study. Currency was strewn amid the rubble, and splats of scarlet marred the white walls beyond the bookcases.

A movement outside the shattered windows. A ragged-looking head peered in. Then a disreputable man climbed through the window and stood scowling at the mess.

Suddenly his bloodshot eyes brightened.

"My God!" he said. "My God—a fortune!"

He began scrambling madly about, snatching up hundred-dollar bills, necklaces, bracelets, sparkling rings, jewels of all kinds. He gasped for breath.

"Great God!" he said.

Distantly, almost like the cry of a baby, a siren began to whine.

A Visit from Morse

February 1977

Loretta, though she was terribly sensitive and rather psychic, had absolutely no premonition of what would transpire that hot August afternoon . . .

One might imagine that the manner in which Loretta had been thinking continually about Morse since those terrible days in the late twenties, when the awful culminating event took place even in accord with Mother's fearsome promise, she would have been little surprised that *something* would happen, *had* to happen. If one dwells religiously on an emotionalized memory regarding someone, practically living it hourly, for over fifty years, emotionalizing it even in nightdreams, something *must* happen. The gods allow it, deem it; they do not let a body crave and want and lick with hate and blood-need for all that time without bringing the image into satisfactory relevance, of one kind or another.

Anyway, so it was with Loretta.

Yes. With Mother lying stretched out in the big brass bed in the shadowed back bedroom, at ninety-seven, after eighteen heart attacks, her face wrinkled and sagged; a sometimes scary mask of blues and yellows and blacks and purples; her muscle-frozen legs swollen for the twice-weekly dehydration shot from the doctor, talking, mumbling incessantly about what she and her long dead husband, Adolph, had done seventy years before, or of what some relative or acquaintance had said, the yellow eyes burning from the mask—would it be into eternity? Hated Mother. But doted on, outwardly, at least, beloved, served, listened to, tucked in, and dreamed about, just like Morse.

Loretta is so kind, so wonderful. Loretta is my sweetie: Mother's stick-a-nins:

"Yes, mm, she has always lived with me, taken care of me, haven't you, darling, mm, mm, never deserted, never lied, always loved, mm, she is made of love, aren't you, dearest, mm?"

Crazy-long limbos of hesitant, whispered monologue dealing with the purchase of a spool of thread, the purplish lips bubbling, "Mm, was it Tuesday, or no! Mm, it was Wednesday afternoon, mm, no, it was Monday. Green thread. Yes. Mm."

The southern August house was hot and quiet, except for the afternoon Soap on the TV, and the stuttering stammer of the $88 air-conditioner that gusted hot air into the dining-room.

Loretta was on the green sofa, where she always sat, wearing a knitted white sweater, wiping her splotched throat with a damp hankie. She was knitting an Afghan in memory of the northern winters, perhaps. Loretta always knitted Afghans, reds and yellows and oranges and whites; this one curled down her knees onto the floor and the needles ticked as on the vagrant, flickering screen the girl kissed the boy, and, leaning over his shoulder, her eyes were wide and agonized over her dear brother, Bob's, alcoholism, and her sister's forays into undisclosed wicked paths of promiscuity.

Loretta lifted her pink-tainted, blue-and-red framed glasses and wiped her perspiring eyes, her fingers trembling. Morse. Morse.

Mother . . . ! Had she or had she not given Mother lunch? Yes, yes. Chicken salad and a raspberry drink of tinkling Kool-Aid. Mother loved Kool-Aid.

Mother had eaten some of it, hoarsely explaining that Loretta and her sister Martha, mm, had been seven and nine, respectively, when Loretta fell on her skates in front of Baumgartner's house and bumped her nose. Mm. Was it a Friday morning, or Sunday afternoon, mm, no, mm, it was Friday noon, because she was preparing a roast, mm, and Adolph was home early from the office, mm, he had to kill a chicken for supper, mm, yes, noon, Friday, because the Chasens were Methodists and did not play cards on Sunday.

Oh, God! I hate you, I hate you. I'm crying and you can't even see it.

Hated Mother, for another terrible reason, too, not just because she was old with her steel-framed glasses propped on that blade of nose, and the Kathleen Norris folded open on her ribby breast, mm.

Yes. She had fed Mother a lunch of chicken salad.

Oh, Morse. Why did you do it? You just simply messed up everything. But, Mother, anyway, she had warned and warned.

"You're my snookums, you're my little sweet-ums, my only one, with Martha and Mary and John, they're loving, too, but you'll stay by Mother, won't you, dear."

"Yes, Mother. You know I will."

"And, really, Loretta, you'd better not see Morse anymore. It's not that I don't want you happy. I do, I do, you know I do. But you're Mother's bunny-kins. So, you'd better not."

"I won't, Mother."

"You'll always be with me, won't you, dear?"

"Yes, Mother."

And the wild lilt of *My Blue Heaven*; just Molly and me and baby makes three, but now it was all changed. But she could remember, couldn't she?

Oh, Morse, I love you, I love you . . .

With the black-and white-checked open Model T Ford with the new coil springs so they just danced around the red brick corners.

Loretta never missed a stitch on the Afghan, and she absorbed rather than realized the blue-gray motions on the TV screen, her glasses steaming, her throat dripping, her body cold under the white sweater.

Fingers trembling sensitively.

Mouth dropping open like a crow's, to be immediately remembered, and closed.

I love you, Morse, she thought. I have always loved and needed you. Her mind thronged with the naked outright of what might have been.

Morse and she had had a brief relationship, held to a few quick dry kisses, with Mother always in the background, never letting him into the house, until that cool, fragrant May night on the porch under the wisteria, he had groped and grabbed and ripped her skirt up and torn her pants down and taken it out before she knew what was happening, her breath in her throat, stopped, and tried to rape her, all the time wildly murmuring filth in her ear, his wet lips chewing her hair. And she had let go a little yell, and told him to go and never come back, and slapped him, and said, "Mother!" and he went and never returned.

Oh, Morse.

It had been an almost. There had never been any others. Loretta had devoted herself to Mother and Dad after the others married, and finally they had come to this southern retirement town and it had been so pretty then, when Dad quit the office, but it was all changed now, with the old ones down on Fourth and Central, the young hippies, or whatever, with long hair and pinned denim, with holes gaping, and drink and dope and crime and rock and roll.

Loretta had studied at Julliard. Violin. It was hot in the attic, now, she didn't quite know where and she did not care, either.

All through the years, she dreamed of Morse and his kisses and that half-naked night and he was forever young to her, forever soft-voiced and marvelous, wearing his smooth gray flannels and the thick maroon sweater with the rolled collar.

And then Dad died, right over there, and she devoted herself to Mother. She had devoted herself to *them* for her entire life, and Mother kept living.

Sometimes she was driven to lust over that night's memory, on the wisteria-fragrant porch. Scrabbling.

And every day, as now, she would think about how much she hated Mother, I don't, I don't, but you do, Loretta, I don't, you do—yes, I do, but I'm her stick-ums, I love her. She hated Mother so terribly she screamed silently with it in the night, and, too, she envisioned returning to that northern town, that brown-shingled house where Morse would forever live, and he would be there, fooling around with the black-and white-checkered Model T, waiting for her, and she would say:

"I've come back, Morse—to you."

"Loretta, darling."

"I love you. I loved you all the time."

"It's all right, Loretta. I love you, too. Now we can get married and ever after be—"

The doorbell rang, the sound shooting through the house, tearing at Loretta's nerves.

The blinds were closed on the door, and she did not move. People seldom rang her doorbell, only salesmen, and on Hallowe'en, when she prepared apples and nuts and candy for the Trick 'n Treat masked prowlers of the ebon night, and, even then, only a few came and candy would be left over, sometimes through the following summer, when it melted and stuck to the silver dish.

The bell rang again . . .

This time, Loretta lay her knitting aside, slowly rose, still gripping the soggy hankie in one fist, and went to the door. She fought with the latch, finally unlocked it, but then the door was stuck. She perspired, and gasped, and finally it swung open with a rush and a man stood there. An old, old man, bald and skull-freckled, with a few white hairs sticking up, hat in hand, purple and veined and bony, a cane, a bright blue suit, white shirt, red tie, incongruous, unwholesome, terrifying. His face, his eyes, burned blackly.

Loretta's fingers trembled. "Wha—wha—?"

"Loretta." An ancient, cackling tone. "I'd of known you anywheres. By God. Yes! Loretta! Don't just stand there, by God. Honey, you ain't changed a bit."

"But—who are you?"

"I'm Morse, for God's sake, Loretta. Don't you remember? I sure do. You little devil, you." And he winked, then said again, "Morse, Loretta. Morse Cheetham. Now, you remember. I can tell." And he did a little dance on his heels, holding the cane tightly, flapping his hat against his bony leg with the crisp blue suit.

Loretta's mouth was open and her glasses steamed, and she dripped perspiration and stared at Morse. She stared and stared in a terrible kind of ruin.

He abruptly thrust past her into the house, aimed straight for the old Boston rocker that they'd brought with them, and sat down, fanning his gargoyled face.

"Phew, man, baby—you keep it hot, hot, hot! Where's your air? Ain't you even got air?"

She firmly closed the door, turned and went to the sofa and sat, still staring at Morse Cheetham.

She was weeping and strangled, her nose running. She mopped at her nose with the wadded hankie.

"Morse," she said.

He leaned forward. "Yeah, honey. I knew you was down here, and I checked everywhere, phone book, everywhere—and I went to the Chamber of Commerce and got your address, and here the hell I am." He breathed heavily. She could smell it. He had been drinking and he was something out of hell.

"I been married four times, wore 'em out, by God, an' they the hell wore *me* out, too. By God. But there's a dance in the ol' dame yet, toujours gai, that's what I always say. Can't keep an old fart down, now can they? How you been, Loretta? By God, you still carry a leg on you, I'll say that."

She was weeping openly, sobbing softly, her mouth a dark hole, eyes streaming, nose plugged and red.

"By God, I got to you, honey. Didn't I? Didn't I? You remember them ol' times, right? Check. Sure you do. You was always a hot one, I recall." He leaned back, fanning and rocking, now. "Phew! Hot in here. Jesus."

His soft-toned voice, such pure English. That's what she remembered.

"Wore 'em out, by God! Had a hell of a life, would you believe it? Made three fortunes and traveled the globe seventeen times." He winked foully, yellow-tusked. "You up to a little bad things, honey, you remember? Still got a leg on you, by God."

Cackling monster; he had grown into this!

"I can still do it, too, by God!"

"Stop it."

"What happened to your mother?"

Loretta hated her mother. She had thrown her life away. Oh Lord. She hated him, Morse Cheetham. She despised them both with all her being, like a flaming sword. She wanted to vomit at the sight of him. But somehow the gods had prepared her, too, when they had revealed to her this living image of memory and lust and invention and dream and wisteria and love and year-in year-out devotion to a lifetime of remembering.

"Just a minute, Morse. I'll get you a drink, huh?"

"'Atta girlie! My ol' Loretta. Just like always." He gaped and winked and rattled his cane against the edge of the Boston rocker. "Make it a stiff one, I carry a jugful. Boy, you sure got a leg on you." He smacked his purple lips wetly. "A drink's perfect, it's so all-fired hot in here, now."

She was already on her way to the kitchen, determined in all ways, prepared for the entirety.

"Loretta?"

It was the weak, husky tone of Mother.

Loretta stepped into the hall, then into the shadowed, curiously smelling bedroom. "Hush, now, Mother. I'll be right there, just a moment, now."

"I hear somebody, mm, did I, mm? Somebody out there, mm, sweets?"

"No."

"I'm hungry."

"Yes, Mother."

Loretta walked away, through the dining-room and into the kitchen. She opened a drawer and took out the turkey knife, then walked slowly, weeping, perspiring, nose-plugged, back into the living-room.

"Keerist, honey," Morse said. "You look good! *Good*, I tell you!"

She stepped directly to the Boston rocker and lifted her arm. It was at this moment that Morse Cheetham saw the knife. . . .

Loretta prepared supper, a roast in the oven, a salad, baked potatoes. She fixed Mother's plate and took it in to her on a tray, set it across the withered, disturbed body.

"Mm, Loretta, dearkins—I'm so hungry, mm, darling, that's good of you. I thought I heard somebody earlier. There's something I must tell you, mm, about, mm, remembered when Adolph went out to band practice with his trombone—"

"Later, Mother. I'm going away, now. I'll be back. There's a program on TV. Something special."

"But, mm, child, darling, I can't possible eat by myself, you know that, mm—what is it, sweetums?"

"After the program, Mother."

And Loretta returned to the living-room and sat on the green sofa and took up her colorful Afghan and stared at the TV screen.

Yes. Love. Morse. Mother.

. . . and gone was the wisteria and the long cool May night, forever and ever, and she would have the TV only, now, for real, and the ubiquitous Afghans, and, of course, Mother. But, mm, Mother would not last for all time, would she . . . ?

"Loretta, dearest—please?"

Weak and husky, from the bedroom, calling.

Well, all right, she would go in there, then, now. Mother did not know what she was eating, and perhaps that spoiled it. But, not really. Loretta would go to the bedroom and cut that meat for Mother, because she knew what the meat was, and that, only that, really mattered.

Junk Yard Blues

Brinker yawned and lumbered to the front of the shack, which was fashioned of old billboards and corrugated iron. He had his eye on Meegins, his helper. Meegins had been acting funny, and twice Brinker had caught him in the shack, staring at the cigar box. There was a good deal of money in the cigar box. He knew he had to stay by the shack, but this was difficult, because there were things to take care of in the yard. And what if somebody came, wanted something?

Brinker lowered his fat, enormous bulk onto a three-legged chair, propped on a box, and yawned again. In the yard, surrounding the shack, were hundreds of wrecked cars, stacks of junk that towered and leaned precariously. Damn it, somebody always trying to steal something. They climb the fence, sneak into the yard. And now, Meegins had his eye on the cigar box.

Brinker gusted a heavy sigh. He rubbed ham-like hands against filthy khaki pants.

He heard running footsteps. A skinny kid, with a narrow face, wearing tennis shoes, jeans and a torn red shirt, ran up to him.

"Yah!" the kid said.

"You're Meegins' kid," Brinker said. "Get out of here—get, now!"

"Yah, yah!" the kid said. He had yellow eyes, and they were pure fyce.

"Just like your old man. No damned good," Brinker said. "I told you to get out of here. Now, you better get!"

"You fat slob!" the kid said. He stuck his tongue out, leaning forward. "Yah!"

Brinker heaved himself off the chair and took a lumbering stride toward the kid.

The kid ran.

Brinker returned hugely to his chair, squatted. He had very little lap. He looked across the yard at the sound of some clanking. It was Meegins, stacking fenders. It would take him all afternoon to stack four fenders.

God, how he hated kids like that one of Meegins'. Sneak thieves. He hated them. Actually, Brinker disliked nearly everybody.

"Meegins!" he shouted.

A tall, gangling, tired, hurt-eyed specimen came lounging across the yard. He wore dirty black jeans, and a ripped sweater that had once been blue. He was badly in need of a shave.

"Now, Meegins," Brinker said, breathing heavily. "I tol' you you got to stack them fenders. You ain't stacking them worth a damn."

"Okay," Meegins said. He grinned lopsidedly. He was sweating in dirty rivulets.

"An' you see to it that kid of yours stays out of the yard. I don't like him, see? You talk to him."

"Okay," Meegins said.

"Okay, okay. That all you can say?"

"Sure," Meegins said in a weak voice.

Brinker was disgusted. "Get back to work. An' see you really stack some fenders. No lollygagging."

Meegins turned and moved away, his lean, boney, bent back a picture of futility. In a few moments, Brinker heard fenders scraping and clanking.

Just then a horn sounded from the other end of the yard. A car had driven in the gates.

Brinker heaved himself up, and moved fatly out toward the car. A neatly dressed young fellow wanted to know if he could buy a muffler from a '59 Chrysler New Yorker. "I need it in a real hurry," he said.

"That's something new," Brinker said with a grunt.

He took the young man over to a rusty fence where some mufflers were stacked. "Now," he said. "You just take your 'hurry' an' look for yourself. There's probably one here," and then he stopped, because he realized he hadn't heard any fenders clanking.

Meegins was not by the fender pile.

"Go ahead," Brinker said to the young man. "Look." He turned and began jogging elephant-like toward the shack. His jowls flapped, and the awesome fat around his waist moved thickly up and down.

He was just entering the shack as Meegins came out. Meegins had the cigar box under one arm, his mouth twisted. Brinker hauled off and struck Meegins on the shoulder. Meegins made a crazy face, his eyes wild, and tried to thrust past.

Brinker stuck his big foot out, and Meegins tripped with a shrill curse. Brinker saw Meegins land on his side, start to get up, and he just fell on him.

Meegins let out a yell.

Brinker's enormous bulk covered Meegins almost completely. The thin man struggled, but it was no use.

"Help!" Brinker shouted hoarsely. "Help! Help!"

He kept shouting, and pretty soon the young man who had been after the Chrysler muffler, hurried over.

"Don't stand there," Brinker said. "Get in the shack. There's a phone. Call the cops."

"The cops?"

"Yes, you damned idiot."

So the young man called police headquarters, and Brinker stayed put, holding Meegins down, till a cruiser came by. Meegins was abject, beaten, when Brinker let him up. They took Meegins away, and a week later Brinker heard he was in the county jail. "Now he'll work," Brinker thought. "They'll put him out on the road, and he'll sweat for his beans."

He had nobody to help him now, but he no longer cared about that. He couldn't get reliable help, anyway.

It was a week and a half later, when Brinker heard the racket out in the yard, a rattle of loose metal. Then silence. He left the shack, walked heavily through the stacks of junk. Damn it, somebody was always trying to steal something.

"Hey, there!"

He stood quietly beside a rusted Packard sedan that had lain in the yard for twelve years, stripped and desolate. He heard stealthy footsteps. There was nothing wrong with Brinker's hearing.

Brinker ran, abruptly, the heavy fat jouncing at his hips, gasping, down between a double row of sadly bent cars.

It was that kid. By God, he still had on that torn red shirt, too. The kid stood by the fender of a smashed, yellow milk truck. *Boardman's Dairy.* The kid held a gun in one hand, and his lips were pressed tightly together. His eyes were pure fyce, yellow and sick.

"Ha, kid. You. What you want?"

The gun was steady.

"What is it, kid?"

"Why'd you do that to my pop?"

"He tried to steal my money," Brinker said. "That's why."

"Get it."

"Get what?"

"Get the money, or I'll blow your brains out."

They stood there in the late afternoon, watching each other. A rat peeked from behind a flat tire, eyes winking with wit, whiskers twitching.

"You, kid," Brinker said. "You out of your head?"

"Yeah. I'm out of my head. Get it up."

Brinker ruffled his sticky hair with one dirty, thick-fingered hand. "Haw," he said. "Haw, haw, haw." He said it, he did not laugh it. "Oh, my."

"You're asking for it," the kid said. He had a thin voice that was rusty sounding, and he kept blinking those yellow eyes.

Brinker suddenly took a step toward the kid, then another. He was grinning broadly. "You gonna rob me? That it, kid? You fixing to rob ol' Brinker?"

"Look out, you fat slob." The kid cursed him.

"Call me fat? Haw." Brinker walked directly up to the kid. "You live over on Twentieth, by the gas house, huh? Where's your mommy?"

"Shut up, or I'll blow your brains out."

"You got a gun," Brinker said. "Use it."

"I'll use it, you fat slob." The kid cursed him again.

Brinker reached out and clutched at the kid's ratty-looking hair. The kid snatched his head back, fright in his eyes, mouth open. "Kid," Brinker said. "Didn't you know the meek shall inherit the earth? You ever hear that? Haw." Brinker stood back and looked at the kid.

"I'd plug you as soon as look at you," the kid said.

"Haw."

"Get on over to the shack."

"I ain't going no place, kid," Brinker said. "An' you're just going home to mama. That's where you belong."

"You fat slob."

"You got a filthy mouth."

"I'll kill you," the kid said.

"Kid," Brinker said. "You got a gun, an' it looks loaded. But you ain't gonna use it, see? Because you're like your old man. You're scared. An' you got a filthy mouth. I don't like filthy mouths. You're comin' with me."

"Get your stinkin' paws off me!"

Brinker grabbed the kid by the arm, and began dragging him back toward the shack. The kid waved the gun around, and started weeping. Dirt streaked his cheeks.

"Right here," Brinker said. He had towed the kid behind the shack. There was a crusty basin on a wooden stool, under a leaking faucet. Brinker reached up to the slanting roof, brought down a gray, worn cake of soap. "I'm gonna wash your mouth out," he said.

The kid strained, trying to break away. He waved the revolver which was huge in his hand, and sobbed loudly.

"Ah, there," Brinker said. "Haw. Here we go." He grabbed the kid by the head, and held him against his big belly, ramming the cake of soap into the kid's mouth. "Lather up," he said. "Haw." He forced the soap into the kid's mouth with the heel of his hand, then struck the kid's jaw. The kid bit off the soap. Then the kid went crazy, and began spitting and cursing and weeping. He tore loose from Brinker's grip, and ran spitting off among the wrecked cars. "The meek," Brinker said softly. He watched the kid climb the fence and vanish down the street.

Brinker yawned and lumbered back to the front of the shack, lowered himself fatly onto the three-legged chair. He yawned again. He shook his head. "Kids," he said into the late afternoon.

Half an hour later Brinker was getting fidgety. He had the feeling he was being watched. Probably that kid. Well, he thought. He rose, went into the shack, picked up the cigar box of money, tied it tightly with a frazzled shoestring, and started again for the door.

"Time to quit," he muttered.

A tall, lean, open-faced, yellow-haired young man stood in front of him as he stepped out of the door. Two others, both heavily built, stood behind the first.

"Here," the yellow-haired one said. "Give me the box, old man."

Brinker stared at him, wrinkling his nose.

"Meegins was right," one said. "He told us straight. It's a cigar box. Is it loaded, old man?"

"Give it to me," the yellow-haired one said.

"Take it from the poor jamoke."

"Meegins?" Brinker said.

"Yeah. Meegins. He worked for you. We been with him, an' he told us all about you, fatty. Now, let's have the box."

"I ain't giving you this box," Brinker said.

"Sure, you are," the yellow-haired one said. He suddenly held a switchblade in his right hand, and the gleaming steel knife snicked open. He stepped up to Brinker and, without a word, sliced his belly deep and wide.

"Uh," Brinker said.

Brinker looked down at his belly. It was bleeding, and it was cut frighteningly. He dropped the box and tried to hold himself together, staring down, musing. He sprawled to his knees, hypnotized at what he saw.

"True contemplation," one of the others said.

The yellow-haired one picked up the cigar box.

"Let's split."

They ran off.

Brinker knelt there, like that, holding things together as best he could. He chewed his lower lip and blinked, the blood covering his hands, dripping into the dust, tiny dusty drops.

"Ah," Brinker said.

He knelt that way for a good ten minutes. He tried to rise twice, but couldn't make it. He was weaving now, holding his belly, when he heard the stealthy footsteps. Then he saw the skinny kid, Meegins' kid, with the torn red shirt.

The kid held the big revolver in his right hand.

"Kid," Brinker said with a gasp. "Go—go phone—call an ambulance. They ripped me open. I can't move."

The kid stood there. Some of the fyce look went out of those yellow eyes, and the mouth revealed the faint trace of a smile.

"Kid," Brinker said. "Hurry, f'God's sake!"

"You stuck soap in my mouth," the kid said.

Brinker stared at him.

"You got my pop in jail."

"Kid, will you—please—?"

"Where's the money?"

"They took it," Brinker gasped. "Took everything."

"I'm gonna blow your brains out," the kid said. He drew a big breath, his eyes shining now.

Brinker stared at him, holding his belly.

"Here goes," the kid said. He gave a short, snarling laugh, and squeezed the trigger of the revolver. He shot Brinker four times in the head, and Brinker rolled over, still holding himself.

The kid stood there a moment, then turned and ran.

Satisfaction

early 1970s

Brenda was as devious as they come. Small, blonde, supple, with a shape that was excitingly rounded in the right places, a heart-shaped face with full red lips, and sad cerulean blue eyes, some said she had a weird mind. She was a loner. She always dressed excruciatingly, with plenty of color, and she commanded the male eye. She worked quietly at her calling, lived in a plush apartment, bothered nobody. She paid her dues. It was even whispered that she was a friend of, and sometimes surreptitiously entertained, Sergeant Newell Saulsbury of homicide. Whether this was true or not, righteous ones questioned. But the police did leave her alone.

She picked and she chose. Libidos raged, because Brenda had that thing, but often she would turn on those sad blue eyes and shake her head.

She read the Bible, and she attended church every Sunday, without fail. She wrote poetry, some of which had been published in magazines, and she painted an occasional picture.

When she strolled down the block, it was an experience to watch. Men appeared out of the cracks in the walls. Sad, sexy, lonely-looking, she chose carefully.

Plenty took it wrong:

"Putting on airs."

"I get my mitts on her, she'll know what for."

"Thinks she's a geranium."

"Yeah. But, man, look at it—just look at it!"

And nothing happened.

She moved through life with a sad grace. Nobody knew where she had come from; she had just suddenly appeared. She had no friends. She played it cool.

"Still waters run deep," a sick old bum said.

That brought a laugh.

"You mark my words," the bum said. "That Brenda gal's got secrets. You wanta watch out for that type."

Winker Conekin, a heavy with the outfit, who invariably used an ice-pick on any contract for a hit, and L. M. Goble, another heavy, strictly a gun man, yearned heartily for Brenda, to the point of incessant day dreams. They had approached her on three occasions each.

"Sorry," she told Winker, "but you boys bore me."

As for L. M., she just lifted her upper lip, and wouldn't give him the time of day.

So word got around, and Winker and L. M. talked it over together.

"I'm telling you, L. M., she's too much."

"She won't give me the time of day."

"I can't stand it. I never had a chick do this to me. I gotta get at it. I gotta."

So they jumped Brenda by an alley, dragged her into a shed behind Burback's Grocery, got what they wanted by force, then beat her up professionally, hauled her naked out into the street, and dropped her head first into a garbage can.

Brenda remained in her apartment for two weeks, recovering. When she again appeared on the street, there was something different about her. She had changed. She walked more briskly now, and some of the sadness had gone from her eyes. She seemed to have a purpose.

Of course, word got out about what had happened behind Burback's Grocery that night.

"Did her good."

"Ain't so rosy now, is she?"

"Maybe we got a chance."

"Wanta try?"

"You first."

And Winker Conekin was surprised when he opened his basement apartment door one evening to discover Brenda standing there. She wore yellow with black trim, and her teeth glistened.

"Hi, Winker."

"Well, baby. Couldn't stay away? Got a taste, and you want another bite, eh? Say, you look okay, now. Didn't really hurt you, eh? Come on in, Brenda, baby."

"It's a business call."

Winker grinned. "What else?"

They sat on the couch and Winker swelled a bit. In his curious life, Brenda could only have come because she admired something about him.

"Snuggle up," he said, reaching for her knee.

"Wait, Winker."

"Aw, now—we didn't really hurt you. Huh? You 'member how it was, eh, baby? Ol' Winker, that's what it takes, every time."

"Maybe later. Not now. This is serious, Winker. I've got something to tell you. You'll see how important it is."

"Yeah?"

"Yes. You're right, Winker, about how I feel." She moved slightly against him, and Winker held his breath a bit, because Brenda was really choice, even with what had happened back of Burback's, and he knew he could well do with a babe like this on the string. You'd never know anything had happened. She was downright beautiful, and Winker knew it.

"How you feel?" Winker asked.

"Yes. I mean, oh, damn it, Winker, it's rough admitting it, but you got to me somehow. I can't help it." She bit her lip. "You just plain got to me, that's all."

"Yeah?"

She nodded. "Because of that. I'm telling you something you've got to know. I know maybe it isn't right, telling—but I've got to. Winker—L. M.'s out to get you."

"What?"

"It's true. He says you been working his territory, getting contracts that should've been his. Now, I know it's tough, Winker, you thinking L. M.'s your friend, and all. But he's going to kill you."

"Yeah?"

"Yes. It's true."

Winker thought about it. His one eye was nearly closed.

"Where'd you get all this jazz?"

"L. M. told me. He thinks I'm his girl, now. See? But I'm not. I want you, Winker—just you. So I got a way—"

"You telling the truth, Brenda?"

"I wouldn't lie."

"After what we done, and all?"

"L. M. thinks I'm his girl. I'm telling you."

"He's going to knock me off?"

"Yes, but—"

"But what?"

"L. M. will be at my place at nine tonight. You could fix him easy. Get the drop on him. See?"

Winker looked at her and pursed his lips.

She moved against him. "I want you, Winker—alive. L. M. will sure kill you. He means it."

"Thanks for telling me, baby. I'll be at your place a little after nine. You stall him. Okay?"

"Yes, Winker."

"Now, how's about a little—?"

"Not now. I'm too worried. Later tonight, after it's all over. Then we can get together."

"Okay, baby."

Brenda left, and went directly to L. M.'s apartment in the Dawsby Arms. L. M. was surprised, too, and he considered Brenda looked so downright beautiful it was a shame.

". . . and that's how it is," she told L. M. "Winker's fed up, you getting all the good news."

"But we split it."

"He don't wanta split it anymore, L. M. He wants all the gravy for himself. He's going to rub you. So the way I feel about you, and all—I can't help myself, L. M. It was something you did that night back of Burback's. It got to me, I tell you." She nuzzled L. M.'s throat. "A little after nine, then. And I'll have Winker waiting."

"But it's your apartment," L. M. said.

"You can break the door," she told him. "I'll go out, then, and when I return, look what I find. Winker, splashed all over the wall. It's terrible. Don't worry, the police'll believe me."

"That rat," L. M. said. "And all the time we been pals."

"Some pals, him scheming what he does."

"An hour till nine. We got time, baby." L. M. was slightly hoarse. "Okay?"

"Wait till after," Brenda said. "Then we'll have all night." She winked slyly. "Okay?"

"Okay, baby."

Brenda returned to her apartment, slipped into white silk pajamas, and waited. She felt nervous. She paced the floor. Would it work? Her two-fold plan was desperate.

At five to nine the buzzer sounded. She opened the door.

"We're early," Winker said. L. M. stood by his side, grinning.

Brenda looked frightened. She backed away.

L. M. and Winker entered the apartment, closed the door. They stood there looking at Brenda.

"Cute, isn't she, L. M.?"

"A perfect picture," L. M. said.

"Shall we play, or just get it over with?"

"Let's just get it over with. I got a date, anyways."

Brenda whirled and made a dash for the bedroom. Winker caught her and threw her brutally against the wall. L. M. rocked on his heels and grinned. "Baby," he said. "You should know Winker and me are real close pals. We're so close we read each other's mind, see? You come on like blasting powder, delivering your message. TNT is subtle, compared, baby. I read you straight off, and so did Winker. Trying to even the score. I suppose you thought even if only one of 'em gets it in the head, it's one less, and you'll squeal to the cops on the other guy. Eh? Eh? That read like the morning paper, baby?"

Brenda did not speak.

"Well," Winker said. "What's it gonna be, L. M. Your way, or mine?"

"Let's make it both ways, pal."

And they did. Winker used an ice-pick on her, and stabbed her forty times. L. M. had a silencer on his .38 and he blasted her five times in the throat. They laid her on the bed, and covered her to her chin.

"She ain't so pretty now," L. M. said.

"She never really had it, L. M. It was all in our heads. Mental, like they say."

"Let's get out of here."

Two days later Newell Saulsbury found Brenda. He didn't explain exactly how he found her, except to say it was a tip from someplace. His eyes were a little misty, though.

He found the sheet of pale blue stationery with the writing on it in a book of poetry beside the bed:

TO WHOM IT MAY CONCERN:

Winker Conekin and L. M. Goble did this to me. They killed me. Both of them did it. I planned it this way, because they hurt me badly. I could not find my way out alone. And they must go too. You can get it out of them just why. I know you have ways to make them talk.

Sincerely,
Brenda.

Sunflower

The moment Gregg phoned and said we were going to Albuquerque for five days, I knew it was the visit to his brother's place. And I said, "Damn it!" I didn't say it out loud, but just thought it very hard, and I thought, "Hot!," too. Because that's all I could think and I said, "Do they have air-conditioning?" to Gregg.

"Air-conditioning?" He sounded as if I'd struck him across the face, or something, and then he laughed and said, "Oh, of course. And a swimming pool, too."

"Who's all going?"

"Don't worry about it. I don't have time now," and he was gone and I knew it would all come to a head, because that's how it was. I didn't want to go. But that would mean disappointing Gregg, or troubling him at the very least.

Then I didn't have anything to wear and that meant shopping, so I went out and shopped and bought some half-crazy things, not nearly so crazy as they might have been. I bought them just simply out of rebellion, that's all, because I am not prone to buying crazy things to wear, like some.

Jonsey was going to fly us out in his *Cessna*, just Gregg and myself, and it was rush, rush, rush in my mind all night long—I didn't see Gregg because he said it was good we rested—because we had to leave early in the morning, and the way it was with Jonsey even after we were in the plane, it was no consolation that he was older than Gregg or me. It was no consolation at all. Flying with Jonsey at the controls was an experience, and especially there were the mountains, and it doesn't matter how beautiful they are, sometimes.

I could feel it all coming to a head, because Gregg just simply didn't say anything at all of consequence. I realized he had his work and he was thinking ahead, but he didn't have to make such a fool out of himself about it, and it *was* supposed to be some sort of vacation, these five days, even if they wouldn't be any vacation at all to me.

I knew how much I loved Gregg, I really did love him a lot, but there was just something the matter all the time, and it was so *hurried*; everything was so hurried of late, and I did love Gregg, but he was a perfect beast most of the time lately. A real beast. I knew Gregg really wasn't being mean in any way, it was just that he had to pay for something somehow. After all, he was getting a lot for his beastliness. And there was so much ahead of us. Why should he avoid talking about it?

But I did love him.

We couldn't land near his brother's place. Jonsey said it was because of the terrain in the Jemez Mountains, and we landed at the airport and took a taxi. A taxi! They didn't even come for us, and right then I knew it was all going to be exactly as I suspected, and I didn't want to go there at all. I'd much rather Gregg and I spent the five days just in Albuquerque, doing something, because there was the ride through the desert into the mountains and it was hot, just as I'd supposed, and I knew exactly what to expect.

You can tell if they don't come for you at the airport. It's something. It's that they'll all be just waiting, and then you walk in, like that.

It was just that I had to do something to Gregg to make him realize the seriousness of it. He didn't talk about anything at all. And there wasn't a serious bone in his body about us. Or, at least it seemed that way. Anyway, he acted terribly grumpy all the way out to the house, and I tried really hard to do something to make him feel better; I stroked his hand twice, and he reacted nicely but he still didn't say anything. He was just grumpy.

It was all so stupid, all of it.

I felt like crying, but I couldn't because right then we were coming up the drive, and it would have to wait.

"It shouldn't really be bad, should it?" I said.

"How do you mean?"

He looked all puffed up as he said that.

"It's my brother. He wants to throw a party. Why should it be bad, or anything like that?"

"I don't know."

Of course, I *did* know, and I could feel it all coming to a head more and more.

"They're just people," Gregg said. "I don't know what gets into you, girl."

"Yes, but it's your family."

"They aren't all my family."

"Yes, but your brother."

"He's just my brother. And besides—there are others."

"That's what I mean."

And right away I felt it worse than ever, worse than before, because whoever else *was* here, they would know more about things, and they would be closer to his brother Norman, and if they were closer to his brother, then they would be closer to Gregg.

There was no telling, no telling at all. But how could they be closer to Gregg, I wondered.

It was ridiculous, and I stepped out of the car, and it was right then as I heard voices over the hedge, that I saw the sunflower. I had to turn my face away. It struck me that hard and I didn't know what it was except that I thought, Maybe I hate Gregg.

It was a huge sunflower. There were several. I suppose they grew them. It was so blatant, so perfect, so big about the whole thing, that sunflower, and it was just as if it stared back at me frowning and scowling, all too largely yellow for words. And they were laughing over the hedge. The house was immense—too much.

"Does he have this much money?"

"How much is this much?"

I just wanted to say, "To hell with you, goddamn you!" but I didn't say anything. I took another look at the big sunflower and wished to God I was with Jonsey flying back, because Jonsey couldn't come. He was busy with something else. Gregg had even asked him.

They were at the pool.

I thought, Just suppose his mother and father weren't dead, after all, and suppose I had to meet them, too, this way.

It was worse than I'd expected. There they all were at the pool, and I didn't know any of them. Not a single one of them. I didn't even know his own brother, Norman.

I wanted to say, "Do we have to?," but of course, I didn't say anything. I couldn't speak, actually, not at that moment. It was ridiculous.

There were just too many of them all clustered sprawling around the big pool, with the trees over-hanging it, the way they did. There were three girls and three men, and then I saw another man coming down the steps, and a woman was saying something to him from the veranda.

"It doesn't matter," the man called back. "Really."

We went straight across the area around the pool right by everybody, and they all looked at me, and kept looking. But we went on across because the man who had just left the veranda, and the woman on the veranda, were both coming to meet us.

But on the way, Gregg just stopped. I mean, he just wasn't there anymore, not with me, and I was all alone. Then the man got detained by one of the girls and the woman stood halfway down the steps with her hands clasped in front of her.

Somebody was laughing very loud about something.

"So you're Donna," the woman said, and I nodded, and we shook hands, and one of the men called, "Hey, Donna, get your suit on!"

I looked around and Gregg was talking to the man and I learned from the woman that the man was Norman, just as I'd supposed.

"It wasn't a bad trip at all," Gregg said.

I was glad he hadn't asked me about it.

I kept thinking about the sunflower, and it was then I saw an even bigger sunflower beside the porch where the steps went down to the pool through the flowers, and it did the same thing to me. I couldn't explain it to myself, what it was. Just that something had to happen, and maybe I hated

Gregg for the whole business. Not just this business today, but the business every day. And not just the hating him for what had happened all along, but just a basic all-over hate.

But I couldn't understand that, and I wanted to cry. Because I knew I loved him, but I didn't want to be here, like this, among strangers. Everything was strange, even the woman, whose name was Louise. And Gregg had never even told me her name. It was that bad. She had to tell me her name and she was Gregg's brother's wife.

I didn't know anyone here, and I certainly didn't want any introductions, because of the way Gregg was acting. I suppose I should have forgiven him, but I couldn't. He didn't stay with me, not at all. I just wanted to sit somewhere and cry, and if I could just get to my room, I would.

"They aren't much alike, somehow," Louise said.

"Aren't they?"

"No. They're quite different."

They were all talking about nothing, splashing in the pool—at least two of them were splashing in the pool. The others were splashing their drinks around, and I wondered if that's the kind of party it was going to be. Because I didn't know Norman or Louise well enough. I couldn't stand it at all, flatly, if that's the kind of party it was.

"I wonder if I could see my room."

Louise took me to my room and smiled and after she was gone, I sat on the window seat up above the pool, where a vine twined around, and cried. It didn't do any good, and I thought of the sunflower. And it was nearly an hour and a half before Gregg came up and said, "What are you doing?"

"Nothing."

"Why don't you come down?"

"I don't feel well. I'll feel better tomorrow."

"You'll have to come down to eat."

He really didn't even care.

I hated him.

"Not yet, is it?"

"In a little while."

We looked at each other, and he looked at his watch, and for the first time, ever, it simply scalded me the way he stood there and looked at his watch. Because it didn't matter *what time* it was.

"They're having a buffet by the pool," he said.

"All right."

"You all right?"

"Of course, I'm all right." But I didn't move from the window seat and I could see he wanted to get down there among them, that was all that mattered.

"They're a damn lot," he said. "But I have to."

"Yes."

I suppose it was because Norman was his brother, and all. But he might have cared just a little bit more. I suppose he did care, but he just wasn't showing it, right then.

"Go ahead," I said. "Go down with them."

He seemed to miss it.

"Well, I'll be down by the pool."

"Yes."

He was stupid. I hated him.

But it was worse than that.

It was later that I finally screwed up enough to go down and eat something, because I knew if I didn't, then Louise would probably come up and ask me why.

I ate some roast beef, and wandered into the kitchen and saw all those knives on the wall, from little ones to big ones with their blades shining in the light from the fire in the front room. And they looked so fine, shining there, and I thought of the sunflower.

They had used one of the big knives to slice the roast of beef. It was very good beef, at that, but the way Gregg was prowling around and staying away from me, I couldn't enjoy everything. Everybody was talking about the same nothings, and I couldn't bear it, and I went to my room after mentioning how I felt to Louise.

"It's just you don't feel well?"

"That's all. I'll feel better soon. I just want to rest."

"I'm so sorry, really."

And Norman looked up once from his glass and twinkled his eyes at me. Gregg was talking to all three of the girls at once.

I went up to my room and undressed and went to bed. I could hear them talking down there, some of them out by the pool, and some of them inside, and the tinkle of ice, and laughter out across the night. I felt awful, and I cried again, because I wanted to go home, but I didn't know how to manage it.

Then in the night it began to come over me stronger and stronger, how much I did not like Gregg, how I hated him.

The house was very still and the knives were still racked in the kitchen against the wall, and they glowed and seemed to breathe, shining with the last of the light from the fire in the fireplace.

They should never have built a fire. It wasn't cold enough for a fire, but they did it for looks, and that was how I didn't like Norman either, on the way back upstairs with the big carving knife.

It was all I could think to do. I couldn't get away, and all I wanted to do was get to Gregg with that knife and show him all the wrongs he'd done, all in one movement.

His door was open, and I went into the darkness, hearing him breathing quietly on the bed. I went over to the bed, and moonlight shone through the window and bathed just his feet and part of the bed in pale light, but I could make out the rest of him.

I got over close to the bed, by his side, and lifted the knife and whispered it.

"I'm going to kill you, I want to kill you, Gregg. So then you'll understand we should be married, I want to get married, not like this—the way this is, I don't like it the way this is."

And I thought of the sunflower; the way it looked at me. I held the knife above him and began to cry softly in the darkness because he didn't understand, and he would never understand, and there he was under my knife, asleep in the pale moonlight and the darkness.

I stood there for a long while, getting ready to kill him in his sleep. And I cried.

Then I went back downstairs with the knife, and washed the fingerprints off it, and hung it up again on the wall. Some of the embers of the fire still showed in the long smooth gleaming blade of the knife.

I went back to my room and lay down on the bed. I loved him. I really loved him. And it didn't matter about what the sunflower had done to me, what these people were, or how they acted. I loved Gregg, and tomorrow everything would be all right.

Shalimar

early 1970s

He was known as "Blue Boy" because he was blue, not under-the-counter blue, although he was sexually aligned—which really brought all this about—but *blue* blue, sad blue, melancholy blue. Categorically, he was out of sight, even though he was pigeon-holed. Some thought he was a blue fink, but that was only because he seldom spoke to anyone or entered into the swing of the scene. He would slowly pass back and forth through The Quarter, even on rainy nights, by the graveyard, maybe, and some of them would see him.

"There goes old Blue Boy."

And in the sunshine, too, a blue note could turn him on, if it was lonely enough, sad enough, and then he might buy a jug and get smashed, and wander the streets looking all hung-up and lost and forsaken, his black denim cuffs freckled with noon's vari-colored vomit, because he liked to eat strange things.

Blue Boy was a remittance kid from a well-fixed family in Bangor, living out his dark, perilous night in delta town: *"be kind enough, Charles"*—his name was Charlie Pelterbridge—*"be kind enough to write monthly so we'll know you're all right, dear, but don't, please, under any circumstances, come home, and we'll send you money enough."*

"Did the moo come in yet, Charlie?" Nikki would ask.

Nikki was the red-haired woman he lived with, and laid with nightly, and sometimes in the afternoon, but all the sad helpless hopelessness of Blue Boy was there because of the auburn-haired girl, Julie, in Bangor, whom he had loved, helter-skelter, like a wild stallion, but deeply, squarely, and who had married another guy, off the cuff. It was all so simple . . . but to Charlie Pelterbridge so completely tragic.

He was one of those who drowned in the everyday business, unable to dismiss or forget.

So at midnight, a June night, when he saw the dimly-lighted face in the curtained window on the court, the second-story window, and heard the soft music, "Pale Hands," he couldn't, at first, believe it.

But then, in a sickening rush of wild anguish, he did believe it. That was either Julie up there, or a girl exactly like her—and he knew he must have her, the face at the window, laughing down at just him.

He returned half frightened to his apartment and laid Nikki.

Then musing afterward, sad, feeling the awesome loneliness.

Could it be?

Had she come to him?

Julie—my Julie?

Each night, then, around midnight—for that was when she appeared—he lounged with strained abandon in the silver moonlight and shadow of the court, overcome with need and fear, shrouded in the scent of Chinese Jasmine, slightly drunk because he needed gin to bring him this far.

He knew he needed to dare go up there, face her in that second-story room, where the music played so softly, where she watched him from the window. And redeeming lust of memory was mixed with dread, begetting a touch of shame, as he remembered and recalled his Julie.

Was it she?

The smell of her hair returned to him, the clinging touch of her wondrous body when they used to nakedly press; the urgent wonder as he entered her.

And looking at the face in the window, yearning, he missed the slight topiary art of the scene, and so succumbed.

First he began to pray, down there in the midnight court, then to silently weep, strained in his eagerness, his urgency, almost his wrath, and the music played, "Pale Hands," again, and she laughed lovingly down to him.

He cried her name. He ran across the court, shoved the purple door open, and stumbled wildly up the odoriferous stairway, narrow, and dimly lit, between high yellow walls of patched plaster.

"Julie!"

He pounded on the big black door, calling softly to her.

"Julie?"

He placed his hands against the wood, waiting with that intense fatigue of promise beyond hope.

And the door opened, yellow light from the room haloed her head.

He reached for her, his heart like a bird's now, and a withered claw-like hand took the young-girl mask away, tore off the auburn wig.

He stared at the ancient face of the shrunken crone, saw her pale phlegm-like eyes, saw her toothless mouth, open, the gray and bloodless lips—and heard the dry leafy laughter, the obscene cackles, saw her clutch at the wilted breasts.

He stared beyond her to the green walls of the room, where hundreds of masks with sightless eyes mocked him, where wigs hung, spun silver, black, and gold, on shadowed pegs.

The music played.

"Pale hands I love . . ."

She beckoned him inside.

He ran from there, down the stairs, into the echoing court.

And now once again, as always, he was Blue Boy, walking the streets of The Quarter, always alone, forever alone, always and forever, even on rainy nights.

Love's Weekend

Dardy first saw him Friday afternoon on the lake shore, and the way he was acting, she knew something was wrong. At first, she did not want him to see her, and she stood in the shadow of the boathouse.

But that was foolish. She didn't even know who he was. Just a tall, lanky, yellow-haired boy, wearing red swim shorts. Very long legs.

Peter would be home at five-thirty. That was two hours away. And her sister, Helen, was coming over from Chicago in the morning. Lots of things to do, really. But she couldn't help being interested in that guy.

She said, "Oh," softly, as the boy slipped and sat down in the lake waters. It wasn't deep. He struggled to his feet, weaving about, then just stood there. He was peering off toward Canada. But something *was* the matter. She should do something. There was no one else in sight.

She had her thick black hair pinned up, to keep cool. If he turned and saw her, she would feel positively naked in the new yellow bikini. It was the first time she'd worn it; skimpier than anything.

Oh God, she thought gently, remembering again that she and Peter had been married nearly a month, and that she loved him.

Helen tomorrow. Why did this thought strike a discordant note? Helen, of course, was older, and too staid to quote, but up until moments ago, she'd been happy at her coming for the weekend visit.

The boy fell again. Was he drunk?

He just lay there in the water, the slow, cool, crystal waves lapping at him.

He came to his knees. She watched, digging her fingers at the side of the boathouse. The shadow of the pier sliced across her oval face, which was rather pale, the dark blue eyes wide and round.

She thought, I've got to help him . . .

He was floundering around in waist-deep water, unable to stand at all.

She ran over there, across the stones, before she realized what she was doing. She stood in the water close to him, staring.

"Is something the matter?"

He staggered backward, sat down again, and began to laugh. Then he stopped laughing, and just watched her. His hair was soaked. He flipped his head and the hair splayed back, showering.

"Quite all right," he said.

Well, you could tell. Breeding. Perfect articulation. And this in view of the fact that he was ill. When they were ill, and still stood up for you, as he was trying to do, then you could be certain.

"I'll help."

"No. No, thanks."

He came to one knee and began giggling. Then he stared down into the water and shook his head. "You're a poem," he said. "A poem in black."

"I'll help you. You'd better—"

"Just to my bed, dark one."

His nose. It was positively running. "Here," she said. "You'd better. Let me. Won't you?"

He came to his feet with a violent effort, bowed slightly, turned and began walking, thrashing through the water, up the shore.

"Come along," he said over his shoulder. "Perhaps you can help, at that."

She followed. He led a meandering course along the edge of the water, until they reached an old fallen oak tree that spanned the shore. Moss clung to its branches. He sprawled across this, landing on his side.

"Oh," she said.

He laughed, lying there, looking up at her. She was leaning across the oak trunk. She stepped over the tree, and he crept on hands and knees up along the shore, until he reached the turfy bank. Here there was a tarpaulin, with two stakes at the front, like a tent. A lean-to, she realized. There was a blanket, and she glimpsed two empty Campbell's soup cans. He crawled in on the blanket, and lay there, staring straight up.

"You may come in, if you like," he said.

She knelt abruptly by the opening. He had rather large feet, not at all like Peter's, but they were beautifully shaped. Very high instep, and deep arches. This meant something, but she could not recall what.

"Are you all right?"

"Now, dark one. Do not worry. No. I am not all right, but I shall be perfect, eventually."

"But what's the matter?"

"Your name?"

She told him she was called "Dardy." "Actually, it's Dardford Sommers. But everybody knows me as Dardy."

"I'm Luke."

She was very worried now. He was perspiring awfully, and his nose was running, and she began to know he was on something. Drugs. Once she had tried grass, and it had done nothing for her. And once Peter came home with some LSD, and they sat there with some Spanada wine and stared at the two capsules for three hours. Then Peter gave a funny laugh, took her hand, and picked up the capsules. They went into the bathroom, and he flushed them down the toilet. They were both immensely relieved.

She knew he was on something.

"I'm coming down," he said. "It's a jarring crash, my dear. I'm kicking, actually. You see?" He said it as if in answer to her unvoiced question. "Now, if you'll read to me?"

"You mean—a book?"

"Yes, love." He reached over his head. He had a perfectly beautiful head, and the hair was drying in curls. The hair was rather long, but not too long. Now in his hand was a thick book. "Page one-thirty-two."

She took the book. While she turned the pages, she thought about the sound of his voice. And thinking about that, she realized the book was a late edition of the complete tales of Edgar Allan Poe—and she had deep feelings of guilt because Peter was working at the AEC, and here she was with this stranger.

"You mean *The Black Cat?*"

"Please. Poe helps me forget. He soothes me. And I already know I like the sound of your voice. It, too, soothes me." He paused. "Dardy."

"Huh?"

"I was just saying your name, that's all. It's a name of summers, which is trying because of your last name—of summer light, and shadows in the hay fields. Of clover and horses. Dardy. Of walks in the woods, by fernery, and deep, dark, shining pools. Of a squirrel in an elm. Of white birch, and nonsense in the swing."

"You don't really want me to read?"

"You have marvelous legs, too," he said, reaching out and touching her ankle. "Peach fuzz and summer light. The light of summer."

"You lived on a farm?"

"I've been there, too, my dear. Now, read."

"Not until you tell me how long you've been *here?*"

"Just last night. But I'm going to remain. Kicking is a process, you see?"

"You want me to read—have you eaten anything?"

"Hunger. Hunger."

She read slowly. He did not interrupt, and at intervals she imagined he wasn't listening, so she would pause. His eyes snapped open immediately, and he frowned. His eyebrows were sandy, and quite thick. They drew together when he frowned. There were shiny places beneath both eyes. She was reading, and she did not know what color his eyes were. It became a minor obsession. She ceased reading. He opened his eyes. Gray, for goodness' sake.

She read on to the finish. She had never read *The Black Cat*, and the story did not help how she felt.

"Thank you," he said. "And now, dear one, I'm going to sleep. It comes upon you like that. But meanwhile, I have nothing to cushion the crash. And it promises to be faithful to the TV extravaganzas, y'know? So if you could procure, say, four downers, sleeping pills, just to ease things, it would be great."

"But—where would I—if you—?"

"It's just that the pain comes on in waves, and the sleep, and if I'm sleeping I don't need the dope, but I do, you see?"

"I've got to go."

"But you shall return?"

She stood up. She still held the book. "I think that's a horrible story," she said.

"Precisely why it's so good. Be sure to come back."

She laid the book at his feet, turned and walked stiffly along the shore. Then she cut quickly up onto the bank, and began walking through sparse woods and grass. There were only vacant lots along here.

She would not think about him. It was late. She had spent more time than she'd figured. Peter would be home, and no dinner ready.

She reached their cottage, white stucco, surrounded by pines, fronting the lake. They were renting. They had planned on coming to the lake for some weeks.

Then she saw the car. Her sister. Helen.

Before she reached the porch, she thought of only one thing, quickly. Helen is here and she uses seconal.

Her sister was in the doorway.

"Dardy. I'd think you'd be here, at least."

"Yes."

Where would she keep them when traveling? In one of her bags, of course. Stupid.

"Where's Peter?" Helen asked.

"Working, natch. When did you get in?" She hugged and was hugged, stiffly. Helen smelled of lavender, faintly. Dardy had never liked lavender. It was a peculiar frontier odor. Like catnip.

They went into the kitchen. "Where have you been?"

"By the lake."

"I was out there. I saw nothing of you, dear."

Her sister was tall, like her father had been, and they had somewhat similar features. That same sharp quality in the shape of the face. Her sister had very little gray hair, only a few strays. But she no longer plucked them as she once had. She wore shorts, now, blue, and a fuzzy pink sweater. She had changed already. Vacations got to them so quickly.

Dardy realized she was looking around, trying to spot the bags.

"I put my things in your room. But where in the world shall I sleep?"

"With me, of course, Helen. Peter will use the sofa-bed."

"It makes me feel awful, putting you out like this." She smiled, took Dardy tightly by both arms. She winked. "But it's good to see you, dear."

"It hasn't been a month, yet."

"I just so wanted to come over. Anyway, Chicago's a mess in August. Ugh, you know?"

"I should."

"Yes. Since the family's gone, I just don't realize, sometimes. Mother, and then Dad. It's as if you weren't there, either. I mean, this last month."

What futility. She wandered into the living room, forgetting Helen, and into the bedroom. She closed and locked the door abstractedly.

He's got to have them, she thought. I know he must have them. He's not the kind to say it and not mean it. About the kicking, too. It must be horrible. She wondered, Would he get worse?

She was in her sister's suitcases. She discovered the small bottle of barbiturates in an overnight bag. She took a few, dropped them into her bikini bra, thought about them melting, which would be evil, and unlocked the door. Helen was standing there, staring at her.

"What's the matter, Helen?"

"Is Peter treating you all right?"

"Certainly. What d'you think I'm—"

"I just wonder, all the time. It worries me. He's so young, Dardy."

"Since when am I ancient? He's very capable. You know that." Why did the words gnaw at her? Capability.

"I suppose it's all right."

"I think I'll shower and dress. Excuse?"

"What will we do tonight?"

This was a shock. She did not want to do anything tonight. She had to get out there and see how he was. Would he be reading Poe by candlelight?

"Peter will think of something."

Her sister looked vaguely around the small living room, at the waterfall print on the wall, at the nearly empty bookcase, at the scarred TV.

"I won't be long," Dardy said.

She went into the bedroom. She undressed and took the seconal capsules into the bathroom. She wrapped them in toilet tissue, because they were out of Kleenex, damn it. She put them on the back of the tiny sink, and showered.

With the wrapped capsules in her hand, she returned to the bedroom. Peter came through the door. "Hi, kid."

What would she do with them?

"You're prepared for me, I see," he said, and took her in his arms, feeling her fresh damp skin. She was stiff, rigid, really, with the damned seconals.

"I've got to dress. Helen will come in."

"Why the hell did she have to come?"

She wriggled free. She couldn't use her hand, because it clutched the wad of capsules. He stared at her. "What's the matter, Dardy?"

"Nothing."

"I talked with Helen. She's fixing dinner. I brought home a steak for tomorrow, but she got here early, so we'll have it tonight."

"Revelations."

He was not as tall as Luke. And there was a great lack, really. She saw it now. A lack she had never even noticed before. Beside Luke, Peter was a baby. A black ball formed inside her, and she just stood there, staring at her husband, feeling this terrible lack.

"Something is the matter."

"Nothing at all," she said lightly. "Now, get out while I dress. And stop staring at my belly."

He left the room.

She dressed in denims and a white shirt, tucked the capsules into the right-hand pocket, brushed her hair, snatched on some lipstick, and went into the other room.

"Dinner's nearly ready," Helen called.

Peter was on the sofa-bed, reading the evening paper, swilling a can of beer.

"Food," she said aloud.

He stared at her.

She hadn't been thinking about anything but Luke. She'd suddenly realized he simply must eat. But how the hell could she get food to him with them here. It was the weekend . . .

Oh God, she thought.

He would be lying out there, all covered with sweat, his nose running, and he might even be shaking now. Seeing things. Hearing things, even.

She sat down in a chair, and stared at her hands. Then she buried her hands between her thighs, and sneaked a look at Peter. He was reading, but she could see one side of his face. He was not like Luke in the slightest. The first time they had made out, 'way back when, he had vouched undying love, and told her she had to marry him. "You have to, that's all."

So she had married him. After months of it. There had never been any recklessness. Just a steadiness. And the thing was, Peter did not look as though he were steady. His mouth was weak, his chin, too. He looked as if he might make a good lush. Actually, he became ill on three whiskies.

Oh God.

They ate dinner in the dinette. She did not know what she was eating, and she could feel the wadded toilet tissue in her pocket. She wondered how she would get out there on the shore.

They took a drive in Helen's car. Peter said it was terrible, her driving over alone. He would have come for her. Her sister loved the woods. They would have a fine time, just a fine time.

They stopped and had beer at Jake's Fish Fry. Peter had been brought up in Florida, and he explained about smoked mullet. And mullet in general.

How they had a crop like a chicken, and ate weeds. "Not at all like other fish."

"That's so interesting, dear."

Dardy seethed.

When they came back to the cottage, her sister was simply exhausted. Peter had had a rough day. So they decided on bed. Peter kissed her, patted her behind, and went to the sofa-bed. So there would be none of that, thank God.

Her sister talked till eleven. Dardy waited for an hour. Then she eased carefully out of bed, slipped into the denims and the white shirt, and left the house. Peter was snoring. He never snored in her bed. Only when alone, which sometimes happened. He said he had a cooperative valve.

She ran all the way, nearly tripped on the fallen oak tree, and found the lean-to. The moon was out, high against froth, slanting glazed whiteness into the shelter.

"Did you get them?"

A shaking hand grabbed her arm. "Wait." She dug in her pocket. Was she doing wrong? No, for God's sake. She handed him the wadded tissue. He was breathing in gulps. He took them all, swallowed them down without water.

"I've got to get you something to eat. I forgot."

"Wait a minute."

He lay back. She could see his stomach move, the beat of his heart. He had been in the water again, because his hair was damp. She could tell. The curls were ironed out. That meant he liked to be clean. Peter was sometimes careless about that.

She waited for some time. Then his breathing began to smooth out. She felt his hand touch her ankle. I'm doing something good, she thought. Helping another human being. Peter would scalp me. He would do worse than that. He's a drug addict, and I'm helping. He's kicking. In my little way . . .

"Can you walk?" she asked.

"Sure."

"C'mon, then. Back to the house. You'll have to wait outside. There's some steak left."

"I couldn't eat, dear one."

"You've got to." It was imperative that he eat.

"I couldn't really walk."

She leaped up and ran all the way back, and went into the kitchen. Peter was still snoring. She made a steak sandwich in the dark, took the half-full gallon jug of milk, and ran back to the shore.

He had not moved.

"Summer nights, too," he said. "Moonlight and summer nights, with your hair in my mouth."

"Here. Now, you eat that. And there's milk."

He drank some milk. It left a ring around his mouth. He was seated Indian fashion. She began to laugh, and couldn't stop. He laughed too. She had never heard such a laugh. Peter brayed like a donkey, an absolutely stupid donkey. But Luke. It gurgled in his throat, and burst from his chest. And she couldn't stop laughing herself, either.

They slapped each other. He pulled her hair. He reached over, and cupped her head, and drew her close and kissed her. "Nepenthé," he said. "Ah, my dear—the moonlight and you."

She sat there. Numbed. Stupid, she thought. Fool.

"Eat the sandwich."

He took a bite and chewed. He chewed for some time. He was never going to swallow. It was endless. Peter was back there, snoring. He finally swallowed, and gulped some milk.

"First in a week," he said.

"Food?" She forgave him the empty soup cans.

"Yes, my love."

"Are you really kicking?"

"You know it. You're married, aren't you?"

"Yes."

"I'm not married. But it doesn't matter unless you think it matters." He paused, then said, "My God, you're sweet, Dardy."

She said nothing. She was sitting on her calves, palms on her knees, looking at him. He lay stretched out again. His knuckle rested against her right knee.

"You like being married?"

"It hasn't been a month."

"Then you're not married."

"I guess not."

"What's his name?"

She told him. Just saying it made her feel guilty. She looked down the shore, into darkness. She could hear the slap-slap of the water. It bubbled gently among stones.

He said, "Why don't you come away with me?"

"I couldn't."

"You could, you know. All you have to do is do it. Just come."

She did not speak.

"Dardy?"

"Yes?"

"It would be very nice. When I'm well, I'm lots of fun."

"You're conceited," she said.

He laughed gently, stroking her knee.

"You're not happy with Peter."

"My sister's here, too. From Chicago. She drove over today."

"You'll have a fine time."

She could have screamed. She just sat there, with him stroking her knee.

"You're feeling better?"

"Much better."

She looked into his eyes. He was staring at her, the moonlight full on his face. She had never seen such a face. He must have been absolutely everywhere. She had been lots of places, but it was all insignificant. He dwarfed her, Peter, life, everything. What would Peter say?

Oh God.

What was she doing?

She abruptly stretched out beside him. He curled one arm under her head. She could feel him tremble. Just occasionally. It streamed through him, like a vibration. They lay there. She listened to him breathe. She compared his breathing to Peter's.

"Dardy Summers," he said.

She said nothing.

His hand touched her. She held her breath.

"Not now, anyway," he said. "Will you come away with me?"

"I'd better go." She was trembling inside. She had never felt anything like this. It was a sweet tingle. "I'll bring you breakfast."

"And read me *The Cask of Amontillado*?"

"All right."

He held her hand, lying there. The moonlight was full on his face.

"Dardy—of the summer's sun—"

She rose quickly, turned and ran over to the oak tree. She leaped across the dark trunk, and ran to the boathouse. For a moment she stood there under the moonshade of the eave. Then she went back to the house.

She stood in front of the medicine cabinet mirror in the bathroom and stared at herself. Then she sat on the toilet, and wept. She stifled the sound with a towel. Finally, it was over. She dried her eyes, then bathed in a trickle of water so it would not wake her sister, and went to bed.

In the morning, preparing breakfast, she knew he would want more seconal. He would need it. *Oh God.*

A motorcycle roared violently to a stop out front.

"Who's that?" Peter called.

She looked out the window. Luke. Straddling a big black bike, looking at the cottage. He gunned the motor, roaring, and blasted the horn.

She walked out in a daze.

He grinned at her. "Hi. Just leaving for the Coast, on my trusty."

"But—you—did you?"

Peter stood in the doorway. She saw her sister, standing behind Peter.

"Luke," she said. "Are you all right?"

"Will you come with me? And read me Poe, every night—and feed me goodies?"

She stared at him.

"I'm on it again," he said. "I didn't make it, my dear. Coming?"

"I can't." It was all she could say, in a small voice. He was watching her eyes.

"Dardy of the summer's sun," he said. "Give my best to Peter."

She wanted to say something, anything. Nothing would come.

He grinned again. His hair was dry now, the curls burnished in the sunlight. He still wore the red swimming shorts. His feet were bare. He gunned the motor. Abruptly, he was riding away, fast, in a shower of gravel. She watched him vanish down the highway.

Turning, she walked slowly back into the house.

Peter looked at her and scratched his head.

"Who was that, dear?" Helen asked.

How could she tell them she didn't know?

Death Window

It was past midnight. She could not sleep. There was some consolation from the nightlight; it colored the bedroom, and when she opened her eyes, she could see the familiar surroundings. There was the closet, two chairs, the bureau and the dresser; she could even make out Stan's framed photograph, see his forehead and his eyes, the mustache he kidded she had married him for. But, where other times, other lonely nights, that photo might have cheered her, provoking love feelings, happiness, a sense of security over finally having married the man she so cared for, tonight it was different.

Tonight she was more frightened, alarmed, than she had been for two weeks, ever since that first night she had heard the prowler and actually seen him running across the back yard from the kitchen window.

Stan had been away that time, too. She had called the police, but they said they could do little or nothing. They sent a uniformed man out to question her, and he looked around the yard. But that was all. And when Stan returned two days later and she told him about it, he made light of it.

"Nothing to worry about, hon."

"How can you say that? I saw him out there. He was looking in the window. I heard something at the bedroom window again last night. And footsteps, running. A shadow. I'm all alone out here. It's three miles to town, Stan. And you—you're away someplace, all safe and sound."

He had silenced her with a finger to her lips, kiss her on the forehead. And smiled that winning smile. He held her and rubbed her back. As if that would help.

"I mean it, Stan. I'm scared. I'm alone so much—"

"You know my job—it keeps me away. I'm sure there's nothing to worry about. The police found nothing, and there's been no other reports of prowlers, Ginnie. . . ."

She had regarded him with all the patience she could summon. She felt sure it must trouble him, but he just wasn't allowing himself to reveal it, for her sake. And he looks so strong, so—so staunch, with that square jaw, and the black mustache, and the steady, assuring, dark gaze. He had fixed her a drink, then, that first time, and he was all love, overwhelming her, so she began to believe as he said.

"Just your imagination. It's autumn. Windy. Shadows out there. You probably saw a shadow." Pausing, he held her chin, grinning down at her. "My sexy little wife's got herself all wrought up over a shadow."

"But, if you only had a job in town, nearby, so you wouldn't have to be gone so long in between—"

He shook his head. "Wish it were different. . . ."

That had been two weeks ago. And it had happened four times since; four times she'd heard the scratching at one of the windows, rushed across to peer out, and had actually seen twice the running man. For it was a man, she knew that. And Stan had been away those times, too. Once in Chicago, once in New York, and twice in Seattle—so far away. He had warned her about his job before they were married six months ago; he headed the publicity department for a line of school books for *Desmount Publishing Educational Service*, and was called to conferences and meetings throughout the country. It was a good job; it paid well, and there was promise of future promotion—near future. So she didn't really want to discourage him. . . .

But she was so worried. Especially now, after reading that story in *Murder Omnibus*. She wished she had not read it, she wished that so much. But she had. She had taken the book to bed, thinking to quell her fright and frustration with hair-of-the-dog; that's what they did for disease, didn't they: fed them inoculations of the disease to ward it off? Well, she'd imagined the promised thrilling stories in the book would somehow cheer her.

None had. They had only worked her up more than before, especially that last one: *Husband's Night Out*. It was like everything else. You run across a word, perhaps, something you don't know, and you ask somebody, or go look it up at the library. And an hour later that word is used, explained; again the next day, and maybe two or three times thereafter. It happened like that with her. *Husband's Night Out* had struck home so forcefully, she had actually wished the author in hell for disturbing her. She had lain there in bed after reading it, afraid to move a muscle, with the book propped on her chest her eyes fastened like twin carpet tacks to the last line: "*. . . just before she died, Helen knew who the prowler was: all the time it had been her husband, Jack, taunting her from the darkness.*"

"Jack" had a job that kept him away from home. "Helen" had done nothing but love him when he came home, worry him about the prowler, and frighten herself to death, almost. Until Jack murdered her. Helen had told the police and they had been of no help whatever. She had called in a private investigator and he had made off with the princely retainer she'd paid him. She had tried to locate him, and found he worked under an assumed name, an out-and-out fake.

And she had died. Her husband, Jack, had made fun of her fears. Well he might. All the time he was plotting to kill her for her money. And he had succeeded . . . the story had left Ginnie hanging there, suspended in an absolute aura of fear.

That story! Why had she read it? What had she been thinking of, hoping she could inoculate herself against fear and possible death, even, *with fear?*

All during the time she'd been reading *Husband's Night Out*, she had silently been—with heart thudding—comparing herself with *Helen*, Stan with *Jack*. There had been such accommodatingly close parallels she had almost been fearful of moving her eyes to read. She had lain there frozen between the sheets, under the blankets, perspiring, rigid, not wanting to know anymore, but hinged to the book like a magnet, gobbling up the horror of discovering your husband, the man you love, was killing you— but not till the last line; up to then it had only been the awful occurrences in her lonely, terrified, besieged life. Ginnie's prowler had scratched at the windows, too—just like in the story. And, like Helen, she always hurried to the window, out of some weird promptings of bravadocio, to frighten him away, or to reassure herself . . . Ginnie did not know which.

She lay there, now, with the book still propped on her chest, afraid to set it aside for fear the secret watcher at the window might accept it as a gesture to enter . . . it was a mad surmise. Yes. Whenever sounds came from the windows, she ran across the room, blind with it, wanting to know, summoning intrepid strength from somewhere beyond her ken.

"Oh, Stan. . . ." The whispered words slipped unbidden past her lips.

But, it couldn't be . . . he wouldn't . . . *would he?*

Why?

She had no money of her own, no luring bank account. She had quit her job, which had just barely supported her before marriage, and leaped completely abandoned into Stan's arms. She had weighed every angle beforehand, as dispassionately as the circumstances of love allowed, and decided to marry him. His friends had been an assurance, though there had been no real doubt.

"Stan's an oddball, but you can count on him in a pinch."

"Well, he used to drink often and a lot, but I never saw him drunk."

"He loves you, told me so himself. Said he'd go to hell for you, Ginnie. . . ."

And, from a liberated woman: "By God, even I'd marry him—if he'd ask. I'd quit work and slave in the kitchen."

There had been other welcome agreement to her own attitude and his best friend had clinched it:

"Ginnie, you'll never find a better, safer man than Stan Wyomore. He saved my life in Nam, under enemy fire. He risked his own life, more than once. You didn't ask for advice, but you've got it. Grab him, Ginnie."

And she had.

And now, here she was—'way out in the country in a lonely house, with somebody scratching nights at the windows, running across the yard, defeating every lawful premise.

Why *were* they so far in the country?

"Always wanted it like this, Ginnie," he'd told her. "Can't stand urban life. Had it up to here. This isn't the last place we live in—I want a lot more than this. But it'll do for a while. And you'll get to like it—"

"I like it already. I love it, Stan."

She had loved it. She didn't admire city life, either. Everything was so beautiful out here. And the town wasn't really so very far away. And it was just a town, nothing more. They shopped there once a week, when Stan was home.

"Baby, I don't like leaving you here all alone, for such long intervals. But it'll change. And soon. A few more months and I'll have that new job. The house's a family thing, and they like me. And I like the work. I'll have a fat salary, and we'll have a better place near Chicago—not in, but near. I'm actually looking around, Ginnie. Wouldn't buy anything without your seeing it first, but there's one place—boy!"

And it had always sounded so good.

Until now. *Murder Omnibus.*

Damn it!

She let the book fall, jerked her gaze to the window. Out there, beyond the drawn green shade, was night. She could hear crickets, katydids. But what troubled her was something she must remedy; she hadn't been able to bring herself to do it, yet. The shade didn't come all the way to the sill— there was a gap. And she could see the dark, gleaming pane.

She still hadn't moved. The faucet dripped in the kitchen, which seemed so far away right now.

Why did they live 'way out here? . . . at such distance from streetlights, from other houses, from people . . .

Jack, in the story, had been a jealous man. Helen had been blind to that; or at least, she had averted her mental eyes. She chose to love him, believe in him, even when there was doubt. What had it gotten her? A knife along the throat. . . .

Ginnie suddenly moved, braced with a surge of bravery. She tossed the covers back, and at that very same instant she heard the scratching at the window.

She screamed a little bursting scream, jumped to the window, and disregarding everything, whipped the shade up. She whirled, bounced on the bed, and cut the bedlight. Then she rushed back to the window.

She saw the face in the night, with the windy moonlight icy behind the shadow . . . the pale face, with the mouth—open, laughing without sound. Then he was turning, running, leaping off across the back yard, by the apple tree. Then, he hesitated, turned, and lifted one arm—a fist, and shook it. The face had been just a white blob, unrecognizable.

She knew he knew she was watching. He shook that fist at her. He knew she was alone. He wasn't afraid. The fear did not show in the way he ran. He ran haphazardly, uncaring, as if staging some sort of dance.

Oh, God! Yes. All she had seen was a pale blob. It could be anybody. It could be Stan.

That's what was in her mind. Stan. Out there, planning something, some reason . . . she had been led to that story. But, no. Stan had actually brought the book home with him last week. He knew she liked mysteries, and somebody had left it in his car.

"He won't miss it. I glanced it over. Looks good."

It had been good, all right. . . .

The shadow moved quickly from the apple tree, now, and out beyond the garage, disappearing in the night.

She stared at the night. Finally, she drew the shade. Her hand was trembling, and her stomach was a knot. What was he planning for her?

It was Stan. It had to be.

The prowler had never appeared when Stan was home.

"*If* there is one, which I doubt—and *if* he's really been here, which I also doubt—now, now, kitten, don't get your hackles up—*if*, I say, then he knows I'm home, and won't appear. But—I don't believe it. Come here, gimme a kiss."

She stood there in the bedroom. Then she took off her nightdress, went to the closet, and proceeded to dress. She knew. She knew she would not remain in this house one more night without protection. A gun. She had to have a gun.

Why hadn't Stan insisted on that much? He hadn't.

He had gone merrily off, and wouldn't return for three more days, till Friday. Where was he? San Francisco. She didn't even have a phone number. He called occasionally, but had told her he could not give her any number so she could phone him herself, because he was always on the move: luncheon engagements, dinners, meetings, conferences. He would never know when he might be at a hotel. Sometimes he pulled out at a moment's notice, under directions from the president of the publishing house.

Well—tight inside, ready to burst into tears and at the same time torn with a strange kind of inner rage—she was leaving. For now . . .

But, that man—he had gone out back by the garage.

Well, Stan—figure it out, baby. Two can play. And from somewhere, out of her past, came the words, "Be bold!"

She slipped on her coat, took her purse and a flashlight, turned on every light in the house, and left by the back door for the garage. She was scared to her toes. She ran lightly, the flashlight beam bobbing ahead of her, and she began to wish she hadn't been so quick to decide. It was awful out here. But, with every step, a kind of wild anger was sweeping her up, coming from deep inside. He had fooled her. She didn't know what he was planning. But he wasn't going to have his way.

Oh, she knew now that it was Stan. She knew it for a fact. There had even been something about the way the shadow moved, that convinced her beyond any doubt. He was a weird kind of voyeur, maybe—some sort of perverted monster. He had worked his love potion on her, and she had succumbed—but now it would change.

She reached the garage, the car, and slid beneath the wheel. She locked the door, realized she was breathing in short gasps and that her heart was ready to burst from her chest—but she was secure. At least, for the moment.

She backed out fast, turned, and came down the dirt road as fast as she dared. She would not return until tomorrow, bright daylight.

Because, now she hated him. Everything that she'd had for Stan was gone, with what was happening. There were sharp interims of doubt, but she erased them with thoughts of what had happened so far, and with the alert mental wave that it was so very pat.

He had her where he wanted her. Out here in the country. She had reported a prowler and they had done nothing. They knew her husband was away a lot. She was alone in the house.

They hadn't even sent anybody to keep watch . . .

She stayed in a small hotel in the tiny town; she wanted something more secure than a motel on the highway.

She did not sleep. She lay there between the strange-smelling sheets, with saffron light from the window bathing the room, and thought about it. The more she thought, the worse it became, until she knew—in a moment of despair—that she could kill him.

He had left her out there, alone, knowing her fear, her terror. He had talked it down. He had actually kidded with her about it.

Well, all right.

She rose harried and haggard in the morning, at seven-thirty, and forced herself to wait till nine o'clock. She wanted nothing to eat. Breakfast was beyond her.

She only wanted one thing. It was something hypnotic in her now, an extension of her fear. She still felt fear. She knew what she must face. Perhaps she would face more than she imagined. Things could go wrong.

She might even die—as he planned. Because that's what he was trying to do; scare her out of her wits, then move in with the coup de grâce.

She bought a gun, signed for it as was demanded by law in this state. The gun was a .32 Savage automatic, and the man in the pawn shop showed her exactly how it worked.

"I want it for rats," she said. "One rat in particular, a big one—very wily. Can't get him in a trap."

"You should really have a target pistol, you ain't done much shooting."

"No. I want this. My brother had one once. I fired it several times. It feels like just the thing."

That last had been the truth. How she wished Bob were alive, still. She would run to him, right now. She knew this. They had been close. Now, there was nobody. Bob was dead. Her parents were dead. She had no real friends out here. They were all far away. Besides, how could she ever explain?

She had only Stan.

She bought cartridges for the automatic, and drove home. In the kitchen, she prepared a meal, and ate it, forcing herself.

She was more frightened, now, being here, where it happened. But there was something else that carried her. The panic, the knowledge inside her that she would kill to live.

When it came down to it, most people would be the same way. Could she go to the police now, tell them she was certain it was her husband?

If she could only check him out by phone . . .

She went to bed early. It was a dark, windy night, dark of the moon, spooky and gesticulant.

She waited. She left the windowshade up. She lay in bed, with the gun in her hand, under the covers, the bedlight on, and waited. She wasn't patient. She was frightened to a kind of madness. The anger had taken over now. She hated Stan so much she could hardly contain herself. Should she shoot to kill?

Minutes ticked past. Two hours drifted by.

The prowler wouldn't come tonight. She was prepared and nothing would happen. And Stan hadn't called.

He must have a secret bank account somewhere, luck-funded for mayhem. But, why did he want her dead?

It was death she considered now.

Suppose she couldn't bring it off, knowing it was Stan. Suppose she couldn't fire the gun. Suppose she missed and the prowler somehow got inside the room?

"Stan . . . Stan . . ." Whispering his name when a worm of inner pleading surfaced. "Why?"

She heard the footstep outside, stiffened, and started to cry. The tears simply welled in her eyes, streamed down her cheeks, and she lay there as rigid as ever. She could not move. It was the invasion of her private world. The shade was up, the window wide for him to see her . . .

And she could see him . . .

The scratching. On the pane, and this time there also came subdued laughter, as if choked off in the throat, but gloating—out there in the night, carrying into the room.

It was the laughter that did it. Stan, laughing at her, playing with her all this time.

She threw back the covers with a single thrust, burst from the bed, and fired point blank at the indistinct white blob of face in the window. She fired six times, sobbing hysterically, calling, "Stan . . . Stan . . . !"

The pane shattered with the first slug, the explosion loud, echoing. The face looked immediately battered. But it was still there, the eyes gleaming, and then that face fell apart with the driving impact of bullets from the .32 Savage automatic.

Ginnie stood there in the bedroom. The gun fell from her grasp, rattled on the floor. Wind gushed in through the broken window, fluttering her nightdress, cooling the damp curls on her forehead.

"Oh, God," she whispered.

She heard pounding feet out there in the night. More panic feathered her breast.

"Ginnie!"

She heard the voice, and then she saw his head poking through the smashed window.

"Ginnie—you all right? You shot him, by God!"

"Stan . . . ?" She was in a state of shock.

"Yes, it's me, darling. . . ."

Then he was scrambling in through the window, standing before her, holding her shoulders, looking worriedly down into her frozen face.

She winced, shrank back . . . he gripped her arms.

"I was out in the field, waiting for him—watching," Stan said, pulling her close. "I came back last night, didn't come in, because I wanted to catch him. I got to thinking and knew you wouldn't lie—I was a dope, kidding you like that. Saw you come back this morning. Where were you—never mind . . . later." He paused. "I realized the cops couldn't help. They have to have something to go on. So I took over. You bought a gun, didn't you— and you shot him."

"Is he dead?"

"He almost doesn't have a head, Ginnie."

He held her very tightly, then, and kissed her cheek, and she should have felt pleasure, relief, reassurance at the touch of his hands.

She did not. Would she ever feel pleasure again? She had doubted him, thought the very worst of him. She had imagined he planned to kill her. And all the time, he'd been trying to protect her. . . .

What could she ever say? How could she live with herself? How could she live with Stan?

A fine trembling began inside her and a sob broke from her throat . . . she would never be able to say, "I love you," again.

Ugly

His name was Haskins. He knew how he looked. He was the monster of monsters, and anyone who saw him recoiled in shock at the sight of such human wreckage. He didn't know how it would all end, he only knew that someday it would all end for him. Even he couldn't stand the sight of himself.

Nevertheless, he was drawn to mirrors. As he was right now.

In his room, he stood before the mirror and tried to look without feeling the awful sickening rush of emotion in his chest. The feeling welled within him, and he hated himself as he knew everyone else hated him.

Women especially.

He swallowed, standing there. Even that minor movement produced an effect in the mirror that made him grimace with disgust. As the disgust registered on his twisted features, he turned and stepped away from the mirror for a moment. Then he came back and faced himself.

The thought uppermost in his mind at all times was, How do I look. Sometimes he had to run and find a mirror, just so he could stare at himself. He could hardly bear it, but he had to do it.

The physical shape of his body was huge, cumbersome, heavy, but not too unordinary. Thin waisted, his stomach and chest bulged out enormously, and his shoulders were like projecting out-of-place cliffs on either side of his long neck.

If he could only hide his face. If he could only look out of his eyes at people and somehow tell them how he felt without their seeing his face. His face.

Haskins stroked his face with his hands.

Little children stood open mouthed, or turned away bewildered. Men stoically held their features and stared him down, or avoided him entirely, as if they hadn't seen him.

But women. . . .

Women.

Haskins savored the very taste of the word on his tongue and said it aloud.

"Women."

Women were startled to the cores of their beings with a horrible disgust. And Haskins knew it.

The thing was that lately Haskins hadn't been able to bear that, either. He was a man, no matter what he resembled. A man had to have a woman.

It had become an immediate problem. But how?

Previously he had somehow managed to evade women; they had not been imperative. Long ago he had relinquished himself to the knowledge that his world had to be a world without women. But lately, the powers within his body had taken over and it was all he thought about.

His chin was like a cantaloupe. His lips were of blubber. His nose was huge and somehow shaped all wrong; it was also clogged so the blubbery lips were forever open as he gasped for air. His eye cavities were on different levels, and he only had one eye. A toy arrow had taken the other when he was a child. The bad eye was a white shield of membrane under his lid.

Oddly enough, the one thing he possessed that wasn't out of place was his hair. Jet black and curly, it combed and brushed to perfection, alive and luxuriant. He took great pride in his hair.

Haskins knew that because his hair was so fine, it only made the rest of him that much more horrible, by contrast.

He ran his hands gently over the waves of his hair.

"Women," he said aloud. "A woman. Girls."

He turned away from the mirror and began to pace the small confines of his room. He moved with a heavy, disorganized stride. Yes. Even his walk was ugly.

"Girls," he said to the four silent walls.

Even prostitutes avoided him, didn't want him. Perhaps if he had been extremely rich, it might have been different. But he wasn't rich.

He could look back on one conquest. He called it a conquest, but he knew the truth. Nevertheless, to him it was a conquest, even if he had paid for it. A skinny streetwalker had taken pity on him one night three years ago, taken him to her room, and tried to help him. He dwelt on the sweet memory of this in his dreams.

Once it had been enough.

It no longer was enough.

"Women," he said to the four walls.

How to get one.

Because it was the getting and the execution of the deed now. No matter how, no matter what he had to do.

He worked as a nightwatchman for a small, out-of-the-way plant where no questions were ever asked of him, where nobody ever spoke to him.

But now it was the sixth night of his yearly vacation.

The sixth lonely night amid a welter of ever lonely nights.

Haskins stopped in mid-stride. He would go out on the street, he had to go out on the street.

He threw on a topcoat and went out into the cool night. It was early, the streets weren't crowded. He moved slowly along the sidewalk, close in against the buildings, lunging, cumbersome, terribly alone.

He started across the street only one block from his room, then stepped back hurriedly as a truck swung around the corner. The truck was going much too fast for this district.

Something flew from the back of the truck and fell bouncing at Haskins' feet. It was a large package wrapped in brown paper and neatly tied with twine.

Haskins stood there staring at the package. He had a mild urge to yell after the truck, but that was all. He frowned deeply, then finally, when nothing happened, went over and picked up the package, hefting it. It held cloth of some kind, he could tell that by the feel.

Abruptly, he hugged the package close, turned and started rapidly walking back to his room. A find. Something to take his mind off his loneliness.

He burst heavily into his room, closed the door, and switched on the light. He tossed the package on the bed, took off his topcoat, then sat down to savor the contents of what he had found. He sat on the edge of the bed, and slowly began to unwrap the package.

There was colorful cloth; orange, red, yellow, blue. His hands trembled faintly. It was a masquerade get-up, something for a mask ball, a fancy dress party. It was a clown's dress.

Haskins' heart beat heavily. He stood up and held out the costume. Something tumbled to the floor and rolled face up and he saw a clown's head leering at him, grinning with wild eyes.

It was the mask part of the costume, a complete head mask that fit over the head to the neck. He grabbed it up and stood there staring at it, the rest of the clown's dress tumbled on the bed.

He grunted suddenly, split his blubbery lips in a tooth-gaped grin, and hurried over to the mirror. In his hurry he was clumsy, but he managed to slip the big mask down over his head and he stood there before the mirror staring at himself in wonderment.

Nobody could tell what he looked like. He was a laughing clown; a happy someone. He was hidden. He stood there and he thought one thing immediately.

"Women."

They wouldn't know what he looked like.

The clown's face laughed back at him from the mirror, the head topped with a long swinging hat peaked and with a flaming red ball on the end of it. When he moved his head, the peaked hat swung around and around. And the clown's eyes crinkled with humor to see such fun.

And through his one eye, Haskins watched this.

He was a diabolically clever-looking clown, the face of the mask was expertly fashioned; humor of all kinds lurked in the laughing face, and altogether it was a handsome face, as clowns' faces go. It certainly was much better looking that Haskins' face.

He stood there for some time. He liked what he saw.

Finally he went back to the bed and picked up the rest of the costume and donned it slowly. There were tassels and ribbons and balls and bells and color of all kinds in heavy pleats. There was no shape to the costume and Haskins liked that, too; it disguised his strange chest and shoulders. Then he found the shoes. They were black slippers, really, with long pointed up-turned silver toes.

He had to climb on the bed in order to see all of himself in the mirror. He jumped up and down on the bed before the mirror and ribbons fluttered colorfully and bells jingled and jangled and the floppy peaked hat whirled around and around.

The clown laughed and laughed in the mirror.

Haskins sported himself for some time like this.

He danced around the room. He approached the mirror from one side, then suddenly leaped into its view, and caught himself there, laughing and happy.

Finally he just stood before the mirror admiring himself. He was immensely happy over his find.

For three days he was happy. Once he even thought of trying to join a circus. He would don the costume and jump and run around the room, and stand before the mirror.

For three days he wasn't Haskins at all. He was a clown.

But there were the times when he didn't wear the costume. They were sick times, moments of hell.

It was on the evening of the third day that he found an answer. Because what good did it do to wear the clown's costume just in his room? No good at all.

He found the answer in the evening paper.

It was on the society page.

Mary Jane Weltings' Costume Party. Masquerade.

He even knew the street where she lived. And before he had finished reading the piece in the paper, he knew what he was going to do. His heart rocked in his chest, and he had to gulp for air at the thought. But he knew he would go to that party.

"Women," he said aloud.

Because that thought never left him.

The party was tonight.

Excitement crowded him and he experienced fear, too, but the urge to do what he thought of doing was too much. He had to go through with it.

He checked the time, then sat back to wait. For nearly two hours, he did nothing but sit in a chair with the clown's costume piled on the bed. Then, finally he got up and dressed in the costume, and went out.

He passed through dark streets and many a dimly lighted alley on his way to the address he sought. Few people saw him. And when he did walk on a main thoroughfare, those who saw him only gave him little more than a passing glance. Some nut dressed up in a clown's costume.

Finally he stood on the same side of the street, at the entrance to an alley, near Mary Jane Weltings' home. He waited there, watching through his one eye. He knew what he wanted to do—but how was he going to do it?

Two carloads of people came to the address and he watched them stream from the cars and enter the house. They were dressed in every conceivable type costume: there was a pirate and a gypsy and a dancing girl, and several disreputable-looking characters. He watched them enter Mary Jane Weltings' home and wished he were one of them. There was an ache inside him that didn't go away, it became worse and worse as he stood there.

There was an alley beside the house and Haskins moved to the edge of the alley, standing in the shadow beside the house. He waited. From inside the house he heard music and laughter and the tinkle of glass. Someone shouted something, and someone was singing.

The ache grew worse. He didn't know what to do. He felt afraid at the things he thought of doing, but he knew he had to do something.

Two more carloads of people came and parked in the street in front of the house. A wind was blowing, and as they moved from the cars to the house, their costumes coloring the night, Haskins suddenly slipped along the wall and mingled with them and entered the door.

He moved swiftly through the vestibule and on inside. Everyone was talking and moving about and everybody wore a mask of some kind, so nobody seemed to think the tall hovering clown was out of place.

Suppose they could see my face, he thought. What then.

The rooms were lighted nicely, and many guests were at the party. A three-piece orchestra was playing music at the far end of one of the rooms. For a long while Haskins did nothing but stand in the shadows and watch.

People danced and talked and ate at the crowded buffet.

There were many pretty looking girls and Haskins had difficulty in breathing when he looked at them.

Haskins didn't want it to end.

"Havin' fun?"

He turned quickly and drew a quick breath. A girl stood beside him, wearing just an eye mask, her red plump lips pursed as she questioned him.

"Yes," he said.

"That's good."

She wore nothing on her legs but long black silk sheer stockings that went clear to her hips. She wore a short little black jacket that thrust out from her full breasts. Her long black hair fell across ivory shoulders that were as bare as the day she was born.

Haskins wanted to touch her.

"Let's dance," the girl said, and before he knew what was happening, he was whirling the girl around the floor as the orchestra played. And he could feel her against him and he didn't know what to do, except that he knew he wanted her.

"My, but you're big. I don't think I know you."

"Maybe not," Haskins said. "You're very lovely."

"I like clowns," the girl said.

Haskins was having trouble not to show that he was trembling to the very core of his being. There was nothing he could do about it. He wanted to yank the girl to him and kiss her, but he couldn't. Not here.

"Do you like the party?" he asked.

"Oh, yes. As parties go," the girl said. Her voice sounded bored and Haskins liked the sound of it. It sent jangles down through him and his nerves were on edge as she thrust against him as they danced about the room.

He tightened his arm about her and she moved in still closer to him, smiling up at him with her plump red lips.

Haskins could hardly contain himself. It can't last, he told himself. He was sweating inside the clown costume. She seemed so complacent, seemed to want to do anything he felt like doing. His nerve came back with a rush and he held her still tighter.

"I like you," the girl said.

"Do you?" he replied.

He was already planning, throwing caution, everything to the winds. Nothing seemed to matter, except that he get as close to this girl as he could. The fragrance of her hair and her body seemed to cloud around him. It was as if she had crawled inside the clown's costume with him. It was all he could do to stay standing up, holding her, dancing with her.

He let his hand drop and it touched her thigh, her hip. She seemed to like it, gave a little wiggle against him. He had read of such creatures but had never supposed he'd hold one in his arms.

"Let's go outside," he said, trying not to gasp.

"But where?"

"We could just go outside. There's a side door over there."

He moved her toward it and she went right along with him.

"You think we should?" she asked, the white nibbles of her fine teeth showing between her red lips.

"Yes," Haskins said. "I think we should."

"All right!"

They went to the door. He looked around to see if anyone had noticed, then tried the door and they stepped outside into the alley.

He closed the door and looked at her and pulled her to him.

"You're rather rambunctious," she said. "But I don't mind."

Haskins was in a kind of frenzy. He couldn't stop what he was doing. His nervous hands sought her out, feeling everywhere on her body as she pressed against him. Suddenly, she reached up and yanked her mask off. "There, see?" she said.

She was very beautiful. Haskins almost wept at her beauty. He fumbled clumsily, pulling her to him, panting heavily under the clown's mask.

"Won't you take off your mask?" she said.

"I'd better not."

"Why?"

"Just not now."

But he wanted to kiss her, too. It was an agony.

Abruptly the girl reached out with both hands and grabbed at Haskins' head mask.

He leapt backwards. But she held to the peaked hat part of the mask and the entire mask came off. It dropped at her feet and she moved quickly closer. And Haskins stood there staring at her with his one eye and his blubbery lips.

The girl took one look and began to scream.

He grabbed her. He held her close and she fought and kicked and screamed as he tried to kiss her.

"You wanted my mask off," he said. "It's off."

"Help me—somebody!" the girl called.

The door on the side of the alley burst open. Someone looked out and she screamed again. An instant later Haskins was surrounded. He didn't know what to do. It was then that one of them noticed his face.

"He tried—he tried—" the girl said.

"Did you ever see anything more ugly!"

One of the men jumped at him and struck him in the face. Haskins fought back. He was crowded in against the wall.

"Who is he?"

"Never seen him before."

"I don't know him."

Somebody kicked at him. Somebody else struck him in the face. All he could see was the girl, it was all he wanted. He was dizzy and fogged and nothing meant anything except that a girl had been kind to him, had let him hold her.

"Beat him up!"

They did. It was done methodically. Between the shower of slugs that struck him, Haskins glimpsed the girl going back inside the house. She was being comforted by someone else.

"Get 'im good."

"Don't worry."

There were at least eight men pounding at him. They broke him to the alley floor and he lay there.

"I'm phoning for the police," one said.

"Do that," another said.

He lay there as they stood over him breathing heavily. He knew he was just ugly. It would never be any different. It would always be this way. There wasn't anything he could do about it.

He wasn't even a clown.

Death Is a Private Eye

I walked into it with my eyes wide open. . . .

It was a Florida summer afternoon, with the sun hot and white in a pale blue sky and the air full of surprisingly cool, pleasant winds coming in from the Gulf of Mexico. I drove slowly by the house out on Tangerine and had a look at it. It was impressive, with the big live oaks dripping Spanish moss, the deep shade, the house itself, glowering stonily in a darkness all its own. I drove once around the block, then parked in front of the house.

I didn't like the fact that this Mrs. Grace Carter had phoned me at my office. Very little business is contracted in my office. It's only a room with a desk, chair, telephone and one window looking down on Central Avenue. I sometimes go there, lock the door, and sit watching people down on the street. Every man likes to be alone occasionally. I pick up what business I get on the run; from tips at headquarters, and other sources. I use the phone once in a while, but nobody ever phones me. I just don't have that kind of business, that's all.

But she phoned. "Come out, please, right away," she said. "Irving Carter's house. This is Mrs. Carter speaking." Her voice was touched with hysteria.

I refused, drank it over that night. What the hell? It might be a fifty-dollar retainer.

It kept bothering me that she should phone me. There are big agencies in town, and they just don't come to me like that. For six years they hadn't come to me like that, so why should they start now?

I got out, slammed the car door, and crunched up a long gravel drive toward the house. Somebody had been playing croquet possibly a month ago. The grass was trimmed around the stakes, and the wire hoops; trimmed without moving them, if you get what I mean. Even the balls and mallets had been left where they'd been dropped, with little ridges of grass growing around them. I kicked one of the wooden balls, and it bounced across a cement patio and splashed into a small artificial lake. I crossed the patio, crossed the gallery, and stared at the brass knocker on the door. It was a heavy sword, about three feet long, hung blade-up. I grabbed the handle, swung it out and let it slam against the brass plate beneath it. It sounded like a battering ram.

The house was sprawling. Somebody with a lot of money had built the place, maybe seventy years ago. Of shipped-in stones. I would have liked to have had the price for transit.

"You're William Death?"

I looked inside the suddenly open door.

It was a woman. They're always cautious about my name, and I don't much blame them. We Deaths were in America to welcome the Pilgrims when they landed, so it's a bit late to think of changing the name now. Besides, my old man was devilish proud of it. He used to say he was Death to everybody, but particularly the ladies. My mother didn't much like that.

"Yes," I said to this woman.

"I'm Grace Carter, Mrs. Irving Carter, that is." She backed inside. I nodded and looked at her. She was worth a long look. She was rangy, tall, strong-looking. She wore an oyster-white dress that clung all over, like scotch tape. Her hair was black and wiry, in rich, heavy waves, and she had hot, smoky eyes the color of charcoal. She had a good chin and a nice mouth; it drooped sulkily, with a full lower lip.

I stepped inside.

She closed the door and leaned against it for a second. The carpet under my feet had the same feel as the grass outside, turfy and rich. It was like a church inside the house, with the sun gleaming through windows and dust motes crawling in the sunbeams. Somewhere in the house a clock chimed three, musically.

"We needed you yesterday—and now it's too late to save him."

Somewhere miles away, in another world, a car horn honked.

She looked at me hard, then ran her left hand across the door. "It's my husband," she said.

Suddenly she was all action, her chin leading her off down the hall toward a sweep of circular stairs. "Come with me, please, Mister—Death."

Tagging along, I tried to see as much of the house as I could. She moved ahead of me up the stairs, though, so I decided to watch her legs.

Somewhere up above us somebody coughed once. It was a male cough. We approached land ahead, in the form of a rail-less platform covered with more ankle-deep carpet, blood-colored, and salted with heavy sofas and chairs like a hotel lobby.

"Rather large," I said.

She didn't answer. She went down the hall, trailing a mild and expensive perfume. She stopped at a closed door, opened it, and stood aside for me to enter.

A man stood, his broad back to me, at the far side of the room in front of a cold fireplace made entirely of black, cast-iron. In its exact center was a burning match. It went out just as I looked, and at the same instant, the man turned and blew his first lungful of cigarette smoke with a grimace of agitation.

I turned to Mrs. Carter. She dry-washed her hands, pacing up and down the room, not looking at either of us.

"Glad to meet you, Mister Carter," I said, stepping toward the man, with my hand stretched out.

He made a noise in this throat, dropped his cigarette. "I'm not—!" he said.

Mrs. Carter turned. The pupils of her eyes were like black tunnels in a coal mine. "I'm sorry, Mister Death. This is Kirk Adams." She wrung her hands some more.

I nodded. Adams recovered enough to step away from the fireplace and stare at me. I stared back. He had sandy hair, clipped very short, and a meaty, pink face that looked harried. His eyes were very clear blue, as though somebody had made two heavy splashes of clear blue water color paint on his eyeballs. His teeth showed all the time and they looked as if they were carved with precision out of a cake of white soap. He wore a gray-brown tropical worsted suit and his hands were freckled on their backs. He was so nervous he was ready to fly right through the ceiling.

The room was furnished like an extra-large living room, only on the heavy side.

"Police? Grace, you said yesterday you'd get a private detective."

"Meet Mister Death, Kirk. That's what he is."

He stared at her, then began to blink rapidly and his eyes watered. Turning, he braced his hands on the fireplace mantel and lashed his head from side to side.

I felt uncomfortable. But I was going to see this out.

"You said this was an emergency," I told Mrs. Carter. "You told me to hurry, that time was essential."

She went to a coffee table, poured three drinks and the bottle neck rattled against the glasses like buckshot in an empty skull. We all sat down, me alone on one sofa, facing them on the other.

I drank and set the empty glass on the floor.

Adams attempted to drink, but most of it spilled down his chin and shirt-front. He held the glass away and pawed at the stains.

Mrs. Carter stared at him for a minute, then looked at me. There was a strained expression on her face, and she rolled her glass between her hands.

"It's terrible," Adams said. He swallowed sharply. "It's something I would never have done, anyway. Never. I changed my mind at the last minute, like I told Grace." He paused, and his knuckles whitened around his glass. "We talked about it, but I never could have. We've decided to tell you the whole story, so you can tell us what to do."

"Dear," she said, patting his knee.

I reached over, took the glass from his hand, and set it on the floor before he spilled the rest of it in his lap.

"We called you," Mrs. Carter said, "because we need your advice—and, of course, your help. Kirk thought it was best, he insisted." She looked at Kirk and smiled.

"I'll tell you the truth," Adams said. "I was going to kill him. I really was." He clawed into this pants pocket. "With this!" He held up a long-bladed fishing knife. "But I didn't!" He turned to Mrs. Carter. "I swear it, Grace!"

"I believe you, darling," Mrs. Carter said. "Kirk was going to kill him."

Adams nodded fiercely. His voice was blurred. "When I got there, outside the door, I knew I couldn't do it," he told me. "I knew it wasn't for me. That's why we need your help. I was just going to talk to him, man to man. I stood outside the door, like that," he said. "I'd had the intent, all right, but it was gone. I couldn't."

"Go ahead, Kirk, tell him," Mrs. Carter said.

He bent his head, shivered, stared between his knees, then looked up at me. "I opened the door and went in," he said thickly. "He was dead. Shot dead." His eyes were very blue as he stared at me.

"My husband," Mrs. Carter said.

"Have you called the police?" I asked.

"Oh, no, of course not!" Mrs. Carter said. "Kirk's sure to be blamed. We had to talk to you first."

"That's not good," I said. "It should have been reported immediately." Neither of them said anything. "How long ago did it happen?"

She sliced the air with her hand. "It just happened. Hasn't been over an hour."

"Where is your husband's body?"

She gestured vaguely toward the rear of the house. "In his workshop. We didn't touch anything."

"We realized we shouldn't move the body," Adams said.

"Suppose you show me." I stood up. "You can tell me about it as we go along." I watched her as she again patted Adams and got to her feet. There was a quality of hardness about her, yet at the same time a shade of sorrow. Whether she felt real sorrow over her husband's death, or not, I wasn't certain. It was plain that Adams, not her husband, was closest to her.

Adams raked his fingers through his hair, and stood. "All right," he said. "Come on, Grace. We'll take him out there."

Mrs. Carter left the room and Adams tried to usher me ahead of himself. I jerked my head tightly. He went on ahead. I could watch them that way, not their faces, but their backs.

We started across the plateau of blood-colored rug toward the sweeping staircase. We started down, had taken perhaps eight or nine steps, when I heard a sound behind me that made the nape of my neck tingle. An anguished, throaty noise, and plodding footsteps.

We all stopped, turned in unison.

"Oh, Tippy!" Mrs. Carter cried.

"Good Lord," Adams grunted. "He's drunk again!"

Tippy drooled at us as he prowled and lurched closer across the blood-red rug. He came along the very edge of the landing, and his right foot swept space with each step.

Mrs. Carter surged past me, her mouth wide and soundless. Her voice burst out, "Oh, Tippy, Tippy, Tippy!" She dragged him away from the sheer drop. He craned his neck, staring at me.

Tippy was someplace between manhood and boyhood, in an interim of mutation that had solidified and in which he would remain. His thick, chunky body was covered with a yellow-and-green banded bathrobe, his legs jutting hairlessly to the floor and stopping in bare, stubby feet. His head was completely bald. He looked at me, white-lipped, open-mouthed, wetly. The whites of his eyes were like skimmed milk, the color of them like rain-washed yellow straw. He was obviously fried to the ears.

"How can you look at him?" Adams said by my elbow. "He makes me want to run—gives me the creeps." He kept raking his fingers through his sandy hair, cropping it like a barber about to use the shears.

"Nora!" Mrs. Carter called, turning toward a partly open door. "Nora! Come down here!"

Tippy pawed at her arm and made droning noises in his throat. He lurched against her and I saw the sick look of despair on Mrs. Carter's pretty face as she repulsed him. He staggered backward, tripped clumsily and sat down. He was startled, patted the floor with his hands, and cooed. The coo changed into a whine. The partly open door was flung wide and a young girl hurried out.

"Nora," Mrs. Carter said. "I've told you never to do that again. Have you no pride at all?"

The girl shook her blonde head and said, "Nope," in a petulant, spoiled-kid's kind of way. She wore white rayon slacks rolled nearly to her knees, and a Kelly-green sweater that was tried to the last strand of fabricated endurance. I felt like bowing. The rest of her was very good, too.

"You've fed him drinks again," Mrs. Carter said wearily. "Why, Nora?"

"Felt like it," Nora said, again with that kiddish petulance of manner as well as voice. "I'll do what I please. You do, don't you—*Mother?*" She said the last word with a viciousness full of bright hate.

Tippy slid along until he reached Nora's ankle. He placed both hands around her ankle, leaned his head against her leg and was immediately asleep. Nora brought a handkerchief from beneath her sweater and wiped Tippy's mouth. As she raised up, she saw me standing head-level with the platform.

She gleamed a white-toothed smile at me. "Who're you?"

Mrs. Carter said, "Never mind, Nora. Take Tippy to bed."

"When I'm ready," Nora said. But, keeping her smiling face on me, she bent and slapped Tippy awake, helped him up and they both went through the door. I heard them start up some stairs. Mrs. Carter moved over, closed the door, then rejoined Adams and me.

"I'm sorry," she said to me. She said nothing more.

We started through the house toward the rear, passing among large rooms dressed in very old and heavy furnishings. In the big kitchen, seated at a breakfast nook was a middle-aged woman in a black dress with a white shawl about her shoulders. She glanced up, and I was startled at sudden, striking beauty. Maybe she wasn't middle-aged and it didn't matter a damn, because a man could go to hell for those eyes, alone.

We went on out the door, across a broad back porch, and into a backyard dotted with orange and grapefruit trees. The yard was enclosed by a high board fence to the rear left of which stood a wooden shed, unpainted, and with green vines climbing its sides and eaves. From the shed came the incessant throb and whine of a motor of some kind.

As we reached the shed, Mrs. Carter said, "Inside, Mr. Death."

The throbbing was loud. On a long bench in the workshop, an electrically-driven motor turned various wheels.

On the floor in front of the bench lay the body of a man. He lay on his back, his round, surprised face stilled with death. Just below his left eye was a round hole. In the center of his gleaming forehead was another hole. Beside him, on the old, worn, plank floor, lay a twenty-two caliber bolt-action rifle.

The dead man was dressed in white flannels, white shirt, and slightly soiled white tennis shoes. A fat man, but of solid build. In his left hand he gripped a foot-long model hull of a sailboat on which he had been working.

Mrs. Carter shut off the motor by a switch near the door. Adams stared down at the body, raking his fingers through his hair, cropping and cropping.

"That is—my husband," Mrs. Carter said. She turned to me. "You'll help us, won't you, Mister Death?"

"How can I help you," I said. Then, at her sudden worried expression and the jerk of Adams' head, I said, "The police have to be notified. Private detectives are not for murder cases. And I'm not. I want that clear."

"It's clear. But we need an investigator terribly. We tried to hire you yesterday. You let us down. At least you can help us now, when we're desperate."

"I don't see how I can help, but I'll do what I can." I watched her carefully. "You know you should have called the police. Yet, you didn't. And," I said, "the set-up stinks."

Her face began to twist up and Adams said, "You have no right—!"

"Let's not argue over the body." I turned to Mrs. Carter. "Is that young girl your daughter?"

"No," she said. "My step-daughter, and Tippy is my step-son." She motioned toward the dead man. "Irving's first wife's children." She sighed.

"He was very despondent over Tippy. I'm afraid he's spoiled Nora in an effort to give her what Tippy couldn't appreciate if he had."

"Tell me," I asked Adams, "just how you came to find the body?"

He cleared his throat, glanced at the dead man, then at me. "Grace and I wanted to be married," he said. "Irving wouldn't hear of a divorce. He laughed at me whenever he saw me, although we'd never mentioned anything like that. It went on for five years, until I couldn't stand it—him hounding me, laughing—and I decided to kill him." He looked at Mrs. Carter. "I knew I couldn't. I came inside and found him—just like that." He stared at the corpse. "Somebody had already shot him with that rifle."

"Maybe he committed suicide," I said.

"Yes," Mrs. Carter said. "Yes! That could be!"

"Only I don't think so," I said. "Is that all you have to tell me, Mr. Adams?"

"Yes." He looked at the tip of his left shoe.

I shrugged, turned to her. "You knew he was going to kill your husband?"

She nodded. "Yes. I tried to dissuade him, but couldn't. Still, I didn't think it right to warn Irving." It was her turn to shrug. "Think what you wish."

"Did your husband carry insurance?"

"Why—yes."

"How much?"

"Two hundred thousand dollars."

My palms got hot. "You want me to find who killed him?"

"Yes. You see, we know Kirk is sure to be blamed. It looks so—so pat." She kept her eyes on mine for a long moment, then broke and tipped her lips with her tongue.

"Adams," I said. "You're a cinch for this. From where I stand, looking at it from the viewpoint the police will take, you'll be behind bars in an hour or so." I shook my head at the pleading movement of his head. "There's not one thing I can do about that. I'm just a private detective. I can go to jail, just like you. We'll all be in jail if I don't report this right away."

They were silent, watching me.

I said, "Who were some of your husband's enemies?" I knelt on one knee by the body and stared at Irving Carter's face, wishing a dead man's eyeballs could leave an imprint on them of their last living image.

"Well," Mrs. Carter said, "there's Howard Huston. Irve—well, ruined Huston. He caused him to lose a lot of money."

I grunted, and checked over the contents of Irving Carter's fat wallet. Then I felt a little odd.

I looked up at a long shadow that suddenly appeared across the floor before my eyes where there shouldn't have been one. Lieutenant of

Detectives, Pat Durkee, stood there frowning down at me. Behind him were
two uniformed cops.

Durkee shook his head. "Never mind putting the wallet back, Bill. I'll
just take it now." He stepped inside, brushing past Mrs. Carter and took the
wallet from my hand.

Pat Durkee and I clinched gazes.

I stood up, patted my pockets, found cigarettes, and lit one. There
wasn't a thing I could say. I was wrong. It was his move. The two harness-
cops remained outside the shed. Mrs. Carter eyed Durkee with level coolness.
Adams had the frightened air of a startled fawn.

"I overheard some of it," Durkee said finally. "You just found the
body?" He hadn't even glanced at the dead man as yet. He put the wallet in
his pocket.

"That's right," I said. "I was going to call you, Pat, right away."

"It's a good thing somebody called me."

"Who called you?" Mrs. Carter said.

He ignored her completely. "You on this as a case, Bill?"

"It interests me," I said.

"I see," Durkee said. He clawed in his shirt pocket, brought out some
apple plug, reached into his pants pocket and came up with a pen-knife. He
whittled off a healthy piece of tobacco, popped it into his mouth, and put
the plug and knife away. He began swishing the chew around in his mouth
with obvious enjoyment.

Durkee was a bag of bones. He stood about six feet in a wrinkled blue
tropical suit, pink shirt, and blue tie that was never tied tight, because the
top button on his shirt was always undone. He smelled of tobacco, garlic
and fish. His hair looked like rusty barbed wire. He was one of the best
fishermen in the district, an expert shot with any kind of gun, drank root
beer spiked strongly with rum as a steady diet, and had worked himself up
until he was a very good homicide man. His eyes looked like those of a cow,
brown and mooey. He had no lips at all, his mouth coming together like a
hard clamp, and his crooked nose was turned up at the end. I liked the guy.

He placed his cud in his left jaw and turned slowly toward Mrs. Carter.
"You want to tell me about it now?" he said.

She told him she hadn't known what to do when Mr. Adams accidentally
discovered the body of her husband. She had realized she should call the
police, but she felt Mr. Adams was on a spot, and Mister Death was here,
so . . . because she'd called him the day before, so, because.

Durkee grunted. "You're Adams?"

Adams nodded jerkily, then looked appealing at me. He told Durkee
simply that he had found the body and left everything else out. "I know it
looks peculiar," he finished lamely.

Mrs. Carter said, "Please. Who called the police?"

"A woman, name of Burley," Durkee said.

I watched Mrs. Carter's lips twist, then her lower lip began to jut.

Durkee said, "This Virginia Burley claims she heard the motor running out here in the shed and hadn't seen Carter for a while. She came out and saw him lying there, so she called the police. It looked like homicide, so I'm it." He cleared his throat, looking at me. "Bill," he said, "I'm allowing for things, but you made a serious mistake. You should have called right away. Will you take these folks into the house and wait with them? Round up everybody else and tell 'em to set."

I said I would, and we went back to the house. As we came up to the back porch, I said, "Mrs. Carter, I'll try to help you." I glanced back and one of the uniformed cops was starting toward us. "Adams," I said, "you're it."

Mrs. Carter's fingers closed on my arm. She had quite a grip. "Kirk didn't do it," she said. "He's sure to be accused. You've got to help! I want you to investigate Irving's past—help free Kirk."

I looked at her. She was some woman, all right.

"They'll have Kirk," she said. "That's all they want."

"Yes," I said. "I want you to make out a list, on paper, of every person you feel had any reason to dislike your husband. Also, each person's address. You needn't let the lieutenant know I asked you. He'll know anyway, but don't you tell him."

"All right," she said. Her gaze held thankful promise.

Adams plucked at my arm with one hand, and cropped his hair with the other. "You really think they—?"

The cop was almost up to us now.

"Yes," I said, "I do."

I was right. Durkee arrested Adams on suspicion of murder. I excused myself while they were talking in the hall, and went on out to my car.

Nora Carter was smiling at me through the window.

"What're you doing here?" I said, opening the door and staring at her. She had on a bright green two-piece bathing suit, and a white robe. The bathing suit gave an even more terrific effect than the sweater had.

She stuck her lower lip out at me, then smiled. "They let me off," she said, nodding toward the house. "I'm going swimming. I wondered if you'd be so kind as to drop me off at a place. I mean a house, of course. I'm going with somebody."

"All right."

"He's a man. Only he's not near so nice as you. I like your double chin."

"That's not a double chin," I said. "It's a cleft chin."

"Well, I like it."

She was about eighteen, acted fifteen, and looked twenty-six.

I got in and started the engine.

"I like riding with you," she said. "Maybe we could go swimming together sometime, huh?"

"Where shall I drop you off?"

"1214 Hibiscus Drive. But you don't have to. I could ride around with you."

"It's only about three blocks. You could have walked."

She chuckled. "I could have," she said. "My, it's hot in your car. Mind if I take my robe off?" She wriggled out of it. I glanced at her. She was propped in the corner against the door, watching me with a wet-lipped smirk, her left leg buckled up on the seat, the other slanting straight to the floor. That leg was curved like a piece of Rodin sculpture.

I said, "Mrs. Carter isn't your real mother, eh, Nora?"

She said, "Uh-uh. But you met my real mother."

My mouth began to open.

"She was wearing a black dress. She's the one called the police when she found Daddy dead."

"Miss Virginia Burley?"

"Yep. That's my mother."

"Don't you think you should stay at the house?"

"Don't start that!" she snapped. "I don't care what they think. They can think what they want. Daddy's dead and nothing can help that. I can't see getting all excited about it."

I cleared my throat.

"Grace doesn't care, and mother does, maybe, but it doesn't matter. And I don't care."

"I see." I turned into Hibiscus Drive, and started looking for 1214. I braked the car. She opened the door, then leaned over by me and gripped my arm with her right hand and smiled.

"I like you," she said. "I really like you."

Nora got out of the car, grabbed up her robe and a red bag with a long red-leather strap on it. She stood on tip-toe and revolved before the open door of the car.

"Like it?" she said.

"It's a nice bathing suit."

"Not the bathing suit—Me!" She scampered up the winding walk, flung open the front door of the low-roofed cottage and vanished inside.

I lit a cigarette. I found the piece of paper in my pocket with the list of names on it that Grace Carter had given me.

At the third name and address I stopped. Alfred Shane, 1214 Hibiscus Drive.

I turned and looked at the low-roofed cottage. The house number was done in chromium-plated scroll-work, and jammed into the front lawn with spikes. The numerals stood a little over a foot high. 1214.

I slid across the seat of my car, and stepped onto the curb. The house door burst open.

It was Nora. She was screaming as she backed out of the door. She cringed backward, screaming in a series of lungless shrieks. She ceased abruptly and ran at me down the walk.

Her eyes were gray holes of horror. She saw me and screamed again. She backstepped, turned to run. I bounded at her, grabbed her arms above the elbows. She kneed me and shrieked. I doubled with pain. Her nails raked at me like the prongs of a fork. I still held her with my left hand. She bent her head, her hair wild and blonde, and sank her teeth into my wrist. I let go.

She ran off down the sidewalk, out across the street and with her legs flashing whitely, headed directly into a field of tall grass. She was barefoot. The sandspurs wouldn't be comfortable.

I looked at the purple teeth marks on my wrist. My stomach felt like it was full of broken glass and torn hunks of jagged tin. I limped along the winding walk toward the cottage.

The living room was furnished in good taste with light-colored wicker chairs, rattan couch, and tables. There were vari-colored scatter-rugs on the highly-polished floors, and a radio in the corner gave out with some poor bop. Afternoon waned softly through partially-closed Venetian blinds.

In the center of the room, I spotted Nora's red bag, lying on the floor, with the usual feminine implements of witchery tumbled out. I scraped them into the bag, hung the strap over my shoulder.

In the dining room, I found her white robe. I wadded it up and stuck it under my arm. Then I saw the hand.

The hand was in the form of a claw, tendon-strained, clutching at nothing. It jutted past the kitchen door-jamb, on the floor. I walked over and stood with my right foot an inch from the hand and looked down into the dead man's face.

I touched the hand with my toe. It went abruptly limp, began to move upward from its twisted position above the man's head, jerked, and flopped on the linoleum floor.

All the shock of sudden death was on the man's face. He was about forty-five, iron-gray hair, medium build, and with a fairly strong-willed face. Three small-calibered bullets had entered his throat. I figured they were twenty-two's again. There was no gun anywhere around. It looked like he had scrabbled around on the floor quite a bit, and finally died beneath the stove, twisted into a knot. A chair was tipped over and blood was smeared in a winding trail all over the kitchen floor.

I went back to the living room with Nora's robe over my one shoulder, and her red bag over the other. There was no phone on the desk. Nothing else was there of interest except a framed photograph of a young man who resembled the dead man in the kitchen. Not the same man, but maybe the same blood. Thinner, he was, with a weaker face, not as much chin and with a rather droopy mouth.

I sat down on the desk chair, and flipped open the top middle drawer of the desk. Letters. Addressed to Alfred Shane. Others to Alfred Shane, Jr. His letters smelled of different perfumes.

I decided against going through all the letters. I found the phone book, got up and shut off the radio, checked Irving Carter's number and dialed.

Mrs. Carter answered.

"This is William Death," I said. "Is Lieutenant Durkee still there?"

"No. I'm so glad you called. They took Kirk away. Kirk is frightened—and I am."

"Do you know Alfred Shane very well?"

"I know him," she admitted. "He was on that list."

"All right," I said. "Look, Mrs. Carter. Where is Adams' home?"

"Over on Bayside. At the Bay-View Apartments. I've never been there. But that's where he lives."

"Did he know Alfred Shane?"

"Yes. Do you think Kirk will be all right?"

I showed my teeth to the phone mouthpiece. "It's a little sticky," I said. "But, O. K., Mrs. Carter. I'll keep in touch."

I heard her gasp, and she said, "My, here's Nora! She's a sight. Nora! Where's the top to your bathing suit?"

I hung up, and dialed Captain Holland's desk, at headquarters. Holland said, "Uh?"

"This is Bill Death. Did Durkee get back there yet?"

"No."

"I just stumbled on a body. Alfred Shane. 1214 Hibiscus Drive."

"Who did it?"

"How do I know?"

"How?"

"Shot."

"Two in one day. They're going nuts."

"It looks like a twenty-two."

"Did you find the body? Is anybody else there? You wait where you are."

I walked out and looked at the body again. The phone began ringing. I turned, still with Nora's robe and red bag, and started back through the house.

I went on out to the car. The phone kept on ringing.

As I parked before the Bay-View Apartments, a hippy girl in too-tight yellow shorts, fuzzy purple sweater and high-heeled shoes, swayed out of the double doorway with three well-groomed Irish setters on leashes, and legged away on the walk lock-step fashion.

The apartment building had an imposing façade of bent glass, brick and cement, modernistically molded, with large windows and balconies.

I shoved through the doors. Lush carpeting of maroon, and a general atmosphere of shine and cheapness. Rap your knuckles against the wall and you likely rap through the wall. I found Kirk Adams' name and apartment number on his mailbox. I went up the maroon carpeted steps three at a time. I found one-oh-two and used my passkey.

Venetian blinds were closed. I walked across and flicked them open. Living and bedroom combined, the studio couch in the corner was still rumpled with last night's sleep.

The police hadn't been here yet. A large bookcase in the two corners beyond the bed was filled with books. Best-sellers, adventure and love-in-the-jungle stuff. A large, brown-covered volume's gold lettering stood out. SEXUAL CUSTOMS OF SAVAGES THE WORLD OVER. I plucked it out and glanced on the inside cover. It was inscribed in red ink: "Kirk: To keep you home on those occasional lonely nights, Grace." I flipped another page to the title page and paused again. Beneath the title, in the same hand and also red ink, were the words, "Or, How To Improve Your Technique!" I glanced further. Certain passages were checked with red ink. I started to put the volume back and something fell from between the pages. It was a photo of Grace Carter. She was holding her skirts waist high, while standing in water, and she had exceptional legs. She was smiling, her jetty hair foaming about her shoulders. I stuck the photo back inside the book and replaced it.

There was a flat desk just outside the bathroom door. I looked in the bathroom, then sat at the desk. There was a large exotic photo of Mrs. Carter on the desk. The lighting was from the rear, playing across her hair and against the outer edges of cheekbone, throat and shoulders. Her lips . . . I reached for the phone, called the Carter address.

A soft voice was musical in my ear. "This would be the detective with the exciting name, would it not?"

"It would be," I said. "Miss Burley. We haven't met, and I dislike having to do this over the phone, but would you mind answering a few questions?"

"I cannot say that I'm delighted, Mr. Death. But if you insist, and need answers. . . ."

"Thanks. What can you tell me of Kirk Adams?"

"You embarrass me, Mr. Death," came the musical voice. "You mean, do I think Mr. Adams killed Irving?"

"I don't mean to embarrass you," I said.

"Mr. Adams very well could have killed Irving," Virginia Burley said. "He had every reason to wish Irving dead. He borrowed money from Irving a year or so ago to start a store of his own, but I believe he lost it gambling. Some eight or ten thousand dollars. Irving tormented the man, Mr. Death. It was a joke to Irving, who didn't really care if he got the money back. Adams couldn't pay. Irving hounded him at every opportunity. And, of course, Irving knew about Grace and Mr. Adams." She paused. "In fact," she said, "Irving came upon Grace and Mr. Adams one time when they least expected it."

"Bad?" I said.

"Bad."

"You don't like Mrs. Carter, I take it?"

"I hate her," Virginia Burley said. "Irving fully understood what was going on. But rather than divorce Grace, allowing her to have her freedom, he let her do as she chose, keeping her on tenterhooks. He pretended he knew little or nothing. He passed shocking remarks at remarkably inappropriate moments. Mr. Adams is so confounded with Grace's ways that he cannot think straight."

"You hate her, yet you live there—why?"

"I felt sorry for Irving. My children are here."

This set-up beat me.

"Eh, Alfred Shane. You knew him?"

"Yes, I knew him. Nora says he was shot. Nora has been running with Mr. Shane's son."

"Something normal, anyway."

"Don't be too certain," she said.

I changed hands with the phone-piece. My palm was beginning to perspire.

"Yes," Virginia Burley said. "Adams found out that Grace was seeing the elder Shane. And Irving knew. Grace only had to cut through the backyards to Alfred Shane's home."

"You're certainly enlightening," I said.

"There's more," she told me. "Kirk Adams escaped the police on the way to jail."

"What?" I nearly dropped the phone.

"You see, they didn't handcuff him or anything. Lieutenant Durkee called only a short while ago, and told me to report it if Adams shows up. He pushed open the police car door and jumped right out while they were moving in traffic. One of the policemen fired a gun at him, but he got away. They think they hit him as they found blood on some bushes."

"He's signed his own death warrant."

I hung up and sat there, staring at nothing. I began opening the desk drawers. The revolver was in the first drawer on the right side and I saw it was a twenty-two target gun. I held it in my hand. It was a six-shot revolver, and five of the shells were spent. One remained. It smelled of recent use.

A twenty-two wasn't good for killing people; too small a caliber. The killer had proved that being a good shot was all that counted; striking a vulnerable point. I was willing to bet that ballistics would prove this gun to be the murder weapon—not the stock twenty-two rifle in Carter's shed.

I laid the gun on the desk and started to prowl the room. I went over to a closet, opened the door. Kirk Adams' clothing was arranged neatly on hangers. I proceeded slowly to check the contents of the pockets.

I heard the door-latch click, and turned. The door opened and Kirk Adams stepped into the room. His face was twisted. The left shoulder of his brown suit was soaked with blood.

He grunted and came at me. He sobbed deep in his throat.

I tried to dodge, said, "Adams! For God's sake, I'm trying to help you!"

"Liar!" he gasped. "You were waiting here for me!"

He swung a vicious right. He was too bushed to connect.

I stepped in low, blocked the right, and let him have my fist in the midriff. Adams gasped, stepped back with a shuffling two-step.

I grabbed for his arms, said, "Cut it out, you fool! I'm trying to help you!"

"Liar," he said weakly.

I released him and something connected with my jaw that felt like a brick-bat. I windmilled backward into the clothes closet, sat on the floor, trying to clear my head.

Adams said, "Now, by God!"

I sprawled out into the room.

Adams moved in. He held his fishing knife raised high. The blade was long, slim and gently hooked at the end. It gleamed as he leaped.

I pushed off with my feet against the doorjamb, and struck him in the shins. He piled over on top of me. I heard a dull *thwack!* Adams was wrestling with the knife. It had stuck into the floor.

As I came at him, he gave up the knife and kicked at me. I tripped and sprawled across the room into the bookcase.

I lunged up and found him facing me with the twenty-two revolver in his hand. He panted, holding the gun in his left hand, his left shoulder and arm dark with blood. With his right he cropped his hair. He licked his lips, and said, "Don't move." Blood ran from his nose down either side of his mouth giving him a kind of Fu-Manchu mustache.

"Don't be a fool," I said. I stood stiffly, trying to get my breath.

He shook his head, his blue eyes narrow and intense, the bright blue color standing out like two glinting marbles.

"There's six shots in this gun," he gasped. "If I have to, I'll use them. I'm a good shot, Death." He changed the gun to his right hand.

"How many shells in that gun?"

"Six. Now, get over against that wall."

He jabbed the gun at the air in front of him.

"Wait, Adams," I said. "Maybe you didn't pull those murders. Because there's only one shell in that gun."

The gun turned to a hot piece of metal in his hand and he nearly dropped it. I didn't move. He checked it, his eyes flicking at me like blue wasps.

"Everybody's against me," he choked. "I didn't do it. I'll show 'em. By God, I'll show 'em. Beginning with you." Two and two made three. His eyes had widened and glazed over, he reeled slightly with loss of blood.

"Alfred Shane is dead," I told him. "Shot with that gun you're holding, Adams."

"Shane?" he said. "Shane, dead, too? My gun."

"Give yourself up, Adams," I said. "They'll only get you. You may be killed. Anybody who can break away from the law like you've done has already worn his luck out."

"Shut up!" He was thinking, cropping his hair, and grimacing. "Carter's done this—Carter! He's tried to ruin me." He choked and began to tremble.

"Carter's dead," I reminded him.

He glared at me and began jabbing that gun at me again, his knuckles white on the butt and fine perspiration on his forehead. His stance was that of a fencer, his right foot thrust forward. He shuffled in at me, jabbing the gun.

"Cut it out, Adams!"

"Hah!" He lunged. I tried to dodge, but the bookcase brought me up short. He whipped the gun down against the left side of my head. I crumpled. Then I thought I heard laughter and everything went away.

She didn't have her three Irish setters with her now. She was dressed the same, with the tight yellow shorts, the purple sweater, and the extra-long, cream-colored legs in spike-heels.

"Well, hello!" The voice was hoarse, low-pitched. I strained, saw something of the room. Dressing table, on the bench before which the girl sat with her legs crossed. The windows were pink-curtained. I tried to raise up. I saw her grin, rise toward me, and then I blacked out again. It was like being smothered with a wet blanket.

I couldn't have been unconscious very long this time, because when I came around, she was still coming toward me, saying, ". . . and a very nasty old bump, too."

I grunted. She took something off the side of my head that felt like a large piece of scalp, then patted my cheek with a perfumed palm. The something was a washcloth. My head buzzed and rocked painfully, and my left ear rang like a continuous gong.

"Right back," she assured me, and started toward the bathroom. I watched the tight molten bunching of her hips. The water started to run in the bathroom.

It hurt my head when I tried to concentrate, so I let my thoughts wander. The one thing that kept beating in my brain was the assurance that there was something bigger than I knew behind the Carter business. It wasn't just a love-nest killing; it wasn't a jealous husband deal. I don't know what it was that kept telling me that. But I felt it.

I tried to remember what I could about Irving Carter. I'd heard of him, of course. Retired, and supposedly with plenty of money. That's about all I knew. There had been plenty more. A wild daughter, a faithless wife and her lover, a previous wife living in the same house, an idiot son.

"Hello, again," the girl said. She approached, her thighs moving with an effortless grace that was pleasing to my tired eyes. She carefully placed the cool washcloth against my head. It felt good.

I began to feel better, the head aching, but not sickishly, as it had done. I sat up, putting my feet on the floor. The room caved in, swirled around, then jarred to an abruptly shocking halt. I'd fallen back on the bed. I sat up again and was all right. I stood. My knees caved, but I felt all right.

She watched me with an elusive grin, her dark blue eyes calm.

"O. K.," I said. "What's it all about? How'd I get here?"

"I brought you here," she said. "You're heavy, too. I had to drag you. Would you like a drink?"

"Sure," I said. "Where're your dogs?"

She went across the room to the dressing table. There was an unopened bottle on it, two glasses, and a pitcher of ice. A closet door, open, to her left, showed empty. "They aren't my dogs," she said. She poured two healthy drinks, plopped in an ice cube each, and returning, handed me one.

"To crime," I said.

She frowned slightly, shrugged, and drank. It was good, and I began to feel almost human. I was hungry. My head ached like blazes.

"We're just across from the room you were in," she said.

We drank. She sat on the bed, crossed her legs.

"All right," I said. "I give up. Who are you?"

"Me? I'm just a gal who lives across the hall from where you got sapped on the head."

"I mean, your name?"

"Cadillac Smith."

"What?" I looked at her, and she was peering at me steadfastly, utterly serious.

"Oh, the name. Yes. Well, you see my father courted mother in a Cadillac. I was conceived in a Cadillac. Then father was—died in a Cadillac. I was born in still another Cadillac on the way to the hospital. A cream-colored one. The Cadillac, I mean. So poor old Mom thought she might as well name me Cadillac, for luck, or something. But all I've seen for the most part since then are second-hand jalopies. My friends call me Caddy."

I stared at her.

"I keep hoping," she said. "You drive a Ford, don't you?"

"You could call it that," I said. "And Smith is just—"

"—a good old American name."

We both drank.

"You have a rather striking name yourself," she said.

I felt for my wallet. She brought it from beneath her sweater and handed it to me. It was warm. "Thanks," I said. "Yes."

She leaned toward me, held my head with her right hand and studied the bruise. "It'll be all right," she said. "The police are over there now."

"Police!" I jumped up, and moved to the door, placing my empty glass on the dressing table. I opened the door a crack and looked through. I spotted Pat Durkee standing inside Adams' room across the hall. He was looking for a place to spit and seemed uncomfortable about it. A uniformed cop was standing in the hallway humming, "Flow Gently Sweet Afton . . ."

"Is that what they get paid for?" she whispered in my ear. She was pressed against me, peering over my shoulder, the warmth of her body and the smell of her getting into my blood.

I closed the door softly and turned toward her. She didn't move and we stood together that way for a few seconds breathing at each other. She broke first, turned her back on me and didn't say anything.

"O. K., Caddy," I said. "You won't spill."

She shook her head, the little bunch of blonde hair bobbing comically. I happened to glance past her into the dressing table mirror and saw her face. She was biting her lip, and I swear there were tears in her eyes.

She whirled. "Why don't you get out of here?" Her chin trembled just a little and then she was hard again, cynical and knowing.

"O. K.," I said. "I've got a hunch we'll meet again, Caddy."

"I hope not," she said. "For your sake, I hope not."

"Where did the man go who hit me?"

"He beat it."

"Give me a break, Caddy."

She pointed toward the door with her hip. "You can't leave until they go, eh?"

"I can leave any time," I said. "But I'd rather not speak to Durkee now."

She filled our glasses again and said with her back turned, "Why were you in that man's room? What'd he do?"

"It won't work, Caddy."

She hesitated, then picked up her glass and hurled it against the wall. "All right!" she said. "Then get out of here!" She moved across the room and stood before the window, looking out. Her hands were clinched in front of her. "Please," she said. "Get out of here, will you?"

I looked at the wall where the glass had smashed, and the whisky was mingling with the pink paint.

"Somebody won't like the way you're acting," I said.

"So, they won't."

I noticed her purse on the chair. A large, black purse. I went over and opened it. She turned, watched me, her eyes saucer-round and blue, her face expressionless as I drew out a .32 revolver. A folded piece of paper caught my eye and I opened it. All it said was, "Call Ralph Flaxen." I put it back.

She sighed, turned back to the window.

I dropped the revolver into the purse, snapped it shut, and put the purse back on the chair.

"Why are you here, Caddy? Why'd you bring me here?"

Silence. The room was becoming darker.

"Caddy," I said and she turned to me, still without expression. "Who is Ralph Flaxen?"

I thought she shivered, but I could have been wrong.

"You've got until the police leave," she said.

"I telegraphed that one, huh? I'm a dope," I said.

"Yes," she said, "you're a dope. A big dope."

I moved over to the door, opened it a crack, and looked through. Adams' door was closed, the hall empty. "They've gone," I said.

She watched me with calm, blinking eyes.

"Goodbye, Caddy—for now."

She didn't answer. I went on out into the hall, closed the door. There was a light at the far end of the hall by a fire-escape door; a red bulb. I headed for the stairs.

Nobody was in the lobby. I hurried outside to my car, got in and started off. The old coupe made a lousy grunting effort, staggered sidewise toward the middle of the road. I stopped and got out.

Not one, but *all four* tires had been neatly sliced with a knife.

"Hey!"

I looked around.

"Hey, dope! Up here!"

I looked up. It was Cadillac Smith, leaning from a second-story window.

"Get a move on," she said. "Get out of here." She vanished and the window closed.

I got Nora Carter's white robe and red bag out of the car and started walking toward town. Cadillac Smith, I thought. What a name. What a dame, for that matter.

It was suppertime and the streets were quiet, beginning to shadow down. I walked nine blocks to Tim Donneker's Service Station. Not a taxi showed itself all the way and the only bus I saw passed me by because I wasn't at a bus stop. I spent most of the nine blocks thinking about Cadillac Smith. Whatever her job had been, she had failed. I wondered who hired her, and what for? She'd made a stab at trying to find out what I was after, and that was all.

Donneker held a greasy rag in one hand and a greasy ham sandwich in the other, his sallow cheeks puffed with chewing. I told him about my car and asked him to take care of it, thinking how four new tires would come out of the expense account I'd tender Mrs. Carter.

"And, Tim," I said, "have you got a car I can borrow? I'll be needing one till my heap's running again."

He had one, a gray, two-door sedan. He gassed it up and turned the keys over to me. "Where's the dame?" he asked.

"What dame?"

He gestured at the white robe and red bag I carried.

"She went home."

There were lights lit in Alfred Shane's home. I parked the car and started up the walk.

"Hold it up," somebody said. A sober-faced cop stepped off the porch, and frowned at me. I knew him slightly, and he remembered me. I didn't know his name. His harness creaked and he had a pose of resting his right hand-heel on the butt of his holstered police .38.

"Durkee said if you was to come by to call him," the cop told me. "Durkee's mad about something."

"Yeah? Who's inside?"

"Nobody," he said, then grinned. "No body, get it?"

"How about his son? He been around?"

"Nobody," he said and started to grin again.

"Mind if I take a look around?"

"I ain't supposed to let anybody in—" He started to grin *again*. He was startling himself with his own jokes.

"Look," I said. "I'll only be a minute." I pushed past him and went on inside. The lights were all lit. I started clawing through the desk and got through one drawer of junk when the cop came in.

He shook his head at me, his right hand jammed on his gun butt in fine fashion. "None of that," he said.

"All right." I quit, and left the house. I thought I saw movement across the street behind a shoulder-high hedge of trimmed Australian pine. I couldn't be certain. I slipped behind the wheel. There was somebody across the street.

I slammed the car away from the curb, cut diagonally across into a driveway, threw open the door and leaped toward the sidewalk. I reached her before she had a chance to take three steps.

This time I didn't give her any leeway with the knee and fingernail etiquette. I grabbed her wrists and shoved my left hip into her hard.

"Whoof!" she pouted. "All right. So you got me. So what?" She kept wriggling and I held her tight.

"C'mon, get in the car." I twisted her arm. She looked at me, her eyes cunning, her lips half-parted. I twisted harder. She began to tremble and her mouth hung open a little more; she surged tight against me, her eyes wide as she said, "Go ahead, brother—that feels good, too!"

I walked her over to the car. She got in and slipped across to the other side of the seat. I climbed in behind the wheel.

"You've got a good start, for one so young," I said.

She was still breathing hard. "Yeah?"

I reached over and yanked her skirt over her legs.

"Bother you?" she said.

I brought the white robe and red bag out of the rear seat. "Here," I told her. "These are yours. You forgot them this afternoon."

I drove away. I glanced at Nora Carter. She hadn't moved, still lay there leering at me, only her mouth was closed, her teeth clenched with her lips pulled back and I could hear the hiss of her breath above the sound of the car.

"Nora," I said. "Where's Alfred Shane, Junior?"

"Went away."

"Where?"

"Don't know."

"This afternoon?"

"Yeah."

"How do you know he went away?"

"Saw 'im. He told me."

"You mean he just went away, without saying anything to anybody?"

"That's right."

"Did he say where he was going, Nora?"

"No." She sat stiffly on the edge of the seat. Her face was chalk-white in the dash lights, and her lips had gone thin.

I looked down. Her hands were clenched into her knees, her fingers biting into her knees. She kept swallowing sharply.

"Hurry up!" she said. "Take me home!"

"What were you doing across the street like that?"

"Watching."

I drew up in front of the Carter place. She flipped the door open and ran off in the darkness toward the house. Her red bag and white robe were still on the seat. I slumped behind the wheel.

I was right back where I'd started.

I opened the door to my apartment fifteen minutes later, and stopped in my tracks. The lights were lit. Mrs. Grace Carter was seated in my most comfortable chair, smoking a cigarette and reading a copy of a police manual of mine.

She looked up as I entered. "Oh, hello, there."

I nodded, slammed the door. They were going to break me down if they kept it up. Then I remembered how Irving Carter had looked with the two bullet holes in his face.

She was wearing a wine-colored dress of some soft material.

"I just left your step-daughter," I told her.

Mrs. Carter's lower lip got sulky and she massaged the back of her neck beneath the thick softness of her black hair. Her eyes got hard, the pupils hollow and dark. "I've washed my hands of Nora."

"Doesn't it bother you having Virginia Burley in the same house?"

Her eyes went cold. "Why?"

"Because she was your husband's former wife."

She shrugged.

"You didn't answer me," I said.

"Do I have to?"

"You don't have to do anything. What do you want?" I asked.

"I've a new job for you. I don't want you to try to help Kirk. Not anymore. I want you to prove that Kirk did kill Irving."

I stared at her. Her eyes were filled with fire now, but she hadn't moved a muscle.

"It's obvious that Kirk Adams did kill Irving. I'm sorry, but that's the way it is. He shouldn't have lied to me, told me he didn't. I would never have called you in. I would have thought of something else, and Kirk and I would have been together now."

"Would you? You don't want Kirk Adams. You've been tired of him for a long time. You wanted something new—and now Shane's dead."

She stared at me with her eyes blank and glazed over.

"Yeah," I said. "And now you don't want me to finish the job I started. Why?"

She cursed me. She stared at me and started to cry, then she began laughing. She bent over double with it, laughing at the floor.

I went over to my bookcase and found my bottle of Irish. I took it into the kitchenette and fixed two whiskies over rocks and brought her one. She was quiet, now. She accepted the drink.

Finally I said, "Have you seen Adams?"

"No." She stared at her lap, then glanced at me. I watched her stand up. She was tall, and she was sure put together. She took her purse from the chair she'd been sitting in and started for the door.

"Just a minute," I said. She didn't stop. I leaped over, matched her at the door, and handed her Nora's white robe and red bag.

She took them. She opened the door and I stood there listening to the rap of her heels as she went down the hall.

I phoned headquarters and was told that I might be able to reach Lieutenant Durkee at his home. I called his home and Pat answered.

"Look, Pat. Did you get the gun, the twenty-two revolver in Adams' room?"

"Gun? What gun?"

I groaned. I told him what had happened to me.

"That's great," he said. "The rifle wasn't the gun used on Carter. That must mean Adams took the gun with him. Where'd you go?"

"Just checking around. Have you heard anything—any reports on Adams?"

"Nope. Nothing."

1. Howard Huston
    Orange Blossom Hotel

2. Pete Springer
    Owner bait camp, Dead Man's Cove.

3. ~~Alfred Shane~~
    ~~1214 Hibiscus Drive~~

4. Walter Blake
    Blake Realty, Central Ave.

5. Roland Smith—?

I read the list over again, then added in pencil:

6. Ralph Flaxen—?

The whole thing was a tangle. I didn't see light anyplace. Grace Carter had had motive enough to kill her husband, but why Alfred Shane? Besides, she had seemed truly interested in helping Adams. But now she hated Adams.

It was seven-thirty. I went out and grabbed two hamburgs and a cup of coffee at a nearby restaurant, then headed for the Orange Blossom Hotel.

It was a run-down, ramshackle wooden building fronting on the bay. I parked the car, got out, went into the four-story hotel. It had swaybacked balconies stretching across the front of each floor, with rotting wooden columns bracing it, strengthened here and there by two-by-fours nailed against the original wood.

The lobby was a dim, dank room with dusty, threadbare, colorless carpet, torn leather chairs, and a desk at the far side. A drunk was asleep on a leather couch, snoring.

I went over to the desk. A fat, grubby-looking clerk got up off a bench and shuffled over to me, clutching a copy of a magazine in one claw. The magazine had no reading matter, but lots of pictures of lush women sprawled across its pages.

"You have a Howard Huston living here?"

"He ain't here."

"He lives here?"

"He did, but he don't no more."

He wanted to get back to his magazine.

"Where can I find him?"

"Ah, try Jack's Place. Across the street, up there. He might be there. I think he's in." He eyed me some more. "I warn you, he's probley boiled."

He wasn't at Jack's Place, but one of the boys—a tattered fisherman of about twenty-two, pickled in alcohol, and in his bare feet, with the wildest shakes I'd ever seen—said, "Listen, listen, listen—Howey's at the boat. The ship, he's at. Over at the ways. Ah, ha, ha, ha! Howey's there!" He did a little dance in front of me and slapped his hands together and some of the other customers laughed. "Excuse me," he said, "I really got 'em. Gotta keep movin'. Excuse me. Gotta keep movin', or I'll die." He shuffled around in his bare feet, quite friendly and amiable, and said, "You'll find him at the ship." Then he stopped shaking, stood perfectly still, and appeared quite sober. "Just two doors down. Tuttle's Marine Ways. The *Gypsy Queen*."

The *Gypsy Queen* was in dry dock, a fishing sloop, up on a wooden rack, with a ladder leading up to the deck. I read the name in the dim yellow light from a bare bulb against the side of a shed, and climbed the ladder.

Loud snoring came from up forward someplace. I started along the deck and tripped over some tin pans, sprawled against a wooden crate and barked my shin. It made a racket. The snoring continued.

I felt through the hole that was the companion way and then reached in with my foot. A ladder went straight down. I stepped down. It was about six steps before my feet reached a curved surface. Moonlight entered at the companionway. There were bunks racked on either side of me, slanting into a triangle at the bow. My head would have bumped the bulkhead if I hadn't bent down. On the middle bunk on the left a man sprawled, snoring. I shook him.

He came awake like a shot, tried to pile out of the bunk. I shoved him back. "It's all right, Huston," I said. "I just want to talk."

He stared at me. He was heavy-set, broad of shoulder, wearing a sweat-shirt and jeans. His face was bearded. He rubbed his nose and said, "Yeah, what is it?" He reached beneath his bunk and lifted an opened bottle of beer. He drank it off thirstily, tossed the bottle to the floor.

I gave him a cigarette, took one myself, and we lit up. His hands shook horribly with the match. I noted his eyes. They were intelligent eyes, for all their despair, and they were waiting and watching.

"Do you know Irving Carter?"

His reaction was immediate and loud. "Get out of here! Get off this ship, you!"

"Now wait a minute."

He tried to get up. I shoved him back. "When'd you see Carter last?"

"Did he send you here to haunt me?"

"No."

"What's he done now?"

"He got himself killed," I said.

He sat quietly, his feet on the floor, puffing his smoke. "So, Irving is dead."

"Yes."

"Who did it?"

"I don't know."

"Who are you?"

"Just a friend."

"So, I'm supposed to have killed 'im, that it? Is that it? And you're a flatfoot, right?"

"No. I just want to talk."

He stared at his feet and dragged at the cigarette until the ash was a popping red amber. "I suppose they'd naturally come to me. I have every reason for wanting him dead. I'm glad he's dead. I would have liked to have killed him mister, believe me. But I never had the nerve."

"Why did you want him dead?"

He reached beneath his bunk, brought up a bottle of beer. Then he grinned and uncapped the bottle with his teeth, spat the cap to the floor, and drank.

"You ever meet his wife—Grace?" he said.

"Yes."

"I used to call her 'wiggles.' She was my wife, once." His voice was hoarse now, and he looked mad, a cigarette in one hand, and his bottle of beer in the other. "Yes, I wanted him dead. Carter broke me, finished me. She was never any good, but neither was I. We were a good pair, Grace and I. I was a doctor, that's how I met her. Then Carter met her, and got her. Only before he took her away, he ruined me."

"What do you mean?"

"Just started talk about me dealing with dope. Things like that. My practice fell off. I drank, gambled. Went to the dogs. Then he loaned me money. A lot of money. Then, when I got started, and on my feet again, he sued me for what I owed him. I couldn't pay. He cleaned me, and took Grace. She divorced me. Mental cruelty. I'm forty-two years old," he told me. "Think of it. Washed up. But the things I cared about, I don't care about anymore."

"Where did Carter make his money?" I asked.

"Ah, nobody really knows," he said. "But I think he was neck-deep in gambling. He either got out somehow before they started the clean-up, or he stashed the money. He worked it somehow, I'm sure of that." He drained the beer, dropped the bottle on the floor. "I think I'll get drunk," he said. "I was weak, I admit it. I listened to him—he had a glib tongue. He was smart. Just a little smarter than I was."

"You know his daughter, Nora?"

He looked at me and leered. "She'll end up in an institution, you watch. I hear she's gone high hat."

"Yeah," I agreed. "Well, much obliged. By the way, d'you know a bird named Flaxen? Ralph Flaxen?"

He pursed his lips, shook his head. "No."

I started up the ladder. When I got to the top, I looked down. "Good luck, Huston," I said. "Why don't you give it a try again? Ghosts don't bite."

"That's all you know about it," he said.

Dead Man's Cove was on the bay.

I found Pete Springer's place finally, after driving through winding jungle roads, getting lost twice, doubling back, and then practically running the car onto his back porch. He rented boats to fisherman and sold bait.

There was a kerosene lamp burning in the shack of a house, and four or five kids scrabbled on the floor as I knocked on the screen door.

A tired-face woman answered my knock.

"Pete here?"

"He's out on the pier." She turned and walked into the room. She was barefoot, and her dress was smeared.

I picked my way past some raddled cabbage palms to the beach, where fiddler crabs scurried in waves and sounded like dry leaves.

The moon was bright and I was thankful for that. I walked past two rotting rowboat hulls, and the hull of a sloop, and found the pier.

"Pete?" I called.

"Yep?" A shadow suddenly stood before me. He'd been kneeling on the pier. Across the water I saw the dark outline of some of the keys.

I stepped closer. He was a thin, small man, with quick movements. His voice was thick drawly south.

"Pete," I said, "I'd like to ask you a few questions."

"Uh-huh. Sho. What about?" He wiped his hands against his flanks and grinned up at me. He had a pleasant face, and a congenial air.

"About Irving Carter. Now—"

"Git out of here!" Moonlight glinted on the barrel of a revolver. "Come on," he said. "Git! The police have been here. I tol' them everything I knowed." He stepped toward me, shoved the barrel into my stomach, and prodded. "Come on, bud!"

"All I want to know is what you know about Carter," I said rapidly.

The hammer of the gun went *snicker-snack* as it drew back. "You want to feed fish?" he said.

I backed off. "All right," I said. "Just tell me one thing, then. Did Carter do anything to you? Do you like him dead, or what?"

He advanced, his voice soft and gentle. "I tol' you to git off of here, naow, didn't I? You think I'm dallyin' round, son? I'd as lief shoot you as spit on you. Naow, git!"

"You didn't like him?" I said.

"I hated him," Pete said, advancing as I backed off. "I wished I'd cut his throat like I'd slit a fish. I had a charter boat, makin' good money. He taken the boat when I couldn't pay 'im money I owed on this yere land I bought from 'im. He skinned me." He leaped at me, poking the gun out. "Naow, git!"

He meant it. He really meant it. I got out of there. Standing by my car, I turned and called, "Say, Pete. D'you know a guy called Ralph Flaxen?"

The gun spat flame in his hand and a slug caromed off the bole of a nearby palm, sang stridently into the jungle, ticking against leaves.

"That was a-purpose," Springer said. "I don't know your man. Naow, where you studyin' next? In the belly?"

I drove down Central, checking on the Blake Realty office. After asking around at a magazine store, they told me that Blake was no longer in town. His offices had been converted into a shoe-shop, and Blake himself had left for the West coast some three years ago.

Virginia Burley answered the door when I knocked with the hilt of the big sword.

"Well, Mr. Death. I'm afraid nobody's home this evening." Her face was rather small, somehow reminded me of a flawless cameo.

"That's fine. I wanted to speak to you, Miss Burley."

She smiled. "In that case, please come in."

I followed her inside. She led me to a large sitting room, with an old carved secretary at the far end, between cases of books that looked aged and dusty.

Virginia Burley was still dressed in black, but it was an expensive cloth with a sheen and she had a good figure. Her hair immaculately in place, with touches of white, surrounding her cameo-like face. Her face was intelligent. But her eyes turned the trick—they did things. I couldn't say what color they were. She motioned toward a high-backed chair and I sat.

"I was making coffee," she said. "Would you care for some?"

"It would go good," I said.

She nodded, smiled cryptically, and left the room. I listened to the dull thud of her footfalls heading toward the rear of the house. I eyed the secretary. It seemed to be in regular use. The leaf of the desk was open, the pigeon-holes crammed with papers, the leaf itself littered.

I made it fast, and started at one side of the desk, going methodically through every piece of paper. It would have taken a long while, and I knew that as I began.

I grabbed a wad of letters from the first pigeon-hole I came to. I yanked them out, and a small note-book came with them.

"I suppose detectives are forced to do such things."

I turned. Virginia Burley stood by the door, with a tray in her hands, with two cups of coffee, cream and sugar on it. She was leaning back against the edge of the door, and had apparently been watching me for some few moments.

"Sorry," I said. "I was admiring this desk. It's a beautiful old piece of furniture."

She set the tray on a coffee table, straightened and stared straight into my eyes.

"All right," I said. "I was snooping. I didn't find anything."

"It's obvious you must have discovered something of interest," she said. "I can see it in your eyes, Mr. Death. You're all turned around because of it."

"I was looking for something," I said. "What, I don't know. In my work, you just keep looking and asking questions. You keep on the move."

"I suppose you're right."

I nodded. "So you keep asking questions and getting in everybody's hair."

She smiled. "You're not getting in my hair, Mr. Death. I admire you for your work. And—I rather like you as a man."

She asked me how much cream and sugar and I told her, "Black, please," and we sat down across from each other in high-backed old flower-upholstered chairs. The coffee was good, strong and hot.

Then I heard the noise for the second time and the nape of my neck tingled like it had before. A hollow, throaty droning, despairful and forlorn. Feet clumped nearer.

I watched her face across from me. She frowned and said, "Excuse me." Her coffee cup clinked as she set it down and moved away.

Tippy entered the room at a shuffling, staggering run. He was dragging something behind him tied to a piece of green twine. I looked. It was the carved sailboat hull that had been in Irving Carter's hand when he died. Tippy stopped running at the sight of Virginia Burley, turned and sprawled flat on the carved piece of wood, cooing and slobbering. He was dressed in a white sailor-suit, with a large blue bandanna tied around his throat. He looked up at her, hugged the sailboat to him. His eyes were shouting something at her with the blank shock of explosion, his mouth gaped and moaning.

"Tippy," Virginia Burley said. She helped the boy to his feet and started him walking out of the room. He stumped along, and vanished. I listened to the stumping movement of his feet and the sound of his voice, lost and forlorn as it faded into the house.

Miss Burley returned and sat in her chair. She looked neither sad, nor troubled, her face was expressionless. Then she said, "My son."

I watched her.

"My son," she said. "Did you see him, Mr. Death?"

"Yes, I—"

"Don't apologize. Don't feel embarrassed. He hates me."

"You can't mean that."

"Ah. He hates me. He possesses two sensations. Hate and love. He hates me. He loves Nora. He is devoted to Nora, of all people. You know why?"

I tried to avoid her eyes. "No," I said.

"Because she gets him drunk. Nora says he should have some fun!" Her face didn't change, her voice was still soft.

"Can't you stop it?" I asked.

"No. She feeds him drink. He's crazy for it. It's the one thing he knows. That, and hate for me. Because he understands that I don't want him to have it."

"Can't he be put someplace?"

She smiled—smiled only.

"Nora could be taught," I said.

"Surely," she said. "What was it you wanted of me?"

"Who is Ralph Flaxen?"

"Really, Mr. Death, I don't know. Why?"

"That's a question I wish I could answer," I said. I stood, told her I had to leave, thanked her for the coffee, started for the door.

"It's been nice," she said. "I hope I don't sound callous about Tippy and Nora. Irving destroyed them."

Irving seemed to have destroyed everybody in his path. "No," I told her. "I don't understand, but I don't believe it's my business to understand." I looked at her and asked myself what was behind that unblinking gaze of hers. I'd probably never know. "You wouldn't know where Mrs. Carter is, would you?"

She shook her head. "No. But Kirk Adams was here a little bit after you called."

"What?"

"Yes," she said. "I bandaged his arm for him, poor fellow. He is in a state. I think he's a little out of his head, the way he babbled, you know? Grace seemed upset because he turned to me for help."

"Did you call the police?"

She shook her head. I tried not to breathe too hard.

"Did he say where he was going?"

She smiled at me, only she left her eyes out of it. "No, he didn't say. He blundered on about how they weren't going to railroad him for these killings. Said he was going to find who did it, if it took him all his life." She opened the door, stared at me for a long moment, and said, "Good night, William."

"So long, Virginia." I nodded, stepped out onto the gallery and the door closed.

The moon was gone. I saw the man's shadow at the edge of the gallery.

"Just keep walking," the flat, quiet voice said. "Get in that car in the driveway."

I tried to elbow my coat out of the way, so I could grab the automatic in my hip pocket. Whoever he was had a very white face that stood out against a dark suit.

"Now, is that any way to act?" he said flatly. "Do like I say. Get over to that car!"

I saw the gun in his hand. "Now listen," I said. "You wouldn't really use that thing, would you?" As I spoke, I broke sidewise and clawed for my gun. In the space of a second, my gun caught in my hip pocket, his gun roared and flamed, and something seared my left side. The shock of it spun me around and I went to my knees.

Two pair of running feet beat a rapid staccato over to me across the gallery.

"You crazy fool!" somebody said. "You hit 'im!"

I tried to get up, still clawing at my gun.

"It was him or me," the flat voice said. "Come on, let's get him into the car."

One of the men lifted me to my feet with one hand, and he didn't grunt.

"You're a sucker to pull a stunt like that," the one who had shot me said. I felt him tug my gun from my hip pocket. "That'll teach you," he added. "Use a holster. It was caught in the lining of your pocket."

We moved off the gallery into the gravel drive. My car was way out front in the street. I glanced that way, saw the headlights go on and heard the engine turn over.

"Who's that out there?" I said. I could feel the hot blood, like sweat, on my left side, beneath my arm.

"A friend of yours," the man who had shot me said.

My eyes were becoming used to the darkness now. I saw a very pale face with a long, hooked nose. The other fellow was a tremendous hulk of a man with a huge heavy-jowled face. He wore a sports shirt of indeterminate color outside his trousers. He also carried a gun, which he put into his belt beneath his shirt. The smaller man ordered me into the front seat, and got into the rear seat himself.

The big one slid beneath the wheel. It was a tight fit. My side was beginning to burn now, where my clothes rubbed against the wound. I got out my handkerchief and slipped it inside against the wound, sopping the blood. It was bleeding pretty badly.

"Where we going?"

"For a little ride. You like taking little rides?"

I lined up the handle of the door, lunged down on it, and threw myself out of the car. I judged wrong. The rear door flew open again, caught me in the forehead.

The thin one said, "Get back in, Jack. You act like a kid."

The big one behind the wheel said, "Lenny, ain't he a card, though? The boss said he was a card." He grunted and turned the motor over. He didn't switch on the headlights, but put the car in reverse and backed swiftly out of the drive. It was a big car, the engine sounded like honey poured over hot-buttered toast.

My side was hurting worse now. "I better get to a doctor."

The little one said, "Listen to him, Corfoni. He wants a doctor. He'll get a doctor, all right."

We were on the highway now, and had started moving forward. I snatched a quick look back. My car moved away from the curb behind us, the headlights glaring into the night.

"Maybe he's hit real bad," Lenny said, "the way he babbles."

These two guys were the type who did killing jobs. They were obviously hired hoods. Men like these were hired from another city to do a job. They came, did their business, and left. But they were ignorant farmer-boys, or city-boys too dumb to know they were too dumb. They never lasted very long, but they played havoc until they were wiped out. I was beginning to feel a little dizzy. "You're both a couple of punks," I said.

"Shall I give him the business?" Lenny said.

"Yeah," Corfoni said. "You might as well."

"A pleasure—" Lenny said, and grunted. The grunt was the last thing I heard. It must have been his gun butt that was laid against the back of my head with close to everything the little fellow had. I piled forward and my head slammed into the dashboard.

Corfoni said something a long way off. I felt his fingers claw into my hair and everything faded. . . .

I came to slowly and sickishly. I was lying on a couch in a dimly lit room. I tried to move, but felt stiff all over and blamed it on my side. But when I went to lift my hands, nothing happened. I was tied down.

My head was a sick roaring, my side burned and throbbed.

From nearby came the sound of the Gulf, the rising drone of the waves, the recessive wash as the water spread itself upon a beach.

A cool Gulf wind blew in at the window above my feet. Straining, I listened. There were voices in the next room, but I couldn't make out what they were saying.

I disregarded the pain in my side and made an effort with the ropes on my wrists. They didn't have me bound to the couch. Only my hands and feet were tied. I could have rolled off onto the floor, but that wouldn't have been so comfortable as the couch. The rope was tight and strong. Too strong.

The room wasn't large; a small living-room. A couple of chairs, two floor lamps, and a table with some magazines on it, and two bottles of beer. One empty, one half empty. Looking at the beer made me realize how thirsty I was. My mouth was like a caterpillar's back crossing a hot stretch of highway under a noon sun.

The voices in the next room droned on. This was the first time in my life I'd ever been tied up, since I was a kid playing cops and robbers. Only then, I recalled, we'd always been able to get untied.

This was different.

I felt warm blood sticky on my side. I looked down, and somebody had removed my suit coat. My shirt was sopping dark with it, and it was getting on somebody's nice clean light tan couch.

A man cursed in the other room. It sounded like Corfoni. Then the voices ceased and a door slammed. Pretty soon a car started, and vanished into the night.

A door opened in the room, behind me. I twisted, tried to see who it was.

"Hello, again."

It was Cadillac Smith. She crossed the room, wearing white slacks and blouse, her hair bunched at the back of her head. She carried a gun. She laid the gun on the table by the magazines and beer bottles and turned to me.

"I told you you were a dope," she said. "But you wouldn't listen, would you, dope?"

"This is getting to be a habit," I said.

"And not a very nice habit, either." She walked up to me and looked down at me. Her white slacks and blouse looked as though they'd just been donned. There was something new in her eyes. Maybe it had been there before, but it hadn't been as pronounced. It was a sadness; a loneliness.

"Do you suppose," I said, "you could get me a dirty old greasy cloth, so I could sop up the blood?"

"Yes," she said. "I'm going to fix you up. I don't care what they say."

"What who says?"

She gnawed on her full lower lip for a moment, then said, "Never mind," turned and left the room.

She returned pretty soon carrying a basin of water, with a washcloth in it, and beneath her arm a box of gauze. She held a pair of scissors between her teeth.

"You'd make a pretty pirate," I said.

"If you don't stop talking like that, I won't do anything for you!" She put the basin down on the floor by the couch. She tore open the box of gauze. Then she started to cut away my shirt with the scissors. "We don't joke around here," she said. "We're very serious about everything."

"That blocks the imagination," I said, sweating as she ripped the shirt away from my side. It felt like my side went with the shirt.

"Did it hurt much?"

"A little."

She stopped peeling the shirt off me and looked at me. She bit her lip, and said, "It looks nasty, but I don't think it's so bad. After I wash it—just hold still now."

I had expected cold water. It was scalding hot. I nearly backed right through the couch.

"Sissy," she said. "Hold still." She slapped the washcloth against my side and scrubbed. She was brutal about it, but she meant to get it clean. After the first few passes with the scalding cloth, my side became numb.

"Caddy," I said. "Where am I? What's all this about?"

"Hold still," she said. "There. It doesn't look half bad. It plowed a hole in you is all, a kind of furrow, like."

"So, you're still not talking? That it?"

She looked at me, laid her hand across my forehead. "You've got a little fever," she said.

"Who wouldn't, with you."

She was very serious. "I wish you wouldn't talk like that." She looked at the wound again. "I think it'll be best if I take your shirt all the way off."

I grinned at her.

She didn't even smile. She took the scissors and rather brutally cut the shirt off me, up my arms, across each shoulder. Then she yanked it out from beneath me and tossed it on the floor.

"You've got nice shoulders," she said.

"I wish you wouldn't talk like that," I said, imitating her. "You've got nice shoulders, too."

"If you don't stop, I'll just let you bleed to death." Then her eyes got funny, and she turned and left the room.

I decided Caddy and I were alone in the house. If there was any chance of my getting away from whoever was holding me, now was the time.

She returned with a bottle of Iodine. "This is going to burn," she said. "But it's all I could find."

"What, no penicillin?"

"He used it all."

"What? Who?"

"Lie still, now." She tore off a piece of gauze, soaked it with Iodine and splashed it on the wound. It felt like she laid a hot poker along my side, and I could almost smell the flesh burn. "There," she said. "You'll have to sit up, now."

She helped me sit up. I nearly toppled over, I was that sick-headed. She started to wind the gauze around me. It wouldn't work with my hands tied. She made a face.

"No. I don't untie them."

"Then I'll just bleed," I said. "How can you do a thing like that, Caddy?"

"I can't do a good job of bandaging," she said. "But if you get away, I'm sunk."

"Why, Caddy—for God's sake, why?"

Her lower lip trembled just a bit, then she got hold of herself. "I'm here because of my brother," she said. "I'm going to tell you. Then I'm going to untie you. They'll be back soon, and I'll have to tie you up again. You can make up your own mind about getting away. I'll do everything I can to stop you. I'd probably even kill you." Her voice was grave. "I mean that."

I didn't say anything.

The room was silent, save for the rushing of the Gulf outside and the wind that came in the window. It played with a few loose strands of her hair as she watched me. Her mouth tightened, but her voice was still grave.

She said, "Irving Carter put my brother in prison. He's in Raiford, right now."

Something clicked in my brain and I said, "Roland Smith."

"You know?" she said.

"No," I told her. "I don't know anything. All I know is the name, Roland Smith."

"That's my brother," she said quietly. "Carter held a grudge against him, because Roland was playing around with Carter's wife."

"Good Lord, another!"

She watched me. "It was nothing, but Carter framed him in a robbery. Framed the whole thing. Roland went up for ten years. A man has promised me he'll get Roland free, if I help him."

"Ralph Flaxen?"

"To you—yes. I have to do what he says. He has a big deal on. You're in the middle of it right now." She turned away. "They're going to kill you."

I sat there, stared at the floor. I could feel the wind blowing in on me and it felt like a cold crone's hand.

"That's nice," I said.

"I don't know what they'll do to me, if you get away." A white line began to show around her lips. "I don't want this!" she said bitterly. "I hate it!" She started pulling the gauze apart with her fingers; strong, capable fingers—soft fingers. "There's nothing I can do. Now I'm going to untie your hands."

As she untied me, I said, "Caddy, tell me everything you know."

"I can't."

"Between us, maybe we could stop all this."

"Sure. And my brother sweats out eight more years in that hole. Do you know what it's like?"

I shook my head.

"If I told you," she said, "I'd lose everything I built for. I don't know anything, anyway. I don't want to. I only know a little. I never knew what I was getting into, believe me." She ceased speaking, and finished untying my hands. The ropes had been tight. My hands were dead weight. I pounded them together. My side began to feel better, I felt stronger already. Psychological effect. My eyes moved to the gun atop the table.

"Yes," she said. "You could do that."

She made a pad of gauze and started wrapping the long bandages around me pulling it tight. She had to reach around me to do it, and her cheek brushed mine. The third time around, I kissed her forehead. She didn't stop. She kept on bandaging. She smelled good, and I didn't know what to do. She finished with the bandage, tied it real tight.

My hands were tingling, jabbed with a thousand needles. I reached out, took her head and she bent down to me. I kissed her lips lightly, and stood. She moved away. She made a little half-gesture with her hand, a helpless movement.

She turned and left the room and came back in a moment with a white shirt. "Here," she said. "It's his. Put it on. It'll fit. Maybe a little tight across the shoulders but it'll do."

I put it on, all the time watching her. When I got it on, she picked up the rope that had bound my wrists and started toward me.

I went over and picked up the gun. It was a .32 revolver and I figured it was the same one I'd seen in her purse.

"Come on, Caddy," I said. "We're getting out of here."

She shook her head. "I can't."

I could feel my side pull, and my shirt was bloody in a couple of spots. "Come on, Caddy," I said. I took her arm.

"No, Bill," she said. "It's too late. They'll get us both."

I jammed the gun into her side. She just didn't budge.

We both heard the car roar up beside the house. The motor gunned and quit. A car door slammed.

"Come on," I whispered. "We've got to get out of here!"

She didn't move. She just looked at me and her eyes were filled with despair.

"They'd only get us, anyway," she said.

I grabbed her arm and yanked her toward the door. She shoved me to the right and we went into a large living room, filled with modernistic furniture, and huge windows overlooking the Gulf. We hurried through two bedrooms, then I saw the open side door. We went outside. Just then a door on the other side of the house slammed.

"That road," she said, pointing beyond the driveway. "It leads to the highway."

"Run," I said.

"It won't do any good," she told me.

We started off anyway, running up a dirt road between a tangle of mangroves and cabbage palms. It was very dark. But far in the distance I heard the sound of passing cars.

"Your car's back there," she panted. "I drove it here."

I grabbed her again and we stopped, panting, listening. I heard somebody yelling back by the house on the beach. "Come on, run!" I said. I stuffed the gun in my hip pocket, took her hand and pulled her along with me.

My side began to twitch and burn. But I knew it wouldn't bleed much with all the bandages on it.

"Do you know where we're going?" Caddy gasped.

"No."

"I can't run much more, Bill. I'm not used to it."

Already my breath was like fire, rasping my throat and lungs. I could imagine what it was doing to Caddy. But she kept pounding along. Then she started to drag on my arm and I knew she wouldn't last. She said, "The Tally-Ho! We might make it to there!"

"You know where it is?"

She shoved me off the road. We started through a field and against the night ahead, I saw the passing lights of cars.

Pretty soon we stumbled across another dirt road, beyond that into sand. The sand pulled at my feet and I knew we couldn't run any longer. We settled to a fast walk, not talking, just slogging.

Caddy was sobbing. It didn't last but a minute before she stopped and said, "I've got to go back, Bill. I've got to."

"Never mind that."

"I've got to. I should never have come with you."

Up ahead, through the sandy, thicketed field, I saw the rear of the box-like joint trimmed in neon. Cars were parked around it and as we came closer, I glimpsed the large green and red sign. The Tally-Ho! We stumbled up a slight incline to a battered, frame back porch littered with crates and empty cartons.

From inside the joint wild music throbbed, lifting into the black night. Right then it started to rain, a warm drizzle, almost a mist. We cracked the screen door and went into a dimly lighted room stacked with cases of drinks.

"O. K., Caddy," I said. "We made it."

We both flopped against the wall, breathing like mad. We stared at each other. Her face was still full of despair.

"You don't know them, Bill," she said. "You don't know them. You think they'll stop?"

"I've got to phone," I said.

She began to laugh. It was a kind of wild, idiotic laughter. "You dope," she said. "You poor dope!"

"Wait here."

"No!" She clung to my arm. "Not now. I won't wait. I'm coming with you."

We came into a small hall, past the Gents room and then the Ladies room. Then we came into the dance floor. It wasn't a large floor, but it was full and the joint was jumping. Tables around the side of the floor were packed with drinking, laughing couples.

"There's the booth," I said. We shoved our way through the dancing couples, the music throbbing in my ears, wild, almost mad. The air was thick with smoke and laughter.

We reached the booth. A man and woman were standing in front of it arguing over whether they should go home.

The door was off the booth. Caddy started saying, "No, Bill! No—no!" I shoved past her, pushed the arguing couple out of the way and reached the phone. I slipped a coin in and dialed headquarters.

The man who was arguing with the woman slammed against the side of the booth. The woman came up to him and slapped his face.

"Bill!" Caddy yelled.

Pat Durkee answered the phone. He said, "Yeah?"

I turned to see what Caddy was yelling about and looked straight down the black muzzle of Corfoni's snub-nosed revolver. He nodded his head toward the back of the building. I glimpsed Lenny twisting Caddy's arm, shoving her across the dance floor. She kept craning her neck, shouting, "Bill! Bill!"

Corfoni took the sputtering ear-piece and slammed it back on the prongs. He jerked his head fatly. "Come on," he said.

As I stepped from the booth, his hand dipped into my hip pocket and my gun went away. We crossed the dance floor, walked stonily down the hall into the store-room. I heard Caddy and Lenny outside. I reached for the door.

Corfoni began hitting me across the middle of the back with the gun. I opened the door. He kicked me in the small of the back. I stumbled across the railless porch, pawed at drizzling, misty night and fell down into a pile of broken bottles and tin cans.

The screen door slammed shut. The music faded.

"Bill!" Caddy cried.

There was a loud, vicious slap. "Shut up!"

I got up. My hands were bleeding. My knees were torn. Corfoni moved up to me, and whipped the gun across my face. I tried to grab the gun, missed. It bit into my cheek. I staggered back holding to the side of the porch. Corfoni stepped in, transferred the gun to his left hand and struck me with his right.

I made a wild dive for him. He simply lifted the gun against my jaw and laughed. I went down again. I tried to get at his legs. He kept moving away and I cut my hands on more broken glass.

"Come on, sucker," he said thickly, breathing heavily. He had no wind. I got up. He jammed the gun into my side. "Come on—over to the car."

The car was parked at the rear of The Tally-Ho!, in shadow. Corfoni shoved me into the front seat, went around the car and grunted in beneath the wheel. Lenny was in the back with Caddy.

"Looka what I got back here," Lenny chortled. "Corfoni. Maybe we oughta stop yet? We could stop on the road a little. Old Smitty's pretty nice, an' she won't be nice much longer."

"You know he wouldn't want that."

"Saving her, huh?" Lenny said.

"That's his business."

The engine turned over smoothly and we lifted out of there. There was only the hiss of tires against the pavement.

"Come on, baby," Lenny said. "Be nice. I can be real nice."

"Stop it!" Caddy cried. I turned around. Corfoni slammed his right handful of gun against the side of my head.

"Stop!" Caddy cried again.

"I ain't going to hurt you," Lenny said.

Corfoni said, "Tame down back there. You wanta mess it up?"

"I wasn't hurting her," Lenny said. There was a loud rip and Caddy cried out. Corfoni braked the car savagely. He turned, reached into the rear seat and swung a vicious fist at Lenny.

"You going to stop?" Corfoni said.

"Ah, I wasn't hurting her."

"I said, 'you going to stop?'"

"Yeah. All right."

"O. K. See you do, then."

"All right. So I'll stop. So, all right!"

Caddy was sobbing back there.

We drove up beside the house on the Gulf. It was a beautiful place. Royal palms stroked at the drizzling night sky and far out on the Gulf lightning flared. Low, growling thunder stuttered in the distance. The rain fell heavier. Still not more than a drizzle.

We piled out of the car. Caddy and I went together, ahead of Corfoni and Lenny.

"Don't say anything about that," Lenny said to Corfoni.

Corfoni jabbed me in the back with his gun. Caddy looked at me and her face was white. Her slacks were torn.

A man walked through the living room of the house toward the front door.

"There's Ralph, now," Lenny said.

We moved across a silvery green lawn. A sprinkler was whirling, watering the lawn in the rain. We walked up some cement steps, through a screen door, across a screened-in porch.

"I don't want to go in there," Caddy said.

"Move," Corfoni said. The door opened and we went inside.

I turned and felt sick inside. I was looking into the cold, impossibly blue eyes of Kirk Adams.

Adams lounged across the room with his hands in the pockets of his gray jacket. He slacked into an easy chair and began cropping his sandy hair.

Corfoni told him how he and Lenny caught us.

"You didn't think you'd get away, did you—Death?" He chuckled as he spoke my name. "Had you fooled right to the ground, didn't we?"

"Who's we?" I asked.

He waved the question aside with his freckled hand. "You're too snoopy," he said. "You've snooped yourself right into your grave."

I watched his unblinking violently blue orbs cut toward Caddy. She moved closer to me.

Adams nodded, then shook his head. "You crossed me," he said to Caddy. "You've cut yourself a piece of cake," he told her. "The wrong piece, sister."

Caddy said nothing.

"Too bad about your brother," Adams said. "He'll have to do his time at Raiford. Outside of Irving, who framed him, I'm the only man alive who can clear him." He shrugged.

Caddy stared at him and there were tears in her eyes.

Adams said, "Lenny here wouldn't want me to do that"—he turned, looked at the thin, flat-voiced hood—"and you'd never speak up yourself, eh, Lenny?"

"Boss, you shouldn't have—"

Adams silenced him with a wave of his hand.

Caddy looked at Lenny, now. She started across the room, pacing slowly. "You cheap, little chiseling rat!" she said. She ran at him, her hands clawing the air.

Lenny took one look into her eyes, cried, "Boss!," and shrank back into the sofa on which he sat.

Corfoni glanced at Adams, and Adams nodded. Corfoni leaped at Caddy, grabbed her arm and flung her across the room. She came up against the wall with a thud, her shoulders shaking.

"Too bad," Adams said. "If you'd played along, Smitty, you'd have cut yourself a piece of real nice cake, like the rest of us. Maybe not so large, but large enough." He turned and grinned at Lenny. "Your brother would have been free." He cleared his throat, looking at Caddy. "You and I could have had fun."

Caddy lifted her head abruptly and glared coldly. The smile left his face. "All right," he said. "That's the way you want it."

"So, you killed Carter and Shane, eh?" I said to Adams.

He grinned. "You think I'm nuts?" he said. "Uh-uh. Not me. I'm Ralph Flaxen. You'll never know how it worked."

"Was Pat Durkee with you when you escaped?"

"The lieutenant?" Adams said. "No. Every man has his price. I bought off two cops who drove me to town. Durkee was in the car behind us. A cop with him winged me. The other two fired over my head. That was a set-up. You know what a set-up is?"

I showed him my teeth.

"You're in the middle of a set-up right now," Adams told me. "How's it feel?" He smiled, turned to Corfoni and Lenny. "You two know your job? You know what you have to do?"

"Sure," Lenny said flatly. "But I don't see why we gotta take him way out there. Why not fix him right here?"

"You're a fool," Adams said. "You want to earn your money? You want to get your money?"

"Natch," Lenny said. He stood, his face pale, and licked his lips. "What you going to do with her?" He explored Caddy with his eyes.

"You don't look that dumb," Adams said.

"Come on, bo," Corfoni said. "We got our work cut out for us. Every man to his own poison, what I say." He looked hard at Adams, then at Caddy. He waddled over to a table, took my gun from his pocket and laid it down. "This is his, boss," he told Adams. "Maybe you want it—I got one."

Adams' eyes narrowed with the amazing blue of them glinting between the lids like lake ice under a winter's sun. "Don't mess this up, you two. Everything depends on keeping things clean." He chuckled at that and cropped his hair with savage impatience.

Corfoni said, "It's going to be funny, watching him dig his own grave."

Adams' eyes flicked to me. "I'm sorry, Death, but that's the way it is. You were brought into this as a dupe, sort of. But you're entirely too snoopy. We didn't count on that."

"Who's we?" I asked again.

"If you'd just have gone on being the dope you're supposed to be, everything would have been fine. This was your first murder case. I suppose you got excited."

I just looked at him. Caddy hadn't moved from against the wall. I saw her eyes peering steadily at the gun on the table. I glanced at her and shook my head very slightly. She looked at me for a moment, then let her gaze slip to the floor.

There was nothing I could say. I wished I had more experience on murder, but probably it wouldn't have helped. In one afternoon and evening I'd been plunged into something I couldn't control, and now I was on my way to be killed.

Corfoni lumbered into another room and returned dangling a length of rope in his hand. Lenny and he tied my hands behind my back, while Adams and Caddy watched. Adams with satisfaction, Caddy with warm horror.

Suddenly Caddy ran across the room and clutched at Adams' arms. "Don't," she pleaded. "Don't do this! Please, don't! I'll do anything you ask—anything! Only don't let them do this."

Adams grasped her hands and pulled them off him. His face was twisted as he said, "So you're gone, hey? Well, too bad, Smitty. It's got to be done. But I'll maybe take you up on the other part."

She rushed at him, pounded him with her fists. He laughed, and shoved her over against the wall again, where she watched, her eyes round with that same old despair.

We moved across the porch and out into the night. It was raining harder now, and the night was black. Down on the beach the Gulf nudged the sands sleepily beneath the drowsy rain. A buoy light far out cast a slow wash of pallid white across the smooth water, freckled by raindrops.

"The shovel," Lenny snapped.

We started around the house and moved beneath the car-port. The shovel was leaning against the side of the house. A large picture window opened from the side of the car-port into the living room and I could see Caddy's back, and Adams facing the window.

Lenny reached for the shovel and we started off.

I glimpsed Caddy move across the room. She reached the table, snatched the gun that Corfoni had laid there and aimed it at Adams.

I saw Adams' mouth move. He flung himself behind a chair. A gun appeared in his hand, roared, spitting flame. Caddy staggered back and my heart lurched. The gun fell from her fingers. Adams stood and walked toward her.

I shouldered Corfoni, tried to break away. Lenny swung the shovel across the backs of my legs.

"Stand still!" Corfoni grunted.

I saw Caddy sprawl on the living room floor. Something went wild inside me. I tried to run. Lenny flung the shovel at my feet. I tripped, sprawled on wet earth outside the car-port.

Corfoni yelled, "You want we should stick around, Ralph?"

Adams called back, "On your way. I'll take care of her!"

I cursed, managed to wobble to my feet and once again tried to run. Corfoni grabbed me. "Come on," he said. "What's another dame? Lots of 'em. Besides, they maybe won't have 'em, where you're going."

We moved across the long sweep of wet grass, past the lawn sprinkler which was still spraying water in the rain, down toward the beach. I was sick inside. I'd had my chance to set Caddy free, but I'd fouled that chance. Now everything had gone wrong.

Lenny's face was paler still in the night, and his sharp little teeth glinted. "We should've brought a umbrella," he said.

Corfoni grunted. "Never mind the umbrella, kid," he said. "Just hang on to that shovel."

We reached a large cement breakwater that stretched out, away from the beach. There was a boathouse between the grass and the water. We walked past that and onto the breakwater.

"Here we are," Corfoni said. "Reach me the flashlight."

I saw a good-sized motor launch, a cruiser, tied to the breakwater. Cement steps descended to the bobbing deck. Lenny went down the steps, and returned with the flashlight.

"Take him aboard," Corfoni said. "I'll cast off."

Lenny jammed the gun into my ribs. We went down the stairs and onto the moving deck of the boat. They had an awning rigged aft from the forward housing.

"Park yourself," Lenny said.

I squatted on the lockers that stretched along the port side. Lenny stood by the wheel, the gun trained on me. I heard wet ropes slap the deck as Corfoni untied the craft.

Corfoni leaped aboard, went forward to the wheel. "You watch him," he told Lenny. "Anything goes wrong, I'll plug you—I mean it."

We were drifting in toward the beach. For an instant I hoped that the boat might ground itself before the engines started. But the engines caught. Corfoni's voice was jubilant. "Here we go, pardner!"

"You sure you know how to handle one of these things?" Lenny asked.

"I was borned on one," Corfoni replied.

He knew his business. We surged around, leaving a white, frothy wake, and the boat vibrated, lifting and sinking with the swell as we headed directly out into the Gulf.

"It's shallow in-shore," Corfoni said. "We gotta go out a ways."

"Whyn't we bump him out there and throw him in the drink?"

"You're a ass," Corfoni said. "Don't you know a body'll float? So he comes floating in one day with holes in him. Is that nice? No, it ain't nice," he answered his own question. "Better he should dig a nice grave for himself on Casket Key."

Land faded rapidly in the rainy mist and the lights at Adams' place vanished. We were in the Gulf. The large rise and fall of deeper water was menacing and bothered me. I was taking my last boat ride—my last ride of any kind.

Someday an archeologist would dig me up, alongside of one of those shell mounds out on Casket Key. "Some pirate," the digger would say. "Maybe he sailed with Gasparilla."

Lenny said, "Say, Corfoni. You think we'll get our dough?"

"We better."

"I don't like it. Dames. Too many dames. Flaxen claims he's got to wait for his dough. He says it's a big wad. I won't like this waiting for dough. I don't mind the work. But I like the dough in my hand."

"Tend to business," Corfoni said, "or maybe you won't have any hand to hold the dough you ain't got."

"I don't like it," Lenny repeated. "Flaxen thinks he's too big. He ain't big."

"He's bigger than you," Corfoni said. "And so am I."

"So, all right. Hey," Lenny said, kicking me in the shin. "How you like taking this cruise? Nice, huh?"

I told him it was grand. I worked at the ropes, trying to free my hands, but they were tied tight. Too tight. The circulation was cut off. If I jumped overboard—and I might manage that—where would it get me? A pass to Davy Jones' Locker. If I stayed on the boat, it was just as bad. And certain.

"Here we go," Corfoni said.

We turned at right angles, the boat careening, and headed in toward land. Only we didn't strike land. We passed through a small, deep channel, between the mainland, Long Key, and some other key that hovered like an ominous shadow off the starboard side.

"There's Casket Key," Corfoni said. "Straight ahead."

I glimpsed a large blackness, blacker than the wet night, looming ahead. Far to the left, against the unseen horizon, the lights from Long Key spattered the jet heavens with white and pink.

In the drizzling silence, with the sound of the boat's motor vibrating through me, and the continuously liquid slosh of the wake of the water, that pressing presence of the Carter house returned. I thought of the veritable hell the house must be, or have been, with the two factions of the family living in it at one time. Virginia Burley on one side, Grace Carter on the other, and with Irving, Nora, and Tippy in the middle. Carter must have been the worst kind of sadist to force, or allow, such behavior. Doubtless he had enjoyed the conflict between the two women.

But why did Grace Carter stand for it? Money. Irving Carter could, if he chose, fabricate a divorce in a matter of hours with his purchasing power. Had she clung on, overlooking whatever pride she had, just so she could grab at the lettuce?

We chugged in along the edge of the key. Mangroves were snarled close against the side of the boat like petrified snakes. Strident crickets chirped, frogs thumped, night-birds screeched, and an animal of the darkness prowled clumsily a few yards away, stumbling along through the key's gagging jungle.

I began to feel hollow inside and then the hollow filled with suspense as I thought about what was to happen to me. I had been fishing and spearing among these very keys at one time or another. Once, several years before, I had brought a girl out to the other side of Casket Key, and we had picnicked and spotted a possum galumphing along the muddy beach beyond us. I remembered the thick, choking jungle in there—pathless, dank, foreboding, where men simply didn't go.

The boat ground against sudden shore-line. Corfoni cut the engine and silence swept over us like a global deafness. Waves lapped. Rain drizzled. Birds whooped. Crickets chirped. Then I heard the loud, blood-choked bumping of my heart as it rocked inside my chest.

"Whyn't we tie the anchor on him, knock him off, and sink him?" Lenny asked. He swallowed. I heard and saw the loud throat-movement as his eyes roved the breadth of jungle close to our side.

"Watch him," Corfoni said sharply. He leaped off the deck with a rope in his hand. He fumbled around on the shore, tied the rope to a cypress trunk. "O. K.," he called. "Throw me the shovel, and bring him along."

Lenny tossed the shovel at Corfoni. Then he jammed the gun in my back and said, "Jump."

I jumped and sank to my ankles in black muck that stank of rotten fish. The rain was a heavy drizzle now and a summer's night had become very cold and threatening.

Lenny stood on the boat's deck, gun in hand, staring bleakly at the bush. "Look, Corfoni," he said. "Whyn't we just bump him off and get out of here? We could strip him. He'd probably get et up before dawn."

"Come on," Corfoni said. "What you ascared of? Snakes?"

"Snakes?" Lenny muttered. "I hadn't even thought of snakes. Keep still about them things, will you?" He jumped ashore, waded through the muck to where Corfoni and I stood.

"Ralph said the middle of the island," Corfoni grunted. "Let's go—you first," he said to me. He shoved me straight at the mangroves.

After we got through the outer shield of tangled undergrowth, it wasn't too bad. We finally reached a spot beneath a large slash pine and Corfoni said, "This will be his gravestone."

"I don't like it," Lenny said. "So, all right. He's hid an' he'll never be found. But all the same, I don't like it. It isn't business, Corfoni. When you bump a gee, you bump him and get the hell away to someplace with a blonde on your lap and a bottle in your hand. You don't monkey around, like this. Ralph's nuts."

"So, he's nuts." Corfoni stepped up to me. He took out a knife, turned me around and slashed through the ropes. Then he handed me the shovel. "Dig," he said. "Dig hard and fast. It won't hurt to wear yourself out this time. Maybe you can kill yourself digging. Then our hands would be clean."

I took the shovel and started to dig. The ground was a rich loam, sandy, and it came away loosely, quickly, easily. Entirely too easily. Corfoni and Lenny sat down on a nearby cypress log. Overhead the sky cried lazily, dripping tears through the thick roof of jungle.

I decided that if it was going to be *my* grave, it would be a good one. I had it about half a foot deep, outlined satisfactorily, with my eyes and mind skinned raw watching for an opening, when I saw the snake.

A large rattler, slick and sickening in the half-light. Corfoni had brought the flash and it fell from his fingers. Maybe the snake had been there all the time. Maybe I'd smelled it, heard it—maybe it sensed a meal. Anyway, there it was.

I'd had my shovel in a big bunch of dried stuff and I flipped it loose. Little wriggling snakes flipped from my shovel. I had dug into a rattler's nest.

I leaped back. The big snake, easily six feet long, slid toward the grave from around the log Lenny and Corfoni were seated on. They had seen it about the same instant I had.

Lenny yelled something and started emptying his gun at the snake. Corfoni went for me. I swung the shovel as Corfoni aimed his gun. The blade of the shovel caught his gun hand and the gun whipped away into the brush.

"I got him!" Lenny sang out. "My God!"

The snake thrashed in a dying attempt to coil, defenseless. Then Corfoni was on me.

I swung the shovel again and again, clubbing at him, and when he retreated, chopping with the blade down into his shoulders and arms. Corfoni was in Lenny's way and the smaller man couldn't fire. He kept trying to get around Corfoni. I beat Corfoni back with the shovel.

I gave the big man a whack. He screamed and dove headfirst into the grave, straight into the squirming mass of baby rattlers.

Lenny shoved the gun at me just as I hurled the shovel at him. I turned, plunged off into thick darkness.

Lenny clicked the trigger on an empty gun.

"Don't leave me!" Lenny screamed. "Corfoni—he's got away! Don't leave me here!"

I heard him crashing after me. But he was headed wrong. I paused, waited. The sound of his wild running was loud at first, his voice wild and afraid—then gradually it faded away, until only the forlorn echo of his cries roofed the suddenly sibilant dark.

I sprawled face down in the muck against the boat's side, started to slip off the shelf into deep water. Heaving, I got back on the shelf of land. I leaped aboard. Standing on the deck, I listened. There wasn't much sound coming from Casket Key. Then as I listened, the mysterious night-life took over again.

I swung the boat around, heading back. I ached all over. My body burned from lacerations of thorny brush. I was mud-soaked. Back there in that moribund dark were two men; one running for his life, the other possibly just now regaining consciousness to find himself in a rattlesnake nest.

I reached the Gulf, headed out a way, as Corfoni had done, then started to the right, up along Long Key, toward Adams' place. I went in as close to the beach as I dared, watched for a certain pattern of lights. Then I remembered the light buoy out on the water.

I saw the cement breakwater before I saw anything else. Then minutes later I was running up the lawn, past the lawn sprinkler, toward the house. I hadn't tied the boat and hoped it would smash itself on the beach.

The house was empty. The gun Caddy had picked up from the table still lay on the floor. The lights were bright.

I wanted Adams. I wanted to feel my fingers curling around his throat, pressing the life out of him. I wanted to kill him. Thoughts of Caddy, what he had done to her, hurt me more than the slash in my side. I wanted to get that man so bad, I shook with it.

I took the gun, hurried outside. The big car was gone. Tim Donneker's car was gone, too. I started jogging up the road toward the main highway, the same road on which Caddy and I had run not so long ago.

I found Donneker's car. It was jammed into a copse of pine off the dirt road, its shadow rising against the paler night sky.

The engine turned over. Apparently Adams had hidden it quickly in case any trace was sent out for it. With the car on the road, I pushed the gas-pedal down, and headed for the city lights, pink against the rain-washed sky.

The rain beat against the windshield and a wind was rising. As I broached the main highway, I saw a string of royal palms lashed by the wind, the fronds beating the air like crazy fingers.

The Tally-Ho! was silent, and lightless, as I sped by. The car's tires screamed on the wet pavement, sounding like tearing silk. I was soaked to the skin, and hurting all over. But the biggest hurt was inside me.

As I approached the Carter house on Tangerine, I recalled coming to it for the first time that afternoon. I turned into the drive, cut the engine and rolled to a quiet halt.

I piled out and hurried soundlessly toward the front of the house. As I passed a lighted window, I looked in.

Tippy was standing in the center of a bedroom, before a bureau. In his hand he held a gun. He stuck the barrel in his mouth and gnawed it. He was standing in a pile of loose papers that he had apparently pulled from the bureau. He kicked loosely at the papers and stumped around the room in his yellow and green banded bathrobe, gnawing on the gun barrel. His eyes were blank with satisfaction. He started out of the door.

I went toward the front gallery of the house, hoping to intercept Tippy in the hall. I glanced back toward the rear, along the side of the house.

The long black hulk of the big car was outlined against the pale, weatherbeaten side of the old shed where Irving Carter's body had been found.

I moved onto the gallery, and entered at the front door. The heavy sword knocker ticked on the brass plate as I closed the door. The mellow sound of talking came from way at the rear of the house, in the kitchen.

Tippy stood in the entrance of the bedroom off the hallway, watching me, still gnawing complacently on the gun barrel. I moved up to him, shoved him into the bedroom and carefully closed the door.

He didn't move after that. Just stood, gnawing and watching with his blank, hopeless eyes. He was chewing on the barrel of what looked like the very same twenty-two caliber gun I'd found in Adams' room at the Bay-View Apartments.

I knew I couldn't just take the gun from him. He might set up a howl. I wished he could speak, but he couldn't. He could only make those horrible throat-noises. He made them now, gurgling over the barrel of the gun. He placed his thumb inside the trigger guard and my heart stood still.

So far as I knew, there was one remaining shell in that gun. If he tripped the trigger, he'd kill himself. Suddenly, he took the gun out of his mouth and slobbered a smile at me. His eyes were so blank and helpless I felt sick. He handed me the gun. I took it slowly from his pale fingers.

It was the same gun, all right. I tucked it into my pocket, and stepped toward the bureau. Tippy stumped along clumsily beside me. There was a framed picture of Nora and Tippy atop the bureau, and an early portrait of Virginia Burley, standing beside a lithe and gay-looking Irving Carter. Was this Virginia Burley's room?

Drawers of the bureau were open. I glanced through them hastily, then rummaged in the papers that littered the floor. Tippy entered into it, lifting the papers with both hands, as he hunkered down, throwing them into the air and cooing.

There were letters from Carter. Love letters. Then I found a marriage certificate. The marriage certificate was stapled to a thick wad of legal-looking documents. I flipped through them. They were divorce papers. The divorce papers of Virginia Carter and Irving Carter. Then my breath hesitated in my throat.

Across the first page of the divorce papers was printed a single word, stamped in large violet letters. VOID. And affixed to that was an explanatory paragraph, witness and notarized.

Things clicked into place. I folded those papers, jammed them into my pocket and looked long thankfulness at Tippy Carter. According to this, Virginia Burley Carter would stand to collect Irving Carter's money due to his death. Grace Carter was not legally his wife and she would receive nothing.

I started toward the door, still not knowing what I'd do. The door opened slowly as I reached for it and Nora Carter slipped into the room.

She grinned at me. She was wearing thin black lace pajamas and there was a gleam in her eyes. Tippy stumbled over to her, clung to her.

I just watched and waited.

"I know everything," she whispered. "I've just heard."

"Fine."

"I've been listening by the kitchen door. They're arguing. There's going to be trouble. They say you're dead." Her voice was edgy.

"Do I look dead?"

"No, you don't look dead. You look good. You look real good and alive."

"Nora—you've got to help me."

She smiled and patted Tippy's head as he snuggled close. Then she shoved him away. He went obediently and stood watching. For a long moment she stood there, looking at me, then suddenly she laughed shortly, went over and took Tippy's hand. "Damn you!" she said, and left the room. I looked at the door as she closed it.

I opened the door, stepped into the hall. Just then, Grace Carter's voice reached me.

"If I'm it, then you'll go too!"

I heard Adams curse. I ran toward the kitchen.

"What's that?" Virginia Burley said.

"Look out!" Adams cried.

A single shot smashed the night. Grace Carter screamed.

"You fool! You fool!" Virginia Burley shouted. "You've killed her!"

I made the kitchen, burst into the full light. Grace Carter was leaning against the table, holding a hand tight against her breast. Blood worked over her white hand. The gun in her other hand clattered to the floor.

Kirk Adams stood opposite her, an automatic clenched in his fist.

"Drop the gun, Adams!"

He looked at me and laughed. The two women stared wide-eyed, one of them dying, the other pale-faced and furious.

Adams said, "You don't want to kill. I do. You'll hesitate, Death. You haven't got a chance."

I stared at the twenty-two in my hand. I knew he was right. I dropped the gun and it smacked the floor. They stared at me. Adams' eyes were as blue as ever. Virginia Burley's mouth worked as she tried to say something. Grace Carter watched her life blood stream out of her, coating her clutching fingers with crimson. She sagged against the edge of the table. "They've done this to me," she said.

I looked at Adams. "It's falling to pieces," I said. "The whole thing's crumbling around you."

A wild light came into his eyes. "Don't say that!"

"I'll say it," I said.

"My hands are clean!"

"Yes," Virginia Burley said quietly. "Our hands are clean. We have done nothing to incriminate us."

"You can cut that out," I said. Her face was still like a cameo, only it was a wax cameo that had been set too close to a flame. Pieces of it began to cascade away; a muscle weakened here, a muscle twitched there. It wasn't nice.

"I'll have nothing," Grace Carter said. "Nothing at all. He lied to me— lied!" She staggered across the room, leaving a trail of blood.

"Your hands aren't going to be clean long," I said to Adams.

Grace Carter cried. Fear was abrupt in every feature of her face. "I can't die," she said. "I don't want to die." She slacked to a bench in the breakfast nook and stared owl-eyed at Adams. "You—you've done this," she said. "You and she planned—my marriage was never legal. And I never knew, not until tonight."

Adams stalked across the room and looked down at her, holding the gun still on me. "Come on," he snapped. "Get outside."

"It won't work," I said.

"You're a stupid, bungling fool!" Virginia Burley said to Adams. Her face was drawn up into a crazy pucker now. She wrung her hands.

Adams said, "Out to the car."

"You've spoiled it all," Virginia cried.

"I haven't spoiled anything. We've got to get rid of this guy!" He gestured toward me. "Then we'll come back. We'll report Grace's death. I'll tell them I've killed her. In self-defense. We'll say she confessed to the murders. Crimes of passion. We'll be as safe as ever."

Some of the fear washed out of Virginia Burley's face. "I always underestimate you, Kirk."

"Never mind," he said. "Get out to the car!"

He handed his gun to Virginia Burley. "You keep this on him," he said. "Keep it poked into him and pull the trigger if he moves."

We climbed into the car, the three of us sitting in the front seat, with me in the middle. As I rested back against the cushions I felt the hard pressure of my own gun in my hip pocket.

Virginia Burley sat tight against the door, half facing me, with her gun poked into my stomach. There was something very evil and hard about her face now.

Adams backed out of the drive, around Tim Donneker's car onto the lawn, back onto the drive and out to the street. We sped away, the motor purring like an expectant cat.

"What did you do with Caddy?" I asked Adams.

His laughter trailed out the rushing window as he leaned hard against the steering wheel. We were headed out Tangerine in the direction of the beaches.

"I left her pretty body in the utility room," he said quietly. "If it'll please you, we'll bury you both together." He laughed again, and I knew that the pressure was beginning to get him. It bit into me, ate at me like cancer. Caddy was dead, gone. She'd been out there when I'd returned from the island.

"I'll get you, I promise that," I said.

Again his laughter, and this time it was joined with the vivid screeching of Virginia Burley. "Listen to him," she said. "How he rants." She peered into my eyes, her own eyes glinting. "I thought you had better sense," she said.

"You've made a play for Carter's money. It'll all go to you now he's dead, won't it?"

"Certainly," Virginia Burley said. "He married Grace Carter before the time limit was up on our divorce, and it nullified the marriage. Grace never knew. He kept it secret because she had already started to play around with Kirk. He decided to use her, torment her, as he has done to everybody else. He approached me. I hated Grace for taking him away from me, and agreed to come and live with him."

Adams interrupted, "You're a witch," he said. "But you've got brains, and that's what counts."

"Maybe not enough brains," I said. "You two have taken the door right off its hinges."

Adams grunted.

"I dreamed this up, honey," Virginia Burley said. "Two years ago, I dreamed this up. We've waited and it's a perfect plan. There are no loopholes, save for what Kirk has made. But they can be covered."

We turned off Tangerine and took the beach road.

"All Kirk had to do was win Grace. It wasn't hard. He worked on her, showed her that he was the same type she was. For two years he's carried it on, but Irving wouldn't let her go. Irving could buy anything. He bought the law, lawyers. Kirk had to kill him. She didn't know she wasn't married to Irving. She knew there was nothing she could do."

"And Alfred Shane?"

"He saw it," Adams said. "He had to die."

"Now," she went on. "Grace is dead. But the plan continues to work, doesn't it, Kirk? You killed her in self-defense."

I reached, grabbed her wrist with one hand, the steering wheel with the other. I whirled the wheel.

The speedometer read in the seventies. It took only a snap of the wrist and we headed in a wild leap off the road toward the abutment of one of the causeways leading to Long Key.

Virginia Burley's scream hung in the air, above the rending crash of metal and broken glass; the savage thunder as we were shot around inside the car. I felt it fly into the air, strike, turn, leap, strike and turn. The engine shrieked, Virginia Burley's scream still hanging in the air. Then it cut off sharply, like you'd cut string with a knife.

I wasn't unconscious. The car rocked. Glass tinkled. Metal ground together. The car steadied, resting on its side. The night was quiet.

Then slowly, crickets chirped again. I opened my eyes. I was staring up into a cloudless sky. Bright stars shone down, winking. Somebody groaned terribly.

I tried to get up, managed to stagger to my feet. I was thrown outside the car, close against the water's edge.

My left arm was useless. It hung at my side. I looked down at a splinter of bone showing white in the night, rammed through the sleeve of my coat. As I stood there, I became dizzy.

Then I saw Adams. He was coming around the other side of the car, with a gun in his hand. He started to fire. His face was a bloody mash. He fired as he walked toward me.

I flung myself at him. We both fell. I didn't think I'd been hit. He dragged away from me, crawling on his hands and knees, muttering to himself. I found my own gun and crawled after him.

He was staring at me, gun level. He fell to one knee.

I kept crawling. We were no more than five feet apart, staring into each other's face. His eyes were wild, his mouth continuing along the left cheek almost to his ear. It had been ripped wide open, into a flapping gash.

I sprawled face down, lifted my head, and blasted at his face. I saw the face disintegrate, blow apart, as slug after slug from my gun found its mark.

Each time I pulled the trigger I thought of Caddy. I squeezed the trigger until the hammer clicked against empty casings. Then I passed out, face down in the wet earth.

Faces swam across my vision. I heard voices. Then everything was black again for another eternity, while I fought up through a tunnel of rushing darkness.

Somebody said, "This is becoming an awful habit. Bill—Bill—Bill. . . ."

I opened my eyes. The room was bright. Caddy looked down at me. Slowly images took on outline. Caddy was bending over me, and beside her was Pat Durkee.

"You're all right," Caddy said.

I tried to say something, but could only nod. She had her arm in a sling, and there was a large patch of bandage on her right side.

"You're all right?" I heard myself say. I grinned at my voice.

"I'll say she's all right, fella," Pat Durkee said. He looked uncomfortable.

"Go ahead and spit," I said. His head vanished, then returned. He was beaming. "Used the window," he said.

Caddy said, "We had a devil of a time finding you in this hospital."

"We?"

Pat spoke up. "Listen, Bill. This here girl of yours bummed rides all the way in from the beach, with her arm and side all shot up. She told us the whole story." He winked. "Everything's jake."

I tried to grin, but that hurt. "Where are they?"

"They're dead," Durkee said.

I told him about the two men out on Casket Key and he went to the phone to put in a call to have them picked up.

Caddy sat beside me on the bed. She was smiling. It was the first time I'd ever really seen her smile.

"Mr. Durkee is real nice," she said. "I was excited when I came into town. He says he is sure he can get my brother out of prison."

"If Lenny isn't dead," I told her. "I'm sure he'll talk." I looked at her. "Get my clothes," I said.

She shook her head. "You'll have to stay in bed a while."

I grinned. "Nothing doing. I feel fine. It's been a rough day, but I'm O. K."

She chuckled. "A rough day?"

"Sure. Today's been rugged."

"Darling," she said. "It isn't today. You've been unconscious for three days. They've been looking everyplace for Lenny and Corfoni. But I know neither of them could swim, so they're surely still out there on Casket Key."

"Three days," I muttered.

"Yes," she said. "The doctor says I have to go now."

"No," I said. "Don't go." I tried to grab her, but my arms wouldn't come up. She bent and pressed her soft lips against mine. I couldn't feel them. Then I realized, my head was swathed in bandages. I cursed, and made an effort to sit up.

Caddy's smiling face faded away as I passed out with the effort. Then her voice reached me. "It's all right, Bill," she said. "I'll be here. I couldn't let you regain consciousness without having me around. Not after all the practice I've had."

And then I didn't hear anything.

Decision

date unknown

This is the only story in this collection whose manuscript, sloppily typed, is clearly a rough draft and not a story ready for submission. There is no return address on the manuscript, and there is a handwritten question mark at the top of the first page.

They had not spoken since entering the hotel room. She was unpacking a suitcase. He had ordered a bottle of brandy from room service, and it had just come up. He opened it and poured a glass. Then he set it on a small table, and went to the window.

"Snow," he said.

"Hmmm?"

"Snow. All that damned snow."

"Well, darling, it's what you wanted to see. You said, just to feel it squeaking underfoot. Remember?"

"I'm not being disparaging," he said. "It's just—so all encompassing."

"Well, I didn't care. I didn't want snow. You wanted snow. Now, you've got it." She chuckled, and pressed a sable coat against her cheek, then tossed it on the bed. "Davos. Skiing. All that."

"Yes," he said. He continued to stare out the window.

"You insisted," she said. "You said you were here once, and you wanted to return. You said you wanted to ski. You insisted on Davos. Now, here we are."

"That's the beauty of it," he said.

"What?"

"I said, that's the beauty of it."

"Oh. I suppose you're right, darling."

"Were you happy in Cairo?"

"What?"

"I said, were you happy in—oh, the hell with it."

"There you go, cursing again, not saying what you mean. What's the matter with you? Must you talk in riddles?"

He sighed. He was still looking out the window.

"Yes. I liked Cairo, for your information. And I thought we should go to Spain. We know so many people in Madrid. It would be simply—"

"I'm frustrated," he said.

"What?"

"Frustrated. There's something the matter. I don't know what it is. I feel sick—sick."

"Oh, dear."

"I'm emotionally upset." He turned from the window, and walked across the living room into the alcove bedroom where she stood beside the bed. She was very beautiful with her long blonde hair.

"What is it?" she asked.

"Anxiety," he said. "Depression. I can't control it."

She watched him anxiously. "Are there any voices?"

He shook his head. "No."

"You're not lying?"

"No. Of course not."

She giggled. "Maybe we should send you back."

"Don't say that."

"Well, maybe you're coming apart at the seams."

"I can't breathe right, even. It's just—I can't explain it. Nothing makes any sense. I've sensed this depression for a long time, but now there's anxiety, too. It's unbearable. Christ. What can I do?"

She stepped close to him, put an arm around his neck. "Poor dear," she said.

He groaned, pressed his face against her hair.

She said, whispering, "Would sex improve your attitude?"

He groaned again.

"We could go right to bed."

He sighed. "Damn it, damn it, damn it."

She leaned away from him, searching his eyes. "You're unhappy here, already. I can tell. You really didn't want to ski. You really didn't want any snow. We can go someplace else. Where would you like to go? Anyplace is all right with me. I was only kidding about Madrid."

He turned and took three paces into the living room, and just stood there. Then he walked over and picked up the glass of brandy and drank it.

"Does it help?" she asked. She had followed him.

"Too soon to tell. Jesus," he said. "I feel like—I just feel like—it's all coming up inside me."

"If you're going to toss your cookies, go in the bath—"

"I don't mean that."

She moved close against him again. "I'll take care of you," she said. "Haven't I always taken care of you?"

He made a small noise.

"Haven't I?"

"Yes."

"There's nothing to worry about, is there? Nothing at all."

"I know." He sighed again.

"What have you to be anxious about?"

"Nothing. Nothing. It's just free floating."

"Why not take one of those tranquilizers?"

"They're no damned good."

"Why should you be unhappy?" she asked. "You have everything. And, I'll always take care of you."

He grinned at her, but his eyes were touched with pain.

"Have another brandy," she said.

He looked at her, staring at her.

She smiled.

He said, "What shall I do? I don't know what to do. God. I feel awful, simply awful."

"Maybe you should take a job, somewhere."

"Oh, God, you don't understand."

"Of course, I understand. But I told you, I'll take care of you. You have absolutely nothing to worry about. Nothing. We'll go wherever you wish. Haven't we always? Don't we go wherever you say?"

"Yes."

"Where d'you what to go? You don't want to stay here in Davos, do you?"

"I don't know."

She was silent.

He was still watching her, staring at her. Suddenly, he said, "I think I'm hungry. I think I'd like a steak. Yes, a steak."

"Would it help?"

"I don't know. Maybe."

She ordered the best they had, and told them to get it right up to the room. It did not take long. The man wheeled it in under silver. There was a bottle of wine.

"Better, now?"

"I'll see," he said.

"I'll just finish unpacking. You eat your steak, darling."

He drew a chair up to the cart, lifted the silver lid, and gazed at the steak. He glanced into the bedroom.

"It doesn't help," he said.

She was humming. She ceased. "You should be like me. I keep doing something. That way, I don't worry about anything. I never worry. Never. Feel better?"

"No."

"Let me worry for you," she said. She chuckled again. "Okay?"

He did not answer. He was staring at the sleek steak knife. He picked it up.

"I'll do all the worrying for both of us," she said. "Isn't that marvelous? I'll take care of you, darling. I'll always—what are you doing?"

"This," he said, and he cut her throat just as she screamed. The sound gurgled. There was a lot of blood, and he stood there, looking down at her on the floor. She moved convulsively, then was quiet.

He went into the other room, dropping the knife on the rug.

He stood before the window and took a deep breath, and smiled.

From the Master of Obsessive Noir. . . .

Gil Brewer

Wild to Possess / A Taste for Sin $19.95
1-933586-10-9
"Permeated with sweaty desperation."
—James Reasoner, *Rough Edges*

A Devil for O'Shaugnessy / The Three-Way Split $14.95
1-933586-20-6
"Brewer's insights into the psychology of sexual enthrallment and obsession still resonate."
—David Rachels, *Paul D. Brazill Blog*

Nude on Thin Ice / Memory of Passion $19.95
1-933586-53-2
"His entire livelihood came from writing works in which lurid narratives were rendered in a punchy, unadorned prose style."
—Chris Morgan, *Los Angeles Review of Books*

The Erotics / Gun the Dame Down / Angry Arnold $20.95
1-933586-88-5
"Showcases the impressive storytelling talents of Gil Brewer, a true master of the noir mystery genre. . . strongly recommended."
—*Midwest Book Review*

Flight to Darkness / 77 Rue Paradis $19.95
978-1-944520-58-8
"Murder, madness, swamps, gators, a savagely beautiful woman . . .it doesn't get much better than this for noir fans . . .crazed and breakneck."
—James Reasoner, *Rough Edges*

The Red Scarf / A Killer is Loose $19.95
978-1-944520-55-7
"There are some neat plot turns, the various components mesh smoothly, the characterization is flawless, and the prose is Brewer's sharpest and most controlled."
—Bill Pronzini, *Big Book of Noir*

"Brewer is a skilled craftsman and he builds suspense slowly and deliberately, leading the reader down an unavoidable path of doom."
—Ron Fortier, *Pulp Fiction Reviews*

Stark House Press, 1315 H Street, Eureka, CA 95501
griffinskye3@sbcglobal.net / www.StarkHousePress.com

Available from your local bookstore, or order direct via our website.